THE RIVER MAIDEN

Meredith R. Stoddard

Moran taing!

Erkita Press

Ruther Glen, VA

Erkita Press
10551 Gallant Fox Way
Ruther Glen, VA 22546

Publisher's Note: This is a work of fiction. Names, characters, places, and incidents are a product of the author's imagination. Locales and public names are sometimes used for atmospheric purposes. Any resemblance to actual people, living or dead, or to businesses, companies, events, institutions, or locales is completely coincidental.

The River Maiden/ Meredith R. Stoddard. – 2nd ed.
ISBN 978-0990433347

For Eric, my careful steward

CHAPTER ONE

Mòrag MacAlpin died when she was six years old, although death can be a relative term. It's sprinkled throughout our everyday language like so much cinnamon on top of our morning coffee. When we're excited, we say, "I could just die!" We get "mortified" when we're embarrassed. When kids know they're in trouble they say, "My parents are gonna kill me!" and of course there is the petit morte of sexual satisfaction. Our pop culture is full of sentient ghosts, vampires, and zombies who interact with the world even after death.

Our most prominent religions are based on what happens after we die. Hindus and Buddhists espouse reincarnation. Islam promises a heaven of gardens with rivers running through it. Mormons even allow you to convert relatives after they've died. Christianity is based on the idea that death is only a temporary condition, and like Jesus, believers will all be resurrected when the Rapture comes. We do our best to change death from a period or even an exclamation point at the end of life into a comma or a semicolon.

Whether little Mòrag's heart actually stopped on that morning in the spring of 1976 is debatable. But there is no doubt that the girl who woke up gasping for breath, cradled in her grandmother's arms that day, was not the same girl who had been picking flowers in the woods just that morning or laughing with her mother as she got ready for her bath.

In that moment, when she stared shivering over her grandmother's shoulder at the limp form of her mother on the floor, the ground shifted beneath her feet and the very sky above her changed color. Nothing was ever the same. And for a child as young as six, the only solution was to become a different person. That was the day that Mòrag became Sarah, and Sarah put away childish things like fairy tales.

***

June 1995
Chapel Hill, North Carolina

Sarah woke up gasping for air. Her heart was pounding. The dream had been so vivid that for a few seconds she didn't see her bedroom, but the bathroom of her childhood home. Its dull, tiled floor was puddled with water from her bath and spotted with blood. Her mother lay unconscious on the floor.

But this time Sarah hadn't come to cradled in her grandmother's arms, with Granny cooing to soothe her. This time she was alone. Granny was gone.

"Again?" Sarah thought as the room began to resolve itself from dream and memory to reality. She'd been having the dream far too often lately—she had the bags under her eyes to prove it. She inhaled deeply, trying to slow her breathing and maybe to prove to herself that she could, that it was air and not bathwater. Nope, it was definitely air…humid, sticky, my-AC-can't-keep-up-with-June air. Sarah cast a look around the room, taking a mental inventory, reminding herself that she wasn't in the holler. She was in her apartment in Chapel Hill, her very messy apartment.

When her inventory reached the clock beside her bed, she sat up with a start. Nine-thirty! The library had been open for half an hour, and if she was going to catch up with her transcriptions she needed every minute. She shot out of bed and threw on a pair of jeans and a T-shirt. She wound her wild and curly hair into a bun and secured it with a pencil. Then grabbed her bag and headed for the door. Between the kitchen and the door she noticed Amy sitting at the table with a cup of coffee and a copy of the Herald. Her bobbed brown hair was slicked back and wet as if it had just been washed. Sarah stopped in her tracks. Amy was usually up and out earlier than this.

"Hey!" Amy said.

Sarah turned back toward the apartment's dining area and stared at her roommate in confusion.

"What are you doing?" Amy's tone implied that Sarah had lost her mind.

"Going to the library?"

"We're going to Grandfather Mountain today. Remember?"

"Right." Sarah stood dumbly in the middle of the living room. Her backpack slid slowly off her shoulder and down her arm.

"You're not awake yet," Amy said. "Put your bag down and go take a shower. We've got to be going in about forty-five minutes if we're going to talk to that folksong class."

Sarah turned and walked back down the hall, still wondering how she could have forgotten about their trip. She tossed her bag into the bedroom and went straight to the bathroom to take a shower. The water revived her memory. They were indeed heading up to the Grandfather Mountain Highland Games to perform. She had even packed her bag already for the trip.

Sarah probably would have remembered earlier if she hadn't spent the better part of the night tossing and turning. She finished her shower and got dressed. She'd had the bathtub dream again. It had been happening a lot more lately—she wasn't sure why, but the result was usually a sleepless night.

"C'mon, Sarah! We're gonna be late!" Amy called as she dragged her own bag out the apartment door.

Sarah scrambled to throw her keys and wallet into her bag and follow. She squared her shoulders, took a deep breath, and stepped into the near-blinding summer sun. They stowed their bags in the back with the tent they had packed the night before.

"Donald is going to be so disappointed if we miss that class," Amy chided as Sarah slipped into the passenger's seat of Amy's Toyota.

"I know. I'm sorry. We're just singing, right?"

Amy let out an exasperated sigh. "The guy teaching the class is a friend of Donald's, and Donald told him we would come and talk about mouth music."

"That's right, the guy from Scotland."

"I don't know what's gotten into you lately." Her friend spoke over her shoulder as she turned onto Ransom Street. "You sleep even less than usual, which I didn't think was possible, and when you're awake you're half-dazed."

"It's just stress, I think, too much to get done before my research trip."

"You know, that stuff's still going to be here when you get back," Amy said, giving Sarah a sidelong glance. "I have to ask you something, and I want you to be completely honest with me. Are you on drugs?"

Sarah, who never took so much as an aspirin, gaped at her roommate. Amy gave her a crooked smile and the two exploded with laughter. Tension flew out the window. "I've been having that dream again, the one about my mother. It keeps me up. You know, because I needed more stress on top of work."

"Well, you can get plenty of sleep today. We've got a long drive ahead of us. I don't mind doing most of it, but you're taking over once we get to the mountains."

"Sounds good." Sarah shifted so she could lean back in the seat and drifted off to sleep just as Amy hit the highway.

***

Dermot was beginning to think she wasn't coming. He'd spent the past week teaching the basics of Gaelic singing to a class of tone-deaf diaspora Scots, and he was nearly at the end of his tether. He had arranged with his friend Donald to get Sarah MacAlpin and Amy Monroe, two award-winning Gaelic singers, to come and talk about puirt à beul today. As of yet, there was no sign of them.

Just as Dermot had settled on the idea that she wasn't coming, a dark head popped through the door at the back of the classroom. This was soon followed by a tallish girl with dark brown hair who seemed to be bouncing with energy. Behind her came another lass. This one was on the short side. She wasn't plump, but had generous curves in all the right places. She had a head of madly curling hair that was the color of honey.

Dermot straightened his shoulders. This was the girl he was looking for. He felt a slight sense of triumph as they settled into desks at the back, trying to make as little noise as possible.

"Mr. Sinclair?" said a girl in the front who couldn't have been more than eighteen and had been making eyes at Dermot. "What about mouth music? We haven't discussed that all week."

"Well, I havena talked about it, because we could spend a whole week on mouth music and still have barely scratched the surface. Does anyone here not have a general idea of what mouth music, or puirt à beul, is?" Dermot surveyed the few hands that went up and decided to explain. "Right. Well, believe it or not, in Scotland, there isna always a fiddler or piper handy. So we ingenious Scots developed a style of singing that allows us to mimic the rhythms of those instruments. This style tends to be fast like a reel or a strathspey. It's meant to give people somethin' to dance to."

At this, Dermot caught Sarah's eye. He gave her a wink and his most charming smile. "It just happens that we have with us two of the best puirt à beul singers in North America today, and if we ask them verra nicely, they might sing us a song or two. Ladies?"

The whole class followed his gaze to the back of the room. Amy jumped up and winked back as she walked to the front of the room. Sarah followed more slowly and addressed the class.

"The lyrics in puirt à beul are really servants to the music and are meant to be more percussive than poetic," Sarah said. "Unlike what you've been studying this week, these songs are strictly for fun, not usually for storytelling or lamenting. So some of the words might not make a lot of sense. They are loads of fun, though." She gave the students a warm smile.

Sarah began tapping her foot, and Amy came in with a verse from a particularly complicated piece. Sarah followed with the next verse. They sped up and ran through the two verses quickly before breaking into rounds that made it sound like there were more than two people singing. Dermot watched as the students nodded and tapped their toes in time. They were good, if a bit clinical. Just as the rounds swirled to a blur of rhythm and tones, the two singers stomped their feet once and sang a third verse in unison. Then they incorporated it into the round, complicating the sound even further. Their listeners began tapping their desks to the complex rhythm.

The singers finished the song off on a single, sharp beat. They were met with applause and myriad questions about how they had learned it and how much work it had taken to make it sound so clean. Sarah answered most of them. She was a born teacher. Dermot stepped to the front of the class to help her, referring to things they had covered earlier in the week. They worked well together, fielding questions and explaining the less obvious aspects of the music. By the time the students trickled out, their teachers were smiling in the afterglow of a well-delivered lesson.

Dermot turned to Sarah and held out a hand, introducing himself in Gaelic. "*'S mise Diarmad Mac na Ceàrda.*"

Sarah slipped easily in the language. "*'S mise Mòrag NicAilpein. Tha mi toilichte ur coinneachadh. Seo mo charaid, Amy Rothach.*"

Amy offered him her hand, clearly understanding what Sarah had said. "I drove most of the way. I'm afraid I'm too tired for the Gaelic right now."

He chuckled. "It's alright. We can stick to English."

"Thanks." Amy gave him a dazzling smile.

"I was beginning to think ye wouldna come." Dermot addressed Sarah's back as she retrieved her bag from the back of the room.

She turned and gave him a smile. "I'm afraid that's my fault. We got a late start this morning. Amy's lead foot is what got us here in time."

"Then ye have my thanks, Amy." He gave Amy a gallant nod.

"Don't thank me. It was fun. Anyway, Sarah did all the teaching." Amy jerked her head in her friend's direction.

"Sarah, you seem to be an expert on the subject."

"She is! She knows more about Gaelic song than anyone around here, even Donald." Amy beamed.

Sarah shrugged, not meeting his eyes. "I know as much as anyone could learn. I'm still just a scholar."

"Where did ye learn it? Ye sing like a native."

"I practice a lot," she replied curtly before turning on her heel and walking out.

Dermot turned back to Amy. "Did I touch a nerve?"

Amy was looking at the door, her brows knit. "She kind of is a native. I mean, she learned at home. She doesn't really like to talk about her family, but I've never seen her react like that before."

"Do they not get along?" he asked.

"There is no family anymore. She was raised by her grandmother, but she died a few years ago."

"I didna mean to pry." He shot a concerned look at the door where Sarah had disappeared.

"And I'm sure she didn't mean to overreact. She'll feel bad about it in a little while. You can apologize to her at the cèilidh tonight." Amy gave him a conspiratorial wink before leaving herself.

***

"He was a hottie!" Amy exclaimed as they settled into the car and headed for the campsite. "And did you see the way he was looking at you?"

"Yeah, like a hungry snake looking at a rat."

"He looked like he meant business, if that's what you mean." Amy smiled a crooked, lascivious smile.

"I am so NOT interested in romance, not even a festival fling." Sarah cut a hand through the air between them to emphasize her point.

"You were kind of short with him."

"I was nice to him. I just don't like talking about my family. You know that."

"Well, I think you overreacted," Amy said in a tone meant to take some of the sting out of her words.

"And I think you just wanted to keep him talking because he's so attractive," Sarah teased. Dermot Sinclair was a handsome man. He was tall, solidly built but not overly muscled. His close-cropped brown hair, simple jeans, and blue T-shirt suggested he dressed for utility, not for show. He looked to be in his late twenties, but something in his eyes seemed much older.

"Are you saying that I can be dazzled by a pretty face?" Amy feigned surprise.

"Oh no. It takes more than that." Sarah's face lit up with a wry smile. "I'd say a pretty face, a nice body, and a Scottish accent."

"Bitch." Amy gave Sarah a playful slap on the shoulder. "In any case, I think your Jon is in for some competition whether you like it or not."

"Good. Maybe some competition is what we need to light a fire under our young anthropologist." Sarah had to admit that she was beginning to get impatient with her would-be suitor.

"That's it!" Amy beamed. "It's that anthropologist training. Jon is observing you thoroughly before he makes his move."

"Right. If that's the case, he should have enough field notes by now to write a book on me."

"He doesn't take notes on your dates, does he?" Amy cringed.

Sarah laughed, picturing her nervous date across the table in a restaurant frantically scribbling notes about how she dressed and what she ordered. "I'm not sure which would be worse, him taking notes or me waiting endlessly for him to make a move."

"Well, there's always our handsome Scottish friend."

Sarah narrowed her eyes at her friend in mock irritation.

CHAPTER TWO

The Friday night cèilidh was a gathering for performers, much smaller and more informal than the grand and well-organized party on Saturday night. On Friday, everyone with a voice or an instrument was welcome to join in, and most did. The drums, pipes, and fiddles could be heard all over the mountain, and a bonfire lit the clearing where the performers camped. Dermot found Sarah sitting a short distance away, watching the dancing and enjoying the music.

"Beer?" He offered her a plastic cup he had filled from the keg.

"Thanks." She took the cup, which was blessedly cold on the June night. She didn't take her eyes from the party around the fire.

Dermot eased himself down next to her and watched with her for a few moments "Listen, I'm sorry about this afternoon. I wasna meaning to upset ye."

"No, I'm sorry. I shouldn't have snapped at you. You had no way of knowing." She was glad for the chance to apologize, although she was still reticent. "I just don't like to talk about my past. Being in the mountains again tends to bring it all back."

"Well, I was too forward. Ye can blame it on my curious nature." He took another sip of his beer.

"You know what they say about curiosity." Sarah shot him a sideways glance that was half sarcasm, half suspicion.

"Och, I've got a few lives in me yet." He gestured toward the crowd with his cup. "I'd expect ye to be in the thick of this wi' yer singin'."

"Oh, I'm not much of party girl. Besides, I'm the scholar. I don't participate. I observe." She gave him a smile that dared him to question her.

"Are ye ever unscholarly?"

She gave a short laugh and almost drowned her answer in her beer. "No."

"Right. Then I reckon I willna ask ye to dance."

"That's wise," she told his back as he rose to go. "I'd probably break your toes."

"Then I bid ye goodnight, Miss MacAlpin, and wish ye happy studying." He strode back toward the crowd.

She watched him go and pondered this last exchange. He'd asked her to dance. Maybe Amy was right. Maybe there was nothing wrong with this man. Still, she couldn't help feeling like he was working her, playing some sort of game. Sarah vacillated between suspicion and self-doubt all the way to the bottom of her beer.

She stared at her cup for a moment, wondering what she had been thinking accepting a drink from a near stranger. In the age of date rape drugs and god knows what else, she was usually careful not to take a drink from anyone she didn't know. The danger hadn't even occurred to her this time. It didn't taste strange, and besides he was a friend of Donald's, and everyone here would know him from the workshops he'd done. He might be forward and a bit too charming, but she didn't think he was stupid enough to drug her with all their friends around. She was being irrational, she decided, and walked toward the keg to get another beer. Just to be on the safe side, she threw away the cup. She would get another.

"Sarah!" The shout came from somewhere in the crowd of people clustered around the keg. "Just the lass I'm lookin' for."

"Donald! I haven't seen you all day. How are you?" She saw her academic advisor elbowing his way to the edge of the throng. He was a short, energetic man of middle age with lively hazel eyes and light red hair. Sarah had found a kindred spirit the first time she had walked into Donald's Gaelic class, and he had proved to be a great advisor and friend.

"Och, I'm grand." He said with a wave of his free hand, the other being occupied with his own beer. Donald's accent always thickened a bit when he'd had a few, and Sarah could tell that he was well into his cups. He gave her a gallant bow, almost spilling his beer. "Will ye join me in a reel?"

"Well, I was just coming to get a beer."

"It'll be there when yer done." He extended a hand in invitation. "C'mon. We'll see if my ol' legs canna keep up wi' ye."

"I'll wager, Dr. Campbell, that my young legs won't keep up with you." She smiled, placing her hand in his.

They reached the other dancers just as the music changed and wove easily into the pattern of the dance. Sarah had not danced like this in some time and was a little unsure at first. Soon, though, the rhythm of the music drew her in and she was weaving and turning with the group.

The partners changed as the dance swirled on, and in no time Sarah found herself arm-in-arm with Dermot Sinclair. He danced with the ease of someone who'd been doing it all his life and turned out to be quite graceful for someone of his height. Sarah glanced over her shoulder to see Donald whirling away with a new partner. He showed no signs of returning.

"I seem to have lost my partner."

"That's alright. Ye havena broken my toes yet." Dermot grinned wide.

"Keep grinning at me like that and I might do it just for spite," Sarah quipped over her shoulder while executing a turn.

Behind her, Dermot placed his hands on her waist and whispered in her ear, "I dinna think you liked me, Miss MacAlpin."

Turning again to face him she replied. "I like you just fine, Mr. Sinclair, for a near stranger who seems to ask a lot of questions."

"I promise no more questions. Perhaps yer disposition will improve." He straightened his face and tried to look earnest.

Sarah winced. "I'd also like you better if you would endeavor not to step on my foot again."

"Just letting you pay in advance for those toes ye promised to break." His eyes sparked with boyish mischief.

Sarah managed to glance at her watch and decided that her time for revelry had run out. She began extracting herself from the arm around her waist. "Oh. I should be going. It's getting late and we're singing early tomorrow. Thank you for the dance."

"Thank ye for no' breakin' my toes." He actually bowed.

"I'm sure we'll run into each other sometime tomorrow."

"Ye can bet on that," she thought she heard him mutter as she walked away.

***

Sarah was still a bit breathless from dancing as she picked her way through the sea of tents and fallen revelers. The music from around the fire wafted over the campsite, and she caught herself wondering if Dermot was still dancing. She told herself that her concerns about him were irrational. In the short time she'd known him, he'd been charming, sardonic, and maybe a little arrogant, which proved nothing beyond the fact that he was Scottish. He'd given her no reason to suspect him of anything other than wanting to be her friend. By the time she reached the tent she and Amy shared, she had determined that she would have to be nicer to the man.

A breeze whisked through the campsite and stirred her hair. It brushed the back of her neck like icy fingers, cold even for the mountains. As Sarah bent down to unzip the tent, a flash of white near the tree line caught her eye. She straightened up and stared into the woods behind the tent, trying to catch a glimpse of the thing. "Hope it's not a skunk," she thought, bending down again and opening the tent. She had crawled halfway in when she was stopped by a sound behind her. It was an odd sound, not a gasp, but like air being sucked in quickly between teeth. Sarah turned her head to look over her shoulder just in time to see a woman turning away and walking toward the trees. From her position half in the tent, she only saw the woman's legs and the trail of her white skirt. Sarah backed out of the tent and took a few steps toward the woods.

"Wait," she thought…but before she uttered a word the woman turned to look back. Sarah's breath caught in her throat as she found herself staring into her mother's eyes.

They stood frozen for a moment. Then Molly turned and walked deeper into the forest. Sarah trailed after her. They wound through the trees and around rocks. Molly always managed to stay a few steps out of Sarah's reach. Even in the dark, she could see the crown of spring flowers ringing Molly's head, just as they had done nineteen years before when Sarah had put the crown there. Molly was moving faster, almost running, and Sarah tried harder to keep up, afraid she might lose sight of her in the trees. She wanted to call out to her mother, asking the questions that had lingered in her mind for years, but she was nearly out of breath. Sarah threw herself forward, trying to catch Molly, but she disappeared around an ancient and sprawling tree. Sarah rounded the trunk and stopped dead.

Molly was standing in the center of a clearing. Her face was a blend of sadness, fear, and anger. She leaned from the waist toward Sarah and spoke a single word. At first there was no sound, like someone had hit the mute button. Then the word came to Sarah in a gust of frigid wind that hit her square in the face.

RUN.

Sarah plunged into the clearing, but Molly vanished just as Sarah reached the center. Sarah spun around, looking for her, but there were only trees and stones and silence. On the ground at her feet was the crown of flowers. Sarah knelt to pick it up. When her hand touched it, there was a flash of white light. Sarah looked up and into the eyes of an old woman whose face was kind on the surface, but her eyes were hard. The woman reached down and took Sarah's hands. She began singing as she pulled Sarah up to stand. The woman's voice sounded old, older than the giant tree on the edge of the clearing, older than the stone, as Granny used to say. It was a song Granny had taught her about the king lost in the mist. The verse ended with the words that had rolled around in Sarah's head for five years—her grandmother's last words, in a language she couldn't understand.

Another flash of light transformed the clearing into a cave and the old woman was gone. The air was cold and damp. She heard heavy breathing behind her and turned. In a silvery shaft of light, a couple was making love on top of a large square stone. The man's back was to her, but Sarah could see that he was fit and young with dark hair. Over his shoulder, she caught a glimpse of honey-colored curls. Sarah stepped closer and to the side until she could see more of the woman. She tried to be quiet. The vision seemed so real she was afraid to disturb them. With a gasp of pleasure, the woman raised her head and turned to her. Sarah felt a stab of pain deep in the pit of her stomach, and her breath caught in her throat. She stared aghast at herself there on the stone with this faceless man thrusting into her. Her other self started a second at seeing her, and then her face seemed calm, self-assured. She knew this would happen.

In another flash Sarah was in the upstairs hall of her grandmother's house. She was standing in front of a door. She didn't have to wonder what was on the other side. She knew. She started to turn away, but the door opened by itself and Sarah saw Molly fall limp to the blood-soaked bed. She ran to the bed as she had done on that day years before. Knowing she couldn't stop it but desperate to ask why. Molly lay lifeless before her, unseeing eyes gazing at the wall above. Sarah lifted her head to see what her mother had been looking at. It was there on the wall, scrawled in Molly's own blood, the only message that her mother had left: *Ruith.*

Run.

CHAPTER THREE

"So then I says, 'Get doon from there, ye daft coo! The lads can see yer knickers!'" The men standing around the only remaining keg at the cèilidh erupted in laughter.

Campbell was entertaining a crowd with ribald tale about his now ex-wife that left Dermot rather un-surprised about the "ex" part. Dermot was wondering about his chances of separating Donald Campbell from his rapt audience. The party around the fire was dying. Musicians were packing up their instruments and drifting toward their tents. The dancing had stopped sometime around midnight. Dermot was nearly ready to drag Campbell away when he spotted Sarah's friend, Amy, standing behind the man, looking worried.

"Donald?" She tapped Campbell on the shoulder.

He spun around to look at her and swayed just a bit. It took a moment for him to focus and for her name to make it to his lips. "Amy!" he exploded. "Will ye no' join us in a beer?"

She spoke slowly and tried to maintain eye contact. "Have you seen Sarah?"

"Sarah?" He almost shouted. "Of course, lovely girl Sarah."

"She left here a couple of hours ago," Dermot spoke up. "Said she was goin' to bed."

"Thank you," Amy said, worry creeping over her face.

Dermot took her arm and pulled her aside from the group. "What is it?"

Amy looked up at him for a moment, chewing on her lip. "She's not at the tent. It was just sitting open, but she isn't there."

"Maybe she ran into someone she knew and went somewhere to talk."

"I don't think so." Her voice rose a notch. "She wouldn't have left the tent open, and I've looked everywhere."

Taking her arm again, Dermot steered her toward the tents. "Can ye think of anywhere else she might've gone?"

"Nowhere that I haven't already looked. Listen, she'd kill me for telling you this but," she gasped for breath as they started walking faster, "sometimes she walks in her sleep. It's one thing when it's around the apartment, but I'm afraid she'll get hurt up here."

"Then we've got to find her." The seriousness of the situation began to dawn on him. "Where's yer tent?"

"This way." She pointed toward the edge of the camp near the trees.

When they got to the tent, Dermot surveyed the area. The tent was partially unzipped, but nothing inside seemed to have been disturbed. "Is this the way she left it?"

Amy stood nearby wringing her hands. She nodded.

"Did you check the woods?"

"Oh, God. Do you think she went in there?" Amy almost cried, looking at the dense forest behind the tent.

"We'll find out. I'll go this way." He waved a hand to the right. "Ye go that way. Start as far out as ye can and work yer way back here."

Amy nodded and started off down the tree line to the left. Dermot ran to the right until the forest gave way to a meadow. He turned back toward the campsite and plunged into the trees. He worked his way through the forest, zigzagging to cover as much ground as possible. He was grateful the moon was nearly full and gave him enough light to prevent him from running into trees. He could hear Amy calling for Sarah, but decided he would get more searching done with his eyes. He looked everywhere he thought she might have fallen or hidden. After nearly an hour of checking every tree trunk and hollow log, Dermot began to lose hope.

He noticed the stones first. He counted eight around the perimeter of the clearing. They weren't tall, and some of them were covered in moss, but he had no doubt it was a circle. They were too evenly spaced to be natural. He was surveying the circle and marveling at the fact that no one seemed to know it was there when he heard her. Peering into the shadow of a giant oak at the edge of the circle, he found Sarah curled up and whimpering like a child.

"Sarah?" He approached her slowly. He wanted her to feel safe. "Sarah, we've been looking all over for ye."

She didn't move or even look up.

"Ye should've told us ye were goin' for a walk." He cooed as he laid a comforting hand on her back. He stepped in front of her and crouched to get a look at her face. In her hands she clutched a crown of flowers that Dermot thought were out of season. "Sarah?"

She lifted her head. Her eyes were red and her face streaked with tears and dirt. A few wet curls clung to her cheeks. Dermot watched patiently as she looked around. He could see her face change as she tried to make sense of her surroundings. He began to think she was coming around until she faced him. Her eyes went wide and wild. She sank back and began frantically scooting away from him in terror.

Dermot reached out to soothe her, but she bolted and ran into the woods like a startled deer.

"Amy! I've found her!" he shouted as he rose to follow Sarah.

She ran faster than he had thought possible. She leapt over rocks and logs and dodged around trees. Dermot stayed as close as he could. He shouted to Amy often so she would be able to find them. Sarah crashed through bushes and creeks without slowing down. Dermot was losing hope of catching her. He tried calling to her once more. She glanced over her shoulder and in her distraction tripped over a root.

She went sprawling to the ground, and Dermot tackled her before she could get to her feet again. He wrapped his arms around her upper body and rolled on top of her. "It's alright, Sarah." He said in her ear. "We're not alone. It's alright."

He heard Amy calling and shouted to her. By the time Amy reached them, Dermot had soothed Sarah enough to roll off her. He still held her, though, not sure that she wouldn't try to run again.

Amy eyed Sarah with a sort of affectionate exasperation. Dermot had thought Sarah to be the sensible one of the pair, the one who took care of Amy. Seeing Amy walk her friend back to the tent with a sheltering arm around her showed him that they were about even in the caretaking department. He stayed with them until they reached their tent and then until Sarah was snug in her sleeping bag. He only left when Amy assured him they would be fine for the night.

***

The next morning dawned through a mist that clung to the side of the mountain. The festival-goers awoke to find a heavy layer of dew coating the camp. Sarah stretched like a cat unfurling itself after a nap in the sun. Through the nylon of the tent, she could hear the stirrings around her and the morning bagpipes waking everyone. She was shocked into awareness by the stinging scratches on her arms. The clothes she'd been wearing the night before were in a heap by her feet and completely covered in dirt. She grabbed Amy's travel mirror and noted a few scratches on her face and the leaves and twigs in her matted hair. Her eyes were red and puffy and her throat felt like she'd swallowed hot coals. Suddenly, the memory of her vision the night before came rushing back. "Run," her mother had told her. She must have been hallucinating.

Sarah put on clean clothes from her bag and unzipped the tent to find Amy waiting outside with two huge cups of coffee. "Drink," Amy commanded, shoving a cup into Sarah's hand. "I've arranged for us to get hot showers."

"Thank God." Sarah took her first sip of coffee and savored it. "I look like hell."

"That's putting it mildly."

"What happened to me?"

"Well," Amy sighed. "If you don't remember, then I'd guess you were sleep walking again."

"Hmm." Yes! That was it. She'd been dreaming about Molly. She'd done that enough times before.

"It's a good thing Dermot found you or I'd still be looking," Amy said while gathering her stuff to take to the shower. Her movements were quick and sharp.

"Dermot?" Sarah could feel her face starting to burn with embarrassment. She made no move to get her own things and instead concentrated on her coffee.

"I know you don't like him," Amy said, starting to gather Sarah's things too. "But he was the only person awake and sober when I went looking for you."

"I understand."

"I hope you do!" Amy snapped. "I was worried sick!"

Sarah laid a hand on her friend's arm and looked her earnestly in the eye. "I do. Thank you."

They finished gathering their things and headed for a dormitory at the nearby college. Amy had made friends with a resident assistant there who let them shower in his hall. It took Sarah half an hour, with Amy's help, to get the debris and snarls out of her hair.

"You look like a wood nymph," Amy observed, holding up a twig with some leaves still attached for Sarah to see in the mirror.

"How did I get to be such a mess, and how did I get these scratches?" Sarah asked, holding up a nearly raw forearm.

"Dermot found you in the woods, and you ran," Amy explained, struggling with a particularly nasty tangle. "I don't know how you live with this hair! You can't possibly get all the tangles out."

"It takes a lifetime of practice." Sarah smiled at the thought of years past when she had cursed her mop of curls. "I ran?"

"Yeah, like you stole something. Dermot must've chased you half a mile." Amy leveled a direct look at her in the mirror.

"It's a good thing he wasn't drunk then. He might have hurt himself."

"Oh, I imagine he's got a few scratches to match yours. He had to tackle you to get you to stop."

Sarah's memory flashed into focus, and she could feel herself face down in the leaves with strong arms tight around her and Dermot Sinclair's voice in her ear. "I wonder where I thought I was going."

"That, my friend, is a mystery to us all."

CHAPTER FOUR

They arrived at the festival early enough that the competing pipe bands were still warming up. A cacophony of wheezing drones and skirling tunes rushed in as Sarah opened the car door and was introduced to the most lasting result of the night before: her head throbbed. She winced and put on her sunglasses in the hopes they would hide the puffiness around her eyes. Amy spotted the movement and reached into the glove box for a bottle of Extra Strength Tylenol. She counted out three of the little wonders and gave them to Sarah, following them with the still half-full cup of coffee. Sarah almost never took pills, but today she needed the fast relief and accepted them gratefully. She silently praised the person who'd thought to make a paper cup large enough to hold twenty ounces of coffee.

As they made their way through the parking lot, Amy arched an eyebrow and gave her friend a wicked wink. "God! I love the sound of the pipers tuning. Don't you?"

"Yeah," Sarah replied flatly before gulping more coffee and hoping the pain in her head would wear off.

"Gets in your bones, doesn't it?" Amy wasn't going to quit. "Rings around in your head all day."

Sarah knew the score. She had made her carefree friend worry and now she was going to have to pay. "Bitch."

"Harpy." Amy flashed their performer passes for the attendant at the staff gate and they walked up the avenue of vendors.

Tent after tent was being erected along the festival's main drag. Before long, every one of them would be decked with racks of plaid and stacks of books watched diligently by their proprietors eager to help spectators get in touch with their Scottish heritage. Some tents were stuffed with books ranging from cookbooks extolling the virtues of herring and grouse to biographies of famous Jacobites. T-shirt stands stood between silversmiths and kilt makers. The girls each had shirts declaring their respective clans. Today, however, they wore jeans and simple black T-shirts that proclaimed her earliest ancestors in plain white letters. Amy's read "Gael" and Sarah's "Pict."

They found their way to the pub tent where they would be performing. The pub manager looked them up and down, taking note of Sarah's appearance. He spoke softly, thinking her hung over, which wouldn't be unusual for some of the performers he dealt with. He had been at the cèilidh too. "I've got programs for you and schedules for this tent. Everything's running about half an hour late, so you're going on at 11:30 instead of 11:00."

"Thanks," they said, taking the proffered booklets.

"There's breakfast in the back of my van if you're hungry." He gave them a fatherly smile.

"You're a good man." Sarah patted his shoulder as they made their way to the various vans and trucks behind the stage. The aroma of bacon and biscuits made it apparent which one was his.

The girls collected plates of eggs, bacon, and homemade biscuits and sat at a table near the stage. Sarah found that she didn't have enough energy to sit up straight and carry the food to her mouth. She propped an elbow on the table and held her head up with her hand, slowly spooning food into her mouth. Not even Granny's scrambled eggs had ever tasted this good. She hadn't even known she was hungry until she had smelled the food, but now she savored every bite.

She was halfway through her eggs when Amy dropped her fork and let out a low whistle. "Damn! Is it me or did the pipes just get a little louder?"

Sarah looked over her shoulder to see what had caught her friend's attention. There, down the alley of shops, stood her savior from the night before, burnished by the morning sun and kilted in red and green Sinclair tartan. He looked every bit the Scottish hero. He was weaving his way through the vendor's crates and tent poles and perusing their wares. His broad shoulders were wrapped in a polo shirt that was just tight enough to show off the muscles in his shoulders. It clung to his trim waist and was tucked into his kilt with military neatness. No one seeing Dermot Sinclair as he was dressed that morning would ever refer to a kilt as a skirt. Sarah didn't think she'd ever seen a man look hotter.

"I swear there is nothing finer than a man in a kilt." Amy craned to see down the lane over Sarah's shoulder.

Sarah stared, mouth agape, and admired the view...until she remembered the night before. She hissed, "Shit! I am not ready for this."

"You're gonna have to face him sometime."

"Well, not now. I…" Sarah searched for an excuse to get the hell out of Dodge, "need more coffee. I'll get you some too."

She sprang to her feet and nearly ran to the booth selling coffee.

Sarah's hands shook as she put cream and sugar in their coffees. Before she headed back to the table she checked to see if the coast was clear. Amy was alone, munching on a biscuit. Sarah picked up their coffees and turned back toward their table and nearly ran right into Dermot.

"Oh!" A few drops of hot coffee sloshed onto her hand.

"Here, let me take that." He scooped up the coffees as she rubbed her injured knuckles.

"Thank you." There was just no escaping this man.

"Morning." He smiled down at her over the top of his sunglasses. There was no trace of the smugness or teasing she expected from him.

She stared at him incredulously, expecting some bit of sarcasm. When she realized there wouldn't be any, she grumbled, "Uh, morning."

"Are ye alright?"

"I'm sorry?"

"Yer hand? Is it all right? Can you carry these?" He offered the coffees back to her.

"Oh! Yeah, I'll be fine." She nodded, still not believing he wasn't going to say anything about the night before. As she looked down to take the coffees from him, she noticed the scratches on his arms. She gasped before she could stop herself.

"Och. Must've fallen on my way back to the tent. It was a rare party last night. Ye should have stayed." He gave her a gentle smile, and suddenly she felt weightless when just seconds before she'd been dragging. It was a sensation something like being poised at the top of the first big hill on a roller coaster, that breathless, gut-twisting feeling that resulted from mixing gravity with inevitability. "Go on and take Amy her coffee. I'll be there in a tic."

She started back to the tent, and Dermot moved up a space in line. Sarah stopped and looked back at the man who had just saved her from what had promised to be the most embarrassing moment of her life. She could have kissed him.

***

The three of them enjoyed their breakfast at the pub tent and hung around until it was time for girls' first performance. Sarah kept the bottom half of her face hidden in her cup of coffee and the top half behind her sunglasses until just before they went on. Dermot began to worry that she wasn't going to be able to perform. The few words she'd said to him had been raspy. When she got up once to go to the loo, he leaned over to Amy.

"Is she going to be able to sing?" he asked.

"Sarah? Yeah, she'll be fine. She's just saving her strength." Amy patted his arm. "See, here she comes."

Dermot looked in the direction of the restrooms just in time to see Sarah trip and nearly land on her face. She managed to catch herself and keep walking.

"Sure she's alright, are ye?" Dermot nodded in Sarah's direction.

"Oh sure." Amy waved a hand as if brushing away his concern. "She's not really awake if she hasn't fallen down a couple of times."

Dermot watched Sarah's approach cautiously, ready to spring into action if she fell again. She noticed him watching her as she trudged back under the tent. "Why is it that you always seem to be around when I'm making an idiot of myself?"

He gave her his most sardonic grin as he leaned back in his chair. "I'm always around. It's just the embarrassing times that ye notice."

"Well, let's see if I can manage not to embarrass myself for everyone. I'll just save the best moments for you." She must be feeling better. The sarcasm was back. She reached around him for her coffee and took one last swig before looking at Amy over his shoulder. "Ready?"

Amy rose and stepped toward the stage. As she passed Dermot, she leaned down and whispered. "Watch."

They had the simplest setup possible: two singers, no instruments, nothing to get in the way, true balladeers. There was no warm-up and no introduction. They just stepped up onto the stage. Sarah took her sunglasses off and laid them on top of an amplifier, then stepped to one of the two microphones. She nodded to the sound tech and closed her eyes. It was 11:30, and the tent had plenty of people in it, but most of them were talking and waiting for the beer to start flowing. They didn't notice the two women standing quietly on the stage.

Ever so softly, Sarah began to sing. By the second line of the song, a few people had stopped talking and looked at the stage. Slowly, everyone's attention was drawn to the pure, simple sound coming from the stage. Amy joined on the chorus, and by the time they finished the first run-through, no one was talking. Dermot wasn't even breathing. It was a lament—one he knew well—about a hunter who returned home after a long hunt to find his sweetheart betrothed to another. He had probably heard fifty people sing the song, but none of them had been like this. This was not the same clinical and precise singer who had taught his workshop about mouth music. Sarah seemed to fully capture the heartbreak that the original singer must have felt. She wasn't singing the song as others did. She was really lamenting, and she held the crowd spellbound. Dermot looked around him and found everyone had their eyes fixed on the women on stage. He even saw tears in the eyes of a bullish kilted man in the beer line. Sarah finished the last chorus alone, and Dermot was not surprised to hear sniffling from various locations behind him.

Then Amy took the lead on an upbeat puirt à beul that had toes tapping all around the tent. It was a very flirty song, praising the virtues of a particular specimen of manhood. The second verse had hands clapping to the rhythm. Sarah picked up the third verse, now coy and beguiling. When they broke into rounds, everyone in the tent was clapping and moving their heads to the sweeping sounds of their voices. Sarah and Amy carried the crowd with them through more laments and dancing songs and Jacobite ballads for nearly an hour. They left the stage to applause that Dermot would not have expected that early in the day and were swarmed with admirers as soon as they got off the stage. Dermot waited patiently by his seat as they made their way through the crowd that now spilled out the sides of the tent. Sarah had put on her sunglasses again, but he could see a new flush in her cheeks and a smile. Amy was grinning wide.

"I'd say that went well."

Sarah nodded.

Amy elbowed Dermot. "And you were worried."

Sarah accepted a bottle of water from the pub manager and drank nearly half the bottle before stopping to breathe. Dermot watched her throat work as she slowly lifted the bottle higher. She was obviously too thirsty to care that some of the water escaped and ran down her chin. She drew the back of her hand across her mouth to wipe away the excess. She was about to put the bottle to her mouth again when she caught Dermot staring at her. "What?"

Dermot shook himself, trying not to hang on the image of her breathless, her full lips wet and red from the cold. Remembering her comment earlier, he said. "I was just marveling at yer ability to not make an idiot o' yerself."

She gave him a slight nod. "Glad you noticed."

***

The ladies spent the hours when they weren't performing watching the athletic competition. Their second performance was even better than the first, now that Sarah was fully awake. Once it was done, they returned to the athletic field for more of their favorite spectator sport. It was on returning to the pub tent for dinner before the cèilidh that they ran into Dermot again.

"Meat pie?" he asked innocently, turning to them from the counter of a vendor selling the very items.

Having spent the afternoon gazing at sweaty, muscled men, the girls' minds were on a rather raunchy bent. Dermot's offer was just too perfect. Both of their faces turned bright red. They managed to stifle their laughter, but the amusement was far too evident in their eyes. Sarah spoke first. "Because you were so gracious to me this morning, I'm just not going to respond to that."

"I will," Amy told her, loud enough for him to hear. She took off her sunglasses and edged closer to Dermot, taking advantage of the fact that his hands were full with his dinner. "So, Mr. Sinclair, were you offering us dinner or discussing what's behind your sporran?" She lightly tapped the leather sporran hanging in front of this kilt with her glasses.

It was Dermot's turn to blush, and blush he did. It started to creep up from the neckline of his shirt and managed to reach the top of his head in a matter of seconds. He nearly choked at the light tap of the sunglasses just over his crotch. "And someone told me that Carolina girls were supposed to be shy and demure."

"Evidently, he's never really been here." Amy gave him a little wink and stepped back.

Sarah came to Dermot's rescue. "You have to excuse her. We've just come from watching a bunch of men toss giant poles to prove who's got more under his kilt. That always leaves Amy a little…excited."

"Just a little?" he feigned worry.

"Well," Sarah arched an eyebrow, and he saw a wicked gleam flicker in her eyes, "the meat pie offer didn't help."

"I'll try to remember that next time." He grinned back at her.

“We will join you for dinner, though.” Amy stepped back to him, just as close as she had before, enjoying how uncomfortable it made him. “That is, if you’re not scared of a couple of hungry girls.”

He flashed his own wicked gleam at Amy and bent lower until he could feel her breath on his chin. His voice was deep, feral, almost a growl. “Are ye so sure ye shouldna be afraid of a hungry Scot? It’s been a long time since I’ve had a good…” He lowered his head a bit and sniffed from the nape of her neck to her ear. Then he whispered, “Meal”

Amy beamed her approval as she watched him saunter over to a table, kilt swinging. She let out a wistful sigh and leaned closer to Sarah. "He’s fun. Can we keep him?"

"Only if you promise to walk him every day and clean up after him."

***

That evening they were trading road stories with a bunch of other musicians before the cèilidh started when a new band showed up. A huge arm reached around Amy and nearly lifted her from her chair. She spun around and let out a squeal of delight when she saw five burley, kilted men in Stetson hats standing behind her. They all crowded around her, and she nearly disappeared in the crush of broad shoulders and grabbing arms.

“Who are they?” Dermot asked.

“They,” Sarah said with a note of affection, “are the Lone Star Scots, a rowdy bunch of cowboys from Texas who happen to play some wonderful music, and if you couldn’t tell they’re all mad about Amy.”

"She seems to be pretty mad about them as well," he observed, watching Amy kiss and hug them all.

"Well, they're all really nice guys, but she's only crazy for Andy. He's the piper, of course. Amy's got a weakness for pipers."

"Sarah!" a tall blonde one bellowed, stepping around the table with outstretched arms. "How the hell are ya, girl?"

"I'm fine," she said, rising to receive his bear hug. "You boys are late. Shouldn't you have been here yesterday?"

"The van broke down around Charlotte. I had the boys push it the rest of the way."

Sarah squeezed his bicep and fluttered her lashes. "You mean you couldn't push it all by yourself?"

He swept his arm around her waist and pulled her up against him. "You shouldn't tease a man, Sarah."

He made a playful bite at her neck, and she giggled like a girl. Dermot told himself that they knew each other while he had only just met Sarah. Still, he couldn't help a stab of jealousy at the easy way she flirted and let herself be handled by the burly Texan. He wasn't the only one who noticed either. He glanced past the man's shoulder and recognized a similar emotion on Amy's face.

Sarah turned back to Dermot, with Andy's arm still around her. "Andy MacAffrey, this is our new friend Dermot Sinclair. Dermot, Andy."

"Nice to meet you, man." Andy removed his arm from Sarah and offered his hand to Dermot.

Dermot took the hand in a firm grip. "Likewise, mate."

Andy turned his attention back to Sarah. "Sarah-girl, you've got to sing with us tonight. There's too many men up there, we need a pretty face with us."

"I don't think so, Andy. I had a rough night last night, and I've been singing all day."

"Alright, then I'm gonna borrow Amy for a bit."

Sarah gave him a wink. "Fine. Just remember you break her, you bought her. "

A few minutes later, the band started to come to life on the stage, tuning guitars and fiddles and warming up pipes. When they were ready, the pub manager introduced the band and the crowded tent erupted with applause. Dermot generally preferred more traditional music to their brand of Celtic rock, but he had to admit these guys were entertaining. Andy proved to be an adept piper, and the fiddle player was fantastic. They gave all they had through a couple of very raucous songs, and the crowd was beginning to get into it when Andy introduced Amy. She and the piper sang a sweet slow duet before breaking into a rock arrangement of "Loch Lomond."

Sarah laughed and applauded when they switched to the next song and Amy stayed on the stage. She turned to Dermot with light in her eyes. "They're not bad, huh?"

"No, not bad at all." He watched her turn, smiling, back to the stage as the next song started. "She's great."

Sarah watched Amy charm the crowd. Smiling, "Yeah. I'm lucky she puts up with me."

"You've been friends a long time?"

"Mmm. About four years. She was trying to take this Art and Anthropology class that I was in, but the class was full. She just came anyway, and kept for weeks even when the professor told her to stop. Eventually, someone dropped out and she took their spot. I liked her persistence, and her sense of humor."

"I can be persistent, and funny." He leaned in so only she would hear. "I think perhaps ye're starting to like me too, Miss MacAlpin."

"Could be," she said with a wry smile. They fell silent for a few minutes, enjoying the performance, before Sarah turned to him, looking pensive.

"Dermot, I have to ask you something. And," she paused, biting her lip, "I hope you won't be offended, because that's not my intention."

He gave a nervous laugh and shifted in his chair to look at her directly. "Alright."

She studied his face a moment and took a deep breath. She switched to Gaelic hoping that no one around them spoke it. "Did you put something in my drink last night?"

Sarah watched comprehension sweep over his face. He leaned forward, full of concern and placed his hand over hers. "Is that why ye ran from me?"

She nodded, shifting uncomfortably.

"Och, Christ! Sarah…" He looked stricken. His face showed nothing but disbelief. "How could ye think such a thing?"

"I don't remember much about last night." She struggled to keep her voice even. "All I do remember is taking a drink from you, which I foolishly drank, dancing, and going back to my tent. Then I woke up three hours later face down in the dirt with you on top of me. What am I supposed to think?"

When she put it that way, it did sound incriminating. He couldn't believe it. She had laughed and joked with him half the day, and yet this had been in her mind all the time. He sat there with his hand on hers, not knowing what to say. He shook his head slowly as if her question could roll right out of it and be forgotten. He tried not to meet her gaze, but he knew she was looking at him.

***

Sarah couldn't believe she'd said it. She had asked him directly; she'd accused him of a crime. He was hurt by it. She read the pain and perplexity on his face. She knew then that he hadn't done it, that he wasn't capable of it. She had hit him, but he didn't leave, didn't strike back. He just sat there, stunned and holding her hand. She looked at his hand on hers and saw the scratches he'd gotten in his effort to help her. "Listen," she said to the top of his head as it hung from his shoulders. "I've only had a few people in this life I could depend on, and most of them are dead. I've managed to keep myself safe for this long by keeping my wits about me. Last night, for the first time in a long time, I let my guard down and something went very wrong. So I reached for an explanation. I'm just trying to make sense of it."

He took his hand away and ran it through his hair, still shaking his head. "Ah, Sarah." His eyes met hers as he struggled to find words. "I didna…I wouldna…"

"Yes, I see that now." Her voice was low, almost a whisper, but there was a hardness in it like a door being slammed shut. "I'm sorry to have upset you." She sprang up from her chair and made a hasty exit. She was mortified. How could she have thought such a thing? How could she have dared to ask him that? He had rescued her the night before, and this was how she repaid him? She hurried back to her tent with tears starting to sting her eyes. She dove in and curled up on her sleeping bag before the tears came in earnest. They weren't just tears of embarrassment, but of loneliness and fear. It was one thing to know she was alone, but it was bigger, more powerful somehow to actually say it out loud.

CHAPTER FIVE

Anemone flowers floated above her, swirling around, a white and pink kaleidoscope. Through the flowers, she could make out the white ceiling and the old-fashioned circular rod that held up the shower curtain. Her mother's arms came around her and held her as they had so often when she was a little girl. She felt a hand stroking her hair and her mother's voice cooed in her ear.

...They won't have you. I won't let them...

Suddenly her mother was there on the other side of the flowery film, her face twisted and hideous.

...let them take you, mo nighean. I won't let...

Her mother's hands dug into her shoulders, holding her under the water.

...Mama? I can't breathe...

...not my baby...not take you...

...Mama, don't...

...do it to you...not while I...

***

Dermot had moved his tent to within sight of theirs so he could keep an eye on Sarah. He was sitting inside with the flap open when he saw her come out. She looked around as if to make sure no one was watching. Then she walked to the back of her tent, not far from the tree line. Dermot crouched on the balls of his feet, ready to follow if she went into the woods again, but she didn't. She eased herself down on the ground and sat with her elbows on her knees looking at the forest. He didn't think she was sleepwalking again. She seemed awake, but deep in thought. She dropped her head into her hands in a gesture filled with such despair that it nearly broke his heart.

"I've only had a few people in this life I could depend on and most of them are dead." He looked away in frustration. He knew he should stay away from her, but part of him wanted to run to her and tell her that she wasn't alone. The other part knew he should stand his ground.

Against his better judgment, he just couldn't leave her alone like that. He approached her slowly and quietly, almost as if he were afraid she would bolt again like last night.

"*A' Mhórag*," he addressed her in Gaelic.

She turned and squinted at him through the darkness. "*A' Dhiarmaid?*"

Damn! He hadn't thought of how to explain his being up and about or coming to her tent. He told her lamely, "I was afraid ye might be walkin' in yer sleep again."

She gave a soft laugh. "I assure you, I'm wide awake. Couldn't get back to sleep so I thought I'd come out here and enjoy the night."

"It's nice." He sat down next to her and looked at the forest in front of them.

"I'd forgotten how much I love nights in the mountains." Her voice was dreamy as she leaned back closing her eyes. "I used to sit on our porch at all hours and just listen to all the little frogs and crickets singing. My Granny used to call them *seinneadairean beaga*." *[Little singers.]*

So her grandmother spoke the Gaelic, unusual in the twentieth century outside of Scotland or Cape Breton. Now he recognized the reasons for Sarah's accent, which was an odd mix of Scots brogue and a western North Carolina twang. It grew thicker as she grew nostalgic. "Was it yer grandmother taught ye the songs then?"

She looked at him a moment as if she just realized they were talking. "Some of 'em. The rest I learned from recordings and other singers."

"Amy said she raised ye."

***

Sarah realized she was sharing more than she had intended, but she didn't care anymore. She was amazed he'd still speak to her after what she'd accused him of. "She did, after my mother died. It wasn't easy."

Dermot must have caught the note of melancholy in her voice. "Ye must have loved her verra much."

She stared at the trees for a few breaths before answering. "I did. I lost her five years ago, and now…" She shook her head and seemed to choke on the words. "Now I just push people away."

"Like ye did me." It was half statement, half question.

She looked out at the trees and nodded slightly. "Like I did you. I even do it to Amy half the time."

"Ye know, ye dinna have to be alone."

She gave him a sideways glance and arched an eyebrow. "Is this the part where you tell me I have a friend in Jesus?" As soon as she said it, she realized she was using sarcasm as a shield. "I'm sorry. I know I don't, but old habits die hard."

They sat for a few minutes just looking at the trees and listening to the night sounds. Somewhere in the distance a whippoorwill called. "Staying in school when a lot of people your age opt for the security of a job, getting up in front of hundreds of people and singing, confronting me the way ye did earlier…I think yer verra brave. "

***

She turned to him with a sad half-smile. "I don't feel so brave lately, but you just have to keep plugging along. Don't you?" she whispered. For a frozen moment, she hid nothing, and Dermot saw all of her: fear, loneliness, and beauty. It pulled at him like gravity.

He was vaguely aware of moving closer to her, of leaning in, but by the time he realized what he was doing it was too late. His lips were on hers. His hand was cupping her face. His thumb stroked her cheek, and he felt the stickiness of dried tears. She returned his kiss with interest. One hand slid up his arm, over his shoulder, and her fingers laced through his hair. Her other hand caressed his thigh just beneath the hem of his kilt. Her lips were soft but hungry against his.

Warning bells sounded in his head. He knew he had to stop, but her tongue danced against his, sending his senses reeling. No! This was wrong. She was not for him. He tore his lips away from hers, but slid his hand behind her head. Her eyes were closed, and she leaned back into his hand like a cat wanting her ears scratched. Before she had been distant and reticent, now she was open and compliant. She was captivating, and he had to remind himself again that she was not for him. She drew his face back toward her own. He stopped her, gently leaning his forehead to hers as she let out a ragged sigh.

"I shouldna have done that," he said, pulling her hand from behind his head and removing the other from his thigh. He squeezed her hands together and stuck her in place with a piercing look. "I'm sorry."

He left, every muscle rigid with frustration. Sarah sat there puzzled and silent.

***

Dermot was still on Sarah's mind when a mountain breeze woke her before dawn. She burrowed deeper into the warmth of her sleeping bag, not wanting to expose herself to the chilly mountain morning just yet. She wasn't ready to face it, to face him. Despite all her misgivings, Sarah had to admit she had enjoyed that kiss. She couldn't remember the last time she'd been kissed with such abandon. Something about that man felt good, like warm flannel sheets, like home. Yet evidently he hadn't felt the same. He'd been embarrassed and guilty and had left her bereft and confused.

"Damn him," she thought, throwing back the flap of the sleeping bag. She quickly threw some clothes on and tied her hair back. The morning air was cool on her skin as she crawled out of the tent. It was early, and most of the camp was still asleep, but Sarah didn't really notice as she headed for the car. She was up before Amy, and it was her turn to go for coffee. She was determined to go on with her day as if nothing were different. She went behind the tent to the edge of the tree line and skirted around the camp on her way to the parking area.

She was coming around a stand of trees just in sight of the cars when she saw Dermot. He was loading the trunk of his rental car. He looked grim. He slammed the trunk closed and stood there a moment with his hands spread wide on the lid, his head hanging from his shoulders. He slowly started to shake his head and pushed off the back of the car. Retrieving the keys from the trunk lock, he stomped around to the door and got in. The engine started, and he swung the Ford Taurus from the space. Gravel spat out from behind the car as he tore out of the parking lot. He was obviously in a hurry, and Sarah couldn't help thinking he was in a hurry to get away from her.

CHAPTER SIX

Early August 1995
Cape Breton, Nova Scotia, Canada

Sarah's trip to Cape Breton had been well worth the cost. She'd gathered dozens of good songs and stories and had even found a few households where Gaelic still lived as a language. She felt thrilled at collecting songs firsthand and interacting with other Gaelic speakers. Any enthusiasm she had lost during her months locked in the library listening to ancient recordings was now restored. She was anxious to get back home and work on her dissertation. Still, she felt as though there was something missing, some song that would link American English songs with their Canadian and Scottish Gaelic counterparts. She could still make her points with the various songs she had, but one song that crossed communities to show an evolution would be the key between good and great.

Sarah walked along the beach behind the campground where she was staying and planned how she would use the songs she had collected. She didn't notice the other woman on the beach until she was nearly on top of her. The young woman cleared her throat. Sarah stopped short. "I'm sorry. I was so deep in thought I almost stepped on you."

"That's alright. I was actually coming to see you," the young woman said casually. Like Sarah, she appeared to be in her mid-twenties with wavy light blonde hair and laughing blue eyes.

"Me?"

"You're the one collecting the songs, aren't you?" The woman gave Sarah an open, friendly smile.

"Oh!" Sarah instantly perked up. "Yes. I am. Do you have a song?"

"My grandmother does. Come on, our house is just over the hill." She pointed to a nearby hill with a narrow sandy path that snaked its way over the top.

Sarah started to follow her, but stopped. She didn't have a tape recorder or even a notebook to write anything down. Well, she supposed she'd just have to use the old knee-to-knee method. She'd learned early that you didn't always get to pick the time to do fieldwork. Sometimes it just happened. The other woman was getting ahead and Sarah rushed to catch up.

"I'm Bridget, by the way," the young woman said as if she had suddenly remembered her manners. She turned to offer Sarah her hand.

"I'm Sarah." They shook and Bridget turned back to the path.

Bridget gave a giggle over her shoulder. "I know. Every old man in the county has been by to tell my grandmother about the pretty American who likes the old songs. You're quite the talk among the over-sixty crowd."

It was Sarah's turn to laugh. "I usually am…occupational hazard."

"You're a..." She seemed to be searching for the term. "Folklorist?"

"Yep." Sarah decided not to get specific. Folklorist was usually easier to explain than ethno-musicologist.

They fell into silence as they climbed their way up the hill. It gave Sarah a moment to study her companion. Bridget was attractive, with the grace and confidence of an athlete, which was totally foreign to Sarah. The closest she ever got to an athlete was in the checkout line in the dining hall. Still, there was something familiar about Bridget, something Sarah couldn't quite put her finger on.

"What do you do, Bridget?" Sarah ventured.

"I'm still a student right now, but I'm hoping to be a geologist," said Bridget as they started down the hill.

"Hoping?" The thought that she might not get her degree had never occurred to Sarah. She simply didn't think of failure as a possibility. She thought briefly about the girls she'd grown up with back in the holler. Most of them probably had several kids by now and not much else. She'd rather spend her days struggling for grants and scholarships than struggling for food and heat.

Bridget looked at Sarah for a moment. "You know, things happen sometimes that aren't part of your plan."

Sarah did know that. Her grandmother's death had nearly derailed her a few years ago. "That's true, but you can't let those things get in the way of what you really want."

Bridget just sighed and looked at the little cottage ahead of them. "Some things are much harder to overcome than others."

The cottage was like many old houses in Cape Breton. It was small and squat, almost like a croft house with a couple of lean-tos added to the back and side. Its weathered walls had probably been white once, but the salt air had weathered them to a crackled gray. The folklorist in Sarah immediately began analyzing the age of each part of the house. It sat halfway up the leeward side of a hill, high enough to avoid any flooding and sheltered from the harsh North Atlantic winds.

"It's lovely," Sarah breathed.

Bridget smiled as they walked on. "Come inside. My grandmother will be happy to meet you."

Inside, a small fire burning in the hearth made it warm and close. The only light seeped in through the small windows. Sarah stood a moment in the doorway, letting her eyes adjust. Bridget's grandmother sat in a straight-backed chair at a small table in front of one window. Her face was turned into the light and looked as weathered as the walls outside. Her left hand rested on the table, her thumb absently rubbing a small stone.

"I've brought the song lady, Gran," Bridget called from the door.

"Oh, come in, come in." The old woman's hands fluttered in a welcoming motion.

Bridget motioned for Sarah to follow her into the room. She pulled a chair up to the little table, and Sarah sat down across from the old woman. It wasn't until Bridget took her grandmother's wrinkled right hand and laid it on Sarah's that Sarah realized the older woman was blind. "Gran, this is Sarah."

"Sarah." The woman nodded at the name as if it were the answer to some puzzle she'd been trying to solve. Despite her age, her voice was clear and strong. "Lean closer, child. Let me have a look at you."

Feeling more than the usual awkwardness of a field worker, Sarah leaned forward and guided the woman's right hand to her face. Her left hand still held the stone. As one hand traced lightly over Sarah's features, the other thumb rubbed the stone even faster. "What's your family name, child?"

"MacAlpin, ma'am." Sarah used the manners her granny taught her.

"MacAlpin, yes, yes." The woman nodded as if she was confirming a match between the name and the features she was feeling.

"I'll make us some tea." Bridget rose and went to the small kitchen just off the parlor.

"So," the old woman started with a commanding air. "You are here to collect Gàidhlig songs, eh?"

"Yes, ma'am. I study old songs." Sarah settled into the questioning. She never liked talking about herself, but it was sometimes part of breaking the ice.

"Where are you from?"

"North Carolina, and you? Are you originally from Cape Breton?" asked Sarah in an attempt to steer the attention away from herself.

"Oh, yes! I've lived my whole life in this house." She trailed off a bit, training her sightless eyes on the window.

"Do you know when your family came to Cape Breton?"

"I once knew a Jamie MacAlpin." The old woman mused before turning abruptly back to Sarah. "What was your father's name?"

This was the question that Sarah always dreaded. Not knowing her father didn't matter much in cosmopolitan Chapel Hill, but she knew from painful experience that in small communities like this one, she was still a bastard. She usually managed to avoid the question by redirecting with a question of her own, but she could tell by the set of the woman's jaw that she had to answer. So she took a big gulp of air and, deciding to match the woman's directness, said plainly, "I never knew my father. MacAlpin is my mother's name."

To Sarah's amazement, the old woman smiled and nodded again. "It's just as well. I never knew mine either."

Sarah let out the breath she'd been holding and took the opportunity to redirect. "What is your name?"

"*Iseabail NicConich,*" *[Isobel MacKenzie]* she answered in Gaelic. "*A bheil Gàidhlig agaid?*" *[Do you speak Gaelic?]*

"*Tha, tha Gàidhlig agam.*" *[Yes, I do.]*

"For how long?" asked Isobel, tilting her head to the side to listen carefully to the answer.

"*Fad' mo bheatha,*" *[All my life]* Sarah replied, not quite understanding why her answer should be so important. Still it seemed very important to the old woman.

The old woman laughed. Her wizened hand found Sarah's on the table and gave it a gentle pat. "I thought I heard it in your accent. You are lucky to have learned so young."

Sarah smiled remembering how her mother had forced her to speak English so precisely for fear that her accent would make her an object of curiosity. "Yes, I am."

"Here's tea!" called Bridget as she carried a tray over from the kitchen.

"Good," said the old woman, turning her chair away from the window. "Pour a cup for Mórag and we'll begin learning our song."

Sarah started at the sound of her given name. No one had called her that since her grandmother died. Granny had always called her Mórag, and Bridget and her grandmother reminded her more than a little of herself and Granny.

"Come around the table, girl, and learn it the old way."

The knee-to-knee method, as it was commonly called, was very personal and laborious. The teacher and student sat together, often literally knee-to-knee. The teacher would sing a line of the song, and the student repeated it as faithfully as possible. The process was repeated until the student could sing the whole song just as it was taught. Even with Sarah's knowledge of Gaelic and her experience with this method, it was no quick process. Although, as usual, it proved worthwhile. Only moments into the lesson, Sarah recognized the tune and some verses of the song, which her grandmother had taught her many years ago about the king lost in the mist.

'S e seo cridhe mo threubh
Bha an rìgh air chall 's a cheò
Thuig e pòg dhi 's iad air a' chlach
Eirichidh e a-rithist

Bhuail stoirm gu cruidh air an eilean
Bha an rìgh air chall 's a cheò
Chaidh an t-eilean fodha
Eirichidh e a-rithist

Dhuisg an rìgh òg air a' chladach
Bha an rìgh air chall 's a cheò
Bha a' mhaidean ri a thaobh leis a phoit mhòr.
Eirichidh e a-rithist

When they got to the last verse, Sarah nearly jumped out of her skin. The words of this verse were exactly the same as she remembered. They made no sense to her, but they matched her grandmother's words precisely, the last words that her grandmother had spoken. The hair on the back of Sarah's neck stood up. Could this be the song she was looking for?

Arbirainn i finaidh banaon chann ur afoinn
Bha an rìgh air chall 's a cheò
Ach ur pham chann ur n fawur breanain
Eirichidh e a-rithist

"That last verse isn't all Gaelic, is it?" she asked. "Do you know what those words mean, *'Arbirainn i finaidh banaon chann ur afoinn'* and *'Ach ur pham chann ur n fawur breanain'*?"

The old woman turned her face toward the fire with a look of what Sarah thought was disappointment, though she couldn't think of why. After a moment Isobel shook her head slowly. "No, I've always wondered myself. My mother always made me repeat them, though, so I would get them exactly."

"Your mother taught you. Can you tell me more about her?" Any information Sarah could get about the song's origin would help her, so she tried to keep her questions open-ended.

Isobel's mother had left Scotland early in the twentieth century to start a new life in Cape Breton, and she had taught the song to Isobel when she was a child. Sarah was reminded of her own grandmother, who left for America to make a new life for herself in North Carolina. Maggie had left just before Britain was ravaged during the Second World War.

Now Sarah had two songs with an obvious shared origin that had evolved in different locations with only small differences. Unfortunately, they both seemed to have come to the New World too late to have influenced music in America. She needed to find more versions, preferably older versions, of this song. Sarah's analytical wheels were turning well before the lesson was over.

Finally, after the sun had gone down and they were left singing by firelight, Sarah repeated the song in its entirety and felt a deep flush of pride when Isobel nodded her approval. "You've a fine voice and a sharp memory, young Mórag. Did your own grandmother teach you songs?"

Sarah enjoyed a long stretch. Her shoulders were sore from leaning in close to the old woman. "Yes, she did. In fact, she taught me one very similar to that one."

"Yes, I thought so. We old women have long memories. Songs like that one stay with us."

Sarah couldn't suppress her smile. She patted Isobel's hand. "Fortunately, they stay with some of us young women too."

The old woman laid a hand on Sarah's and gave her a squeeze. "You're a good child. Your granny taught you well."

"That she did," Sarah agreed. "Can I come back tomorrow and record you? That way I won't miss the differences from my granny's song."

"Of course, of course." Isobel waved a dismissive hand as if Sarah didn't need to ask.

"I'll drive you back. It's dark now." This from Bridget, who had been listening quietly.

"That would be great. Thanks. I'm afraid I would probably get lost if I tried to walk back the way we came." Sarah rose to go, but Isobel, whose hand still covered Sarah's, restrained her.

"I've something for you." She groped around the table for the stone she had laid aside earlier, the same one she had been rubbing when Sarah arrived. Finding it, she pressed it into Sarah's hand. "Here you are. It's a little piece of Alba, and you should have it."

"Oh, no I couldn't." Sarah tried to return the stone, but Isobel just shook her head. "You've already given me so much."

"No, no. You're alone in the world. You need something to remind you of your family." Isobel was firm.

Sarah was thoroughly nonplussed and slumped back into the chair. "How…how did you know that I'm alone?"

Isobel leaned in close to Sarah and gripped her hands. "I know. I can feel it in the air around you. I can hear it in your voice. You guard yourself well, wee Mórag. Don't stop. You will know who you can trust."

"I…" Sarah felt a chill run up her spine. Were these just the mad ramblings of an old woman or something more? "I don't understand."

Isobel raised a leathery and wrinkled hand to stroke Sarah's cheek, finding it easily. "You will."

"We'd better be going," Bridget interrupted gently. "Gran, will you be alright while I run Sarah back to her place?"

"Of course I will. You girls go on then." Isobel turned back to the now-darkened window and folded her hands together.

***

Granny died with a song on her mind, the one about the girl in the river. She wasn't singing by the time the last breath left her. It was just a movement of her lips, with no wind behind them. They formed the words of the language Sarah could never understand—but Granny's eyes were fierce, as if the words should have meaning for her, as if Granny was frustrated they didn't.

That's the way it had been between them the last year or so. Whenever Sarah had come home from college, Granny had watched her like she was waiting for something to happen. Sarah thought she knew what it was. Granny must have been worried Sarah was going to go mad like Molly had. From what Sarah had heard, it wasn't until Molly had left the holler that things had started going wrong. Sarah worried about that herself…always had.

That's probably why Sarah hadn't gone far to college, just to Appalachian State in Boone. She came home on the weekends to help Granny. It had been a Tuesday, though, when the sheriff had called her to tell her Granny was in the hospital. Someone had gone up to the house looking to buy some liquor and found her in the garden. She'd been barely conscious.

The doctor said it was a heart attack and that she'd been lucky it hadn't killed her on the spot. It was still killing her, though, or at least it made her so weak she hadn't been able to leave the hospital. The doctor whose name Sarah couldn't remember had shaken his head, looking grim, and said, "It's only a matter of time."

Sarah had stood outside the door to her Granny's room for several minutes, seeing not the wide industrial hospital door but the scarred old wooden door at the end of the upstairs hall, the door to Mama's room. It had been thirteen years since the day she had opened that door to find her mother dead in a pool of her own blood, but now it felt like yesterday.

Sarah closed her eyes, swallowed past the lump in her throat, and pushed through the door. She half expected to open her eyes and find the plaster walls and bloody bed. Instead she found the dimly lit but clean hospital room with Granny lying in the bed and bristling with tubes connected to various machines and monitors.

She sat in the chair beside the bed and took Granny's hand in hers. Sarah didn't pray. They'd never been much for praying anyway. They gave thanks for what they were given, but they didn't ask for things, not like the Christians did. Instead, she held her Granny's hand and focused on passing her energy through the place where their skin touched, lending her strength as Granny had always done for her.

After a time, Sarah looked up to see Granny's eyes on her. She cleared her throat, but her voice still cracked a little. "*A' sheanmhair.*"

"Wheesht, *a' nighean,*" the old woman whispered, her voice a mere crack in the silence. "*Seinn comhla rium.* We dinna have much time."

Granny began to sing, her voice fluttering back and forth between strength and weakness.

Bha an rìgh a' siùbhlach, gu tùrsach
Bha an rìgh air chall 's a cheò
Shuidh e ri taobh na h-aibhne lan smaointinn

Eirichidh e a-rithist

Sarah picked up the song and began singing with her. Their voices went in and out with emotion and their hands grew warm where they touched.

Shnàmh mhaidean air an uisge
Bha an rìgh air chall 's a cheò
Dè tha a' cur drag ort a rìgh?
Eirichidh e a-rithist

Granny kept singing through the many verses of the ballad, though Sarah could tell she was losing strength. The last verse was barely a whisper, and the last line even less as Granny's lips kept moving, but her breath was gone.

Arbirainn i finaidh banaon chann ur afoinn
Bha an rìgh air chall 's a cheò
Ach ur pham chann ur n fawur breanain
Eirichidh e a-rithist

Sarah rested her forehead on the railing of the hospital bed and let her tears fall as the monitor let out a long bleating note. In seconds, the room was swarming with staff who shoved Sarah out of the way in an attempt to revive her grandmother. Sarah knew it wouldn't help, but she backed away and let them try, too stunned by grief to do anything else. She watched in a daze as they worked frantically to chase away death.

Soon she was distracted by a new smell. It was not the astringent hospital smell, with its slight burn of rubbing alcohol. It was summer flowers and wood smoke, just like home in June. Sarah looked up above the buzzing workers around Granny's bed. Over their heads on the clean white hospital wall was the word. The last message that her mother had left on her bedroom wall on that evening in June thirteen years ago: *Ruith!*

Run!

***

"I'm so glad I ran into you today. She's been after me to get you over here since old Dougal MacIsaac told her you were in town," Bridget told Sarah with the easy familiarity of an old friend.

"I'm glad you did too. I'll be leaving soon. I hate to think I could have missed that." Sarah watched the little cottage grow smaller and smaller in the side mirror as they drove away.

"I hope it's something you can use."

"Oh, I can definitely use that. Every song helps, but that one is so close to another that my grandmother taught me that it might prove very important to my thesis." Sarah spent the rest of the short ride to the campground deep in thought, turning the song over and over in her head, picking out the differences from the song she learned as a girl.

Bridget turned into the drive of the campground where Sarah had rented a cottage for the month. Sarah had come to love the little cluster of cottages hugging the pristine beach and its little community that centered on the restaurant at the front of the complex overlooking the beach. She turned to Bridget. "You can drop me off here if you like. I think I'll grab a bite to eat."

Bridget parked the car in the small gravel lot next to the building. "Would you mind some company?"

"Not at all." Sarah gave her a smile. "It'll be nice to hang out with somebody my own age for a change."

Bridget was laughing as she got out and locked the car. "Too much of the senior set?"

Sarah shook her head. "Never too much. I'm just used to going home to a roommate and friends at the end of the day. It's been kind of lonely up here."

"I can imagine." Bridget was looking at Sarah as she opened the restaurant door and nearly walked into a nice-looking blonde man in the typical campground attire of jeans and T-shirt. He gripped her elbow to keep her from bouncing into the doorframe. "Oh! Excuse me."

The man let a slow smile slide across his lips and drawled, "No problem," before stepping around her and out the door.

Bridget looked back and scanned his wiry body. She looked at Sarah with just a touch of the devil in her eyes. "I might have to start hanging out at the campground more often."

Sarah couldn't help laughing. They were both still giggling when they settled at a table on the deck. It offered a great view of the beach and the hills surrounding the campground.

They ordered a couple of beers and burgers and sat back to wait, enjoying the scenery. Sarah looked thoughtfully out to where the waves crashed against the shore. "I've gotten very used to the sound of the surf. I don't know how I'm going to sleep without it when I go home."

"You'll have to get one of those CDs with the wave sounds on it." Bridget leaned back and took a sip of beer. "So what do you do with a PhD in folklore?"

"That's a good question. Teaching is pretty much the only option. There might be a few museums that can keep folklorists on staff, but they're few and far between. Even teaching positions are scarce. Right now, only four universities in the States even have folklore departments."

"That's a pretty narrow field."

Sarah raised her glass and took gulp. "Let's just say I'm not in it for the fame and fortune."

"So why are you in it?" Bridget asked.

"It's tough to explain sometimes." Sarah took a deep breath, letting it out slowly and giving herself time to collect her thoughts. "My grandmother raised me in the mountains. We didn't have much, and most of what we lived on came from the land. I grew up much the same way that our grandmothers did. And all those legends that we read about in books and home remedies and songs that you hear on grainy old recordings, those were part of everyday survival for us.

"So few people live that way today, with the whole picture in mind. We might not need a legend to help us remember that you don't take without giving back or which berries are edible and which ones aren't, but there's a lot of wisdom in those old ways that can help us today and maybe tomorrow. I can't stand the thought of that dying with our grandmothers' generation. It's not so much why I do it as it is why I can't NOT do it." Sarah looked up to find Bridget regarding her with a soft smile. "Sorry, I can get a little preachy about it."

Bridget leaned forward shaking her head. "Nah. If I had grown up that way, I might feel the same. I learned those ways from my Gran, but I never needed them the way you did."

"Didn't you grow up around here?"

"My mom and I lived over in Halifax. But I spent every summer here, and Gran made sure I knew every song and legend she could cram into that time." Bridget tipped her glass in Sarah's direction. "That includes that song you heard today."

The young man who was waiting tables on the deck brought their burgers, and Sarah gave him a smile. "Thanks, Angus."

After a few bites of her burger, Bridget asked, "So if you knew that song, why do you need to record Gran singing it?"

"Well, there are small differences between the two that I don't want to get confused. Did you ever play the telephone game when you were a kid? Where one person whispers something and each person whispers the same thing down the line? When you get to the end the message is completely different."

"Sure."

"Well, that's basically how oral traditions work. Each person or each generation teaches it to the next. And each time it's passed along, it changes a little bit. But the changes that happen can tell us a lot about the evolution of a community, or the changes that happen from generation to generation. I want to compare those changes, those differences. So I need to have a recording straight from the source."

Bridget nodded. "Makes sense."

Sarah took another bite of her burger, thinking absently that hamburgers always seemed to taste better when eaten at the beach. "What about you? Why geology?"

Bridget put down her burger and picked up a French fry. "You might be surprised to hear my reasoning isn't too much different from yours. I've always been fascinated by rocks. Ever since I was a little girl, I've just tried to learn everything I can about all of them. I would pick up rocks from wherever we went. Then I'd take them home and research everything I could about them. What made their color or shape what it was? Why were they shiny or not? How did it get where I found it? I just can't imagine doing anything else."

Bridget took a bite of the French fry and chewed. Sarah could see her wheels turning.

"Do you have that rock my Gran gave you?" Bridget asked. Sarah took the rock out of her pocket and placed it on the table. "What do you see?"

Sarah wiped her hands on a napkin and picked up the rock again to examine it. The stone was an oval, no bigger than a fifty-cent piece, and flat with a depression in the center. It was a brownish red, with tiny black and white flecks throughout as if someone had sprinkled it with salt and pepper. All its edges were worn smooth and polished to a high shine with rubbing, and Sarah couldn't help wondering how long Isobel had used it for a worry stone. Who might have used it before her?

"I see the land where that comes from, rocky and remote," Sarah said. "I see the people who must have lived there and what their lives were probably like, trying to eke a living out of the little patches of soil between crags." She ran her thumb around the worry-worn edge as she'd seen Isobel do earlier. "I see generations' worth of worry and care polishing it."

She really could see those things in her mind's eye, as if she'd been there. She looked up to find Bridget grinning at her. "You see their spirit. I see their foundation."

Bridget held out her hand, and Sarah placed the rock in it. Bridget used a close-trimmed fingernail to point out the different components within the stone. “I see feldspar and quartz, muscovite, biotite. I see the process that went into making it millions of years ago, and I see how it got to where it was. Did you know that Scotland is one of the oldest landmasses in the world?” Sarah shook her head, no. Bridget leaned forward, warming to the topic. “It hasn’t always been part of Britain. It spent millions of years moving around the northern hemisphere. It’s held every climate, from tropical rainforest to tundra to desert, and this rock is old enough to have seen it all. Just like your legends and songs tell you about the people who lived there. I think this rock tells a lot about the environment of those people and how it influenced their evolution, and it still does.”

She leaned forward and handed the stone back to Sarah, who regarded it with another level of understanding. She thought of a line from the song she’d heard that day: *“‘S e seo cridhe mo threubh.”*

She looked up to meet Bridget’s eyes. Her new friend gave her a significant nod and translated: “The heart of our people. Like the saying goes, ‘Old as the stone.’”

“Hmm. That was a favorite saying of my granny’s.” The stone felt much heavier against Sarah’s palm now. She curled her fingers around it in a protective gesture and felt it warm as it absorbed her body heat. It was a few moments before she spoke again. “So, what do you plan to do with your degree?”

Bridget shrugged, “I’d kind of like to teach, but I’ve also got a line on a job with an oil company in Scotland.” She ate another French fry and looked out to the beach in thought. “I like the idea of teaching, but that oil company money sure would pay off my student loans a lot faster.”

Sarah laughed. “That does sound tempting. But with your passion, it would seem criminal not to teach.”

Bridget gave a noncommittal look. “We’ll see.”

CHAPTER SEVEN

Mid-September 1995
Chapel Hill, North Carolina

Sarah bounded up the stairs of Greenlaw Hall two at a time. Excited by her good news, she was looking forward to some reward for her hard work and something to take her mind off the nightmares that had been keeping her up at night. She'd been head down transcribing tapes in the Folklife Collection since getting back from Cape Breton, scouring the tapes for any song similar to the one she'd collected there that matched up with Granny's. She had managed to submit one article to a journal earlier in the summer and had just heard back from the editors.

She wove her way through the stream of undergraduates whose class had just let out, eager to tell Donald the news. She rounded the corner on the fourth floor and in her excitement began speaking before she reached Donald's door.

"Donald, you're not going to believe it. My—" The words caught in her throat. Standing in the middle of the books, papers, and general clutter that was Donald's office was Dermot Sinclair. Sarah's brain was slow to process the sight of the man she had last seen running away from her like his tail was on fire.

"Ah, Sarah. Look who's come back to us." Donald beamed.

"Halo, *a' Mhórag*." Dermot looked vaguely guilty, as if he'd been caught with his hand in the cookie jar.

Several seconds passed before she was finally able to manage a flat, "Hi."

"What were ye saying when ye came in just now?" Donald looked at her expectantly.

"Hmm?" She looked blank for a second, "Oh! My article is going to be in the journal next quarter. They really liked it." Somehow, the momentum had gone right out of Sarah's big news.

"That's great!" Donald said with genuine pride. "We'll drink to it tonight at the pub, but right now I've a class. Sarah, could you show Dermot to Dr. Peterson's office? I really have to go," he said, rushing past them and out the door.

Sarah tried to think of some excuse, but Donald disappeared around the corner. She glanced over to where Dermot had come to stand beside her. The consolation was that he looked about as nervous as she felt. He shifted awkwardly, as if he thought he might need to flee for his own safety.

"Well," she said, resigning herself to the task, "Shall we?"

They stepped out into the hall, and she closed the door behind them and made sure it was locked. Sarah tried to think of something innocuous to say, but she found herself at a loss. She wanted to scream at him and ask him what he was doing there, but her kinder, gentler side reminded her that he had ignored some of her potentially embarrassing actions and she really should give him the courtesy of returning the favor. As she ushered him back into the hall, she tried to make her voice sound as casual as possible. "So, how was your trip?"

"Och fine, uneventful." He gave her a relieved smile as he followed her around the corner to the stairs.

"Are you staying long?" she hoped that didn't sound too curious.

"I expect to be here for the rest of the semester. I'm doing some research," he explained to her back as she led him up the stairs.

"Really, what are you researching?"

"Gaelic influence on American folksongs," he replied.

Sarah nearly tripped over the last step, but Dermot caught her arm and held her upright. "Thanks," she mumbled and gently but firmly pulled her arm away.

Fortunately, Dr. Peterson's office wasn't far from the stairs, and they were there in just a few steps. Sarah showed him the way and was turning back to the stairwell.

"Oh, Sarah." She turned back to face him. "Thank you." His smile said that he knew just what she was doing by ignoring the kiss and that he was glad. Sarah supposed she should feel relieved that they seemed to understand each other so easily, and of course she should be glad that he hadn't come back to renew his mistaken attentions of the summer. Somehow none of that seemed very comforting. Sarah still wasn't sure why he was here, but his research topic certainly didn't bode well. She had heard horror stories from other graduate students and even some professors about research work and even whole papers being stolen.

***

Sarah collected her coffee and made her way to their usual table. After her disturbing encounter with Dermot, she felt very much in need of the relaxing atmosphere at The Daily Grind. Located between the Student Stores and the Undergraduate Library just outside of the area that was affectionately called The Pit, the outdoor coffee shop offered an oasis of relaxation at the busy center of campus life. Sarah and her friends usually camped there every morning between classes. It was their time to relax, get the requisite dose of caffeine, catch up on gossip, and enjoy one of their favorite pastimes: people watching. That morning Sarah had arrived first. Now, coffee in hand in her island of serenity, she had managed to gain control of her racing thoughts and calm herself enough to be nearly fit for company.

"You are not going to believe who I just saw talking to Dr. Peterson!" announced Amy, arriving with her usual commotion.

"Dermot Sinclair."

Amy flopped into one of the green plastic chairs, obviously disappointed that Sarah was already aware of the surprising news. Sarah hadn't told Amy about that ill-advised kiss at the festival, but Amy had continued to comment unmercifully about what she thought was his obvious interest in Sarah. "You've seen him?"

"I have," said Sarah. "I showed him to Dr. Peterson's office."

"Do you know why he's here?"

"Who's here?" Barrett Markham asked as he planted his coffee on the table next to Amy. Roguishly handsome, disarmingly witty, and sometimes painfully direct, Barrett was one of those men most women would give their eye teeth for.

Of course, Barrett wasn't interested in any women. His eyes were only for a boyfriend who had graduated the year before and was now living in New York. Since the departure of his own romantic partner, Barrett had become an insatiable gossip, living vicariously through the rumors about other people's exploits. He had already heard the public version of the Dermot Sinclair story from Amy.

He understood completely when Amy said, "Sarah's kilted wonder."

"Ooo," Barrett cooed with a knowing nod.

"No, there's no 'Ooo' about it," Sarah said into the plastic lid of her cup.

"Do you know why he's here?" Amy asked.

"He says he's here to study Gaelic influence on American folksong." Amy and Barrett both emitted sharp hisses of surprise. Sarah nodded, "Exactly."

"Hey y'all." Meg Riley quickly deposited her bags in the next available chair before making a beeline for the counter.

"Hey, Meg," they called in unison.

"So," Barrett began with his usual candor, "any idea what his game is?"

"Not a clue, but I'm sure we'll find out soon enough. It looks like he's staying until the end of the semester," sighed Sarah.

"Well, that gives you plenty of time to figure out what he's up to." Barrett tried to sound positive.

"Let's just hope I figure it out in time."

"You two are always so suspicious!" chided Amy. "Why does he have to be 'up' to anything? Maybe he really is interested in it. Ya know, you don't have a complete monopoly on the subject. Anybody can choose to study it."

"A, we're suspicious because we grew up fatherless freaks in small towns. You learn very early that you have to guard yourself."

Barrett nodded in affirmation. "To thine own self be true."

Sarah gave him a smile. "And B, consider the evidence. He's a graduate student in need of a dissertation topic. If he had this topic picked when we met this summer, he never mentioned it. So he's casting about, and this acquaintance of his mentions that he has a student whose interests are along his lines, and she's already done a boatload of research. Donald innocently sings my praises, as we know he does, and our Mr. Sinclair thinks he's found the answer to his problem. So he comes out here for a small trip to test the waters, see if she knows what she's talking about and if it'll be worth the risk to steal her work. Assuming, of course, that no one in Scotland will know about the American working on the same subject."

"Wow." Amy sat back, giving her friends an incredulous look. "You should write for the X Files. I think your conspiracy theory engine is on overdrive. A, did you ever think that your childhood has made you hyper-suspicious? B, your evidence is all circumstantial."

"Besides," Meg piped in, having returned with her coffee during the prosecution, "maybe he's here and he picked your subject because he wants to be close to you." Meg's boyfriend had recently transferred to neighboring Duke University to be closer to her.

"Well, it's a pretty thought, Meg, but somehow I doubt it," said Sarah.

"I don't know about that, Sarah. He was certainly interested in you last summer, couldn't keep his eyes off you."

Sarah dismissed this with a wave of her hand. "Springes to catch woodcocks."

Theater major Barrett picked up the Shakespeare reference and ran with it in his most theatrical voice: "When the blood burns, how prodigal the soul lends the tongue vows: these blazes giving more light than heat, extinct in both."

"Exactly." Sarah nodded before turning back to Meg. "Sorry, Meg, they can't all be like your Jack."

***

Now that Dr. Peterson had given him the Folklore Department welcome and told him how to get into the folk-life collection, Dermot was free to get to work. The first thing on his list was to find Sarah. Judging from the look on her face when she had seen him, he thought he had some fence-mending to do. The trick would be finding her on the huge campus. The obvious place to look would be the Folklife Collection in Wilson Library, but he didn't think a library would be the ideal place for what he feared would be a confrontation. He remembered Donald telling him that, at some point in the day, nearly everyone on campus passed through The Pit, so he decided it was the perfect place to start his search. He turned to the right and before going fifty feet spotted her.

She was holding court at the outdoor coffee shop, but this was a different Sarah from the one he had met last summer, or even the same one he had surprised just half an hour before. She had the same honey-colored hair that glinted gold in the sunlight, the same carefully erect carriage, but this Sarah was sharper, keener, more worldly. Even surrounded by friends, she was cool and aloof, smiling wryly while everyone else roared with laughter as the spiky haired and thoroughly pierced young man beside her told some outrageous story. This wasn't the vulnerable woman he'd had kissed in the mountains. Then he realized he had seen her like this before, but the memory of their kiss had wiped that memory away. This was the Sarah who didn't like strangers or talking about her family, the Sarah who feared date rape drugs, City Sarah, guarding herself like a fortress.

"Hallo again, Sarah, Amy." He smiled and tried to look as innocent as possible while four pairs of eyes turned to him.

"Dermot!" Amy exclaimed, shooting Sarah a mischievous glance. "It's good to see you again."

"It's good to see ye too." At least one of them seemed happy to see him.

"Sarah was just saying how excited she is that you're here to help out with the research," Amy added with her characteristic wicked smile. The other two at the table exchanged a look that told Dermot Sarah had probably said something quite the opposite.

"Of course," Sarah beamed a little too brightly. "Two heads are always better than one." At that same instant, Amy winced noticeably.

The spiky haired, pierced one tipped his coffee at Sarah and said, "Amen to that," as if he meant something entirely different from academic research.

"Oh, Dermot, these are our friends Barrett Markham and Meg Reilly. Kids, this is Dermot Sinclair," said Amy as she leaned forward to discretely rub her shin under the table.

Dermot smiled charmingly at Meg, who was exactly what the old ballads would have called a "nut brown maid," with chestnut brown hair, hazel eyes, and a dimpled and sweet smile. Barrett, on the other hand, was as guarded as Sarah, but in a different way. Where City Sarah was cool and aloof, Barrett hid behind animation, wit, and flamboyance. He struck Dermot as the kind of person one could see socially for years and never actually know. Dermot could also tell Barrett was sizing him up, although it didn't seem in the competitive way that a boyfriend would.

"Well, children," Amy said, making a show of standing up and retrieving her bag. "It's almost time for class."

"Oh, yes." Meg jumped up with a little giggle. "Can't be late."

With that, the two girls trotted off to the quad.

Barrett lingered, looking at Sarah as if trying to gauge the situation. "I really do need to go. I'll talk to you later." He squeezed her free hand and turned to Dermot. "It's nice to meet you. I'm sure we'll run into each other again."

"It's nice to meet ye as well." Dermot nodded. Turning back to the table, Sarah made a very imposing figure despite her small stature. How was he to begin with her?

"Did Dr. Peterson point you in the right direction?" Sarah asked.

Expecting a confrontation, he generously gave her an opening. "That depends on which direction ye think is the right one."

Sarah almost smiled and made a sharp noise in her throat. "I can think of a couple of directions that would work for me."

"Including right back to Scotland, I'm sure," Dermot said as he sank into a chair next to her.

"That's one of the nicer thoughts." The hint of a smile hadn't left, so he pressed on.

"Sarah, I'm really sorry about that kiss last summer." He focused all of his attention on her. "I had no right to do that, and if we're to work together I wouldna want that to get in the way."

A corner of her mouth kicked up in a smirk as if she was enjoying this apology. "Well, I will say that you surprised me, but I won't say I didn't enjoy it."

He sat looking at her for a moment, not able to think of a single thing to say through the sawdust that seemed to have formed in his mouth.

She gave a brief shake of her head. "Don't worry, Sinclair. I think I can manage to be a grown-up about it. You don't have to apologize anymore. And that brings us to the subject at hand. Just how much work do you expect us to be doing together?"

With that settled, Dermot was able to breathe easier. "Och, well. I've seen some of the transcriptions that ye've done, and I think I can help ye finish those. I'd like to talk about what ye found in Cape Breton. Plus I have a wealth of resources from Scotland that could help us both."

"So you propose that we share resources, but I'm wondering just how much work you've done on this topic." She paused for a calculated sip of coffee. "It seems to me that I'm doing a lot of research so you can swoop in and write a paper based on my fieldwork. Just what is the thesis of your paper?"

Suddenly, Dermot felt a bit like a worm wriggling on a pin. He hadn't thought about exactly what his thesis was, and he didn't know hers. If he made one up now, he could pick one that was too close to hers, but not having one left her suspicions open. “I hadna really thought that far yet. I thought I would look at what’s here and then choose from there.”

Sarah gave a brief nod as if this confirmed what she’d thought. “You’ve always been candid with me, Dermot, so I’m sure you won’t mind what I’m about to say. Did you come here to look at my research and pick a topic, or did you come here to look at my paper and steal my topic?”

Dermot flushed. He had to admire her spirit. For the second time since they’d met, she was asking him point blank if he meant to commit a crime against her. He kept any sharpness out of his tone, though he was definitely frustrated, “Tell me, Sarah, d’ye always accuse colleagues who show interest in yer work of theft, or should I feel special?”

Her tone was positively sweet. “Oh, no, I’m the one who feels special. Here I am, a mild-mannered graduate student working away on my dissertation and this handsome, intelligent, devious Scot comes halfway around the world to take advantage of all my hard work. I’m actually flattered.”

Dermot was so frustrated he had to remind himself to breathe. He leaned closer to her, so close he could smell coffee with a hint of hazelnut on her breath. “Sarah, if I were really after yer work, do ye not think I would have kept going up on that mountainside? What better way would I have to bring yer guard down? If ye really think about it, I think ye’ll see that yer theory has some holes in it.”

“Still, I think you’ll agree that your interest in me has been a bit suspect from the start.”

“I can see how ye can think so little of others when ye obviously think so much o’ yerself.” She visibly stiffened at his words. “I can assure ye that my interest in ye, with the exception of that one demented moment, has been purely professional. What exactly have I done to give you such a poor opinion of me?"

***

She just looked at him for a moment. Right. How could she turn this back around to her advantage? "That's simple, Dermot, every time I begin to trust you, something goes wrong. I was starting to be comfortable with you at the cèilidh, and a couple of hours later I woke up in the woods with no idea how I got there. I know it wasn't your doing, but you have to admit it's pretty scary. Then I trusted you enough to tell you a little about myself. I even kissed you, and you ran away." He started to protest, but she held up a hand. "I think we both know there was no family emergency like Donald said that morning. Then just when I'd nearly forgotten about you, here you are stepping just a little too far into my world for comfort."

Dermot leaned back in his chair in exasperation and regarded her for what felt like minutes. "Someone's done a real number on ye, haven't they?"

Suddenly she felt like she was walking around with a damaged goods label on her forehead. She rose slowly from her chair. Stung. As she pulled her bag onto her shoulder, she gave her parting shot. "Well, Sinclair, perhaps you'll find out someday, if you can stick around long enough this time."

"Och, I'll be around," she thought she heard him mutter as she walked away.

CHAPTER EIGHT

Sarah checked in at the desk and grabbed her tapes for the day. She hoped she would get through them without falling asleep. She'd been having that awful bathtub dream forever, but its frequency usually varied with her stress level. It seemed different now. Now she was having it so often that it was causing her stress rather than reflecting it. What was worse, her work seemed to be slowing down because she was too tired to keep up her usual pace. There was a library's worth of tapes to go through, searching for the recording that would prove her thesis. Maybe her transcriptions would help the next poor student looking for something on those tapes.

She eyed the box, estimating hours in lengths of acetate. She would be at this for a while. She headed down through the study carrels. Someone had once told her that a person could die in the carrels of Wilson Library and no one would find the body for years. Sarah almost believed it as she opened the door to the listening room that she'd come to think of as her cave.

She loved it: total isolation. Nothing else mattered here. There were no demands, no bills to pay, no grades, no department politics, and no bathtub dream. There were just the voices on the tapes and the paper in front of her. She slid the headphones on and popped in the first tape.

She didn't know how long she had been at it when the vision came. She had been listening, writing, and rewinding to listen again for some time when she came upon an interview with a man. He was retelling his own version of Frankie Silvers in a deep, gravelly voice. It was so distinct and soothing that Sarah stopped writing and just listened.

The tape was old and there was a pre-echo where the sound had printed through one layer to the next on the spool. It sounded like two men speaking in rounds, one faintly beginning a sentence to be followed by another saying the same thing a couple of beats later. The result was hypnotic, and Sarah closed her eyes to listen harder.

In a moment she wasn't hearing the words anymore, just the deep, soft, lilting voice. Then another voice joined in, one that was not on the tape. Sarah's breath caught in her throat. Her heart beat faster. She knew this voice. She had heard it before, always rumbling too low to be understood, just shy of a whisper. The fine hairs on her neck and arms bristled. The room grew suddenly cold and Sarah knew she was not dreaming.

The voice spoke faster, the rhythm becoming like a chant, an incantation. Her heart sped along with the chanter, faster and faster until she thought it would burst. Suddenly everything went black, and she heard her grandmother's voice rasping the words, the last ones she had spoken in a language Sarah didn't recognize: "*Arbirainn i finaidh banaon chann ur afoinn, Ach ur pham chann ur n fawur breanain*"

With a rush of warm air, she was back in her listening room. The vision and voices were gone, and she again heard the low rumbling voice on the tape. She sat shaking for what seemed like an eternity. She nearly jumped out of her skin when the tape player stopped with a deafening thwack.

***

For the five days after his return, the only contact he had with Sarah was the occasional nod in the halls of the library or around campus. Sometimes he would catch a glimpse of her in the study carrels with her headphones on writing furiously or listening intently with her eyes closed. She didn't seem to care anymore that he was there, nor that he kept checking out her transcriptions of the tapes. She had done some fantastic work on those transcriptions. Her ear for Southern American dialect was nearly flawless. And her transcriptions from Cape Breton were solid. However, he noticed some hints of Gaelic phrasing in some of the recordings she had missed and some of her translations from Cape Breton were open to interpretation. He thought he could offer a different perspective.

As he'd come in today, he'd passed her a few carrels down and considered knocking on her door and offering his help then and there. No doubt she wouldn't appreciate the interruption. When he had walked by her door she had appeared rapt, not writing but just listening. She'd seemed in a world of her own. The next time he saw her outside the library he would talk to her about helping. He turned back to his work and began making notes on the tape he was listening to. He had been at it for nearly an hour when he was startled by a crash and a muffled curse outside his door.

He whipped the carrel door open and found Sarah on her knees in front of him scrambling to gather audio tapes back into the box that she had just dropped.

Her head jerked up, and her stricken eyes froze the smirk that had been growing on his face. "Hell!" her voice quavered as she turned back to the tapes scattered on the floor. "You would be here."

He knelt beside her and started helping her pick up the tapes. He noticed her hands were shaking. "What's the matter Sarah?"

"I'm fine," she snapped and continued shoving tapes back into the box, not bothering to put them in order. "I'm just tired."

"That explains why yer dropping things," he whispered, not wanting to attract attention in the quiet library. "But not why yer shakin' like a leaf."

She balled her hands into fists to stop the shaking, and tears welled in her eyes. Another student walked by and eyed them with curiosity. Dermot covered Sarah's fists with his hands and leaned close to her ear. Keeping his voice low so they wouldn't be overheard, he said, "Ye dinna have to tell me, but step into my carrel so ye can collect yerself."

She nodded, and Dermot picked up the box of tapes in one hand while keeping her steady with the other on her elbow. He ushered her into the private study carrel, which was just large enough for one person to sit at the built-in desk. Dermot, being tall, had discovered on the first day that he could rest his head on one wall and prop his feet on the other comfortably while listening to the field recordings. Sarah leaned on the desk, trying to collect herself while Dermot leaned his back against the door, making sure to cover as much of the small window as he could so they wouldn't be seen.

***

She wrapped her arms around herself, trying to still her shaking limbs. Of course, she would make a fool of herself right in front of him. Nightmares stealing her sleep apparently wasn't enough. Now she was having visions in the daytime? As usual, Dermot Sinclair was right at hand when she felt the weakest, and as usual he wasn't doing anything to take advantage of the situation. She wondered again why she couldn't shake the feeling that he meant her harm when he kept doing things to save her even a little embarrassment. The conflict just made her shake even more.

Dermot saw it, and with a muffled curse stepped closer and started rubbing her arms and shoulders, trying to warm her. He still carefully kept himself between Sarah and the door, so no one would see anyone but him in the carrel. Canoodling in the private carrels was a surefire way to get kicked out of the library.

Sarah gave up her pretense that she would be alright in a moment and buried her face in his shirt. She didn't cry. She just stood there against him, inhaling his scent; clean and inherently male; spicy, and smoky, and more soothing than she would like to admit. She buried her face a little deeper, and after a few seconds his arms closed around her shoulders.

***

He held her, not saying a word until he felt the shaking stop, and then he held her a bit longer. He didn't know what had upset her so badly, and he was sure she wasn't going to tell him anytime soon. There was no point pressing her. It would only upset her more, and he couldn't afford to do that. He had told himself he wasn't going to touch her like this, that he would be able to resist her. He pulled back and placed his hands on her shoulders. She looked at him, and her gaze fastened on his lips, as if she were remembering the kiss three months ago. Dermot cleared his throat and sought her eyes with his. “Are ye alright, now?”

She nodded as if she were afraid to speak.

“Do ye feel safe enough to go out?”

Another nod.

He reached past her and gathered his papers, stuffing them into his bag. “Then let’s go down to the coffee shop and have a nice bracing cup o’ tea. I’ve something I want to talk with ye about.”

Again she nodded, and Dermot picked up both of their boxes of tapes and steered her to the collection desk. Dermot breathed a silent sigh of relief when he noticed that none of Sarah’s usual crowd was at The Daily Grind. He wasn’t sure either of them was ready for their usual brand of verbal sparring.

“Have a seat. I’ll get ye a cup.” He placed his own bag down at a table that was set back from the usual Pit crowd. He purchased large cups of tea for both of them and loaded Sarah’s with plenty of sugar and milk. When he returned to the table, she was aiming a thousand-yard stare in the direction of The Pit.

“Thanks.” She cleared her throat. “I know I probably disrupted your afternoon.”

“In fact, I was just thinking about ye when ye appeared on my doorstep.” He gave her a gentle smile.

“I’m not usually that clumsy. I just haven’t been sleeping very well lately.” She worried a jagged scratch in the tabletop with a fingernail. “I guess it’s catching up with me.”

"Maybe ye need a break. Yer in that library all the time."

Sarah turned her head, stretching her neck. "Maybe you're right. Good thing it's Friday. I was going to work some more this weekend, but I think I'll declare a two-day moratorium on transcriptions."

His smile widened. "That's the spirit. Relax for a couple of days."

She looked sheepish. "I'm afraid I'm not very good at relaxing. I usually end up sitting at home and obsessing about the work I'm not doing."

"Then ye need something to take yer mind off of it."

"Yeah, well, you let me know if you find something. I've been working on this so long it seems like breathing. I don't always think about it, but I can't live without it."

"What are ye doing tonight?"

"You're not asking me out, are you?" This time she did smile to let him know she was joking.

"Ahhhh…no." He returned her smile. "I'm trying to make sure that ye won't just go home and obsess about the work you're not doing."

"You don't have to worry about that tonight. This is a coffee Friday, so I'll be surrounded by plenty of friends and conversation."

"What is coffee Friday?" Dermot asked, wondering if this was some strange University of North Carolina tradition.

"You met Meg the other day, right?" He nodded. "Well, Meg lives in a house about a block away from mine, and she and her crazy housemates invite the entire world over for coffee every other Friday afternoon."

"That's very generous of them. Obviously, the whole world doesna show up or I'd have heard about it before now."

"Well, it's difficult to communicate an invitation like that to the whole world. But the invitation is always open." She winked, and his heart gave an extra little knock. "Now, you said you wanted to talk to me about something."

He shook his head. "It'll wait till Monday."

"Thanks." She gave him a genuine smile, not the guarded one he was used to but a full-on I'm-really-glad-you're-here smile. He felt something move deep inside him as if puzzle pieces he didn't know he held quietly slid into place with a light but definitive snick.

"Well," she sighed. "I'd better get home. I'm making cookies for this afternoon. If you want to come, it's the blue house on Ransom Street just off Cameron."

CHAPTER NINE

Grandma Maggie's shortbread was still warm on the plate when Sarah and Amy stepped onto the porch of the little blue house on Ransom Street. They didn't bother knocking. Everyone was welcome on coffee Fridays. The blue house was the home of five undergrads who were all English students, but beyond that there was little else they had in common. Meg was cheerful and sweet but could be fierce when crossed. Jane was all elegance with a little whimsy thrown in. Monica was a guy magnet, pretty and earthy with a sensuality that always seemed to mesmerize men. Trish was willowy and ethereal, and Katherine was pink and athletic and rarely home. Despite their differences, they made a nice little family and got along so well that they regularly opened their house to all of their diverse friends.

Inside the house, some of the girls who lived there were bustling from the kitchen to the dining room, setting out coffee pots and plates of treats. The dining room was a study in contrasts, with vibrant salmon pink walls and a black lacquer table pushed against one wall. Matching black chairs were scattered about, and an antique couch with beautiful if worn woodwork and incongruous pea green upholstery rested against another long wall. Sarah loved it.

They made their hellos and set their cookies on the table and headed to the tiny kitchen with its bright purple cabinets to see what else needed to be done. Meg was bustling in and out while Trish the house chef was whipping cream for fresh gingerbread. Jane was fiddling with a boom box and some CDs, and soon Edith Piaf could be heard warbling in the dining room. Sarah felt the tension in her shoulders drain away. These girls, with their openness and enthusiasm, were a balm to her jagged and chapped emotions. She'd been so stressed about her work, Dermot, and the visions/dreams that she couldn't remember the last time she'd really relaxed.

Dermot had certainly helped take some of the edge off in the library earlier. She could still feel his arms around her, and her nose twitched a little with the memory of his scent. She wasn't sure why he was so persistently nice to her when she tried so persistently to push him away. She was starting to wonder why she kept doing it when he'd really never done anything to deserve it.

***

May 1976
Kettle Hollow, North Carolina

Sarah jumped when she heard the door to Mama's room upstairs open and close. She held her breath as her heart beat in time with her mother's footsteps through the hall and down the stairs. She reached a shaking hand out to gather the crayons scattered across the worn table. Maybe if she cleaned up her mess, Mama would feel better.

She put the crayons neatly in her box and closed it. She rose to go put the box in its place on the little bookcase in the parlor, but Mama was blocking the doorway. She stared hard at Sarah, like she was a problem that needed to be solved. It was the same way she looked at the puzzles they liked to work on to pass the time when they got snowed in. Sarah stood beside her chair, awkwardly shifting from foot to foot and wondering what to do. She never knew anymore how to behave around Mama, not since the bathtub.

Now Mama lived like a ghost…there but not there. She rarely ate, though she sometimes came to supper, like now. Her skin hung from her bones. She almost never spoke. Some days Sarah tried to make Mama feel better, but it never seemed to work. Just today, she had painted a picture for Mama at school. It was the prettiest picture she'd ever done. She ran all the way home from the school bus stop with the paper streaming behind her like wings. She was so excited, sure that something so lovely would cheer Mama up.

Sarah had found Mama and Granny in the vegetable garden. They'd been digging up weeds and their hands were covered in dirt. She went straight to Mama, who was on her knees between the rows. "I made this picture for you, Mama! Look!"

Mama looked up. Her gaunt face was smudged with dirt, and some of her hair had come down to drift around her face in little wisps. For a second, just a second, her mama smiled at her. Looked her right in the eye and smiled at her like nothing was wrong, and Sarah could almost see the old Mama. The one who used to play with her and love her.

Then Mama looked down at the picture, and it all changed. Her eyes darted across the picture from one thing to another, taking in the castle and the princess, flowers, and sunshine, and her face became a mask of rage. Sarah watched as the old smiling Mama drained away and was replaced by something terrifying. Mama slowly lifted her hand to touch the painting. Sarah thought about pulling it away because Mama's hand was so dirty. The fingernails were green from the weeds, and there was black soil in every crevice. Before she could, Mama grabbed the painting and tore it from Sarah's hands, crumpling it and causing the thick paint to flake off and scatter in the dirt like confetti. A raw wounded sound came from Mama's throat as she slammed the painting to the ground and began to stab it with the trowel that was in her other hand.

"*Tiugainn leam, m'eudail,*" *[Come with me, my treasure]* Granny said, grabbing Sarah gently by the shoulders and pulling her toward the house. Sarah went, still watching Mama over her shoulder as she began to throw dirt on the painting that was now in tatters. "*Tha Mamaidh glè sgìth.*" *[Mama's very tired.]*

That's what Granny always said; Sarah had heard it a thousand times in the last couple of months. She wanted to ask why Mama was so tired. Why didn't she eat? Why didn't she play anymore or talk above a whisper? Where was the mother who had loved her? She wanted to ask her Granny all these questions, but she couldn't seem to get them past the big lump in her throat.

So she just cried. She hated crying. It made her feel like such a baby. Big girls in first grade didn't cry. Babies cried. She hated Mama for making her cry. Granny tried to make her feel better with a biscuit with honey on it. Sarah tried to take a couple of bites to show Granny she was alright. She'd show Mama too. She'd get out her crayons and draw a picture just as pretty as that painting, but this time she would give it to Granny or Old Duff.

That's why her crayons were all over the place when Mama came downstairs for supper. Mama stood there staring at Sarah until Granny stepped between them. She put a bar of soap in Mama's still-filthy hand and gave a short nod toward the sink. "*Nigh do làmhan.*" *[Wash your hands.]*

Mama didn't argue. She just turned to the sink and began scrubbing the dirt off her hands. Sarah took the chance to step into the parlor and put her crayons away. She stayed in the parlor, but watched through the door as Mama stayed at the sink, giving her hands a good, hard scrub with hot water. She was still scrubbing when Old Duff came in through the back door. He usually only stayed around the farm in the winter, but Sarah knew he was here still in the late spring on account of Mama. Duff was the only way that Granny could get a break from caring for Mama.

He came in and took off his old and patched over-shirt and hung it on a peg by the kitchen door. Sarah liked Old Duff. Most people called him a drifter or a hippy, but he had kind eyes and always a good word for a lonely little girl. She glanced over to her little shelf on the bookcase and the box of tiny wooden animals that Duff liked to carve for her.

Without a word, he stepped up to the sink where Mama was scrubbing her hands. Steam rose from the sink. Duff whispered something to Mama that Sarah couldn't hear as he reached over and turned off the tap. He grabbed a towel from the rack beside the sink and used it to gently dry Mama's hands. Mama let him, but she never looked at him. She would shift her eyes everywhere but at Duff's, like she was afraid to look at him.

"*Tha am biadh deiseil,*" *[The food is ready]* Granny said in her brisk manner as she set the serving dishes on the table. Sarah went into the kitchen and straight to her chair, which was next to Granny's. Mama and Duff sat on the other side of the table. As always in spring, supper was made up of whatever they could get from the garden and the forest. Tonight it was fish Duff had caught that morning, along with greens sautéed in bacon grease and mashed potatoes and some sliced radishes. There were also the biscuits Granny made every morning.

Since Duff started coming into the house for dinner, they had fallen into a routine of eating supper and talking about their days. Duff would talk about the wildlife he'd seen and what he would go hunting for the next day. Granny would talk about the still and how it was working and what plans she had for the garden or foraging. They both made a point of asking Sarah about her school day and the antics of the other kids in school.

They were almost like a normal family. Granny and Duff tried very hard not to act like there was a ghost sitting at the table, but they all knew she was there. She would pick at her food. Sometimes she even took a bite, but most of the time she just pushed it around her plate and stared at the table. The rest of them tried to ignore her. She made it easy.

"Did ye have your spelling test today?" Granny asked. She always spoke English at the dinner table on account of Duff not having the Gaelic.

Sarah swallowed the bite of potatoes she had just taken and mumbled. "No, ma'am. That's tomorrow."

"Then we'll go over your words while we do the dishes." Granny nodded. Spelling and dishes was also becoming a routine.

"Sing any good songs in music this week?" Duff asked her. He loved to hear Sarah sing.

"There is this one funny song about a cat named Don Gato. He falls down and breaks a bunch of bones. It sounds kinda sad, but the song is really funny."

"Well, sometimes you gotta laugh or else you'll just cry," Duff said with a wink. "Maybe you can sing it for me when you're done with—"

Suddenly Sarah felt eyes on her and looked up to find Mama watching her. Silent tears streamed down her face. The others noticed too and stopped talking. They all sat there staring at Mama while she stared at Sarah. Mama looked so sad, but Sarah didn't believe that look anymore. She'd seen little else but sadness from Mama in the last couple of months, and her sympathy had just about run out, especially after Mama had destroyed her painting.

Feeling a little reckless, Sarah did something she had never done before. She lifted her chin ever so slightly and looked her mama right in the eye. She waited to see if Mama was going to say anything, maybe explain why she had destroyed the painting, why she had turned herself into a living ghost. Mama didn't say anything. She just sat there staring at Sarah with fat tears rolling down her sunken cheeks.

When her mother didn't speak, Sarah just shrugged and went back to eating her dinner. She cut off a bite of fish with the side of her fork and was scooping it up when she heard Mama's fork clatter onto her plate and Mama's chair scrape across the wood floor. With an explosive energy that none of them had thought her capable of, Mama had sprung up from her chair and tried to reach across the table for Sarah. Her fingers, hooked like claws, went straight for Sarah's throat. Fortunately, Duff was quicker and stronger. In a flash, he was on his feet. He wrapped his arms around Mama, pinning her arms to her side. At the same time, Granny jerked Sarah's chair back from the table and put herself in front of it in case Mama got loose.

Mama and Duff struggled for a moment until the soothing rumble of his voice saying, "Easy, Molly, easy now," found its way through the rage that had once again clouded Mama's brain. When he got her calmed down enough that he could get a better grip on her, Duff walked Mama outside into the yard. Granny went to the window to watch them. No doubt Mama would calm down a lot faster without the sight of her daughter. Little Sarah pulled her chair back up to the table and picked up her fork again. She stared down at her plate for a few seconds, but couldn't bring herself to eat anymore. She pushed her plate away and stalked out of the kitchen and up to her room.

***

September 1995
Chapel Hill, North Carolina

Sarah was sitting at the bottom of the stairs in the little kitchen full of chattering girls. She hadn't meant to drift away into her own memories, but they just seemed so much closer to the surface lately.

"Hey, Dermot!" she heard Amy's distant voice pipe up. Sarah peeked around the refrigerator and saw the front door. Dermot had just stepped into the oddly tame, cream-colored living room with a plastic grocery bag in his hand. Sarah rose to welcome him. She intercepted him in the dining room as he was surveying the colorful décor with a look of surprised delight. Sarah beamed at him. "You came."

He turned to look at her and started to speak, but only croaked awkwardly. He cleared his throat before trying again. "I've brought a pound cake." He lifted the grocery bag and gave a shy shrug. "I'm told that's the Southern thing to do."

She laughed and took his hand, pulling him to the kitchen. "C'mon, let's get a plate for this."

The kitchen was conveniently empty, and Sarah found a plate and started slicing the cake and arranging it. Still laughing.

"What's so funny?"

"You did the Southern thing, and I did the Scottish thing. I brought shortbread. Granny Maggie's recipe."

He just smiled and shook his head. After a moment, he began to look around and noticed the purple cabinets. "It's ah…quite an interesting décor they have in here."

She arched a brow at him as she offered him a piece of pound cake. "You should see the bathrooms."

"Are they as colorful as this?" He nodded at the cabinets, taking the cake and leaning back against the fridge as Sarah leaned back into the counter.

"Mmhm," she said around a bite of pound cake. "The one down here looks like the inside of a cantaloupe. I love it. Let's introduce you to the gang." She stepped into the dining room and deposited the plate of cake on the table with the other goodies. Then took his hand to lead him back outside, where most of the guests were sitting on the porch or the lawn.

Sarah introduced Dermot to the others who frequented coffee Fridays. The usual gang was there, Barrett among them, and of course the girls who lived in the blue house. There were a few new faces that even Sarah didn't know. She towed Dermot through them, introducing him to everyone and making conversation.

They were in the dining room talking to Jane when Sarah had an odd creeping feeling, a prickling, itchy feeling on the back of her neck like she was being watched. She looked around but saw nothing unusual.

She noticed Amy flirting with a guy who looked vaguely familiar. He had shaggy blonde hair that wasn't really long, but wasn't short either. His build was wiry, and he moved with a lazy sort of grace that Sarah knew Amy would find attractive. "Do you know who that guy is that Amy's talking to?"

Jane looked over her shoulder and shook her head slowly. "I don't think so. Maybe one of the others invited him. I think Monica said she was inviting some new people."

"Hmm. I think I recognize that twinkle in Amy's eye."

Jane cocked her head and watched as Amy gave a throaty laugh at something the new guy said to her. "Yep. Definitely seen that look before."

"I hope he's better than the last one," Sarah muttered into her coffee cup just as the man in question turned to look at them. He smiled and tipped his head to her in a slight nod.

"Anything wrong?" Dermot asked, and Sarah started to wonder if there was anything he didn't notice.

"Nope. Let's go sit on the porch."

He followed her out to the porch. Sarah settled on the swing while Dermot leaned on the post. After a few minutes, she felt his eyes on her. He'd been watching her since he arrived. No matter who she introduced him to, his eyes always seemed to return to her, searching. Even the ever-enticing Monica got little more than a glance. Sarah found it disconcerting, but she was sure it was due to her change in attitude.

Sarah was just trying to think of the best way to address it when Amy bounced over with a couple of friends, including the blonde guy. She threw an arm around Sarah's neck. "There's a party on Green Street. You up for it?"

"Don't think so. I'm kind of drained. I'm gonna try to get some sleep."

"D?" She looked at Dermot in invitation.

"Ah...no. I'm not much of a partier."

"Suit yourselves." She pointed to Dermot and then to Sarah. "Walk her home. It's getting dark." Then she bounded off with her friends.

"Pick a driver," Sarah called after them, to which Amy pointed to shaggy blonde, who held his keys in the air.

Others began drifting away from the little blue house, and Sarah decided it was time to leave. She went to the dining room to retrieve her plate. When she came back to the porch, Dermot was waiting.

"D'ye mind if I walk you home?"

"I wouldn't want you to get in trouble with Amy." She grinned, and they strolled out of the little yard and down Ransom Street. "Actually, I was hoping to talk to you."

"Oh?"

She took a deep breath and blew it out of her mouth slowly. "I owe you an apology. I've been rude to you more often than I like to think of, and I'm really sorry for that."

He seemed nonplused but nodded, keeping pace beside her.

"I don't even know how to explain why. I'm really not just crazy. Let's just say that you've been nothing but kind and gracious to me even when I…didn't deserve it, and…ummm…I appreciate that. So…thanks. Friends?" She offered him her hand.

"Friends." He nodded and took her hand. Instead of letting it go, he pulled it into the crook of his other arm and held it there as they kept walking. Sarah found she like the solid feel of his arm under her hand, all muscle and sinew. She had to resist the temptation to curl her fingers into his arm just to feel the strength there. Walking so close to him made her feel like nothing in the world could bother her. She couldn't remember ever feeling so safe. Before she knew it, they were in front of her building.

She pulled her keys from her pocket and indicated a small brick-front building that was divided into eight apartments. "This is me."

He gently took the keys from her hand and walked her to the door of her apartment. She was thinking how old-fashioned and kind of charming that seemed as he unlocked the door and handed the key back to her. "Well, I'm glad you've changed your mind about me."

"Me too." She smiled, and her eyes drifted to his lips. They were curled up at the corners in something that was not quite a smile.

"Goodnight then." He surprised her by turning and starting for the outside door. Sarah gave herself a mental shake and stepped into her apartment. She had the door half closed when he turned back, "And Sarah?"

"Yes?" She peeked back into the hallway.

He gave her a roguish smile. "Be sure and lock the door behind ye."

She looked puzzled but nodded and closed the door, which she did remember to lock.

CHAPTER TEN

Dermot cracked an eyelid and looked around his room to see what could be causing that infernal knocking. Having arrived after the semester started, he'd had a tough time finding an apartment and had settled for a tiny one-bedroom in a basement on the corner of Rosemary Street. It was close to campus, but the noise that made its way down the stairs from the street was taking some getting used to. This morning there was a persistent knocking disturbing his much-needed sleep. He'd had a quiet but a late night. After leaving Sarah, he'd spent much of it strolling up and down Ransom Street like a sentry waiting for Amy to get home in the wee hours. He knew Sarah had locked the door, but he just didn't quite feel comfortable with her there alone. He'd fallen into bed around 2:30 and had been sleeping soundly since.

Obviously that noise was not going to stop anytime soon, so he might as well get up. As he passed his front door on his way to the tiny bathroom, he realized that the knocking was in fact on his very own door. A quick peek through the peephole had him running back to his room for the nearest pair of trousers. He jumped into them and still had a hand on the button when he opened the door to Sarah.

The little bit of sun that made it down from the street to the dark hallway struck her hair, turning it into a honey-gold halo of curls. She was poised to knock again, but let her hand fall as her eyes made a slow perusal of him in the doorway. "For once I seem to have you at a disadvantage."

"You always have me at a disadvantage, you just havena noticed it before," he grumbled, stepping aside so she could enter.

"Goodness. A little grumpy this morning?" Sarah stepped inside, her green eyes flashing like a cat that had gotten into the cream.

"No, I just didna get much sleep."

"Well, then it's a good thing I brought coffee." She retrieved the large cup she'd held pinned between her chest and forearm while knocking on his door and offered it to him. She had one for herself in the other hand. "Donald told me where you're staying. I hope you don't mind."

"Uh…no, no…mm…" He accepted the coffee, sounding like an idiot. He was just so surprised to see her and still half asleep.

She gave him a gotcha grin. "Drink up and put on your walking shoes. You've been here for over a week and I'll bet all you've seen is The Pit, Greenlaw, and the library."

"Well, I have been to the grocery store," he grumbled.

She continued on as if he hadn't said a word. "So we're going to remedy that. It's a beautiful day, and I'm gonna take you around to see the sights."

"That's verra nice of ye." He looked surprised and wary.

"Well. I owe you a little niceness. Besides, this'll help me keep my mind off work. You wouldn't want me to go back to being that ball of stress you ran into yesterday, would you?" She gave him a look that said she knew he wouldn't turn her down.

"Right, then. Did Amy get home alright last night?"

"More like this morning, and not alone. So I'm sure she'd tell you she got home just fine."

"Ah. Do ye have time for me to take a quick shower?"

"Of course, I'll just poke through your stuff while you get cleaned up." She gave his things in the living room area a speculative look.

He rolled his eyes and made for the tiny bathroom. He sincerely hoped she was joking about that last part.

***

By the time they had walked from Rosemary Street to the Bell tower, his head was cleared of sleep and filled with information about the campus both basic and apocryphal. She'd pointed at Silent Sam, the Civil War memorial statue on the North Quad said to fire his gun whenever virgins walked by, the Old Well, and the earliest building on campus. She'd also told him about the ghost in Playmakers Theatre and other campus legends. After the Bell Tower they walked on to the Smith Center and she'd shown him some of the trophies and memorabilia from the decades of champions displayed there. Football was more his sport, or soccer as they called it here. They took the bus back to Franklin Street, and Sarah walked him past some other landmarks and businesses that had been there for ages.

They had lunch at a place with the decidedly unappetizing name, The Rat. The Ram's Head Rathskellar was one of the more unique places Sarah had shown him. After descending into an alley and entering by a dark, nondescript door, they'd been ushered through a rabbit warren of rooms with varying themes and wild décor ranging from trains to the circus to graffiti until they were finally deposited at a small booth set into a recess in a wall. The ceiling was composed of glass bricks that intermittently darkened as people walked over them on the sidewalk above.

"So how does a nice Scottish boy end up with such an old Irish name?" Sarah asked, smiling as they settled into the booth. Until now their conversation had been about the town and university. She'd done most of the talking, and neither one of them had asked any personal questions.

"Ach…Well, my mother is a scholar of Celtic mythology and a bit of a romantic. Diarmaid and Grainne is one of her favorite stories. Plus it means 'envy free,' so I think she was trying to set me on the right path." He reached for a menu.

"And what about your father?" She placed a hand on his menu, gently pinning it to the table and shook her head.

"Oh…uh…I never knew him. He was out of the picture before I could remember anything."

"Ah." She gave a knowing nod as the waiter, an older black man, approached the table. "You're not diabetic or lactose intolerant, are you?"

He gave a nervous laugh and shook his head. She looked at the waiter and said, "Two sweet teas and two lasagnas."

The man nodded and walked off without writing anything down.

She turned back to Dermot with a pointed look and asked, "Did you always want to be a folklorist?"

"Ach, no. I wanted to be in the army like a lot of other boys, and I was for a time. Injured my knee and was discharged." He suddenly looked serious. "One of the toughest things I've had to do, leaving the army, but there wasna much choice. I cast about for a year or so before I figured on joining my mother in what I reckon ye could call the family business, history."

"And you prefer oral history to the written history."

"Aye." He gave a firm nod. "What about you?"

"Oh, I don't think I ever really had a choice. I grew up in the mountains in a tiny town and we weren't really…social. But I was fed on legends and stories from the mountains and Scotland. The characters in those stories were my friends. So it seemed like coming home when I stumbled across a folklore class and discovered I could make it my career."

"Did you not have any friends?"

She gave that little ironic laugh he was coming to find adorable. "Precious few. Most of the men around there were afraid of my grandmother, and the women in town were not friendly to us. Small communities like that tend to be suspicious of women living alone like we did. It also didn't help that Granny was a moonshiner who supplied most of the strong drink in town."

His jaw nearly hit the table. "A moonshiner, like with a still in the woods?"

She nodded. "Exactly like that. 'The Devil's Awa wi' the Exciseman' is a song I learned at a very early age."

At just that moment the waiter returned with two glasses and a pitcher of the sweetest iced tea Dermot had ever tasted. He took a sip and grimaced, causing her to giggle.

"Do you have any siblings?" she asked when she'd recovered.

"No. You?"

She gave a brief shake of her head and took a sip of tea.

"Your mother…died?" He cocked his head inquisitively.

"Mmmhm. I was six. My granny took care of me."

"How?" his voice was gentle.

"Very carefully, and with a lot of wisdom." He couldn't be sure, but he thought she'd deliberately misunderstood his question. He'd meant to ask about her mother's death. He was about to clarify his question when the waiter returned and placed a small dish in front of him that appeared to be filled with toasted cheese. Dermot eyed it suspiciously as the waiter placed a similar dish in front of Sarah.

She giggled again as he looked at the plate. "This is The Rat's lasagna, commonly known around campus as the Bowl O' Cheese. Your body can only stand to eat it once a year at the most. It's sinfully rich, but delicious in a comfort food sort of way."

"How d'ye eat it?" He eyed the steaming dish as if it were an explosive device to be defused.

"The best tip I can give you is to lean forward, or you'll be wearing it." She dug her spoon into her dish and used the edge to deftly carve out a piece of the concoction that did, in fact, prove to be lasagna.

Comprised of two noodles on either side of a layer of ricotta with just enough sauce to be decent and smothered in mozzarella, the "lasagna" was truly an experience. Dermot used a fork to break through the top layer of toasted cheese and lift up a bite but was confounded by the half dozen rubbery sauce-flinging tentacles of melted cheese that hung from his fork. He leaned forward and was about to put the bite in his mouth when he heard a distinct snort from across the table. He looked up to see Sarah red-faced and doing her best to stifle her laughter.

"Sorry," she said between giggles as sauce escaped and landed on his shirt. "I wasn't trying to embarrass you or…ruin your shirt. This really is a local favorite."

"Aye, well. I'm not one to buck tradition." He shoved the offending bite in his mouth and let the cheese drip down his chin, grinning at her. Sarah let go into full-on belly-shaking guffaws that proved contagious, and they dug into the rest of their lunch with good humor.

***

"This is one of my favorite spots in town." She was facing a space where the leaves of the forest parted and you could see all the way to Durham from the top of the hill. After lunch they'd spent the afternoon walking through the arboretum, talking about everything and nothing. Mostly, though, Dermot had spent the afternoon watching the autumn sun play off her hair and face. She'd been a new woman this afternoon. The tension that seemed to have drawn her tight as a bowstring when he'd first met her was all but gone. She was relaxed and vibrant, and when her eyes weren't covered by that veil of tension she'd worn before, quite beautiful.

As the afternoon light started to fade, she led him up a residential street to a seemingly out-of-place stone castle. Yes, a castle that she'd informed him was the home of some society called the Order of the Gimghouls. They'd strolled past the castle and up a little trail to where a boulder topped a hill Sarah identified as Piney Prospect. Hidden by trees, he never would have known this was here, but the view was spectacular, and Sarah hadn't taken her eyes off it since they'd arrived.

"I can see why," he said. Despite being able to see the bustling traffic of the roads below and the city of Durham in the distance, there was a stillness here that enveloped them. They were separate from the town around them and the city a few miles away.

"Have you heard about the murder that happened here?" She'd stepped up onto the rock. He resisted the urge to take her arm and pull her back from the edge. The drop wasn't long or steep, but it was enough that he couldn't see the ground on the other side from his position behind her. "Back in the early nineteenth century there was a guy, a student named Peter Dromgoole, who fell in love with a girl in town. According to legend, they used to meet here."

She gave him an arch look and continued, "Of course, back then there were only about 130 students, all guys, and not much of a town. So you can imagine that there weren't that many eligible ladies around. So Peter Dromgoole wasn't her only admirer. One thing led to another, and Peter challenged another guy to a duel. They fought right here…" She gestured to the clearing around them.

"Peter was mortally wounded, and their seconds laid him on the rock. Being young and privileged and not really knowing what to do, the killer and the two seconds dug a shallow grave and rolled this rock over it to hide the body. They say he haunts this spot to this day," she added in her best Vincent Price voice.

Dermot was silent. She eyed a dark stain on the rock, and for a moment her eyes looked so sad he almost took her hand. Instead he cleared his throat and asked, "Does he?"

"Oh, I wouldn't know about that." She glanced at him over her shoulder. "The only ghosts I see are all my own."

He could tell her gaze had turned inward even as she turned to face the open vista again. "So you are haunted, aren't ye?"

She cocked her head and narrowed her eyes at him in an appraising look. "Who isn't? I mean, it could be my outcast childhood or the people I've lost or something else. For you, maybe it's your absent father, losing your army career, or whatever caused that knee injury. I think it's hard to make it to adulthood without being haunted by something. Some of us just keep our ghosts closer to the surface."

She turned her gaze back to the view, which allowed him to study her. She blinked into the strong breeze coming up the hill. The sharp elegant lines of her profile contrasted with the riot of curls dancing in the wind. Though he'd never seen her mother or granny, he could almost feel them there. He had no doubt she felt them too.

She was right. They were all haunted by something. Dermot wondered once again at the cruel trick of fate that had put this woman in his path, along with the knowledge that she wasn't meant for him. "What happened to the girl?"

"Oh, no one even remembers her name. Some say she died of a broken heart, but who really knows?"

CHAPTER ELEVEN

Just over a week later, they were sitting at The Daily Grind with Dermot, arguing the finer points of translating a particular story from Cape Breton when Amy bounded up to their table and alighted in the chair next to Sarah. She broke a bite off of the scone Sarah had been eating and popped it into her mouth. It was the first time Sarah had seen Amy dressed and out of the apartment in what seemed like days. Judging from the noises that had been coming through the walls, Sarah was surprised Amy could walk.

Sarah gave her a sideways glare. "Ah. I see you made it out of bed this morning."

"Yeah well, classes and all." Amy winked and grinned at the two of them.

"Have ye been ill?" Dermot asked innocently.

Sarah let out a brief snort. "If by ill, you mean love sick-"

"I think love sick might be pushing it, but I've definitely been, umm…occupied." Amy had the look of a cat who had been swimming in cream.

"And where is lover boy?" Sarah sighed and shook her head.

"At work, and he does have a name, you know."

"Oh, I know. I've heard it. Repeatedly."

"You really will like him once you get to know him." Amy took another bite of Sarah's scone.

"I'm sure I probably will, whenever he's not otherwise occupied."

"Who is he?" Dermot broke in. The girls looked at him as if they had forgotten he was there.

Amy's cheeks turned pink as her face split into a wide grin. "His name is Ryan. I met him at the last coffee Friday."

"And he's just dreamy," Sarah interrupted, resting her chin on her clasped hands and fluttering her eyelashes comically.

Amy stuck out her tongue before adding defensively, "Why don't we all have dinner tomorrow night and you can get to know him?"

"That's actually not a bad idea," Sarah said. "Too bad I'm busy tomorrow night. Jon's getting back today." She thought she really should sound a little more excited about her sometime-boyfriend returning from fieldwork in Mexico.

"Oh well," Amy said, rolling her eyes. "There's a reason to jump around."

"Come on, Amy, he might not be the warmest coal in the fire, but he's got hidden depths."

"Who's Jon?" Dermot asked.

"Jon," Amy supplied with a sneer before Sarah had a chance, "is Sarah's pet project."

Sarah's look whipped back to her. "That's not fair."

"He's a cold fish, Sarah. I'm just trying to prevent you from wasting your time."

"Just because he's not that excitable doesn't mean he's a cold fish. He's just not the kind of person who shows a lot of emotion. That doesn't mean he doesn't feel it." Sarah gritted her teeth and shot a glance at Dermot, wishing he wasn't hearing this argument but knowing that Amy wasn't going to drop the subject.

"Oh, and how exactly would you know? Does he suddenly turn into Casanova when you guys are alone?"

Sarah met Amy's glare and cut her eyes over to Dermot, hoping to remind Amy they had an audience. Said audience appeared to be politely looking elsewhere, but she was sure he was listening with avid curiosity. "Can we continue this later?"

"Why not? We always do. Oh. Don't forget, we're singing at Skylight on Friday. One last show before the class deadlines start." Amy left her bag and walked over to the coffee cart.

"Right." Sarah sighed and gave Dermot a sheepish look. "Sorry you had to see that. It's an old argument. Amy obviously doesn't think much of Jon."

"I think I got that."

"Well, I believe I'll take off before she gets back rather than risk a repeat of that conversation." She rose and grabbed her notes and bag. "I'll give you a call later."

He was gracious enough to give her a nod and a kind smile, though he did not take the opportunity to leave as well, as she'd hoped. As she neared the library, she looked back to see Amy returning to the table where he still sat. Amy would no doubt fill him in on her many reasons for not liking Jon Samuels. Sarah took a deep breath and reminded herself that Amy wouldn't get so irritated about the Jon situation if she didn't care so much about her.

***

"What am I doing here?" Sarah thought, sitting across the table from Jon at the Groundhog Tavern. This was quite possibly the most boring meal she'd had in ages. Jon had been back from Mexico for a week, and they'd spent hours in each other's company with very little to show for it. He'd prattled on about things he'd done in Mexico and the leading academics he'd worked with ad nauseum, and he'd not once asked her about her trip to Cape Breton, her summer, or anything more pointed than where they should have dinner. The self-absorption might have been forgivable if he'd seemed to have missed her even a little. Oh, he'd kissed her and hugged her the first time she'd seen him, but then they seemed to just fall into the same routine they'd had before he left. It felt like he returned to her after spending the summer away the same way he had returned to his apartment or his car.

She'd finally brought up her own experiences over the summer without his asking, and he'd listened and commented on the progress she'd made with her research. Still, when she'd started to talk about the trouble she'd been having sleeping, his eyes had seemed to glaze over a bit—like she was sure hers were doing now. She tried to focus on what he was saying, something about the Mayan descendants still living in the Yucatán and their local legends, something that in any other situation would have fascinated her.

So she nodded and mhmm'ed while she studied him. One of Amy's complaints about Jon was that he even looked boring. He wasn't bad looking, just nothing to shout about. His glasses shielded chocolate brown eyes. His hair was somewhere between blonde and brown. Amy called it "hair-colored." His face was not quite round, but more round than oval. When he'd first arrived home, he'd had a beard that made him look interesting and almost rakish, but naturally he'd shaved it the day after getting home, saying that it itched horribly. He was of medium height and medium build and generally medium. If Sarah had to describe his looks in one word it would be "academic." Amy would say "nondescript," and that would be when she was in a good mood.

Still, Jon hadn't really changed. He had always been self-absorbed and unemotional. He'd always lacked a certain initiative in their relationship, which hadn't really bothered Sarah before. Why, then, did it seem to bother her now? Maybe it was the time they'd spent apart, or maybe this summer's events had changed her. She shifted uncomfortably on the bench and absently pushed the fat, overcooked noodles around her plate with her fork. It was Spaghetti Wednesday at the Groundhog Tavern, something Jon rarely missed. Maybe all of Amy's harping had finally sunk in and affected how Sarah viewed him—or, and she hated to think this, but maybe it was because she had someone else, someone far more interesting to compare him to.

She tried to dismiss Dermot Sinclair from her mind by reminding herself that he wasn't interested in her, but it didn't really work. There was no question that Jon's academic looks were no match for Dermot's rugged handsomeness, but she told herself that kind of thing just wasn't important. The real difference was one of attitude. For all that Dermot didn't seem interested in her romantically, he was interested in her as a person and not just professionally. They were becoming friends, and unlike Jon, Dermot asked her questions about herself and really listened to the answers. Of course, maybe that was because they'd just met. If he stuck around, maybe they would fall into the kind of complacency that Jon seemed to be feeling and that a lot of couples and friends eventually fell into.

That had to be it. She and Jon were just too used to each other. They needed to do something, spice things up. She'd been seeing Jon too long to just give up or let Amy be right that easily, and he really was a good guy even if he couldn't eat spaghetti without wearing a little. She sighed, spying the flecks of sauce on his T-shirt. She was going to have to do something to prod them in the right direction.

***

"Jon," she broke through some story about a giant tropical spider that had found its way into his room in Mexico and made a home in one of his work boots. He broke off mid-sentence and looked at her. They were just a couple of blocks from her building. She'd been trying all the way home to think of the best way to broach the subject of their relationship and hadn't come up with anything better than, "Did you miss me at all when you were in Mexico?"

"Of course," he said incredulously. He put an arm around her waist and gave her a little squeeze. "You know how I feel about you."

"No, I don't think I do." Damn! She was trying really hard not to sound peevish, but clearly wasn't succeeding.

"Oh…well, I care about you very much." He sounded completely puzzled, but not indifferent.

She sighed and slid her arm around his waist. "I know. I just have this feeling sometimes that we're spinning our wheels, but we're not really going anywhere."

His steps slowed, and she matched him. He seemed to chew over what she'd said for a few seconds. "Where exactly do you think we should be going?"

They strolled on as Sarah chewed on her lip for a minute. "Maybe I'm saying this wrong." Sigh. "I feel sometimes like we each have a lot of passion for our work, we definitely have that in common, but we don't seem to have a lot of passion for each other. Do you see what I mean?"

They stopped walking in front of her building. He turned to face her and gently said, "Is that kind of passion necessary in a relationship?"

"Well, I think it helps."

"Bear with me." He held up a hand to forestall her. He took her hand in his and stroked his thumb along the lines of her palm and looked into her eyes. Suddenly, this wasn't the guy who never missed spaghetti night and prattled on about digs and pot shards. He was totally focused on her. "Would it be better to have passion driving us at each other, only to flame out in a few months, or to have a long, abiding affection that lasts for years…decades?"

This was the guy she'd first been attracted to: wise and steady. She lifted their hands and pressed his to her cheek. "I don't think it has to be one or the other. Isn't it possible to have the abiding affection with occasional flares of passion?"

"Oh, I think we might manage a flare or two." He gave her a warm smile and turned his hand to cup her cheek. He brought his lips down on hers with a firmness that was unusual for him, but still wouldn't be called passionate.

Sarah stepped into him and held him in place by threading her fingers through his hair and letting go of her own passion. She opened her mouth and kissed him with a fervor she hadn't felt in some time. By the time she ended with a playful nip at his lower lip, they were both breathless.

"Well," he gave her a lopsided grin. "That was certainly passionate."

She bit her lip and peeked up at him through her lashes. If the streetlight had been a little brighter, she was sure he would have seen her blushing. "Hmm."

He stepped back to her and, holding her face in his hands, gave her a couple of firm, quick kisses. "I have a very early class tomorrow, but I think we should talk more about this. I'll give you a call, hmm?"

She nodded and smiled. "Mm-hmm."

He let her go slowly before giving her another quick kiss and walking away, down Ransom Street. Sarah held her breath and stood in front of her building, not watching him and wondering whether that would be enough spark or if she was just trying to hold on to something that was never really there.

***

"Bloody idiot," Dermot thought as he watched Sarah letting herself inside and closing the door. He didn't even have the decency to walk her to her door and make sure she was safe. What kind of a man was that? What kind of a man left a woman standing on the street when she'd kissed him like that? He'd wondered after talking with Amy if this Jon Samuels would be trouble. In the few blocks from Franklin Street to her apartment, he'd figured out that Sarah's attachment to him was more a problem than the man himself. He wasn't sure what Sarah saw in him.

At least she was home safe, he told himself. He turned down the street and started heading for his own apartment. Walking easily now, not having to worry about being seen following her. He was tired from walking all over town and ready for his bed. He tried to tell himself that he wouldn't see Sarah kissing Samuels when he closed his eyes.

CHAPTER TWELVE

Dermot could hear the blaring fiddle music from the street as he neared the apartment. He glanced through the front window to see Sarah in the kitchen chopping something just out of view and bobbing up and down in time to the reel that was playing. He wondered how she could move like that and wield the large kitchen knife safely, but her hands looked sure. Amy had left the door ajar, knowing he would be there shortly.

"Have you had dinner yet?" she'd said when she'd called earlier.

"No, why?" He could hear loud music in the background.

"Sarah likes to cook when she's really working on a problem, and she's in the kitchen right now making her famous beans and rice. There'll be plenty, so you should come over. Plus I think she wants to talk to you."

"Why is that?"

"I have a feeling it's work related. She said something about finding something in the collection. That's all I know."

"Ah." Even then he had noticed the music in the background. "Are you having a party?"

"No, it's just us. Music helps her think." Possibly by drowning out any other noise, Dermot thought. Amy pleaded, "Please come over, or I'll be eating beans and rice for a week."

It hadn't taken him long to walk there from Rosemary Street. He really hadn't had dinner, and this was a welcome surprise. He knocked on the door when he got there, but with the music so loud no one heard him. Shaking his head at their carelessness, he pushed the door open and stepped into what sounded like a cèilidh in full swing. Amy was cleaning up the living room and looked up at him just as the music picked up a new beat. She waved to him as Sarah let out an excited "Yip" in the kitchen. Amy jumped to meet her and the two danced side by side to a jig. They seemed to float above the floor, managing not to hit anything in the tiny kitchen. For a second it made Dermot wish he could dance.

The song ended, and the girls came back to earth breathless and threw their arms around each other. They grinned at Dermot. He could do nothing but grin back.

"Good," Sarah asserted between gasps. "I hope you're hungry."

"Starved. I hope the famous beans and rice I've heard about is famous for being good."

"Oh, it's goooooood," said Amy.

"So what is this thing that ye found?" Dermot asked as Sarah turned back to the pot on the stove. Amy handed him a beer from the refrigerator.

Her green eyes glinted with mischief as she glanced at him over her shoulder. "The Holy Grail."

Dermot nearly spit his mouthful of beer all over the kitchen. He managed to choke it down and cleared his throat. He was glad she had turned back to the pot so she couldn't see his face. The hairs on the back of his neck prickled as he tried to draw out more information. "I wasna aware ye were looking for that."

"I might as well have been. I was beginning to think what I found today didn't exist." She laughed. "But there it was in the collection, just waiting for me to find it."

The knots of tension in his shoulders eased, and he tried not to let his relief show in his voice. "So, what is it?"

"You'll see. First, we eat." Sarah lifted the lid of a pan that contained bright yellow saffron rice and stirred. "Somebody get some bowls. The rice is done."

***

"Mmm!" Amy enthused at her first bite of beans and rice. Sarah thought she must have outdone herself. Dermot closed his eyes, savoring the way the sweet onion contrasted with the smoky cumin and the fresh cilantro. Sarah took a moment to enjoy their reactions as they continued making inarticulate sounds of satisfaction.

She loved feeding people. Cooking was one of the joys of growing up with Granny that had never been complicated. Cook good food, and people will enjoy it. No one cared if the cook's father was absent or her mother was crazy—or that her grandmother was a moonshiner. It was just feeding people, and she was good at it.

She was glad Amy had invited Dermot. Maybe he would have some insight on her song. Though they'd been working together for weeks now, she hadn't really discussed the specifics of her dissertation with him. She supposed that could be blamed on the lingering suspicion that he might be out to steal her work. Although the more she got to know him, the more absurd that seemed.

She studied him as he ate with relish. He must have felt her eyes on him because he looked up. He blushed slightly as if he were a little embarrassed to be eating with such enthusiasm. She couldn't help thinking that his Celtic scholar mother would have taught him the significance of eating at her table, the bond of mutual trust and protection signified by Celtic hospitality. He held her gaze as his smile slowly faded and gave her solemn though almost imperceptible nod. He knew. She gave him a hint of a smile and returned her attention to her own bowl.

***

Sarah laid three sheets of paper on the table side by side. They had cleared away the dinner dishes and were standing in front of the table, nursing beers and full bellies with equal lassitude.

"This one is a transcript of a song my grandmother taught me. This one, I collected over the summer in Cape Breton, and this is what I found today. Essentially the same song, but in English. I transcribed it from a tape in the folk-life collection," Sarah said, pointing to the third of the sheets. She gave the other two a few minutes to read the three different versions of what appeared to be the same song. "They all have the same tune and the same subject. I think these are the key to my dissertation. I want to trace the evolution of this song from Scotland to the New World, from Gaelic to English."

Dermot studied the songs again one by one. "And you think there is a source in Scotland because…?"

"Because of the similarities. A lot of Scots migrated here and to Cape Breton, but there hasn't been a lot of movement between the two colonies. For these songs to be this similar, there has to be a unified source."

"That part about the stone makes it seem Scottish too," Amy chimed in, looking closely at the Cape Breton version.

Dermot studied them a moment more before looking up at her. "This is very old; the bit about the stone and the cauldron of plenty, the symbolism is ancient...you dinna find unknown ballads this old."

"Right. That's what I thought. But I've been combing Childe, Buchan, and every other collection and analysis that I could get my hands on. I haven't seen it anywhere else. Have you?"

He quickly looked back at the table, shaking his head mutely.

"Where was the American one collected?" Amy leaned toward the table to read it.

"In the mountains near Franklin, from a man named Simon Budge in the twenties on a phonograph. At first I thought he might have learned it from Granny, but she didn't come over until 1939."

"And the Cape Breton song? You collected that?" Amy shifted her gaze to the song in the middle.

"Mmhmm, remember I told you about that woman Isobel MacKenzie and her granddaughter?"

"Right, the blind lady."

"What blind lady?" Dermot asked, dragging his eyes away from the transcriptions. Sarah quickly related the story of the evening she spent in the little cottage in Cape Breton learning the song from Isobel MacKenzie, leaving out the odd feeling of familiarity she'd felt with Isobel and her granddaughter. "Hmm...when did she come over?" Dermot asked.

“Actually, her mother came over, earlier than Granny but still twentieth century. She even had a worry stone from Scotland. In fact, she gave it to me.”

“That might explain why theirs are so similar. They haven’t been over here that long.”

“But still long enough to change according to their surroundings. Granny’s maiden comes from a river, but the Cape Breton maiden comes from the sea like a selkie.”

“Hmm…” Dermot leaned closer to look at the one from Sarah’s grandmother. They all seemed to be working under an unspoken agreement not to move the papers, as if moving them apart might break the connection between the three songs. “Is this transcribed from your memory or directly from her?”

Sarah looked down at the paper with longing. “My memory. She passed away before I got a chance to record her. She never wanted me to write any songs down. She said that was the lazy way to learn them. Granny taught knee-to-knee or not at all.”

He made a mumbly sort of grunt that seemed to suggest some repressed opinion. “What’s this last verse? That’s not Gàidhlig.”

“I don’t know. I had to write it phonetically because she would never let me write it down. At first I thought it was Welsh because of the softer consonants, but I haven’t been able to translate it, so either my spelling is way off or it’s an archaic form.”

He spent a moment almost silently testing the words on his lips. They were neither Gaelic nor Welsh, but something in between, and they had none of the Latin that had been injected into the native British languages by the Roman occupation.

"It's almost exactly the same in every version," Amy pointed out.

"That's why I still think it's significant. You know how some songs turn to gibberish after being passed down by word of mouth? It could just be some untranslated verse that got jumbled by hundreds of years of the telephone game, but each version is just too close. And when Granny taught it to me, that was the part that she drilled me the most on, like it was the most important."

"But she never told you what it meant?" Dermot shot her a questioning look to which Sarah just shook her head.

"Did your lady in Cape Breton know?" he pressed.

Sarah shook her head and looked thoughtfully at the Cape Breton version. She thought back to the shock she'd felt hearing those words from Isobel MacKenzie. "If she did she wasn't saying, but I don't think she did. Her experience was the same as mine. Her mother taught it to her, and she had to learn it exactly, but she was never told the meaning."

He returned his attention to the papers on the table, shaking his head.

"And these are the only versions you've found?" Amy cut in.

"I was hoping to find a version of the song in a collection in Australia. I had a professor friend of Donald's looking for me, but there was nothing."

"What about this Budge guy's family? Maybe he passed it down." Amy straightened up, taking pull of her beer.

"It wouldn't surprise me. I need to try to find out if anyone in the area remembers him. If I'm lucky, his family is still there, and he taught them something about it."

"When are you going?" Amy knew Sarah well enough to know that she would not wait long. She was driven enough that if she knew the next step, she wouldn't hesitate to take it.

"Not sure. That depends on when I can rustle up the money, time, and equipment for a trip, but I definitely think it's my next step."

"Well, dinna go without me, aye?" Dermot gave her a fierce look as if he feared she would hare off to the mountains by herself. Sarah wasn't sure if he was being protective or looking to piggy-back off of her work.

"I wouldn't dream of it." She returned his gaze. They were each caught for a moment, the other's eyes not willing to look away. There were times when Sarah thought Dermot was becoming a friend, and others when she was sure he was hiding something.

Amy nearly jumped, looking at her watch, and the spell was broken. "Crap! I've got to get ready. Are you sure you don't want to go?"

"Very sure," Sarah assured her. She had no interest in going to the annual seventies dance at the Cat's Cradle. She loved dancing and disco, but the seventies dance was always a crowded, sweaty, loud affair, and Sarah was in too thoughtful a mood to enjoy that environment.

"Okay, if Ryan gets here before I'm out, be nice," Amy said before hurrying down the hall to her room.

With the tension broken, Sarah and Dermot returned to discussing the songs on the table. They had just gotten to the imagery of the sickly king when there was a knock at the door.

***

Dermot was relieved to see Sarah glance through the peephole in the door before opening it, though he could tell by the set of her shoulders that she wasn't very enthusiastic about the person she was admitting. He was clearly dressed for the dance in orange corduroy bell-bottoms and a powder blue polyester shirt complete with butterfly collar. His blonde hair looked as though it hadn't been cut in some time. His cheekbones and nose were defined to the point of sharpness. They would have been his most prominent features if not for a pair of sharp blue eyes that sparkled with smug humor. He wore a beard just unkempt enough to obscure the exact line of his jaw. Overall, he gave an impression of amiable rakishness. Still, something about him set Dermot's teeth on edge.

"Hi, Ryan," Sarah said with just energy to be polite.

"Hey, Sarah." He gave back a wolfish grin.

"Come on in, Amy's still getting dressed." Sarah stepped back, letting him into the apartment, and waved her hand toward the living room. As Ryan sauntered in, she waved a hand in Dermot's direction. "This is our friend Dermot."

Dermot offered his hand. "Dermot Sinclair. I'm glad to meet ye."

"Ryan Cumberland." He ambled over to the couch and sat down, seeming completely at ease. Dermot knew he'd been spending time there, but didn't like how comfortable Ryan seemed to make himself in their apartment.

"So you're the guy from Scotland?" Ryan asked. Dermot thought he detected a hint of Southern twang in Ryan's accent.

"That's right."

"Yeah, Amy told me all about you. So you guys a couple yet?"

Dermot and Sarah spoke at the same time. Startled by the bold question, Dermot said, "Well, that's direct."

"We're not together." Sarah gave her head a brief shake.

Ryan's smile grew as he looked back and forth between them. "Oh? Guess I misunderstood."

"Mmm…So, Ryan, are ye a student?" Dermot settled himself in a chair across from Ryan. He had to remind himself not to make it seem like an interrogation. He softened his tone with a friendly half-smile.

Ryan gave a little tilt of his head before answering. "No, I work construction, mostly carpentry. I'm working on the new grocery store they're building in Carrboro."

"Where are you from? Your accent doesn't sound like it's from around here," Sarah asked.

"Oh, a little place in the Florida panhandle. I'm sure you've never heard of it. We didn't even have a stoplight." He smiled tightly as if to say the subject was closed.

She returned his smile with a tight one of her own. "Yeah, I grew up in a town like that."

Dermot pressed on. "You and Amy met at the blue house?"

"That's right. I met one of those girls at the library, and she invited me for coffee."

"At the library, but yer not a student," Dermot said skeptically.

"Yeah, I was doing some research." Ryan looked sheepish and nodded at Dermot. "You know what I mean, right?"

It took a second for his meaning to sink in, but Dermot did know what he meant. He arched a cynical brow at the man.

Ryan looked off to the side and made an "aw shucks" sort of movement with his shoulders. Dermot was about to ask him more about his job when Ryan's face lit up. "There's Amy!"

Behind Sarah and Dermot, Amy had stepped out of the hall and was showing off her costume right down to strappy platform sandals. She looked stunning in a shimmery silver halter top that flowed and clung in just the right places and white bell-bottoms that flared out to cartoonish proportions. She had further smoothed her dark hair with a flat iron so it hung perfectly straight. The effect was just right.

"What do you think?" Amy asked, beaming and taking a model's pose with one leg in front.

"Wow!" Ryan said again as he came around the couch to take her hand and give her a kiss. "You look perfect."

"He's right, Amy, very nice," Sarah affirmed.

Dermot just nodded. He watched Ryan and Amy together. Amy seemed besotted, but he'd known that. For his part, Ryan seemed just as focused on Amy. As far as Dermot could tell, they seemed completely absorbed with each other.

"We'd better get going or we'll never find a place to park," Amy said, grabbing a tiny purse just big enough for her ID and some cash.

"After you." Ryan gestured toward the door before turning to Sarah and Dermot. "It was nice meeting you. I'm sure I'll see you again."

"I'm sure," said Dermot.

"Have fun," Sarah said as she followed them to the door.

When she'd shut it behind them, she turned back to the room, her brows knit together in thought.

"What?" Dermot asked.

"I don't know. Can't put my finger on it, but something about him just feels off. He sure seems to like Amy, though."

"Aye…"

"I guess I'm just protective. She'd do the same for me." Sarah sighed as they sat back down on the couch. "I have to admit, it's kind of nice to see Amy settle on one guy for a while instead of bouncing from guy to guy."

"Mmmphmmm…" Dermot hoped for Amy's sake that this guy was alright. Still, he would have to keep an eye out.

"It's a good thing I speak mumbly-grunt, or you and I would have a hard time communicating." Sarah bumped his shoulder before giving his knee a pat. "I'll get us a couple more beers and we can watch some TV. I could use some mindless entertainment."

CHAPTER THIRTEEN

It was one of those fall days that makes a person never want to go inside. The leaves on the giant oaks on campus were aflame with fall colors. The sun shone bright, and there was just enough chilly breeze to put roses in cheeks. Everyone on campus seemed to want to be outside. Students and faculty alike postponed work to play Frisbee on the quad or sit on a blanket and read a book.

The Ransom Street crowd, as Dermot had come to think of Sarah's friends, seemed to own the tables in front of the cafe on the corner near his building. Some would come and go as their classes and jobs demanded, but there always seemed to be someone there. Its proximity to this favorite campus hangout was one of the few things that made Dermot appreciate his tiny basement apartment. He'd just been walking past the cafe when Amy and Barrett had invited him to go see some new sculptures on display at the Art Center. Since they had assured him that Sarah would be along any minute to join them, he rushed around the corner to his apartment to drop off his rucksack.

He dropped the bag by the door and stepped into the bedroom to grab a light jacket. He checked his appearance in the mirror in the bathroom and was about to leave through the back door when a knock sounded on the front. Thinking it was one of his new friends, Dermot didn't bother to check the peephole before opening it.

"Sinclair." Walter Stuart stood on his threshold, his patrician nose wrinkling at the state of the dingy hallway.

Dermot immediately stepped back to let the older man enter. Stuart had a way of sucking the joy out of any room. As he stalked across the threshold of Dermot's little apartment, casting a jaundiced eye about in a slow inspection, the pretty autumn afternoon that everyone else was enjoying seemed worlds away.

"Cousin!" Dermot turned back to the open door to find James Stuart grinning at him. Where Walter Stuart was like a black hole, his nephew James was quite the opposite. Movie star good looks, charisma, and a general bonhomie made James the center of attention no matter where he was. Were their situations different, Dermot fancied that he and James would still be friends, as they had been when they were schoolboys. Time and tide seemed to have put an end to that, though James called on their friendship often enough.

"James." Dermot gave him a nod of acknowledgement.

"It's been so long since we've heard a report from you that we thought we'd stop by and see how things were going," James softly chided him.

"Stop by? Ye're a bit far from home for that." Dermot was wary.

"We're on our way to the Louisiana for a meeting about drilling permits," Walter put in, his tone making it clear they would brook no more questions.

Dermot just glared at the older man for a few seconds, reminding him that Dermot was the one with the information he wanted. "Aye, well there's not been much to report. I've connected with her and am working on gaining her trust. That's what I told you last month and it hasna changed."

“I find it hard to believe that it has taken you this long to gain the woman’s trust,” Walter spat out with disapproval.

“She’s got a suspicious nature, as any woman alone in the world should.”

“And we’re about to offer her the world on a platter,” James said, holding out a hand as if the proverbial platter rested on it.

Dermot turned to his cousin, trying to be diplomatic. “Aye, your world, not hers. She’s worked hard for what she has, and she’ll not leave it easily.”

“But I’ll—” James started to say something before the older man cut him off.

“She really has no choice in the matter. You would do well to remember that.”

Dermot moved closer to Walter, nearly stepping on the tips of Stuart’s perfectly polished shoes. His voice was soft but his tone firm. “I know my duty as much as you know yours, but I also know that she must be willing. Right now, she doesna know a thing about it. I think her gran kept her in the dark to protect her.”

“Perhaps the time has come to tell her.” Walter would not be cowed by Dermot’s show of aggression.

“If you tell her now, she’ll think you a mad old man and laugh in your face,” Dermot scoffed.

“Meanwhile you’re risking her life by leaving her ignorant. Our enemies could be stalking her right now.” Walter’s voice rose a notch, and he stepped even closer. They were like two rams about to lock horns.

“You mean like we’re doing?” Dermot matched his voice to Walter’s. “I am capable of keeping her safe. Is that not a steward’s job?”

"Just make sure you don't forget it." Walter pointed a bony finger in Dermot's chest and seemed about to give him a proper set down.

Just then a knock sounded on the door. Dermot closed his eyes for a second, willing it not to be Sarah. He was turning toward the door when he heard her voice. Cheerful as everyone else on a bright fall day, she asked, "Hey, Dermot, are you in there?"

***

Sarah was beginning to think he wasn't there. She'd waited at the corner when Amy said he would be right back, but she'd gotten impatient. Finally, he opened the door and she stepped into the apartment. "Amy and Barrett said we were going to the Art Center to see the new sculptures. Are you still—" She stopped her chattering when she noticed the two men standing in Dermot's living room. One was just past middle age and dour looking. He had gray hair cut close and wore a very formal suit. He had a calculating look and a tilt to his head that suggested he believed himself to be a cut above. He looked like a man who ran things.

Sarah had to stop herself from staring openly at the other man. He looked to be in his late twenties and was probably the most attractive person Sarah had ever seen. Chiseled features, deep-set crystal blue eyes, and close-cropped hair of a rich dark brown worked together perfectly on this man. "Oh! You've got guests. I'll just…uh…see you later…"

"This must be the lovely and talented Sarah you've told me so much about." Mr. Handsome stepped forward, extending his hand, which Sarah shook without even thinking.

His voice was a smooth rumble, his accent cultured and very British. He didn't release her, but brought his other hand up to clasp their joined hands. Sarah noticed none of this as she seemed mesmerized by his intense blue gaze.

Dermot cleared his throat. "Sarah MacAlpin, allow me to introduce my cousin, James Stuart."

"It's...it's a pleasure to meet you." There was something familiar about James Stuart, but she couldn't quite put her finger on it.

"And James's uncle, Walter Stuart." Dermot indicated the older man, who stepped forward to shake her hand. Sarah managed to pull her attention and hand from the Adonis before her to shake hands with the older man.

"Miss MacAlpin." His smile seemed warm enough, but Sarah couldn't help feeling a bit like a fly shaking hands with a spider. He did that thing so many men do when shaking a woman's hand: he didn't grip her hand so much as allow her to grip his. By the look of him, Sarah thought he was a man who always tried to have the upper hand, and she was sure he wouldn't have given a man such a weak handshake. Maybe it was just a pet peeve of hers, but Sarah hated when men intentionally weakened their handshake for women—it suggested a subtle misogyny and dishonesty.

"We're here for some business in the Research Triangle and thought we'd stop by and see how my old friend Dermot is getting on." James was obviously better at making small talk than his uncle. "He told me you were lovely, but now that I've met you I can understand why I haven't heard from him for weeks."

Sarah couldn't conjure up any other response to this but to blush beet red.

James stepped closer to her, giving her his most dazzling smile. "We were just about to invite Dermot to dinner with us this evening. Could I convince you to join us?"

Sarah looked over at Dermot. He looked tense, but he didn't give her any hint as to his feelings about the invitation. "Actually, I'm afraid I already have dinner plans tonight."

"Ah. Well, we'll be in town a few days…perhaps another time." If he was disappointed by her refusal, he didn't show it. Sarah got the impression that no one said no to James Stuart for very long.

"Sure," she said, still trying to puzzle out where she'd seen him before.

"Well, cousin, I think we'd better be going. Can we expect you for dinner?" James shifted his gaze back to Dermot.

"Aye, I'll be there."

"Seven o'clock at the Sienna, then."

Dermot nodded. "Seven it is."

"Sarah, it's been a pleasure to meet you. I trust we'll see you again soon." James gave her another dazzling smile and stepped past her to the door.

Walter followed, his eyes focused on Sarah as he gave her a nod. "Miss MacAlpin."

Sarah nodded as well and tried to suppress a shiver as the older man walked by.

Dermot closed the door after them and stood with his hand on the knob for a few heartbeats.

"I get the feeling they aren't exactly your favorite relatives," Sarah broke into his reverie.

He snorted. "James is a good enough fellow, but I could do without the likes of Walter Stuart."

"Mmm, I get the feeling he's a man who typically gets his way."

He turned to her and gave her a direct look. "By hook or by crook, ye can count on it. I canna say I havena benefited from knowing him, but everything you get from Walter comes at a price."

Sarah couldn't help hearing that as a warning, but she couldn't fathom why Dermot would think she needed it. He was clearly off kilter. "Well, you can worry about that old spider later. Are you going to the Art Center with us?"

He ran a hand through his hair roughly as if he could scrub the last few minutes from his brain. "Aye, I am. Let's go."

***

It wasn't until much later, as they were walking back to Ransom Street, that Sarah felt comfortable asking Dermot about his cousin, James. While Amy and Barrett strolled in front of them down the street, she broached the subject. "Your cousin looks so familiar. Where might I have seen him before?"

He shrugged. "Och, he's all over. He and Walter between them run Alba Petroleum. It's the biggest energy company in Scotland, and they have investments all over the world. He's sort of the public face of the company. Naturally, Walter is in the background calling all the shots."

"Well, since I don't really read the business section of the newspaper, I don't think that's it. I just can't shake the feeling that I've seen him somewhere before," she said as they turned onto her street.

"I think they did some feature on him in some American magazine last year."

"Yeah, I don't really read that stuff. Maybe Amy knows something."

Hearing her name mentioned, Amy joined in. "Something about what?"

"A magazine feature on James Stuart."

"The actor?"

"Uh, no, the Scottish businessman."

"Oh, that James Stuart." Her eyes lit up. "He's delicious."

"What do you know about him?" Sarah asked, glancing at Dermot.

Amy looked up as if reading a mental list. "Billionaire, business man, philanthropist, and just about the hottest guy on the planet." She glanced at Dermot and gave an embarrassed shrug. "You know, if you're into that polished, old-school movie star kind of look. Why do you ask?"

"I just met him," Sarah said with just a hint of mischief.

Amy's eyes nearly popped out of their sockets. "Huh? Where?"

Dermot blushed and looked resigned. "In my apartment."

"Wait a minute." Amy stopped and waited for them to catch up to her and Barrett. "What was he doing in your apartment?"

"Well, he's my distant cousin." He tried to emphasize the "distant" before Amy got any ideas.

"No kidding? Wow, Dermot, you've been holding out on us. Here we just thought you were some nerdy folklore guy." She gave him a wink.

"Aye, well, it was sort of a surprise visit. I didna know he was in town."

Amy and Sarah shared a look, and Dermot got the feeling there would be much discussion of James at the apartment that evening.

***

"Oh. My. God! You met James Stuart! Is he as hot in person as he looks in the magazines?" Amy gushed as soon as the apartment door was shut on the guys.

"Since I don't think I've seen him in any magazines, I'm not sure, but I will admit I was kind of dazzled."

"How did he sound, all sexy and Scottish like Dermot?"

"Uh, no, more cultured and precise, not like Dermot at all. He's very charming, though. He was very friendly."

"Like how friendly?" Amy asked.

Sarah looked pensive. "He invited me to dinner."

"Wow, when?"

"Tonight." She waved a dismissive hand. "I can't go, though."

"Why not?!" Amy looked as if Sarah had lost her senses.

Sarah went to the kitchen to get a glass of water. Partly because she was thirsty, but also because she didn't want to see Amy's face when she said, "Because I have a date with Jon."

"Oh! Is it spaghetti night at the Groundhog again already?" Amy followed her to the kitchen, her tone dripping sarcasm.

"Don't start, Amy." Sarah gave her a quelling look. "It's that Anthro Department mixer I told you about."

"Right. I love how Jon remembers he's supposed to have a girlfriend whenever there's some department social thing."

"That's not fair. I'm just as busy as he is. We don't get a lot of time for these things."

"So, that's why he didn't show up for our last performance?" Amy held up her hands in surrender before switching gears. "Okay. What are you wearing?"

"That chocolate brown sheath with the turquoise shawl."

"Ooo! I have the perfect necklace for that." Amy went to her room to retrieve the necklace, bringing it to Sarah's room.

Half an hour later, as a freshly showered and elegantly dressed Sarah was putting on her makeup, Amy stood leaning against the doorframe. Her arms were crossed, and she looked thoughtful.

"What is it?" Sarah eyed her friend in the mirror. "Is my skirt caught in my underwear?"

"Har-har. No, but I do think I should point out that you're trying to figure out how to fund a research trip to Scotland and Mr. Filthy-Rich-Scottish-Philanthropist just dropped into your lap and invited you to dinner and you turned him down." Her tone turned serious. "I know you like to keep everything all official when it comes to money. I know you hate asking directly for it and I know why, but sometimes you just have to go for it. You could spend the next six months trying to cobble together something for a Scotland trip. This guy could help you get there tomorrow. Is your comfort for a few minutes really worth the delay?"

Sarah turned around to face Amy and leaned a hip against her dresser, letting Amy's point sink in. She sighed. "I freaking hate it when you're right."

Amy arched a brow. "You must be miserable all the time."

Sarah narrowed her eyes and let out a low growl before reaching for the strappy heels that would complete her outfit.

"Well, all is not lost. He did say they would be here for a few days and maybe we could do dinner another time."

Amy brightened. "You need to have dinner with this guy. Even if he won't fund you, just think of the connections you could make."

Sarah turned over the possibilities in her mind and almost didn't hear Amy say, "And it can't be too much of a trial to sit across the dinner table from all that hotness."

***

The reception room at the art museum was filled to the brim with anthropologists and graduate students. Every one of them seemed just a tad fidgety, as if they weren't quite comfortable in their nice clothes. There was minimal decoration, but the lights had been dimmed and projectors positioned around the room displaying slide shows of various artifacts from different cultures on the walls. As an ice-breaker it was somewhat effective, giving the typically bookish anthropologists something to talk about. The result was clusters of academics milling around the various projections and chatting over their cocktails and hors d'oeuvres.

The most senior of the department's professors moved between clusters in the vain attempt to get people to actually mix with people who weren't in their immediate field of study. They were helped to a small extent by the various spouses and dates who insisted that their partners move occasionally from one cluster to another. This was Sarah's role tonight, as Jon had briefed her in the car.

"I need your help tonight. You're so much better at this stuff than I am," he'd said as he pulled into a rare parking space near the museum. Sarah had been thankful she wouldn't have to walk too far in her heels.

"What stuff is that?" she had asked, checking her lipstick in the mirror.

"You know, being sociable and outgoing. I need to make a good impression tonight, especially with Dr. Jackson." He turned to face her with his hand on the back of her seat.

"Why him? I thought he was the European cave painting guru."

"He is, but he's also putting together a team to go to Chaco Canyon this summer, some comparative study of cave paintings and carvings there. I really want in on that team."

She gave a knowing nod. "Because of the pre-Columbian connection."

"Right. I might just find the connections I need to finish my research if I can get out there." He toyed with one of her earrings.

She gave a soft girlish laugh. "Sounds familiar. I'm trying to get to Scotland for the same reason."

"Well, we'd better get going. You look beautiful, by the way." He released her earring and brushed the backs of his fingers down her cheek before reaching for his door. Sarah reached for her door, knowing from experience that Jon would not think to open it for her.

Sometime later, Sarah spotted the all-important Dr. Jackson talking with some other graduate students in front of a slide show of Gravettian Venus figurines. Wallace Jackson always reminded Sarah a little of Bill Cosby. He had that a special blend of intellectuality and irreverence that she found disarming. She'd taken one of his classes and enjoyed it, but was sure he wouldn't remember her. He was one of America's foremost authorities on Upper Paleolithic art, from cave paintings to figurines, and he discussed those topics with the same sort of boyish enthusiasm that Cosby used to talk about Jell-O Pudding Pops.

When Sarah managed to drag Jon away from a slide show of Incan grave goods, Dr. Jackson was deep in conversation with another professor on the nature of Venus figurines. The figure on the current slide was typical of the type of figurines they were talking about: headless and footless points at the top and bottom with a center made up of pendulous breasts and hips of exaggerated roundness. Found all over Europe, the figures had been a topic for debate over the last hundred years, with varying theories as to their meaning and purpose. The professor Dr. Jackson was talking with as Sarah and Jon joined them was sure they were idols of a fertility cult, while another in the group made the suggestion that they were pornographic and that the figurines represented the Upper Paleolithic ideal of beauty. Like any good teacher, Dr. Jackson listened attentively to their theories, though Sarah was sure he had heard them all before.

As the slide changed to show the Venus of Willendorf, Jon put in his two cents on the side of the fertility theory. The Willendorf figurine was often used to support this theory, as many interpreted it to be of a pregnant woman. Where many other figurines displayed enlarged breasts and hips, this one added a very rounded belly. It was also unusual in that it had a head that rested almost ball-like on her shoulders and appeared to have a cap of tight curls. Though she had seen the figurine many times before, Sarah found herself studying the enlarged display of it closely.

"Why does it have to be one or the other?" Sarah broke in without looking away from the figure.

Her interjection was met with silence, and Sarah wondered if she shouldn't have spoken up.

"Go on," Dr. Jackson prompted.

"I just don't see that the two are exclusive of each other," Sarah explained.

"You think they sexualized pregnancy?" the other professor asked, surprised.

"I don't think it's a big jump. Our modern sensibilities are what make us want to separate the two. But I think it's more than just sex or human fertility. I think they're fetishizing the idea of plenty." Sarah, warming to the topic, turned to face the others in the group. "I mean we're talking about mostly nomadic hunter/gatherers here, right? They struggled for every bite of food they ate. Not to mention, you don't get that physique hiking all over central Europe. I'll bet that not very many of them looked like that. I think the roundness isn't just about being fertile as people. It's about hoping for a fertile world."

"I think you're creating a false synthesis there. You're implying that they would have made a connection between sex, human fertility, and something as basic as food," another professor interjected.

"Really? I don't think that's such a difficult connection to make. Plenty of cultures do it. Look at the Celts, who in all likelihood descended from these people. Their lore is full of cauldrons that give never-ending food or healing medicine. They're sometimes depicted connected to specific families.

That same round cauldron/womb shape appears in many cultures, and it's usually associated with production or regeneration."

"That's the folklorist talking. Those are later cultures. We're looking at Paleolithic people. Would they even have the mental capacity to make those connections?" Jon put in.

Sarah had to disagree. "Dr. Jackson can correct me if I'm wrong, but I don't think these people were that much less evolved than us physically. You're assuming that our collective human knowledge has developed in one straight line from then to now. History is filled with examples of knowledge that was lost and then regained. There's evidence of prehistoric brain surgery, steam-powered machines in ancient Alexandria, and Mayan astronomers. All of that knowledge was wiped out by disaster or conquest, and we're just starting to regain it. So who's to say these people didn't know more than we think they did?"

***

"I can't believe you did that," Jon seethed as soon as they got far enough away from the building to prevent being overheard.

"Did what?" Sarah slowed her steps to look at him.

"You completely upstaged me, after I told you I needed to make an impression on Jackson. Now he'll probably remember me as the grad student with the preachy girlfriend." He stopped walking and turned to her, his face full of derision. "And what was that drivel about Celts and cauldrons anyway? We were talking about Paleolithic Central Europe."

"Drivel!?" Jon had never been insulting before. Sarah tried to resist the impulse to argue, but she lost. "Okay, I'm not going to get into an argument with you about the theory of Aryan migration out of the Indus valley into Europe, but my points were sound. And anyway, you're a grown-ass man. You shouldn't need someone else to help you make an impression. And if you can't play the department politics game, then maybe you're in the wrong business."

"Oh, and exactly what business do you think I should be in?" He squared his shoulders and stepped closer. Sarah cocked her head, looking at him as if he were a stranger. It was probably the most passion Sarah had ever seen him display, and it just left her feeling cold.

"Clearly not one that involves relationships with live people." Sarah sounded as if the wind had been taken right out of her. She turned away from the direction of the car and toward home. "Good night, Jon. I'm going home."

"Sarah, what are you doing? You can't walk home in those heels."

She stopped and turned back to find him standing exactly where she'd left him. "You just read me the riot act for having a mind of my own, and you're worried about me walking home in heels! What am I to you, a flipping accessory?"

He held up his hands in a conciliatory gesture and walked to her. "Of course not. I was upset. It's just not how I had hoped things would work out tonight. Come on, let me drive you home."

"Tell me, Jon, just how did you hope things would work out tonight?"

He looked around to make sure there was no one from the party listening. “Come on, Sarah. Can we talk about this in the car?”

She tucked her clutch under one arm and folded her arms in front of her, planting her feet firmly on the sidewalk. The message was clear: she wasn’t going to budge.

“Fine. It’s hard to make an impression on people when you’ve always got your head bent over a book or artifact, and you know I don’t do well in interviews. You’re beautiful and funny and you can be charming and all those things I’m just not. I hoped that you would help draw some attention and draw me out of my shell, make me seem like more than just a student. Instead you made me look like just the guy who was with you.”

Sarah’s shoulders slumped and she gave a tired sigh. “Why are we doing this, Jon? What is our relationship about?”

“What do you mean?”

Sarah was surprised that he actually looked confused by her question.

“You only call me when you don’t have some colleague to go to dinner with or for something like this.” She waved a hand toward the museum. “When we’re together, you talk about anything and everything you’re doing, but you never even ask about what I’ve been doing.”

“We’re independent.” He shrugged.

“Independent or indifferent? I’ve been stressing out about my dissertation and how I'm going to finish it for weeks and you haven’t even noticed. When I mentioned it earlier, you told me I looked good and we needed to go inside. I mean, am I your girlfriend or your PR tool?”

He took too long to think of what to say next. Sarah watched as an internal debate went on behind his eyes. Tired of waiting, she lifted her foot and dropped the corresponding hand to unbuckle her shoe and pull it off. Without taking her eyes off him, she switched feet and removed the other shoe.

"Sarah, don't."

"Goodnight, Jon," she said over her shoulder as she headed for the street, shoes dangling from her fingers.

"Sarah, wait…"

She didn't.

CHAPTER FOURTEEN

"Meet me outside in ten minutes. I need a run," his cousin commanded through the phone line without preamble before cutting the call off with a sharp click.

"Oh aye, yer highness, and just how high would ye like me to jump then?" Dermot grumbled to his empty apartment as he set the phone back in its cradle. He'd long accepted the difference between his position and that of James Stuart, but it was rare that James chose to remind him of it so baldly.

He'd just stepped out of the shower when the phone rang, and he had been about to grab a bite in his tiny kitchen before heading to campus. His plan was to catch Sarah as she walked to campus. Instead he headed back into his bedroom for his workout clothes and trainers. Sarah would likely be sleeping in after last night anyway.

Ten minutes later, his hair was still damp and amplified the slight chill in the air as he stepped out of building to meet the limousine that pulled to a stop in the middle of Rosemary Street. James stepped out of the car, looking as much like a movie star in a track suit as he did in Armani. He leaned back into the car to give the driver instructions on when they would be back, then straightened and smiled at Dermot. The car pulled away.

"I've been going mad using treadmills for the last week. This seems the perfect town for a good run…and for little reconnaissance." James grinned at him. "Which way?"

Dermot waved a hand in the direction of campus, and the two started out at a steady jog. As they reached the campus they picked up the pace and began a proper run. Dermot led James the conventional route through the North Quad to Cameron Avenue, then down Cameron off the campus and into the town. As they passed Sarah's building, Dermot lifted his chin in its direction to give James a subtle indication that this was what he was looking for. They turned left and headed back toward campus. At Pittsboro Street, they turned left and then left again between some official looking buildings and ran through a parking lot.

Behind the parking lot and running between the main streets was a sort of alleyway cleared for utility lines running to the university's power plant. The lane was lined with trees and even had sidewalk on one side. It was frequently used as a shortcut by students living on that side of town to get to campus, but at this time of morning it was deserted. More importantly, it ended almost directly across from Sarah's apartment. Dermot had used it many times to watch her comings and goings. In fact, Sarah had been the one to show it to him one day as they were walking back from campus.

Ever competitive, James saw the open space as an opportunity and picked up his speed. They had always challenged each other as boys, and even as late as secondary school Dermot had been able to match James stride for stride. Since then, however, their training had gone in different directions. James had competed in track and field at university as a sprinter and had retained a lithe runner's physique, while Dermot's army training had been more about endurance than speed; he had also gained considerable size on his cousin, adding muscle to his already tall frame.

Still, Dermot thought he could keep up with James at least as far as the two blocks back to Ransom Street. He pushed himself and managed to run faster than he had in some time. James still outstripped him by several yards. His cousin pulled to a stop before he would have burst out of the bushes that separated the end of the lane from the street.

They stood behind the screen of bushes, bent over, hands on their knees, trying to catch their breath. James caught Dermot's eye and grinned. For a brief moment they were kids again, boys racing for nothing more than bragging rights. All that was between them was friendship and a shared childhood. They slowly straightened and gave each other a couple of good-natured slaps on the back before looking around to see if anyone else was in the lane.

"Convenient spot, this," James said, nodding in the direction of Sarah's apartment building.

"Aye, though ye have to watch out for people coming down the lane." Dermot guided James back a few steps to a break in the bushes that allowed him a more direct view. "But no one's mad enough to use an unlit wooded lane after dark."

"Watching here often at night?" James teased mildly.

"Only when she's out with her mates or on a date. Most nights I'm with her at the library working." Dermot shrugged. "She and her roommate are great friends with the hens in the blue house on that far corner. There's a lot of visiting back and forth."

"Date? Anyone in particular?"

"She's only got time for one, an anthropologist, but I don't think he'll be a problem. They had a fair row last night. I think she may have told him to shove off." Dermot kept his eye on Sarah's front window and couldn't help wondering how she was feeling about that argument this morning.

"So that's what she was doing last night," James said, giving him an assessing look. "And I take it that's where you went after dinner."

"Mmm, some faculty to-do at the art museum. I spent my time skulking about in the bushes and following her home when she wouldna get in his car." Dermot's tone left no doubt as to his feelings about skulking in bushes.

"She walked home in the dark?" James was incredulous.

"Barefoot," Dermot put in, remembering how furious he'd been last night both at Jon Samuels for not insisting on seeing her home and at Sarah for being careless enough to walk home barefoot in the dark past frat houses guaranteed to have broken glass on their sidewalks.

"That must have been some row." James gazed back at the red brick building. "Which one is hers?"

"First floor, far right."

"What's she like?" James asked, sounding a bit nervous.

"Lonely, and a wee bit skittish about it," Dermot answered without taking his eyes from her window. "She's a fair amount of friends and they'd do anything for her, but I get the feeling she keeps a lot inside. She's quick-witted and funny and charismatic, but she holds it back like she's learned to be on guard most of the time. She's no more family to speak of, and I think she feels that lack keenly."

"Well, she has us now," James said, throwing a companionable arm around his cousin. "You like her, don't you?"

"Aye." Dermot nodded. "We've become friends. For all my opinion matters."

"It matters, old friend, more than you think." James gave Dermot's shoulder a squeeze. "And if you're friends now, then I'm going to need your help all the more."

"I know. I'll just be happy when it's in the open and I can stop slinking about in the shrubbery." Dermot turned away from Ransom Street and they started walking back down the lane toward campus.

They picked up the pace when they reached Pittsboro Street, and nothing more was said until they pulled up near Dermot's building. James signaled for his car and turned to Dermot. On his face was a look of such sincerity that Dermot, who had already been thinking about where he would catch up with Sarah, gave him his full attention. "I know you aren't comfortable with this, but you're doing us a great service. Your dedication won't go unrewarded."

Dermot's mouth firmed into a tight line, biting back all the thoughts that leapt into his mind about his reason for being there. But that was Walter's doing. He was fairly certain James wouldn't know anything about that. "Just knowing that my mum's taken care of is reward enough, James. The rest is no more than any other Sinclair would do."

"Still, Dermot, I want you to know how grateful I am."

Dermot believed it too. James meant every word. Dermot just nodded, unable to get the words past the lump in his throat. James gave him one more pat on the shoulder as he slid into the limousine.

CHAPTER FIFTEEN

It was about mid-afternoon when Sarah got home. She had tried for the better part of the day to focus on work, but she couldn't seem to get her mind off her argument with Jon. It had been two days, and she hadn't heard a word from him, not even a call to make sure she got home alright. This left her to believe one of two things: either he was still angry with her or he simply didn't care. Given the nature of the argument and that Jon wasn't a very emotional person, Sarah was inclined to believe the latter, thus confirming her point in the argument.

She was stewing on this as she stepped into the hall of her building. She could hear her phone ringing from outside and hurriedly fumbled with her keys to unlock the door. She dove for the phone that sat between the kitchen and breakfast room and barked her shin on one of the chairs.

"Agh! Hello!"

"Hello, yourself. Is everything alright?" There was no mistaking the precise cultured tones on the other end of the line, nor the hint of a smile in his voice. James Stuart was on her phone. When Sarah had been able to get her mind off the fight with Jon, she had managed to do a quick library search on James Edward Stuart. He was indeed a philanthropist and, to Sarah's delight, one that gave a lot of money to Scottish heritage projects and supported the Scottish independence movement. He was also a bit of a playboy. Sarah found no end to the tabloid articles linking him to various models, starlets, and socialites, and he was on her phone. "Sarah?"

"Yes, it's me, James. I'm fine…I just tripped diving for the phone." She rubbed her sore shin.

"Ah. I suppose the accent gave me away?" He flirted like a champ, even over the phone.

"Well, we don't get a lot of folks calling that sound like they should be narrating a Rolls Royce ad, if that's what you mean." Crap! Probably should have kept that one in her head. James, however, let out a hearty laugh.

"I see now what Dermot meant when he said you were disarming," he said with a little laugh. Sarah wondered what else Dermot had told his cousin about her. "I was calling to ask you to dinner. Nothing formal…just the four of us."

Sarah hoped the "four of us" meant James, Dermot, and Walter—well, maybe not Walter. "Umm, sure, that sounds great. When?"

"I was hoping you'd be available tonight. I know it's short notice, but we're leaving for Louisiana tomorrow."

"Oh, no. Tonight is fine." She didn't have plans and didn't dare miss the opportunity. "Umm, where did you have in mind?"

"The concierge here recommended a French restaurant in Durham. I thought we'd give that a try."

"Do you have the address?" she asked, scanning the counter for a pen and paper.

"Don't worry. I'll send a car for you. Say around seven?"

"Oh, sure." She checked her watch. It was three o'clock. "Seven is fine."

"That's grand. I'll see you then." He hung up.

Sarah put the phone back in the cradle and tried not to feel a little giddy. "I might just get that funding after all."

She was about to bounce down the hall to let Amy know her good fortune when she thought of the one and only piece of clothing she owned that would be appropriate for the restaurant she thought James meant lying in a crumpled heap in a corner of her room where she'd thrown it after her fight with John.

"Shit!" She ran to the closet and surveyed her wardrobe. There wasn't much call for dressing up in the life of a folklorist. High heels and skirts weren't exactly conducive to walking across the huge campus or hiking from place to place doing fieldwork. The few dresses she had were sundresses that were out of season. The brown sheath she had worn the other night was her only nice dress. She had chosen it for its simplicity and the fact that she could put almost anything over it, making it appropriate for any occasion or weather. There just wasn't anything here that would do.

She went to the corner and picked up the dress. Holding it up by the shoulders, she examined it. It had a network of wrinkles and outright creases crisscrossing the whole length of fabric. The skirt didn't even hang right. In four hours, she could probably get it washed and dried and ironed. But did she want to? She couldn't help looking at the wrinkles and thinking about Jon and the other night. Was that really what she wanted to be thinking of when she needed to be on her toes? When the result of this dinner could be so important to her work?

Sarah racked her brain for a minute, trying to think of what else she could do. She could try to buy something, but she didn't want to tap into her savings in case she wasn't able to get funding. She had set aside a chunk of the money she had inherited from her grandmother to keep as a safety net, and she had managed to last a few years without touching it. She would if she had to, but didn't like the idea. She'd have to borrow something to wear.

She tossed the brown dress onto her bed and stepped across the hall to Amy's door and knocked softly. There was no answer. She knocked again a little more firmly. Still nothing. Amy often wore headphones while reading, and thinking this might be the case, Sarah eased the door open a crack. She would just see if Amy was there and awake. She widened the crack a little further and spied them on the bed. Amy and Ryan were sound asleep and curled into each other. The comforter had slipped a little and Sarah could see the curve of Amy's shoulder where her arm was reaching across him. Her head rested on his shoulder and his arm curled around her. She could see Ryan's head turned to rest his cheek on the top of Amy's head, a sleepy and contented smile on his lips. Whatever she thought about Ryan, he certainly seemed to make Amy happy. Given her recent troubles with Jon, Sarah couldn't begrudge that.

Sarah eased the door shut again, not wanting to wake them. Maybe she would catch Amy later after their nap. In the meantime, she would have to find another solution, and she had a feeling the Ransom Street girls were just the ones to help. She left the apartment quietly and headed a few doors down to the little blue house on the corner.

***

After much fussing, debating, and wardrobe raiding, they settled on a combination of borrowed items from the girls of the blue house. Monica contributed a vintage, emerald-green, belted dress with an A-line skirt and boat neck and a matching clutch. This was topped by a light brown cashmere shrug of Jane's and burgundy loafers of Meg's. The result struck just the right balance between ingénue and sophisticate.

In addition to looking the part, spending the afternoon at the center of a storm of girls all laughing and clucking and working to help her soothed Sarah's raw feelings from the other night. She wasn't worried anymore about Jon calling or not calling. After the counsel of her friends, she found she could be more philosophical about the situation. Her personal life would sort itself out or it wouldn't. Tonight was business, and she was going to be successful.

That's what she told her reflection as she gave herself a last once-over before walking outside to the waiting car. She wasn't sure what she had expected when James had said he would send a car, but it certainly wasn't the sleek black limousine that awaited her at the curb. The driver, a large man in all black with a cap pulled down to shade his eyes, opened the door and handed her into the car. Sarah perched on the long seat next to the door and surveyed the cavernous interior of the car. It shouldn't have surprised her that one of the richest men in Britain wouldn't be riding in a simple sedan. Despite her chic outfit and pep talk in the apartment, the car made her feel like the country girl from Kettle Holler who had wandered into an alien world.

That feeling didn't ease much when the driver handed her out of the car in front of the poshest restaurant in Durham. "Nothing formal, just the four of us," James had said. Right.

The restaurant door was at the back of a courtyard dotted with tables between potted shrubs and lit with fairy lights. Despite the slight chill in the air, every table in the courtyard was occupied with couples enjoying dinner under the stars. The effect was lovely and would have been romantic if the weather weren't a little chilly. Inside, the cream-colored walls, dark stained trim, and candlelight created an atmosphere more suited to a date than a family dinner, but Sarah wasn't going to quibble.

Since it was Friday night, the entryway was crammed with more couples waiting for tables. Sarah had to weave between the parties clustered near the podium, where a harried looking maître d attempted to keep peace and maintain order. Sarah had to dodge around a woman describing her new drapes to a friend with a rather expansive gesture for such a crowded space and arrived at the podium at the same time as a perturbed looking man in a navy sport coat and green tie covered in crossed golf clubs.

The maître d looked inquiringly at Sarah and she opened her mouth to speak, but Golf Tie held up a staying hand in her direction and said, "Oh no, my wife and I have been waiting for half an hour. There is no way this girl is taking our table!"

Sarah gaped at him. "I haven't even…"

But the man ignored her and glared at the maître d, who appeared unruffled. He raised a conciliatory hand and said, "Mr. Holding, I will be seating you and your wife as soon as a table is available. Now, I have not heard what this young lady needs, so I could not give her a table ahead of you."

"Thank you, I'm with—" Sarah began, but she didn't get out more than a few syllables before Golf Tie started in again.

"No! We've been waiting too long as it is. No one is getting seated until we do," he said firmly and sidestepped, effectively boxing Sarah out from the podium.

For once Sarah wished she was wearing heels so she could dig one into the top of this guy's foot. As it was, she stared daggers at his back. She was just opening her mouth to give him an angry Southern girl's lesson in manners when she felt a warm hand rest firmly at the small of her back and a Scottish accented voice rumble in her ear.

"Usually we like to keep James's outings on the quiet side. Much as he might deserve a set-down, I dinna think our friends would appreciate the scene," Dermot whispered.

Sarah took a deep breath while she reined in her temper. She let herself be distracted by a moment of girlish pleasure at the feel of Dermot's arm around her and his breath on her ear. She had managed to keep things with Dermot platonic since the ill-fated kiss last summer. But after fighting with Jon, scrambling this afternoon, and almost having to fight just to find them, it was nice for just a second to lean back into his arm and turn to find him so close. Without thinking, her eyes fixed on Dermot's lips. They were full and firm in a grim line as he shot Golf Tie a dirty look over her head. Then they softened as his eyes focused on her. Sarah lifted her eyes to his and saw a flash of something, maybe the memory of that kiss last summer.

Dermot made a sound somewhere between a sigh and a grunt before using his hand on her back to steer her out of the entry way and toward the back of the restaurant. As they were leaving, Sarah couldn't help looking over her shoulder to find Golf Tie staring after her. She gave him a saucy wink.

***

"There she is!" James was grinning as he stood when Dermot ushered Sarah to their table. He rose from his seat in the corner and came around the table to kiss her cheek in greeting. Sarah hoped she didn't blush too much when he said, "You look lovely, my dear."

"Good evening, Miss MacAlpin," was the more formal greeting from Walter Stuart, who politely stood as she arrived at the table.

They were seated in a back corner of the restaurant nearer to the kitchen. A half wall separated their table from the pervading buzz of the dining room, giving an illusion of privacy. Dermot left her to the care of James, who pulled out the chair next to his.

"Thank you." She smiled, taking the seat that placed her, like James, in the corner near the wall. "You certainly picked a popular restaurant. If Dermot hadn't come along, I might not have made it back here."

"It does appear to be very busy tonight," James agreed, looking a little dubiously around the dining room. "I hope you don't mind, I've allowed the chef to choose for us."

"That's fine with me. I probably would have had a hard time choosing for myself. This isn't typical graduate student fare." Over Dermot's shoulder, Sarah could see into the kitchen. From the general buzz and the nervous looks the chef kept giving their table, Sarah thought it was safe to assume that the chef knew exactly who James Stuart was. She expected the dinner would be the best he had to offer. Just then a waiter stepped through the swinging kitchen doors bearing a charcuterie platter.

"I trust you'll enjoy it then." James turned his full attention back to her and gave her a warm smile. Sarah wasn't sure if it was a genuine quality or a practiced skill, but when he turned to her with those dazzling good looks and that smile, he made her forget about everything else in the world. As if he weren't a billionaire playboy and she weren't a student, but they were just two people talking and having a good time. It was so disarming that she didn't even notice he was putting food on a small plate until he set it in front of her. "Dermot has told us that you met through a colleague last summer?"

It took Sarah a few seconds to recognize the conversational prompt. She gave her head a quick shake.

"I hope he didn't tell you too much about when we met. I wasn't very friendly to him." She gave Dermot a sheepish glance and found him in his seat with his back to the kitchen, scanning the dining room as if watching for something.

"She was a great help with my song workshop. She has a beautiful voice." He smiled at her before returning to scanning the room.

James raised his eyebrows. "I'll have to hear you sing sometime."

"Oh, it's hard to study folk songs without being willing to sing yourself." She was surprised to feel herself blushing. "You said you were going to Louisiana tomorrow. Then what?"

"Then back to Scotland..." They continued making small talk about travel, work, weather. The conversation was light, pleasant, and mostly included the younger people at the table. Walter Stuart did not seem to have much to say, but Sarah caught him studying her a few times. She occasionally tried to draw him into the conversation for the sake of politeness, but his answers where generally short and his participation never lasted for long. She found it almost as disconcerting as Dermot's wandering eyes. He joined in the conversation, but his attention was always divided between their table and the rest of the room. He ate little, and even when the chef came out to inquire about their meal, he mumbled praise and went on scanning.

James, on the other hand, was affable, funny, and charming. Sarah found herself thinking that if this had been a date, it would be going very well. Except of course for the presence and behavior of their companions.

It wasn't until they got up to leave that Sarah was clued in to the reason for Dermot's behavior. They had paid the check and were chatting amiably at the table. Dermot, however, did not take his eyes from the door. Sarah glanced over her shoulder out of curiosity just at the moment that she saw her driver from earlier in the evening step inside and give an almost imperceptible nod in their direction.

"Alright." Dermot returned the nod and stood. He stepped back from the table, blocking the kitchen door while James rose and gently pulled Sarah from her chair. Walter rose and began strolling toward the door. James guided Sarah after him with a hand on her back, and Dermot brought up the rear. The driver opened the door, and their party sailed through it and into the courtyard without breaking stride. There were two limousines waiting outside. The car in the lead was being held open by another driver, and James led Sarah to it, handing her in himself as the driver scanned the courtyard and street.

Walter and the other driver made a beeline for the second car, while Dermot joined Sarah and James in the first. He closed the door and they were off.

It was only a matter of seconds from table to curb and was carried off like a choreographed ballet. Obviously, everyone else had done this before, and Sarah found the idea of being swept along in it without warning a little disconcerting.

"Is the life of an oil executive really that dangerous?" she asked James, noting that Dermot settled himself next to the door.

James gave her a reassuring smile. "That all depends on where I am. In some countries, yes, it's very dangerous. Here, we're more concerned about paparazzi than thugs or kidnappers."

"Aye, James is popular fodder for tabloids at home." Dermot's tone was mildly teasing.

"Ah. It must drive you crazy, to constantly be worried about being watched," said Sarah.

"You get used to it after a while, and you can find ways around it." James shrugged. "If I don't tell anyone where I'm going I can usually escape. Sudden changes are hard for them to plan for. Tonight, though, between the hotel concierge and the restaurant staff and anyone you might have told, there were too many people who knew our plans. It's times like that when you have to be careful."

***

"Would you care to walk the last block or two?" James turned to her. They had dropped Dermot off at his apartment as it was on the way to Sarah's, and the two of them ridden the few blocks from Rosemary Street in companionable silence. James had been gazing out the window in thought, and Sarah had been wondering about the best way to broach the subject of funding.

"If you think it's safe." Sarah welcomed the night air over the confines of the car, but she was still conscious of his concern about being photographed.

He gave her that same warm smile, the one she was coming to think of as his spotlight smile. It was the kind of smile that said, "I could be doing anything in the world, but right now there's nothing I'd rather do than talk with you." It was a powerful thing. "I think it will be alright."

She nodded, and James signaled the driver to pull over. Sarah felt a little awkward strolling down Cameron Avenue with a limousine coasting along behind them, but she tried not to let it show as James tucked her hand under his arm and walked in the direction of her building.

"Dermot tells me that you're research is similar to his," James said softly.

"It is." Sarah inhaled deeply. Time to dive in. "Actually, that's something I wanted to talk to you about."

"Oh?"

"You see, I've been collecting songs in Cape Breton and here in the States. I've done just about everything I can in North America. What I really need now is to go to Scotland where I can research and collect songs to compare to those I've gathered here."

He squeezed her hand on his arm. "Well, then you must come to Scotland."

"I hope I can. I'm trying to get funding to go for at least a semester so I can finish my research." She kept her eyes trained on the street in front of them. She couldn't look at him. It galled her to think that he was mentally adding her to the list of people who were probably asking him for money all the time.

"Hmm." If he was bothered by her mention of funding he had the grace not to show it. He seemed to think for a moment as they continued walking. "I do a bit of funding for some cultural preservation projects. Perhaps we can manage a work exchange. I'll have my assistant call you with some names of contacts you might try."

Sarah tried not to embarrass herself by signaling a touchdown or dancing a jig right there on the street, but her insides were doing cartwheels. "If you think that could be worked out, it would be a great help. I have a lot of experience at fieldwork and I'm fluent in Gaelic."

He laughed. "Yes, I've heard. But I'm not the one you'll have to convince. I can only arrange introductions. There are no guarantees, but I think we can find a place for you."

"That would be such a big help." She gave his arm a little excited squeeze. They turned the corner onto Ransom Street and the limousine pulled past them to park in front of Sarah's building a block away. She watched the driver get out and stand beside the car, keeping watch, and she thought again about the man beside her.

"Dermot certainly seems to have told you a lot about me." She tried to sound conversational, but she had to admit to herself she wasn't comfortable with the idea of them gossiping about her.

James shot her a slightly embarrassed look. "Ah, well. That's my fault I suppose. I asked."

"Ah." Sarah wasn't sure what to make of that.

"I confess. He told me about you before, but after I met you…I…well…" For the first time that night, he seemed tongue-tied. Sarah looked away, giving him a moment to figure it out. They were in front of the blue house, and she spotted Jane and Meg chatting on the porch swing.

"Hey, Sarah," Meg called out with her usual cheeriness.

"Hey." Sarah gave her a friendly wave, but kept walking. She doubted James wanted to meet anyone just then.

After they crossed onto her block, Sarah decided to close the subject herself. She released his arm and turned to face him. "James, I…I think that as long as I'm trying to work on a project that you're funding we should keep things on a professional footing. I would hate to have it said that I owed my position to any, umm…entanglement with you."

He opened his mouth as if he might disagree and took a step toward her. His hand slid along her waist. "And," she continued before he could interrupt, "I'm sure that you would rather avoid the kind of gossip that that sort of relationship would generate."

Just then they heard a shout and scuffle coming from her building. Before she could think, James grabbed her by the waist and whisked her around the car. Pushing her to her knees near the back door, he sheltered her with his body and kept a firm hand in the middle of her back keeping her down. After a moment, there was a thud on the other side of the car and the driver said, "Clear."

James pulled her up solicitously, helping her brush the gravel and dirt from her knees. He then ran his hands down her arms as if checking for injuries. He gripped her hand firmly and used his other hand to lift her chin until she met his eyes. "Alright?"

She was thoroughly shaken, but it wouldn't help to admit it so she just nodded. James rested his hand for a few seconds on the back of her neck, warming the tense muscles there before he slid an arm around her and steered her around the car to the yard.

"What was that about?" James asked as they stepped up onto the curb. The driver held a squirming man in jeans and a sweatshirt pinned face first to the car by a massive forearm across his shoulders and an arm twisted behind his back. For all the fuss, he didn't look like a threat.

"This clown was staked out in the hallway. Had something in his hand." The driver was slightly winded, but no less in command of the prone figure.

"I was just waiting for my girlfriend!" came a weak voice from the obviously shaken captive.

"Jon?"

"Sarah?" The figure struggled under the weight of the driver and managed to turn his head to face them. "What the hell is going on?"

Sarah turned to James, pleading. "It's okay. I know him, you can let him go."

James gave her a thoughtful look and turned to the driver. "You said he had something in his hand, what was it?"

"He dropped it in the hallway," said the driver, not releasing his hold on Jon.

Before James could stop her, Sarah darted to the hallway of her building and came back holding a much-trampled bouquet of flowers. "Here's your dangerous weapon. I hope you're not allergic."

She handed the flowers to James and stepped around the driver to Jon.

"Let him go," said James, sounding deflated.

The driver released Jon's arm and stepped back. Jon turned around, still leaning on the car. He gave Sarah an accusing look.

"Umm…Jon, this is James Stuart. James, this is my boyfriend, Jon Samuels."

James extended a hand to Jon and turned on his spotlight smile. "Awfully sorry about that. I've had a spot of trouble before. The man was just doing his job."

Jon spent several seconds looking from James's outstretched hand to his face and then Sarah's before accepting the olive branch. Sarah let out a breath she hadn't been aware she was holding.

"James and I were just discussing funding for my trip to Scotland." She hoped James would remember her request to keep things professional.

"Yes, we were." He handed Jon the flowers, their bright heads flopping around on broken stems. "But I see that you have some things to talk about, so I won't keep you any longer."

He took Sarah's hand and drew her aside to bid her goodnight. "I'm sorry. I hope this hasn't put a damper on an otherwise pleasant evening."

"It's definitely been interesting." She gave him a nervous smile.

"You're sure you're alright?" he asked, glancing significantly at her skinned knees, which were just starting to sting.

She nodded before glancing around his shoulder at Jon, who stood now next to the car watching them intently. "I'm really fine. I'd better go and talk to him."

“Right. I’ll have someone call you about your work.” He gave her hand a squeeze and kissed her cheek. “Please, don’t hesitate to call me if there’s anything else I can do for you.”

She nodded, and he released her hand with one last gentle squeeze. The driver, having straightened his uniform, stood waiting by the open car door. She stepped up to where Jon was standing and waved as the car pulled away from the curb.

CHAPTER SIXTEEN

The Sienna Hotel was arguably the best hotel in Chapel Hill. From its Italianate fountain out front to its Egyptian cotton linens, it was the most luxury available in town. Naturally, that was where James and Walter Stuart were staying, and of course they were in the finest suite the Sienna had to offer. Dermot hadn't expected to see them again before they left town, but he had been summoned to the suite early this morning. He paused outside the room door for a deep, preparatory breath.

He didn't relish the idea of listening to a recounting of how things had gone last night after they had dropped him off. It had been difficult enough to sit at the dinner table and watch James work his considerable charms on Sarah. It was some consolation to see that she seemed just as thoughtful and guarded with James as she had been with him when they'd first met. He kept telling himself that it was meant to be and he had known this was coming from the start. Still, no amount of warning had prevented the emptiness he'd felt when that limousine drove off last night with Sarah inside.

James and Walter were sitting at a small table eating breakfast when Dermot was admitted to their hotel suite by one of last night's drivers. The two men seemed preternaturally calm amid the bustle of assistants and porters packing up their belongings. It wasn't until Dermot arrived at the table to see James buttering a piece of toast with more force than necessary that he realized his cousin was quietly seething.

"I thought you said the boyfriend was history," James accused without a greeting and without even looking up from his toast.

"The argument they had the other night seemed to put an end to things. Do you know differently?" Dermot had been about to take a seat in the vacant chair, but James pinned him to his spot with a look.

"He was waiting at her apartment last night when we got there. Ian over there thought he was a photographer when he saw him lurking in the hallway and did what he was supposed to do. After Ian roughed him up, it was all tea and sympathy from Sarah, and he didn't leave until this morning." The last words were squeezed out through his cousin's perfect white teeth.

"Ah." That did come as a surprise. To be honest, he hadn't thought Samuels cared that much.

"You're going to put a stop to it." James pointed at him sharply with a wedge of toast.

"I don't think that's a good idea. If I do it, it'll get back to her that I was involved, and that will make doing my job damn near impossible."

"I'm glad you remember this is your job." James leaned back in his chair, wiping his fingers on a linen napkin. "It seems to me that you're enjoying an easy life in this pretty little town at my expense."

Dermot cast a significant look around the posh suite. "Oh, aye. That basement flat is living it up alright for all the time I spend in it. Ye know, when I'm not skulking about in the shadows. She trusts me now, and that'll be ruined if I go after Samuels."

James studied Dermot from his seated position just long enough to make him uncomfortable. Dermot shifted from one foot to the other, but never took his eyes from his cousin's. At length, James said in a milder voice. "You may not like it, but you're our man here. We can't risk involving anyone else." James leaned forward again. He took a bite of toast and chewed thoughtfully. "You said yourself, the boyfriend is soft. If you do it properly, he'll be too afraid to talk to her, much less tell her about it."

Dermot watched James chew his toast and felt like he himself was breakfasting on broken glass. This was what all his army training and education had brought him to: a glorified bodyguard for a woman who didn't know she had or needed one. Now he was supposed to play the hired thug.

"I don't believe we should have to remind you, Sinclair, of just what is at stake here." Walter, who had thus far been silently observing, spoke up. He looked pointedly at Dermot for several seconds. "Oh yes, I visited your mother just before we left. You'll be happy to know she's doing quite well in her new home."

Dermot eyed the older man as he would a snake, and Walter Stuart glared back at him. His eyes spoke volumes, and Dermot read the message loud and clear.

"Oh, I know just what's at stake here, more I'd say than you do, auld man," he said in a voice full of quiet menace. He turned to his cousin and leaned across the table, his accent thickening with emotion. "She's everything that ye could want and more. She has a sharp mind, and beauty and grace to match it. She doesna even know all that she's capable of. But if ye ever want to win her, and ye should, ye'll have to treat her like more than a pawn in Walter Stuart's great chess game. She's a person, aye? Not just a lucky corner of the gene pool. I'll take care of Samuels. You make sure ye're prepared to take care of her when ye've the chance."

With that, he lifted a piece of bacon from his cousin's plate and strode out of the suite without another word. Ten breathless minutes later, he was back in his apartment waiting for someone at the nursing home to pick up the phone. He paced back and forth, his knuckles white on the receiver.

"Leith House Rest Home," a cheery voice said across the line.

Dermot tried not to sound cross after it took so long to connect. "I'd like to speak to Seonag Sinclair, please."

"She may be asleep. She usually takes a nap at this time," came the voice after the brief delay that he had to remind himself was caused by the distance and not the woman on the other end.

"Then I'll need ye to wake her. I really must talk with her."

"May I tell her who's calling?" The woman's tone was far less cheery now.

"It's her son, Dermot."

"Just a moment." The phone went silent. After a minute ticked by, he was beginning to fear the woman had hung up on him. Still, he made himself wait until several minutes later the woman returned. "She's awake. I'll transfer you to her room."

The phone only rang once before his mother answered. "Halo? Dermot?"

"Mam." His shoulders slumped with relief, and he finally sat down. "How are ye?"

"Och, I'm fine. Where are ye? I havena seen ye in ages." Not only was she there, but she sounded alert and healthy.

"Aye, I know." Guilt ate at him for not being able to visit. "I'm in America."

"America? Whatever for?"

"I'm helping James Stuart with something."

"Mmm. I remember James. Nice lad. Shame his mother never let him be a regular boy." He could picture her face in his mind, her head shaking with that last comment.

"How do ye like yer new home?" If she was being treated like anything less than a queen, he would have Walter Stuart's head.

"It's alright. The people are nice, but it's not home. I miss my garden and the fire. Would be lovely to have a peat fire, but ye can't do that in a place like this." She sounded wistful, and he hated that she couldn't live alone anymore. Still, if the people were treating her well, that was the most important thing.

"But the people are treating ye alright?"

"Och, aye. That lass that answered the phone is very nice. How are the Americans treating ye?"

"They're fine, friendly. I've made a few friends."

"Oh that's nice." They chatted on for a while about nothing in particular. Dermot was just happy to hear her voice and to have a real conversation. It had always just been the two of them. He'd gone with her from university to university for as long as he could remember. She was a true scholar, one of the best in her field.

Still, eventually the conversation turned, as it always did. "Ye seem like such a nice lad. Ye should meet my Dermot, of course he's a bit younger than ye."

"Mam, it's me, Dermot." He tried not to choke on the words.

"Och, no. Dermot's at school this time of day. He's a grand student." He could hear the pride in her voice, and felt his eyes burning with unshed tears. She had always been proud of him.

Knowing her period of lucidity had run out, he said goodbye. "I'll be home in December, and I'll visit ye as soon as I get off the plane. I love ye, Mam."

***

"Did I hear someone leaving early this morning?" Amy said as she poured a cup of coffee in the kitchen. It was midmorning, and she was just venturing out of her room, but she looked dressed for the day.

Sarah had been taking advantage of the quiet morning to get some work done. She currently had the kitchen table covered in index cards that she was reviewing and rearranging into a semblance of an outline. "Oh. That was Jon."

"Really?" Amy made no effort to hide the shock in her voice. "So he finally apologized, huh?"

"I guess you could say that. Where were you last night? You missed all the excitement."

Amy brought her coffee to sit at the table. She pulled her knees up and propped them against the table, cradling her coffee cup with both hands. "Ryan and I went to a party in Durham. Some guy he met at Duke lives just off campus. We didn't get home until late. How did your big dinner with the Laird of the North Sea Oil Rigs go?"

Sarah leaned back in her chair and picked up her coffee before giving Amy her full attention. "It was great. We had a good time."

"What's he like?" Amy did her best impression of a twelve-year-old girl asking for details on a friend's first kiss. Sarah rolled her eyes before answering honestly.

"The only word I can think of is charming. He says all the right things. When he talks to you, he makes you feel like you're the only other person in the world. He holds open doors or his driver does and stands when you stand and gives you his arm when you're walking." Shields your body with his when there's danger, she added in her head.

"And…?"

"And he thinks we can find a work exchange with one of the heritage projects he funds. He's going to have his assistant call me with some contact info."

"Wow. That was easy," Amy said, taking a sip of coffee. Sarah thought she caught something sharp in Amy's tone, but wasn't sure.

"Yeah. It almost felt too easy. I guess because it means so much to me, I expected to have to work harder for it."

"I guess." Amy shrugged. "So what was the excitement that I missed?"

Sarah groaned. "Jon was here when James brought me home after dinner. He was waiting in the hallway with flowers. Unfortunately, James's driver/body guard saw him before I did and assumed the worst. In about half a second I was on the ground with James shielding me and Jon was pinned against the car."

"Are you serious?" Amy's eyes went wide.

"Yeah, apparently James has had some threats and problems with photographers following him. His security is pretty tight. You should have seen the maneuver to get us out of the restaurant last night. In Jon's case, I think the driver was a little overzealous."

"Well, I bet that was an interesting way to end the evening. What did James say?"

"He seemed a little put out over the confusion, but he apologized to Jon and me and left right after."

"What about Jon? Was he alright?"

"Well, after being thrown up against a car and having his shoulder nearly dislocated, he wasn't in the best mood, but I don't think he was really hurt. I brought him inside and gave him some ice for his face and a beer." Jon had been more shaken than angry at being manhandled by James's driver. He had stayed on the couch for some time, not speaking and holding the ice to his face, which was beginning to bruise where it had hit the car. Sarah thought his pride was more bruised. In the meantime, she had given him some privacy and changed out of her dress into some sweats and a T-shirt. She busied herself in the kitchen, trying to salvage what she could of the flowers he'd brought her.

She was snipping the stems and arranging now shortened blooms in a jar when he came quietly into the kitchen. He leaned a shoulder against the doorway. "I'm sorry about the other night."

She stopped what she was doing, scissors open just above the break in one of the stems. "I'm sorry too. I shouldn't have come down on you like that."

"No, I deserved it. I haven't called you because I knew you were right. I guess being a boyfriend is another one of those social things that I'm not very good at."

She turned to him, opening her mouth to protest, but he held up a hand to stop her. "I have been taking you for granted. And the truth of it is, until you walked away from me the other night I didn't know how I really felt about you. I'm still not completely sure, but I do know that I don't want to be without you. I'd like us to take Fall break to go away, just the two of us, and try to work it out. I booked us a cabin in the mountains, and I thought we could talk and do some things together away from school and work and papers." He sighed heavily before adding, "That's what I came here to say tonight. I didn't expect to find you on a date with—"

"Oh, no. That's not what that was. We were—"

"It's okay, I wouldn't blame you. It was just a shock." Jon carefully set the half empty beer bottle on the counter and turned to leave.

"Jon, wait." Sarah took his hand and pulled him back into the kitchen. "That guy was James Stuart. He's a philanthropist who I'm hoping will help me get the funding for a semester in Scotland. We had dinner with his old uncle and Dermot. He was just driving me home."

Jon looked down at their hands. "I may not be the most perceptive guy, but the way he was looking at you seemed more proprietary than professional."

She had gotten that feeling too, but she didn't want to talk about James anymore. "I can handle that. He's a billionaire playboy. He'll only be interested in me until the next supermodel crosses his path. I'd rather talk about this trip you've planned."

They had talked about the trip, about their fight, and about where their relationship was going. There were still a lot of questions and not many answers, but Sarah felt like they were on a firmer footing, and the trip to the mountains would give them an opportunity to take a deeper look at their future. In the end Jon had slept on the couch, not wanting to push their new accord too far. He had come to her room and kissed her good-bye before slipping out early that morning.

"So, you're going away with Jon when Hottie MacMoneybags is so clearly into you and would probably fund a trip to the moon if you played your cards right." Amy was incredulous when Sarah finished her story.

"Umm…I'm going to ignore the implication that I would sleep with someone to get funding."

Amy had the grace to look embarrassed. "Okay, forget the funding part. How could you even think of choosing Jon with all his awkwardness and emotional laziness over a guy who looks like he just walked off a movie screen and is obviously interested in you?"

"First, MacMoneybags is leaving town today and isn't likely to come back any time soon, if ever. Second, even if I were interested in him, which I'm not, I wouldn't do anything about it while I was dependent on him for funding. That would just feel wrong and probably ruin my professional reputation. Third, the man dates models and actresses and worries constantly about paparazzi. What would he want with a frumpy grad student from Kettle Holler? And anyway, who the hell would want a relationship carried out on the cover of every tabloid in the checkout line? Just the thought makes my skin crawl."

"Well, when you put it like that..." Amy took a sip of her coffee, arching a brow over the rim of her cup. "Still, you have to admit it's got to feel pretty cool to think the option is there."

Sarah could feel the blush creeping over her face. "Yeah, okay. It does feel kind of good."

They laughed until Amy glanced at her watch and unfolded herself from the chair, downing the rest of her coffee. "I've got to get going. I'm helping out with that labor lore conference this weekend."

"Wait. Did you say Ryan is here?"

"Yeah, but he's sleeping. He'll clear out as soon as he wakes up," she said over her shoulder as she ducked out the door. Sarah couldn't help feeling a little put out at the idea of Amy just leaving Ryan in their apartment. They didn't always see eye to eye, but Amy was the closest friend she'd ever had. There hadn't been many people she could be friends with growing up. She glanced down the hall at Amy's bedroom door, telling herself it was no big deal. But she still felt uneasy.

She got back to work arranging and categorizing her research. She was so involved that an hour later she reached for her coffee only to find it stone cold. She went to the kitchen to get some more, hoping that the coffee in the machine was still warm. She had completely forgotten about Ryan in the bedroom until she heard his bare feet padding down the hall.

Determined to ignore him, Sarah continued pouring her coffee and adding sugar. Without a word, Ryan stepped up close behind her and reached around to take a mug from the hooks under the cabinet. He was far too close for Sarah's comfort, and from the way he paused behind her before sliding to the side to reach the coffee maker he knew it.

He poured himself a cup of coffee and stepped back to lean on the door frame, blocking her from leaving the kitchen. He was wearing nothing but a pair of jeans that he hadn't fastened all the way. She hadn't noticed before how muscular he was. "So, Amy says you're going to be leaving soon."

"I'm not sure about that yet." She turned to face him, trying not to show how much his presence bothered her.

He took a thoughtful sip of coffee, but didn't move from his spot in the doorway. "Heard you spent some time up in Canada last summer. Meet anyone interesting up there?"

Was he trying to make small talk, or was he getting at something? Sarah leaned back against the sink opposite the door. If he thought he was bothering her, she wasn't going to show it. "Lots of people. Anyone in particular that you're wondering about?"

"Nah, just trying to be friendly. You know, you really should try being a little nicer." He pushed away from the door and sauntered closer to her, taking another sip of coffee. When he got close enough, he set his mug on the counter and set his hands on either side of her, pinning her in place. He leaned down, bringing his face close to hers. "Amy knows you don't like having me here. Funny thing is, she really doesn't care."

He wasn't going to intimidate her. Sarah had met her share of bullies before. She lifted her chin and glared at him. "Amy and I have been friends for a lot longer than you've been around, and we'll still be friends long after you're gone."

"But that's where you're wrong." The corner of his mouth lifted in a smug leer. "You'll be gone long before I will."

He pushed away from the counter and retreated to Amy's room. Sarah stood in the kitchen and counted to ten slowly, before walking to her room and grabbing her purse. She had to keep reminding herself that this guy made Amy happy. She didn't trust herself to be diplomatic, not today. She would take some of her reading to a café and soothe her nerves with some tea. She hated bullies.

***

June 1982
Kettle Hollow, North Carolina

The humid early summer air felt like water in her lungs. Her head hurt from squinting in the bright sun, and her clothes rubbed in the heat until her skin felt raw. She was sure that the noise on the school bus was twice as loud as usual and the Corbett sisters were twice as mean.

She could hear Tanya and Ronnie Sue Corbett whispering to each other two seats in front of her as the rickety bus bounced and rattled its way up Scotch Hollow Rd. Their greasy heads with their stringy flat hair were bent together. Every couple of minutes one of them would cast a look over her shoulder, dark-eyed and gloating. She'd heard similar whispers punctuated by words like "tetched," "crazy" and "suicide" so often over the last few years that she was sure they were talking about her.

Most people around Kettle Hollow had given up talking about her mama, but the two youngest Corbett girls rarely missed a chance to torment Sarah about it. "Dinna mind them, *a'nighean*," Granny would say. "They just need someone to bully the way they're bullied by their kin." Granny also said they were getting up into their mid-teens and would likely be quitting school and getting married soon and wouldn't trouble her anymore. Granny's reminders usually worked, but it was hard to remember Granny's wisdom today.

The brakes squealed and the bus came to a creaking stop at the head of the road that led home. Sarah waited for the Corbetts to get off first. Johnnie, Royce, Tanya, Ronnie Sue, and Buddy filed out mostly in order of their age. Johnnie and Royce, the big twins, were sixteen and seemed huge to Sarah. At their age, they had stayed in school longer than most of their older brothers and sisters, and there were plenty. Sarah suspected they had been allowed to stay in school to prolong their football careers, which were impressive by the county's standards, not that they were going to try to go to college or anything. Lord knew, the Corbetts didn't value education enough for that to be the reason.

Tanya and Ronnie Sue were what Granny called Irish twins, which is to say that at fourteen and thirteen they were slightly less than a year apart in age. What they were, as far as Sarah was concerned, was partners in crime. Sarah didn't usually take much notice of Buddy Corbett. He was her age, but he hadn't been in her class since the school started separating students by their abilities. Sarah was in the advanced classes; Buddy wasn't. He wasn't like his sisters or his brothers, who seemed to dominate any conversation within a ten-foot radius. Buddy was skinny and quiet and kept mostly to himself.

Sarah got up and followed the Corbetts down the aisle. She jumped from the bottom step, and her feet kicked up a cloud of red tinged dust from the dirt road. She took her time stepping away from the bus, hoping the Corbetts would head up the road ahead of her. When she couldn't delay any longer, the bus doors closed and the bus driver set the bus to rattling on down the road.

Sarah shaded her eyes with her hands and looked up the road. Johnnie and Royce were already halfway to the turn-off that went to the Corbett's farm. Buddy was heading for the trees near the road as he often did, and Tanya and Ronnie were slow-walking their way up toward their turnoff right between Sarah and her own home.

There was nothing to do but get moving. Sarah squared her shoulders, slung her book bag over a shoulder, and started walking. As she came up behind the other girls, she heard them shushing and giggling quietly.

"Dinna mind them, *a'nighean*," she heard Granny's voice say.

Sarah made to walk by them, swinging wide enough not to be tripped. She'd learned the dangers of walking too close to Ronnie Sue the hard way.

When Sarah was just a couple of feet past them, she heard Tanya sneering, "I heard she went crazy and jumped off that cliff."

Then Ronnie said, "Oh, she went crazy alright. Everybody knows that, but I heard she was drunk and fell."

Sarah had plenty of practice ignoring rumors about her mama, but it was so much harder today than usual. She hunched her shoulders slightly, as if that would somehow stop the sound, and kept walking.

"Darlene Keith said Miss Molly was a witch and got what was coming to her," Tonya put in. "Says Ole Maggie is a witch too."

Sarah bit her tongue and picked up her pace, trying to get out of earshot. She wanted to defend Granny from that rumor, but she knew any response would only make things worse.

“Hey, it was today, wasn’t it?” Ronnie Sue called out in a louder voice.

Sarah just kept walking.

“Hey, girl, I’m,” there was a slight grunt, “talking to you!”

A second later, Sarah realized what that grunt had meant when a rock slammed into her shoulder with enough force that she had to fight to keep her balance. She rolled the shoulder, checking for any real damage, but she didn’t stop walking.

“Maybe she’s crazy like her mama.”

Sarah wasn’t sure which one of them said that. Her blood roared in her ears.

“Mama said Miss Molly was a whore in the city. That’s why she came back here with no man when she got pregnant.”

The other one laughed. “Ole Duff’s whore maybe.”

That was it! Sarah’s chest heaved and she stopped, dropping her book bag into the red dust of the road. If she had lived through her mama going crazy, she could handle two low-bottom girls who didn’t know when to shut their mouths. Hadn’t Duff been teaching her how to defend herself?

Sarah turned. Her tormentors had stopped when she did. They stood there, laughter and triumph in their eyes. They had finally gotten a reaction, and they smiled like two sharks smelling blood in the water.

Sarah crossed the twenty or so feet to the Corbetts with a dozen things running through her mind. But talking wouldn’t shut them up. Talking would only draw out more cruelty. So Sarah did the only thing she could think of.

She walked straight up to Ronnie Sue Corbett and punched with every ounce of strength she had right in the girl's stupid buck teeth. Sarah knew she'd probably split her knuckles, but hitting Ronnie felt so good she didn't even care.

Tanya, the older and taller of the two, raised her hand to hit back, but Sarah was ready. She lifted her foot and hooked the older girl's knee with enough forced to make it buckle. Tanya landed flat on her back in the dirt with the wind knocked out of her. By that time, Ronnie was back, swinging with one arm while shielding her mouth with the other. Sarah ducked under the swinging arm and delivered a punch to the girl's kidney that sent her sprawling on top of Tanya.

Sarah straightened her shoulders and brushed at some of the dust that had been stirred up. She looked at the sisters with an evil grin. "Maybe my granny is a witch, maybe I am too. And maybe my mama haunts these woods where she died. Keep talking about her like that, and I'll tell her ghost to haunt you too."

She looked away, focusing on a point in the woods just off the road and spoke dramatically in Gaelic. It was nonsense, just a poem she'd learned when she was a little girl, but they didn't know that.

Sarah turned and went back to where she'd dropped her bag and bent to pick it up. The Corbett girls were getting slowly to their feet. She didn't pay them any mind. She was pretty sure they wouldn't come after her. Sarah began walking calmly toward home.

She glanced over her shoulder at the girls. Ronnie Sue had one hand on her mouth and the other rubbing her lower back. Tanya was standing beside her sister, looking daggers at Sarah. The big girl took a step in Sarah's direction as if she would pursue her. But then a mournful sort of keening sound came from the forest, and the branches of a tree that hung over the road right above the Corbett's heads started to shake.

Tonya and Ronnie Sue looked up at the shaking branches in terror. They grabbed their bags and started running in the other direction like they were being chased by a ghost.

Of course, it wasn't a ghost. From where she stood further down the road, Sarah could see Buddy Corbett in the tree jumping up and down on the branch that hung over the road and making whatever creepy noises he could. When his sisters were out of sight, he looked over at Sarah and smiled.

***

Dermot suppressed a shiver and cursed the Stuarts as he pulled the zipper of his dark hoodie up higher and jammed his hands into his pockets against the chilly October night. He was glad Samuels worked late, but he'd rather have stalked the man in warmer weather. He had seen Sarah tucked away safe at home before coming over here to stake out the building that housed the Anthropology Department. They had worked the better part of the day sorting and cataloguing a jumbled box of recordings in the folk-life collection at the library. Luckily, in the course of small talk Sarah had unwittingly told him right where the man would be.

He hadn't been quite sure of his plan until he got here. Fortunately for his purposes, Howell Hall backed up to Coker Arboretum, a place where no sensible student went after dark. By day, the arboretum was a beautiful wooded park covering about half a city block in one of the oldest parts of the campus, but its thick trees and shrubs made the walking paths in the arboretum a real danger at night, especially for the ladies of the nearby dorms. It suited his purposes just fine tonight, and the later Samuels worked, the less likely they would be interrupted. So he settled himself into the bushes between buildings to wait.

It was near midnight when a side door of the building opened and a tall, thin man in khakis and a rugby shirt stepped out. He stopped in the pool of light by the door, looking both ways before sliding a backpack onto one shoulder. Dermot had only seen Jon Samuels from a distance, but he was sure this was his man. He stayed hidden but on high alert, waiting to see which direction the man took. Samuels turned toward the handful of parking spaces behind Davie Hall and closer to the arboretum. Perfect. He would have to pass Dermot's hiding spot to get to the cars.

Dermot had picked up a small stone when he arrived, thinking he could use it to distract Samuels and gain the element of surprise. He inhaled slowly and waited until Samuels stepped close to his spot. At just the right moment, he sent the stone skidding across the brick walkway behind Samuels. When the man turned around startled by the sound, Dermot silently stepped from the bushes into his path. As Samuels turned back to the parking lot, he all but walked right into Dermot.

"Shit! Look I don't—" he started to say as he took a tentative step back, but Dermot cut him off.

"Do ye know me?" His voice was gravelly and low. His accent was thick as he used his broad shoulders to block the path.

"Sh…should I?" Dermot heard the nervous tension in his words and responded with a wicked grin.

"Well, if my lass had spent the better part of the last month in another man's company, I think I'd want to know him." The words were a friendly reproach, but his voice still held a threatening quality.

"Oh, you're Sarah's friend." Samuels took another step back, but seemed to relax the tiniest bit, as if having a mutual acquaintance made the situation just a touch less dangerous. "The Scottish one."

"Aye, the Scottish one." Dermot stepped closer. He was only a couple of inches taller, but he had a good thirty pounds on Jon and used every bit of it to his advantage. "I reckon if ye'd listened to a word Sarah's said to ye, ye'd know my name by now."

Samuels's face hardened. He seemed to decide to brazen his way out of the situation and moved to step around Dermot. "Well, I'm working on that, though I don't see how it's any business of yours."

Dermot turned to walk beside him and threw a heavy arm around Samuels' shoulders. "That's where ye're wrong. Why don't we take a little walk and discuss it, aye?"

To anyone walking by, they looked like two young men strolling home after a couple of beers, but Dermot used his strong arm around Jon to steer him into the thick wooded darkness of the arboretum.

"How long have ye been seeing Sarah, Jon?" Dermot continued in an easy tone as they left the brick pathway.

"About a year," came Jon's choked answer as he attempted to look over his shoulder, probably in the hopes of seeing someone who could help him.

"And what is her dissertation about?" Dermot kept his tone matter-of-fact.

"Umm, folksongs?"

"Ye dinna sound very sure of that. And how far along is she with it?" They had reached the trees, but Dermot continued walking them deeper into the park.

"She's still researching. Look, I get it…I've been a shitty boyfriend. I've already told her I want to change that."

Judging them to be well inside the park, Dermot slowed their walk and released Samuels's shoulders and turned to face him. It was nearly pitch black in the arboretum, and Jon looked around frantically for an exit.

"I've come to care a great deal for our Sarah and I'm not alone." He began slowly stepping forward. As intended, Samuels took a step in retreat for every advance Dermot made.

"So in the year that ye've been dating, how long have ye been in the same place?" Dermot took another step.

"Six months?" Jon mumbled.

"And in those six months, how often has Sarah chosen what ye did on a date?" Another step forward.

"I don't know. She usually lets me take the lead." Retreat.

"And how many of her performances have ye been to?" Step.

"That's not really my thing." Jon made to step back again, but was caught up on the trunk of a giant live oak. He whipped his head around to look at the tree, then back to Dermot, who was impossibly close.

"What do ye like the most about Sarah? Is it the way she cares for her friends, her tenacity, her good cooking? Or is it how when she smiles at ye, it's like she's cradling your heart in her hand?" Dermot suddenly found that he didn't feel as sorry for his blatant intimidation of this man as he had earlier. Samuels just stared at him blankly.

"Ye don't know, do ye man?"

Samuels hung his head and slumped his shoulders. In the space of a few minutes, he'd been nervous, belligerent, fearful, and now his emotional well seemed exhausted. The man seemed to shrink against the rough trunk of the tree. Dermot pressed on, like pushing his thumb into a raw wound. "Ye're right. Ye have been a shit boyfriend. And all along, Sarah has been defending ye when every one of her friends has been telling her ye werena worth her time. Ye've been traveling all over Central America while Sarah has been here missing ye and despairing over yer apparent lack of interest. Oh, I've seen it. She puts on a brave face, but it hurts her."

Though they'd been spoken softly, his words struck like daggers. Dermot knew he had the man on the ropes. He shifted slightly, making sure his broad shoulders blocked out any moonlight. His tone was gentle but firm. "Ye see, Jon, Sarah has become special to me…and to some verra powerful people. Now, we would hate to see Sarah spend another year, or month, or even another week learning what you and I already know. That no amount of trying is going to make ye worthy of her."

He softened his tone a little further as he laid a gentle hand on Samuels's shoulder. "So do Sarah a favor. Do yerself a favor, and move on. Let Sarah go her way, and my friends and I will let you go yours. I wouldna care to have this conversation again. Hmm?"

Samuels's head hung from his slumped shoulders so Dermot almost didn't notice his dejected nod. He kept his eyes on the ground, and Dermot used the opportunity to slip into the trees just as silently as he had stepped onto the path before. When Samuels looked up, he thought himself alone. He gripped the strap of this backpack tight with both hands, looking around as if he were afraid Dermot might appear again. When he felt sure enough that Dermot was gone, he took off at a run toward the nearest light he could see.

CHAPTER SEVENTEEN

Fall break! Sarah thought briefly that she might be a little old to feel this excited about school being out for a couple of days, but she felt almost giddy. She had spent the better part of the week tracking down and contacting all of the names on the list that James's assistant had given her. Applications were done and essays sent off, on top of her usual work. She had dropped off this week's transcriptions with Donald and finished her classes. She had practically skipped home. When Jon had suggested getting out of town for the break, Sarah had thought it would be a nice diversion and give them some much-needed time together. Now that she had a few days' worth of anticipation built up, it seemed absolutely essential. She grew more excited with each step that brought her closer to her apartment.

She was mentally running through a packing list for her weekend bag when she stepped into the cool shaded hallway of her building and saw the envelope with her name on it sticking out between her door and the frame. She recognized Jon's handwriting as she slid the envelope out and unlocked the door. Juggling her keys, envelope, and backpack, she stepped inside and kicked the door closed. She didn't even wait to take off her bag but dropped her keys on the table and opened the letter, half expecting to find a love note and instructions for when Jon would pick her up.

As she slid out the single sheet, a smaller piece of paper fell out and fluttered to the floor. Sarah bent to pick it up. It was a business card for Highland Vacation Rentals. She opened the letter, hoping he wasn't going to ask her to meet him there. She didn't relish the idea of driving several hours by herself to get to the mountains. She unfolded the letter to see what Jon had to say.

Sarah,

I realize now that I can't really give you the kind of relationship you deserve. You should have a partner, someone who can appreciate you for the person you are and not just for what you can do for him. That kind of relationship requires time and effort. You seem to be able to manage working on your dissertation and maintaining a relationship far better than I can. Maybe if we had met later in our careers we could have managed it, but right now I just can't. I'm sorry that I've wasted your time.

The cabin is paid for from Thursday through Saturday nights. The card is from the rental company. They can give you directions. Maybe you and Amy or some of your other friends can enjoy it.

I'm really sorry, Sarah.

Jon

Sarah let the backpack slide off her shoulders and drop at her feet. She sank into a chair, reading the letter again and thinking she must have misunderstood. When she'd read the letter two more times, she went to the phone and dialed Jon's number. Not only was he not answering, his machine wasn't even picking up. Sarah thought maybe that was a good thing. She wasn't entirely sure how she felt about this development yet. So she wasn't sure what kind of message she would have left for him.

She went back to the table and picked up the card from the rental company. She tried to think of who she knew that might not already have plans for the break. Amy was heading home for the long weekend. Sarah thought most of the Ransom Street girls were doing the same.

After a few minutes of glassy-eyed staring at the card, Sarah managed to focus on the address. The rental company was at least based in Franklin, North Carolina, which was the closest town of any size to where what she'd come to think of as the "Budge version" of her song had been recorded. She'd done a little more research and had narrowed down the area a little more, but she still didn't know if Simon Budge had any family left there. As she'd told Dermot, though, there was only one way to find out. It seemed to Sarah that Jon had just unwittingly given her a free place to stay while doing some fieldwork. It was the perfect opportunity.

Sarah checked her watch. It was four o'clock—if she hustled, she should be able to check out a recorder to take with her. She had her own small tape recorder, but the university had much better equipment. If she could manage to get it before five, she could check it out for the weekend. She grabbed her bag and was out the door in a flash.

***

"Hey, remember when you said not to go do fieldwork in the mountains without you?" As usual, Sarah jumped right in without preamble. She sounded like she was about to burst.

"Aye."

"Got any plans this weekend?" She sounded a little too cheerful.

"I thought you were going away with Jon this weekend." He held his breath, waiting for her answer. He'd been watching her for days since his encounter with Samuels. He'd wondered when the man would get around to breaking their plans or if he'd have to pay him another visit.

"That's over. Jon cancelled on me," she said with just a hint of anger.

"Ah, so you want to use the time for fieldwork?"

"Yep. As my consolation prize for being dumped, Jon gave me the cabin he'd rented, which just happens to be in Franklin close to where the Budge recording was made." To his relief, she sounded more excited than hurt.

"What should I pack?"

"Rugged, relaxed clothes, preferably a bit worn. Sturdy shoes or boots if you've got 'em. We might have to do a little hiking."

"When do we leave?"

"First thing in the morning. Pick you up around six?"

"Right. I'll see you then." The line clicked before he'd even taken the phone away from his ear.

***

Dermot unfolded himself from the front seat of Sarah's Civic. The car hadn't seemed nearly so small when she'd picked him up that morning, but after five hours of driving, his knees and back were screaming. Living in a college town like Chapel Hill meant walking nearly everywhere. His body had not been prepared to be folded into the little compact for so long.

A quick glance over the roof of the car suggested that Sarah was in much the same state. She placed her two fists in the small of her back and pushed forward, bending herself into a bow in an attempt to work out the kinks. When she'd finished stretching, she began to survey the small cabin while absently kneading the muscles in the back of her neck. He knew she must be tired. He'd helped with the driving on the highways, but when they had reached the mountains she had taken over, not trusting his left-driving ways.

He'd actually been a bit relieved. Driving on the right took concentration, and he had found Sarah more than a little distracting. She hadn't talked about Jon, and the one time he'd asked about it she'd said, "I don't want to talk about that," with such finality that he wasn't about to ask again. Instead they talked about their fieldwork experiences: getting doors slammed in faces, listening to fish stories, charming old men and women in the hopes of unlocking their memories.

When Sarah took over driving, she had begun to sing. At first she sang along with the radio, but when they found themselves out of range of a station, she just sang whatever came to mind: Gaelic songs, spirituals, ballads, new songs of every genre. Her repertoire seemed endless. As he listened, he realized that he hadn't heard her sing since the summer. He wasn't sure whether it was her dissertation or issues with Samuels, but he didn't think he had ever seen her relax as much as she did when she sang. With her voice washing over him, Dermot closed his eyes and allowed his mind to drift. She had thought him asleep and lowered her volume, but she didn't stop. He could have listened to her voice—low but clear, just above a whisper—forever. Time slipped away, and before he knew it they were pulling to a stop in front of the rental agency office, where they had checked into the rental.

"Well," she said, dangling the key. "Let's see what Jon has treated us to."

He looked at the little log building. It couldn't be more than a couple of rooms and maybe a loft. A charming porch stretched across the front and was just big enough to hold a pair of rocking chairs. A stone chimney peeked over the steeply pitched roof, and Dermot noticed firewood stacked under the porch. "Open the boot and I'll get the bags."

She reached into the car and pressed the release for the trunk before stepping up the simple plank steps to unlock the front door and step inside.

Dermot grabbed their bags from the trunk, leaving the recording equipment, and headed for the house. He found Sarah standing in the middle of the main room with her eyes closed, drawing in a deep breath. She let it out slowly and turned her eyes to him. "The folklorist in me says it's a classic hall-and-parlor style cabin with a loft. The country girl in me says it smells like home: old construction, wood smoke, and forest."

"Is this what yer house was like then?" he asked, setting the bags down just inside the door.

She answered over her shoulder as she headed for the kitchen, which took up almost half of the cabin. It was divided from the parlor by a half wall and support beams stretching to the bottom of a loft. "No, we had a proper farmhouse with a second floor and everything, even indoor plumbing."

"Please don't tell me there's no plumbing." He followed her to the kitchen, watching her open and close the few cabinets.

"You're in luck," she said with a giggle, pointing to the faucet in the sink. "They've at least modernized the plumbing and put in electricity."

He began looking around and found a door just past the small kitchen table. He opened it and found the bathroom complete with a long, deep claw-foot tub under a window that offered a vista of pure mountain forest. Dermot let out a low whistle. "No outhouse for us."

Sarah came up and glanced around him to survey the bathroom. She stiffened. "No shower?"

"I guess people on vacation are more interested in a relaxing bath." He shrugged. All the color had drained from her face as she eyed the tub. Her breaths came quick and shallow, and he thought he noticed sweat on her temples. Fearing she was going to faint, he took her by the elbow and pulled her back from the doorway. "Are ye alright?"

"Hmm." She seemed to collect herself. Her mouth pressed into a firm line, and she took a deep breath as stepped back into the parlor, looking around at the furniture. There was an armchair next to the fireplace with a couch facing it. There was no sign, however, of another door leading to a bedroom. She turned around, scanning the room, and found a ladder in the corner made by the kitchen wall and the back wall of the cabin. The sleeping loft took up the half of the cabin that was above the kitchen, leaving the parlor ceiling open to the roof.

Sarah climbed the ladder. Dermot heard her moving around in the loft, but she didn't say anything. He climbed up after her, being careful not to bump his head on the ceiling. He found a cozy sleeping loft with a full-sized mattress and box spring on the floor beneath the peak of the roof. The linens looked luxurious. Fluffy pillows were piled along the head of the mattress where it met the railing. Rustic crates stood in for night tables on either side of the bed and held a pair of small lamps. A small chest of drawers and a mirror stood against the wall opposite the bed, where a small window let in just enough natural light.

If this were in fact the romantic getaway it was intended to be, the setting would be perfect. Dermot couldn't help the brief pang of jealousy. A sigh that sounded far too close to what he was feeling came from his right. He turned his head to find Sarah on her knees in the corner under the eaves at the far end of the loft, leaning over an open trunk. Dermot looked quickly away, trying not to relish the mouthwatering view her position offered him. Of course, the only other place to look in the loft was at the bed.

She glanced over her shoulder at the bed and then at him. "There are extra linens in here and plenty of pillows. I'll flip you for the couch."

He cleared his throat, looking dubiously at the ceiling just inches above his head. "Ye will not. I'll sleep on the couch. I'd likely knock my head on the ceiling up here in any case."

Sarah sat back on her heels and gave him a direct look. "You don't have to. Your feet will be dangling off the end of the couch. We can trade nights."

He gave her a sharp look, though the corner of his mouth quirked. "Do ye really think Seonag Sinclair raised her son to let a lady sleep on the couch when there's a bed handy?"

Sarah threw up a hand in mock irritation. "Fine, but I'll do all the cooking."

"That's probably safer anyway. I'll get yer bag." He climbed down the ladder. Sarah followed him with the extra sheets and blanket slung over her shoulder. She went slowly so she wouldn't trip over the linens. He placed a hand on her back for the last few rungs. He told himself it was just to make sure she was safe.

***

Sarah struggled for control before she laughed herself right off the couch and onto the floor. Dermot was a raucous storyteller and had just been telling her about the summer he'd tried to teach James to tickle trout.

"Och aye, ye laugh now, but it wasna so funny when James threw the fish out of the burn and it landed right smack in the collar of his mam's Chanel suit," Dermot said, snickering. "And her standing there wi' her hands on her hips and her eyes shooting hellfire down on us."

"She sounds terrifying!" Sarah managed to say through another bout of belly laughs.

"Oh, she's a right dragon is Anne Stuart. She knew all that James was destined to inherit, and she was not going to let him forget it for an instant." He stopped laughing and looked into the fire, taking a swig of his beer. "I'll never forget when they sent him off to school in Switzerland. We'd been best mates before that, near inseparable. Mind ye, I don't think

Anne cared much for James spending all of his time wi' a poor relation. Och, I was miserable that fall. It's never been the same for us since."

Sarah rested an elbow on the back of the couch and leaned her head on her hand, watching him. He sat with his feet kicked out in front of him and crossed at the ankles, his beer resting on a thigh. The firelight played on his features, making them look even sharper, and his hair showed every shade of brown from amber to oak. "It can't have been easy on him growing up with that kind of pressure. I can't imagine being a kid and knowing right from the start what you were meant to do…not having any room to dream about what you want to be when you grow up, always having to worry about who's watching and what they're thinking."

He grunted in assent, watching the flames lick around the logs. He'd built the fire while she'd cooked dinner after they made a run to the grocery store. After dinner they sat down to exchange stories and plan for the next day. "What was it like for you growing up? Did ye have a mate to get in trouble with?"

"Nope, no pals for me." She gave a little self-conscious gust of laughter. "I was wild. I mean, I pretty much lived in the woods. I came inside to sleep. We stayed in during the winter, but as soon as the trees started budding in the spring, I was out the door. Granny was usually busy with the still or the garden or the house. When I got older I helped, but I didn't really have anyone to play with. The forest was my friend."

"Your gran didna worry that ye'd get lost or hurt?" He gave her an incredulous look.

"I'm sure she did, but…" She had never put into words before how she felt when she was in the forest. "It's tough to explain. I've just always known what to do in the woods, like some kind of instinct. It's never felt scary or dangerous to me. It's always felt like home."

"No childhood friends to romp in the forest with?" He turned to study her.

Sarah took another swig of beer and stared into the fire for a few moments. Dermot waited patiently. When she began to talk, it was through the fog of faraway memories. "One summer, I guess I was about thirteen, I made friends with Buddy Corbett. His family lived over the ridge from us, which was convenient because his daddy was one of granny's best customers. Buddy was the youngest of the many Corbett children. The joke was that they named him Buddy because they had so many they couldn't think of a better name they hadn't used already.

"Buddy was like me. His mama was too busy to keep an eye on him, and his daddy was usually too drunk to care, so he got to run wild in the woods most of the time. I ran into him one day while I was out foraging. We started talking and decided to meet again. Most of that summer, Buddy and I played and foraged up and down the mountain. I showed him what was edible, and he loaned me his fishing pole. We made a pretty good pair."

***

June 1982
Kettle Hollow, North Carolina

The cool water of the stream soothed her sore knuckles as the dappled shade relieved the pain in her head. She'd stopped by the stream to soak her hand, hoping the water would keep the swelling down. Maybe Granny wouldn't notice.

All her life she'd been trying to ignore the whispers around her. First, they had whispered because she didn't have a daddy. Then because her mama was crazy…then dead. Sarah got so tired of it, so tired of this stupid town.

Kettle Hollow was little more than a post office, filling station with a little store, and a diner. There was a bar out in the woods on the other side of the holler, but no one was supposed to know about that. People in Kettle Hollow had nothing to do but go to church and gossip, and since she and Granny didn't go to church, people mostly gossiped about them.

Sarah couldn't wait to be shut of the place. She'd be damned if she was going to live out her life on this mountain making moonshine and putting up with all the talk. Not that Granny heard it. She had dirt on just about every man in town, and some of the women, on account of everyone getting their liquor from Granny. She made sure they knew it too. Maggie MacAlpin was no fool. She didn't always see how they treated her granddaughter, though.

The kinder folks just looked at her with pity. Others treated her with suspicion, like they thought she caused her mama to go crazy, or outright fear as if madness was contagious and she carried it. Then there were the mean ones, like the Corbett sisters. Sarah thought of them as the enforcers, pack animals whose job it was to drive out the sick or injured or damaged like her.

A soft rustling nearby let her know she wasn't alone. She braced herself to move quickly in case it was one of the girls.

"Is it true about your mama, that she was crazy?" a quiet voice said behind her.

Sarah turned and eyed him irritably. "I don't know, Buddy. Is it true your daddy's a drunk?"

"Yeah," he said, baldly lowering himself onto a nearby rock, his knobby knees rising nearly to his armpits. His voice cracked just the tiniest bit.

"Hmph. I reckon crazy is as good a word as any other for what my mama was."

They sat for a time, both stunned into silence by the other's frankness. Sarah spoke first. "Thanks for helping me scare them back there."

He chuckled. "No sweat. I don't think I'll ever forget the look on Tanya's face." He made a terrified face before breaking into more laughter. Sarah realized she liked hearing him laugh. Buddy wasn't anything special as twelve-year-old boys go. He was gawky, and his hair could do with a comb, but his brown eyes were warm and his teeth weren't bucked like his sister's. "I could never have scared her like that without you setting it up. What was that you said?"

"Just some old poem I learned when I was a kid."

At that, Buddy laughed even harder, and Sarah found herself laughing with him.

When he had gotten control of himself, he said, "That's some right hook you've got. Where'd you learn to fight like that?"

"Oh, here and there." She shrugged. Sarah never told anyone about Duff teaching her to defend herself. He had told her it was their secret.

"Well, I don't think they'll be bothering you for a while."

"I hope they don't make trouble." She thought, not for the first time, that there might be some consequences for her actions.

Buddy shrugged. "I don't think so. Our mama doesn't want us talking to you at all. I don't reckon they'll want to explain how they were picking on you."

Sarah absorbed that bit of information and silently added Ada Corbett to the list of people she was looking forward to leaving behind when she left Kettle Hollow. They drifted again into silence, though more comfortable than before. They both seemed content to watch the late afternoon sun sift down through the trees and play off the water.

"How's your hand?" Buddy asked after a while.

Sarah lifted her hand and wiped the dripping water off on her shorts before holding it out for him to see. To her surprise he took hold of it gently and turned it to examine her reddened knuckles from different angles. There was a small split in the skin over the joint of her middle finger, but it wasn't bleeding anymore.

"Does it hurt?" His brown eyes sought hers.

"A little."

He smiled warmly not letting go of her hand, "Well, I don't think it'll leave a scar."

***

"He even kissed me one day. It was my first kiss." She arched an eyebrow at him. "It was awkward and sweet, like all thirteen-year-old kisses, but it was enough. A few days later, Mrs. Corbett came across us in the woods, and I thought her eyes were going to pop right out of her head. We weren't even doing anything, but the sight of me just set her off. She yanked Buddy up by his ear and dragged him off, telling him all kinds of horrible things about my granny and my mother. I didn't see Buddy much after that except to pass him in the halls at school. He was never mean to me like some other kids, but he was never really my Buddy again."

"What was it she was saying about your mother?" Dermot asked.

Sarah glanced at him. "You know she died when I was six. Well, there were some rumors."

"What kind of rumors?" He straightened up and faced her across the length of the couch, mirroring her pose by resting his head on his hand.

"Mostly about how she died." Sarah shifted to face the fire. Years of avoiding the topic of her mother made it hard for her to talk about it even with Amy, but between the beer and the dreamlike quality of the firelight, she felt she could tell him at least some. "The official report was that she got lost in a fog on the mountain and fell off a cliff, but a lot of people thought maybe she jumped."

"Why would they think that?" His voice was soft.

Sarah studied him. Would he judge her like everyone else had? "My mother was kind of a tragic figure in our little town. She was beautiful and smart and talented and everyone knew it. Then she went off on a trip when she was about nineteen, to Scotland actually. She came back a year later pregnant with me and something in her seemed to have shut down. At least that's what I was told. It was like a light had gone out inside of her. Unmarried young mother plus unknown absent father plus small town equals an infinite supply of rumor and innuendo."

"Which is only amplified by an unexplained early death." He gave a sympathetic nod.

"Exactly." She relaxed just a fraction. He seemed to understand, and he wasn't judging. "To her former friends, I was the thing that had robbed them of their bright star. To everyone else, I was the daughter of that sad woman up the holler and the granddaughter of the woman who sold illicit liquor."

He lifted his head and reached across the back of the couch to lay a comforting, warm hand on her arm. "That was the rumor. What was the truth?"

Green eyes met blue as she searched his gaze for what seemed an eternity. She swallowed hard past the lump forming in her throat.

"The truth was so much worse." She turned her eyes to the fire as she sipped her beer. "Maybe I'll tell you someday. But for now, I think it's time for bed. Since the phone book got us nowhere, we'll want to be at the courthouse when they open tomorrow."

He watched her stand and stretch before he stood too. He slipped the bottle out of her fingers saying, "I'll take care of these and lock up."

She gave him a long look. "Thanks."

CHAPTER EIGHTEEN

"I think we're about to run out of lunch options?" Dermot said, looking slightly worried as he and Sarah barreled down a country road south of Franklin.

"I want to get as close as we can, otherwise there will be no point in eating out here," Sarah explained. "You can't just walk up to a house in the hills. You've got to know someone or get an invitation. So we're here to get an invitation."

"Right, that's not unlike some places in Scotland."

"I'm sure, but over there I doubt you run the risk of getting shot if you approach a house unannounced. This looks like the best place." She pulled off the road into the gravel parking lot of a squat, beige cinderblock building with a faded sign that might have read Parker's or Parson's.

Dermot looked dubious as he climbed out of the car. "Best place for what?"

"Best place to get an invitation." She smiled at him over the car roof.

"As long as the food is edible," he grumbled on the way in.

They had spent the morning pouring through deed books at the Macon County Courthouse in the hopes of finding land owned by the Budges. When they checked the phone book the night before, they hadn't found any. So they had headed for the courthouse, and after she'd given Dermot a quick primer on how the property records were organized, he had proven to be a great help. Still, it had taken both of them searching the better part of the morning to learn that the Budge land was on the southeast side of town at the far end of a lonely looking road.

"If you were in Scotland, where would you go to connect with people in a community?"

"The pub."

"Exactly, only around here instead of pubs, we have diners like this." She waved a hand to indicate their surroundings. It was like any local diner in the mountains: wood paneled walls, knickknacks on little shelves, old enamel signs, Formica tables and cracking red Naugahyde upholstery. The menu hung over the counter listing items like cube steak, meatloaf, eggs and brains. A chalkboard below it announced the Friday fish special. It was nearly two o'clock so there were not as many diners as Sarah might have liked, but she had a feeling in this area everyone knew everyone else and strangers in the diner would be the talk of the town in no time. In fact she was counting on it.

"So we have lunch?" Dermot looked hopeful. Sarah had no doubt he was near starving.

She couldn't help giggling. "Yes, now we have lunch."

Just then a young woman with limp dishwater blonde hair sauntered up to their table and placed silverware wrapped in paper napkins in front of them almost without looking, as if she'd done that very thing thousands of times.

"What can I get for ya'll?" she asked. She was plain and bone thin, with grey eyes and a heart-shaped face. Sarah estimated her age to be around twenty, but she looked ten years older. Sarah had grown up with dozens of girls just like her. Her nametag read "Billie," but it could just have easily read Tanya or Ronnie Sue—or Sarah.

Sarah put on her friendliest smile and waited for Billie to look up at her before saying in her best Western Carolina drawl. "I think I'll have the fish special and a sweet tea. How about you, Dermot?"

Billie shifted her gaze to Dermot. Sarah wasn't surprised to see the woman's eyes widen and her nostrils flare with interest. The waitress straightened her shoulders as Dermot looked over the menu. Sarah thought approvingly that he knew the reaction he was getting and was milking it. The friendlier Billie was to them, the faster they would find what they were looking for.

"I'll have the fish special as well and an iced tea." Dermot laid the Scottish accent on like cream on scones, and Sarah could almost hear Billie's girlish sigh as she wrote down their orders.

"Can I get you anything else?" her voice was suddenly breathy.

"Ah dinna think so. Sarah?" He looked at her. He knew exactly what he was doing. Sarah just shook her head no, and Billie left the table to put in their order.

"Well, that should do it. She'll probably bend over backward to help the dreamy guy with the accent."

"Dreamy?" He cocked an eyebrow.

"Don't give me that. You know exactly the effect you had on her. I bet old ladies are crazy about you."

"It's just like unlocking a door." He winked at her. "Ye just have to find the right key. Don't tell me ye havena batted yer pretty lashes at more than a few old men to get the stories and songs out of them."

Sarah had to giggle and turned her Southern accent to high. "My granny didn't raise no fool."

She was rewarded with a deep, rumbling laugh. She liked the way the corners of his eyes crinkled when he smiled.

They chatted while eating their fish and chips and nodding greetings to the locals who came through, giving the curiosity generated by their presence time to build. When they had finished, Billie came for their plates. “Can I interest ya’ll in some pie?”

Dermot gave her a charming smile. “What kind do you have?”

Billie beamed at him and cocked out her hip, resting the arm that was holding the plates on it. This naturally had the effect of offering him a better view. “We’ve got apple, pumpkin, and lemon meringue. I made ‘em myself this morning.”

“I think I’ll have pumpkin.” He shot a questioning look at Sarah.

“I’ll have the apple,” Sarah said, though Billie hadn’t taken her eyes off Dermot.

The woman suddenly remembered there was another person at the table and turned to Sarah. “You want a slice of cheese on that?”

“Is it cheddar?” she asked, hoping it wouldn’t be American.

“It’s hoop cheese from the dairy down the road.”

“Then I will definitely have some.” She thought she might regret it later, but it had been a long time since she’d had apple pie with homemade cheese.

The waitress shifted the plates in front of her and sauntered off, clearly hoping Dermot was watching.

He turned back to Sarah. “What on earth is hoop cheese?”

She laughed. "It certainly doesn't sound like much, does it? It's a farmer's cheese that's made fresh and spoils quicker than most aged cheeses, which is why you don't find it in a lot of stores. Around here it tends to taste like cheddar, but creamier. It's fantastic on apple pie."

Billie returned bearing two slices of pie that she set in from of them along with their check. "Is there anything else I can help ya'll with?"

Sarah spoke up. "Actually, there might be. We're folklorists from Chapel Hill. We go around collecting old stories and songs that people pass down."

Billie giggled. "Well, you're in the right place for that. People 'round here got long memories."

"We're counting on that," Dermot said. "We're trying to update a recording we found in our archives. It was made in the 1920s by a man called Simon Budge. D'ye know any Budges around here? We'd like to see if he passed the song on."

The woman nodded in the direction of the road and a cluster of buildings just past the diner that included a gas station with an attached garage. "Randy over at the garage is a Budge. I don't recall him saying anything about a Simon, but he might be able to help you."

"How long is the garage open?" Sarah asked.

"Well, the garage closes around five, but the filling station is open until eleven. Randy usually works the late shift." She glanced at the clock hanging on the wall at the end of the counter. "In fact, if you sit tight for a bit, he should be in here for his lunch break soon."

Sarah gave Dermot a smug look. "Perfect. Then we'll just enjoy our pie and wait for Randy."

As it turned out, they didn't have to wait long. Around the time they finished their pie, Randy Budge strolled in and found a seat at the counter. Sarah thought he had the look of a country boy. He was tall and lanky with a loose-limbed gait that suggested he always did things at his own pace. His worn jeans showed the kind of work he did, and she thought the mud on his much-scuffed work boots suggested that he spent a good share of time in the hills. As Billie leaned across the counter talking to him and nodding in their direction, Sarah wondered if Randy didn't have a side business that kept him in the hills.

When he turned toward their table and started to amble over, Sarah shot Dermot a look that said, "Let me handle this one."

Up close Sarah realized that Randy wasn't much older than she was, though his tanned skin and stubble made him look older. So did the hint of suspicion in his brown eyes. "Billie said ya'll are looking for Budges."

Sarah stood and smiled, offering him her hand to shake. He took it and gave a brief firm shake. "You could say that. I'm Sarah MacAlpin. I'm a folklorist. Have a seat."

Sarah scooted far into the booth so Randy would have room to sit next to her. As he did, she couldn't help but notice the familiar and slight tangy scent of mash. "This is my research partner, Dermot Sinclair."

Randy gave Dermot the once-over and brief nod, not friendly but not unfriendly. He looked back at Sarah. "Folklorist?"

"We study oral history and traditions that are passed down in a certain community by word of mouth. The kind of stuff our grandparents teach us: legends, songs, skills. I'm partial to mountain people. I grew up around Boone. My partner here is from Scotland, and he's researching mountain people whose ancestors came from Scotland."

"Uh-huh." He looked as if he didn't quite believe there was anything about their culture that people in Chapel Hill should be interested in. "Billie said something about a song."

"Yes, we found a recording in our library that was made in this area in the 1920s of a man named Simon Budge. He's singing a song that we haven't heard anywhere else in the mountains. It's a very unusual song because we've only ever heard it in Gaelic and only from recent Scottish immigrants, but he sang it in English. We want to find out whatever we can about him and where he learned the song. Does his name ring a bell?"

He still looked like he didn't quite understand why they would have come all the way up there over a song, but he did seem to think about it. "Can't say that it does, but you never know. You might talk to my granddad. If this man was alive in the '20s, granddad might remember him."

Sarah perked up immediately. "Is your granddad around here?"

Randy let out a grunt. "He lives up in the hills at the end of Nickajack Road. Why don't ya'll come on out tomorrow? I'll meet ya there."

Sarah grinned. "That sounds great! What time is good for you?"

"After lunch. Round two o'clock?"

"We'll be there." She offered him her hand again and tried not to betray her surprise when he held it just a little longer and she felt his thumb glide over her knuckles. She gave him a winning smile. "Thanks again."

Randy got up and went back to the counter and his lunch. Sarah looked over at Dermot feeling pretty pleased with herself.

***

...white and pink swirling around in a bright kaleidoscope. And the mumbling.

...They won't have you. I won't let them...

Molly was there on the other side of the flower film, her face twisted and hideous.

...let them take you away from me. I won't let...

...Mama?...

...Not my baby...never take you...

...Mama, I can't breathe...

...won't do it to you...not if I...

The dream again. Sarah couldn't catch her breath. She knew it was a dream. She wasn't actually under the water. The flowers weren't really floating above her. Molly wasn't really there.

"You're not here!" she shouted in her dream, in her mind.

Thunk! There it was, that awful sound, that sickening thunk of porcelain meeting flesh and hair and bone that meant Granny had saved her and doomed her. She couldn't count the number of times she'd heard that sound in her dreams since that day, but it never got easier. It should have been the sound of salvation, but Sarah always thought of it as her mother's death knell.

Molly's face went blank with shock and fell toward her landing in the water just an inch from Sarah's. Her voice came through loud and clear, as if the water weren't there and Molly whispered to her.

"I'm always here."

***

Dermot shifted again on the couch to ease the pain in his neck. It had just started to feel better after the previous night, and here he was again trying to get comfortable with a thin pillow against the wooden arm of the couch. He wouldn't even consider letting Sarah sleep there, but he couldn't help missing his futon back in his apartment in Chapel Hill. After a pleasant dinner and more easy conversation, Sarah had climbed up to the loft and gone to bed. He lay there on the little couch with his feet hanging off the arm watching the fire and hoping to get just a few more minutes of sleep than he had last night.

Still, whenever he closed his eyes, he saw Sarah: Sarah cooking, Sarah driving, singing, Sarah's face by firelight. Letting her do this by herself was unthinkable, but staying with her in this little cabin was too cozy, too close. It was so much easier to remember the real reason he was here when he had his own place to go back to. It was hard to think about her as someone else's when he put his toothbrush next to hers on the edge of the sink or saw her rumpled and half-asleep in the morning.

He finally managed to drift off and was nearly asleep when he heard a loud gasp from the loft. His eyes snapped open, and he looked hard into the dark in the direction of the sound. The angle was such that he couldn't see Sarah from where he was, but he could hear her taking deep, rasping breaths as if she couldn't get enough air. He was at the ladder in two strides, but her voice stopped him just as he put his foot on the first rung.

"It's okay. Just a dream." Her voice was weak, and she still struggled to catch her breath.

"Are ye sure?" He climbed another rung on the ladder.

"I'm sure." She sounded stronger, and it was clear she didn't want him coming up. "I'll be fine. Go back to sleep."

Dermot suddenly recalled her sleepwalking incident that summer and remembered chasing her through the forest on Grandfather Mountain. He began to question the wisdom of her sleeping in a loft with nothing but a ladder to get down and nothing up there to prevent her from simply walking off the edge. He also realized that the possibility of him getting any sleep that night had just flown out the window.

CHAPTER NINETEEN

Sarah pulled the car to a stop at the mouth of the deeply rutted driveway at the far end of Nickajack Road. They had left the main roads miles back, and the road they were on had taken so many twists and turns that Sarah was no longer sure which direction was which. They sat for a moment, both searching for any way they could see her little car making it through the ruts that marred the nearly overgrown dirt path through the dense trees. There was no way the suspension in her Honda could handle those ruts. She wondered if she even had the ground clearance for it. If they hadn't been told that a person lived back there, they wouldn't have believed this to be anything more than a logging trail.

"Looks like we're going to have to hoof it," Sarah said as she backed out and repositioned the car to the side of the road. "Hope you wore your hiking shoes."

"I did. Are ye sure about this? I feel like we're heading into the heart of darkness in search of Kurtz."

Sarah giggled and made a ghostly "Oooo" noise. "Say 'heart of darkness' again."

Dermot gave her a puzzled look. "Heart of darkness. Why?"

"It just sounds so much more sinister with your accent." She winked and laughed, her head shaking as she repacked the recording equipment and her notebook and purse. "I'm sure we'll be fine. This is more like home to me than our little cabin. Granny had a truck that could make it to town and back, but we walked almost everywhere."

"Aye, but what about what's up there?" He lifted his chin in the direction of the driveway. "Don't you worry about safety, or who ye're going to meet? Ye dinna know what's through those trees or what their intentions might be."

"Come on, you've done fieldwork. We stroll into unknown situations and hope to find what we're looking for. It's the nature of the beast."

"Aye, but I'm a lot bigger than you, and I know how to defend myself."

Sarah studied him, her head cocked to the side, wondering where his anxiety was coming from. She was actually a little annoyed by it. It wasn't as if she hadn't done fieldwork before or as if she wouldn't again. She didn't need him to point out the dangers. She batted her eyes. "Well, now you can defend weak li'l ole me too."

"Sarah—" he started, but she held up a quelling hand. She didn't want to hear anymore, nor did she want to argue.

"Come on, mother hen. We've got to get walking." She tossed the words over her shoulder as she headed up the driveway.

The walk was hard, but not unpleasant. The canopy of trees kept the sun off them, and the fall colors were a feast for the eyes. The driveway wound its way through the forest, running alongside a stream, but just enough above it to make flooding unlikely. Though it was almost entirely uphill, the slope wasn't steep until near the end. As they neared what appeared to be the last curve, Sarah stepped off the dirt track to walk through some dried fallen leaves. Her steps made a constant rustling that was loud enough in the quiet forest to be heard at a distance. "Walk in the leaves. Make as much noise as possible."

"Why?"

"Friends don't sneak up to a house. Besides, I suspect that our friend Randy has a still up here somewhere. We don't want him thinking we're ATF."

"ATF?"

"Alcohol Tobacco and Firearms. They're the agency that tracks down moonshiners."

"What makes ye think he has a still?"

"Instinct, I guess, and I thought I smelled mash on him yesterday."

He shot her a look. "I didn't smell anything funny."

Sarah shrugged. "It was faint. I only noticed it when he sat next to me. It's a smell you don't forget."

Dermot followed her lead and stepped into the leaves to add his rustling steps to hers. The result was a cacophony of dry rustling that sounded like a herd of buffalo.

Sarah thought her instincts were right when they came around the last bend in the driveway to find a ramshackle house and an ancient weather-beaten barn in a small clearing. Randy Budge stood on the porch in front of the door. Propped against the wall within easy reach of Randy's right hand was a shotgun. Sarah could feel Dermot tense next to her.

"Afternoon, Randy," Sarah called out as they approached the house.

"Ya'll walked?" He looked incredulous. Out of his work clothes, Randy wore jeans and a flannel shirt. He could have been standing on that porch in 1995 or 1895; his look and manner seemed out of another time.

Sarah shot a look over to Randy's truck parked next to the house. It was a giant jacked-up affair with enormous wheels and a suspension that appeared ready for anything. She gave an embarrassed shrug. "I'm afraid my little car just wasn't up to the driveway."

"I'm sorry. I shoulda warned you about that." He ducked his head in apology, but didn't move from his spot at the top of the porch steps. The guy who had seemed taciturn and aloof yesterday seemed shy even a little awkward today.

"Randy!" came a gruff voice from somewhere inside the open door behind him. Randy turned toward it. There were no lights on inside, so the open door looked like a black hole. From the dark emerged a man with a face like leather topped by a wild shock of white hair. His build was wiry, and his movements slow and deliberate. He gave her a welcoming smile, revealing that he was missing more than a couple of teeth. "You gonna keep a pretty lady waiting in the yard all day?"

"Sorry, Granddad. C'mon up, ya'll." Sarah thought she caught a slight blush in the Randy's cheeks. The younger man ducked his head and stepped aside, allowing Sarah and Dermot to step up onto the porch.

Sarah turned her most winning smile on the older man. "Hi, Mr. Budge. I'm Sarah MacAlpin. I'm a folklorist from Chapel Hill. This is my partner, Dermot Sinclair. It's nice to meet you."

The old man's eyes flicked to Dermot, and Sarah thought she might have seen a flash of something in that look, but she couldn't place it. He shifted back to her smiling. "Knew a Maggie MacAlpin once, up to Kettle Holler. You kin to her?"

Sarah couldn't help but smile back. Any foot in the door helped on a trip like this, and Granny just might have provided it. "Yes, sir. She was my grandmother."

He sobered. "I was mighty sorry to hear she passed."

"Thank you, I miss her every day."

"I'm sure you do." He nodded solemnly before smiling and giving her a wink. "But save that sir business for the law, girl. Around here, I'm just Budge."

Sarah couldn't help liking him. He reminded her of Old Duff, who had helped Granny distribute her wares. He travelled up and down the mountains doing whatever work he could find, but he always carried a supply of Granny's best in his overloaded old pickup. He would sell it wherever he went and bring Granny back the profits. Duff had drifted in and out of their lives with the seasons. He liked to winter in a cabin on their land further up the holler, but of course he had stayed all through that one year, the toughest year of Sarah's young life.

Budge waved her over to two straw-bottomed rocking chairs that sat next to the door and eased himself into one of them while Sarah took the other. Dermot sat down near them on the top step while Randy leaned on a post.

"Well, Budge, I'm hoping you can help us out. We found a recording in the library down in Chapel Hill of a man named Simon Budge. It was from the 1920s so I'm sure he's not around anymore, but I was hoping he might be kin to you."

"Might be, might be…" Budge rocked his chair slowly, looking thoughtfully at the trees in front of the house. After a moment he slapped his thigh. "Hooo! I tell you, your Granny made the best peach brandy. I don't suppose you took up the business."

Sarah tried to be patient and let him lead the conversation. Sometimes just letting people ramble was the best way to get the information she wanted. “No, Granny never wanted me to. I helped her before I went to college, but I never ran the still after she died.”

He gave her a sly look. “Well, now since you’re not making it, maybe you might tell me the secret of that peach brandy.”

Sarah leaned closer to him and in a conspiratorial whisper. “I’ll tell you what. You help me out with this information, and I’ll tell you the secret.”

Budge let out a belly laugh that shook the whole porch. He leaned over to address his grandson. “You want to get that still up and running, this girl can tell you how. She might even have some tips for an old moonshiner like me.”

He turned to Sarah. “Let that boy take you over to the shed and show you this still we just got. I think he can use some PRO-fessional advice. Ya’ll pick up some stump water on your way back and we’ll talk about Simon Budge.”

Sarah bit her tongue. She didn’t really want to go look at a still, but she reminded herself to relax and let things come. She’d get her information eventually. “Alright. You’ve got a deal.”

Budge nodded, and Sarah believed he did have something to tell. She turned to the steps as Randy pushed away from the post and followed her ushering her toward the tree line.

***

Dermot stood while Sarah walked down the steps and across the yard. He thought about stopping her, going with her, calling the whole thing to a halt. He knew she was following the old man's lead, hoping to get her answers, but he didn't like the idea of her leaving his sight with a man they didn't really know in a place this remote. They were really at the mercy of the Budges, and he wasn't sure exactly what that meant.

He stood there dithering about whether or not to follow them when the old man growled behind him. His voice sounded like a lower, stronger version of the one he'd used with Sarah. "Sit down, chief. She's safe with him."

Dermot stilled. So it was like that, eh? He turned back to Budge. The old man had undergone a change while their backs had been turned. His back was straighter. His impish grin was gone. Even his eyes looked sharper. "I'm not the chief."

"Oh, and I reckon they just send any ole steward." One bushy white eyebrow arched in doubt.

Dermot drew up to his full height, trying to look like the best man for the job. "Hmmph. I was best suited."

The old man glanced off in the direction that Sarah and Randy had walked. "She is the one, isn't she?"

"They seem to think so." Dermot followed the old man's gaze.

"How much does she know?"

"Hard to tell. She studies auld songs like the one she's asked ye about. She learned it as a girl, but if she knows the connection she's isna talking about it. Her mother died when she was young, and I don't think her Granny told her everything." He came up the steps and sat in the rocking chair next to Budge. To his surprise he found that he was actually relieved to be able to talk about his position with someone other than James or Walter.

Budge shook his head and pulled a cigarette out of the pocket of his threadbare flannel shirt. He took his time lighting it and took a long draw of smoke, blowing it out in a cloud that swirled around his head. "Why didn't Maggie tell her?"

Dermot had wondered the same thing since meeting Sarah. He shrugged. "I canna say. Maybe she was hoping Sarah wasn't the one. I think the knowledge didn't sit well with Sarah's mum. Maybe she was afraid of losing Sarah too."

They sat for a few more minutes in companionable silence, both wondering at the reasoning behind the choices of an old woman who was no longer around to explain them. When he had finished his cigarette, Budge stubbed out the butt in an old oyster shell that rested on a wobbly table against the porch railing. He didn't look at Dermot, but kept his eyes on the place where the trail they had taken disappeared into the trees. "How much should I tell her?"

***

Sarah followed Randy along the narrow trail that led through the woods. About two hundred yards in, they came to an old shed that was overgrown with vines. If Sarah hadn't known what to look for she never would have spotted it. Randy opened the door and went inside. Sarah waited outside. The shed looked big enough, but years of being on her own had taught her that enclosed places and strange men didn't mix. Randy stepped back out with a lit lantern. He handed it to her and stepped away from the door. “The still’s just inside to the left.”

Sarah studied him for a few seconds, wondering if going into the shed was wise. There were any number of ways this scenario could play out if Randy or Budge weren’t the good ole boys they appeared to be. Randy had barely looked at her since they had arrived, but there was nothing in his manner that was the least bit threatening. He must have understood her hesitation, because he lifted his eyes to hers and looked completely earnest when he said, “You’re safe with me, ma’am.”

Sarah watched him for a second more before she nodded and stepped inside. The shed was cool from the shade of the forest. It was also bigger than it looked from the outside. She thought they must have built it around a cave or dug it into the mountain. To her right were shelves stacked to the roof with glass jars and jugs. Along the back wall were stacks of sugar and corn meal as well as a number of pieces of scrap metal and odds and ends. It reminded her of Duff’s cabin with its dingy windows and bits of metal and wood hanging, leaning, or laying wherever he had left them waiting for him to put them to whatever use had made him pick them up. To the left sitting on top of some empty burlap bags was an old copper still in pieces.

***

1985
Kettle Hollow, North Carolina

Sarah was coming around the side of the house with a basket full of apples when she spotted the ramshackle rust-colored Ford pickup truck coming down the drive. The cap across the back was held on by rope. There was a giant crack in the windshield, and more rope held the bumper in place. She doubted it would be legal to drive it anywhere that Duff wasn't already known to the local law, but there weren't many places in the mountains that Duff wasn't known. Through the windows in the back, she could see all the things that he had salvaged over the summer. He would spend the winter cobbling the scraps of wood and metal and wire into useful things that he would leave in his cabin or sell to anyone who was looking for a cheap whatnot that did whatever.

The truck rattled to a stop in front of the farmhouse and the engine didn't so much cut off as gurgle slowly into silence. The driver's door opened and out climbed the man, looking as haggard and careworn as his prized pickup. His clothes were worn to threads, and his jeans were spattered with mud from the knees down. His greasy hair hung over his shoulders, and his scraggly beard fanned out across the top of his shirt. Most people in Kettle Hollow wrinkled their noses at him and did their best to ignore the old drifter, but he was the closest thing to a daddy Sarah had ever known.

He spotted her at the corner of the house and strolled over to meet her. The corners of his eyes crinkled when he smiled, and Sarah could see that he'd spent much of the summer out in the sun. He reached out and took the basket from her. His hands were rough but mostly clean. "You puttin' these on the porch?"

She nodded and followed him as he carried the apples to the porch and set them down next to the door. When he straightened he opened his arms to her and she stepped into them resting her head on his chest. His threadbare flannel shirt felt soft under her cheek and he smelled of earth and sunlight.

He held her a moment before stepping back and putting her at arm's length. "You musta grown a foot this summer, girl. How old are you now?"

She shook her head. He said the same thing to her when he returned to the mountain every fall. "You know darn well, I'll be fifteen next week."

"And pretty as a picture." He chucked her under the chin gently. "I'll bet you have to beat the boys off with a stick."

Sarah huffed and rolled her eyes. "Yeah, they're just lining up to ask out Crazy Molly's little girl."

His eyes sharpened and his voice cracked like a whip, but his touch was still gentle when he pulled her back to face him. "Hey! You don't talk that way about your mama. She loved you more than you know. And if anyone else is talking about her like that, you just point them out to me."

Mòrag's eyes stung with unshed tears. No one else ever stood up for her and her mama like Duff did. Even Granny would just pretend not to hear the rumors about Màili's death and her state of mind those last few months. Duff was a different story. He'd even had to leave town in a hurry a couple years ago after getting in a fight over someone bad-mouthing Molly. He was their champion.

***

October 1995

Sarah shot a glance at the door. Randy Budge was sitting across the trail on a fallen log. She stepped closer to the still and bent to examine it. She held the lamp closer and scanned the various tanks and tubes. She wasn't sure what the old man wanted her to tell Randy. Sarah would bet a semester's tuition that Randy knew how to make moonshine, but she would go through the motions and answer whatever questions they had. If that was the quid pro quo that it took to get answers out of Budge, Sarah would tell him everything she'd learned about moonshine from Granny.

She straightened up and went back outside, turning the lantern wick down until the flame went out. She sat down next to Randy on the log. "I don't think you need me to tell you that coil's shot."

He gave a soft laugh. "Nah, I figured that when the old man brought it home. He knows it too, but the tanks are still good."

"Yeah. What does he want to add another still for?" She knew they must already have one. Though it wasn't in this shed, there were plenty of places on this mountain where they could be hiding it. Based on the supplies in the shed, Sarah was guessing it wasn't far away.

Randy glanced at her. "He wants to make something more than just corn liquor. He's got his mind set on barley. When I told him your name last night, he told me about your Granny making whisky."

Sarah nodded. "She did use barley, but you have to malt it. It's not like corn, you can't just add yeast. She malted corn too when she used it."

"I was afraid you were gonna say that. That'll triple our work time and cut our yield."

Sarah shrugged. “But it’ll increase the quality, and you can double, maybe triple your price. As long as you can distribute it.”

Randy made a confident snicker. “Oh, we’ve got that covered.”

They sat there for a few moments each lost in their own thoughts. Sarah could almost see the wheels turning in Randy’s head, calculating supplies and yield and costs. She knew all the considerations well enough. Sarah hoped she was giving him something he could use.

After some time he looked at her. “Was your Granny the one that made the cough medicine?”

Sarah laughed. Granny’s cough medicine was a special run of liquor that included a distillation of horehound, licorice root, and Echinacea. It was mixed with simple syrup to make it a little easier to swallow but only a little. She had sold it and sometimes given it away all over the area. Sarah was a little surprised to hear that it had made it this far afield. She guessed Duff might have distributed it along with the moonshine. “Mmmhmm. My apologies if you were subjected to that as a child.”

Randy laughed too. “Well, it was better than castor oil and it worked, or at least it knocked us out so we didn’t cough for a while. Where’d you get all the stuff that went in it?”

“We foraged or grew it ourselves…even the barley. Granny didn’t like having to buy supplies. If all she bought was sugar and jars, then she could just tell the law she was making jam.”

“No one ever found her barley growing?”

She gave him a smile that said he should know better. “No one who told. We had a lot of land, and she would plant in small patches. We were pretty remote anyway. Anyone who did find them was probably a customer."

By unspoken consent, they both rose and started back. Randy put the lamp back in the shed and grabbed a couple of jars of clear liquor before closing the door. They continued chatting about moonshine on the walk back. Sarah hadn't even thought about the task of making moonshine since her grandmother had died. For years now, it hadn't been a craft to her so much as just something her grandmother did to put food on the table. She found that it was actually nice to remember the work. Budge was right: her Granny had been good at it, and it felt good to be able to be proud of that.

***

"This is Sarah MacAlpin interviewing Alex Budge, October twelfth, 1995, at his home in Macon County, North Carolina. Also present, Randy Budge and Dermot Sinclair," Sarah said into the microphone before setting it down on the little table facing Budge. They had returned to their original seats on the porch, each with a jelly glass of Budge's best stump water to sip while they talked.

"Simon Budge was my granddaddy," Budge said with great significance, looking directly at Sarah. "And he did teach me that song you're talking about. But I'm not much of a singer, so I'll tell ya the story he tolt with it."

"Alright." Sarah would keep her talking to a minimum as long as Budge kept going.

"My people come from Scotland back in the colonial times and they been passing this story down all along. I can't say how much it's changed, but here 'tis, as I learnt it." He leaned back and took a deep breath as if he were getting ready to sing after all. When he spoke again, his voice had a faraway dream-like quality.

"Long ago, when Scotland was just a wild place with different tribes running their own territories, this family came over from Ireland and made to take over the place. They wanted control of the land. Now, some say they were more civilized than the tribes that were there before, but I don't know that that's true. They say these fellers tried to get the tribes to all work together, but the old folk, that's what my granddad called the old tribes, they weren't havin' it. They fought over everything, and some of 'em made friends with the new tribe and some of 'em resisted. The new people maybe didn't mean any harm, they just thought their ways were better, and they couldn't get why some of the old folk didn't want to change.

"So one day the king o' the new folk goes out wandering to think. He's trying to figure out how he can get everybody to come over to his side and get along. So he gets tired and he stops by a riverbank. While he's settin' there, up swims this girl. Now, she's about the prettiest thing the king's ever seen and she's wavin' to 'im, 'Come on in, the water's fine.'" Budge gave a beckoning wave.

"So he goes in for a swim. Only this girl is so pretty he doesn't pay attention and they drift downstream to an island. Now the king thinks they're lost, but she says it's her home and he should come and meet her family.

"She takes the king to meet her father, but her pa is old and sickly and lame. The king starts to wondering who's gonna take care of this girl and her people when her pa dies. He thinks they've got to be pretty poor if they're just living on this island, and he's never even heard of her tribe before. But then she takes him over to the hearth and shows him their cookpot. It's a big ole iron kettle, and every time he sees someone go to the kettle and put in a bowl or a ladle, it comes up full of food. He keeps watching and thinking that kettle's got to be empty, but they still keep comin' up with food, and they're not even scraping the bottom.

"Then she takes him and shows him a cave that's hidden under a hill and in that cave is a big stone. And she tells him, 'This is the heart of our people.' Only he's got a different heart in mind. Remember, she's the prettiest girl he's ever laid eyes on. So he kisses her right there in the cave and tells her that he loves her and wants to protect her when her father dies.

"Now, just when that happens, a big storm like a harrican comes up and hits this island.

"When the king wakes up, he and the girl aren't in the cave anymore, but on shore. And the island is gone. But they find that big iron cookpot on the beach. So he takes her back with him and makes her his queen. They work to bring the tribes together. The old folk see that she's with him and she's one of them. And they see that he's got this cookpot that never runs out, and they start coming over to his side.

"It goes slow, but by the time their son becomes king, all the tribes have come together, and since his mother taught him the old ways and his father taught him the new way, he was a good king."

"In the recording, Simon Budge sings a couple of lines that I didn't quite understand," she said.

Sarah sang the lines as she had heard them in the Budge recording. Her voice was clear with that breathy twang that was commonly referred to as the "high lonesome sound." It was more the sound of Simon Budge than the sound of her grandmother.

Arbirainn i finaidh banaon chann ur afoinn
Bha an rìgh air chall 's a cheò
Ach ur pham chann ur n fawur breanain
Eirichidh e a-rithist

"Do those words sound at all familiar to you?"

Budge took a thoughtful sip of his moonshine and stared at the liquid for a few seconds as he rolled it around in the bottom of the old jelly glass. Sarah couldn't tell if he was thinking about the words or about the contents of the glass. The old man lifted his head and glanced over at Dermot before meeting Sarah's eyes. "I reckon I've heard 'em before. They sound familiar, but I can't tell you what they mean. I don't think my granddad knew either, least not that he told me."

Sarah nodded. "Did your granddad ever tell you any names for this king or the queen?"

Budge took another sip of moonshine from his glass and shook his head. He blew out a breath so thick with fumes that Sarah had to blink fast to keep her eyes from watering. "No. He never said names. He did say that the queen's people were older than names. Old as the stone, he used to say."

There it was again, that old expression she'd heard countless times from Granny and Bridget MacKenzie. "Do you know where in Scotland your people came from?"

"Can't say I do." Budge shifted in his chair and took another sip of moonshine. "That museum in Franklin says the

Budges are Lowlanders. Way I figure it, we been here so long it doesn't much matter."

It mattered to Sarah. It could help her trace the source of the song. She tried not to show her frustration. She glanced over her shoulder at Randy. He was leaning against the post and gazing out at the mountain. Turning back to Budge, she said, "Did you teach that story to your grandchildren?"

"Aw, most of 'em don't have time for an old man and his old stories. Except for Randy over there. He likes learning the old ways." He gave her a wink and a devilish grin. "And you have a lotta time for tellin' tales while you're mindin' a still."

She smiled back at him. That was a fact she knew all too well. She'd learned many a song by the ever-present beat of a thumper tank. She was glad she had found Alex Budge. Even if he hadn't known the legend behind the song, she'd have been happy to know him. She laid her hand over his gnarled, work-worn one where it rested by his glass on the table. "Thank you for talking with me. I appreciate your help."

He turned his hand over to grasp hers, his face serious. "I'm glad you could record it. You'll make sure people remember."

She gave his hand one last squeeze before switching off the recorder and beginning to gather her equipment. Dermot pushed himself up off of the top step to help her. Sarah looked over to where he'd been sitting and noticed that his jelly glass was empty. She hadn't taken more than a couple of polite sips. There hadn't been much in the glass, but it was strong. Fortunately Dermot seemed pretty steady.

Sarah was just stepping down from the porch, Dermot by her side, when a thought occurred to her. "Hey, Budge?"

"Mmm?" He had been looking into his jelly glass in deep concentration.

"You know a man they call Old Duff?" She realized that she missed the old man and felt guilty for not having done more to keep track of him.

Budge let out a hearty belly laugh and slapped his knee. "Shoot, girl! Everybody in the hills knows Grant MacDuff! He comes round this way at least twice a year."

Sarah couldn't help smiling back at the man with his dirty, worn clothes, missing teeth, and jelly glass full of stump water. He and Duff and Granny were why she did what she did. Their beauty and their humanity hit her so hard that sometimes it took the breath right out of her chest. They were people who lived and died in these hollers, and without someone like her, their culture would die in these hollers too.

"Well, next time he passes this way, you tell him I was here." She felt tears pricking the backs of her eyes and tried to swallow past the lump in her throat. "Tell him I remember everything he taught me."

The old man gave her a solemn nod. Sarah started to turn away again, but his voice stopped her. "Wait! You never did tell me the secret to your granny's peach brandy."

Sarah gave him a knowing smile before walking back up the porch steps. Slowly, she leaned over Budge's chair and planted a kiss on his weathered cheek before whispering Granny's secret in his ear.

Budge looked at her closely as if he could verify the truth of what she said in her eyes. After a couple of seconds, he burst into gusty laughter that was accompanied by more knee slapping. "Ha! I knew it! I just knew it!"

Sarah and Dermot climbed into Randy's truck for a ride back down to their car. When they pulled away from the house, they could still hear the old man laughing.

CHAPTER TWENTY

Spring 1987
Kettle Hollow, North Carolina

"Duff?" Sarah called as she came up to the still. Granny had sent her with a jar of stew and some biscuits for Duff, but when she got there he wasn't anywhere in sight. She noticed his whittling sitting on the log next to the camouflaged shelter. They didn't have to work too hard to keep it hidden since most of the local law were in Granny's pocket for one reason or another.

She turned and addressed the trees behind the shelter. "You can come out now. It's only me." No response. She turned in the other direction, scanning the trees and setting the bag with their lunch on the log. His silence was starting to make her nervous. "I brought your lunch."

She felt more than heard him, like a disturbance in the air behind her. She braced herself for a fight, but he didn't attack the way she expected. Not quick and hard, but quiet, so that she was in his hold before she had a chance to fight back. He clamped one hand over her mouth and the other around her waist, pulling her back tight to his chest. In her position, she was immobile.

Quick as lightning, she thought through her options. She couldn't reach his head to throw him, and he held her too tight for her to twist and land an elbow. For an old man, he was mighty strong. She could stomp on his instep, but she didn't think it would get her very far. Eliminating most of her options for breaking his hold, she kept herself still, muscles bunched and listening to him breathe against her ear. Her patience paid off. His breath started to slow down, to normalize. He thought he had her beat and started to relax his hold just enough.

As soon as Sarah felt his muscles shift, she let go of every muscle that she had been holding tensed. Suddenly she was dead weight. He wasn't ready for it, and she slipped right out of his hold and crumpled to the ground. As she fell, she swept a leg against his, knocking him off his feet. He landed flat on his back with a thud.

The next sound Sarah heard had her rolling her eyes in exasperation. He was laughing—not just laughing, but rolling on the ground and guffawing. "By God, girl you do listen to me."

Sarah got to her feet, brushing the leaves and dirt off her clothes. "Of course I do, old man!"

"Well…" Duff got to his feet a little more slowly, brushing himself off. "It's hard to tell sometimes with you teenagers."

"Yeah, I'm such a typical teenager." Her voice dripped sarcasm.

"More than you know, baby girl." He looked at her fondly before reaching over to ruffle her hair. "More than you know."

She gave him a disgruntled look, but deep down she loved it when he called her "baby girl." "Granny sent your lunch."

"Good. Sit down and eat with me," he said, easing down onto the log by the shelter. He liked to pretend he was decrepit, but Sarah knew better. She'd done enough tussling with him over the past couple of winters to know that Duff was as strong as a man half his age.

She took a seat next to him on the log and untied the kitchen towel that Granny had wrapped the biscuits in. Duff opened the jar of stew and inhaled. "I sure am gonna miss your granny's cooking when I take off."

"Do you have to?" Sarah asked, picking up a biscuit. She felt shy about asking Duff to stay, but she didn't want to be without him. "I mean, it's my last summer up here. I won't be here next fall when you get back."

He stopped with the spoon halfway to his mouth and studied her. With a sigh, he said, "Well, now. If I don't go sell all that liquor, how is your granny gonna pay those extra college expenses? That scholarship don't cover everything."

Sarah sighed, absently crumbling her biscuit and dropping the pieces on the ground. She tried to sound strong. She wasn't sure she succeeded. "I know. I'm just going to miss you."

"Baby girl, when you get to Boone and start going to classes, you'll have so much to do and so many new friends you'll forget all about Old Duff."

She shook her head. "Not possible."

"Not only possible, but probable." He gave her knee a gentle squeeze. "Just as long as you remember how to take care of yourself."

She let out a short bark of laughter. "With all of your little pop quizzes like just now, I'm not likely to forget."

His face grew serious. "You just make sure you don't. You're small, so your best tool is going to be surprise. Let your opponent underestimate you, and you can use that to your advantage, but don't expect them to do it twice."

"Yes, sir." She rolled her eyes.

"Yeah." He nodded. "You just let those Appalachian State boys know you're not there for fun and games."

"Duff?" She looked down at the biscuit in her hand, unable to look at his face when she asked him, "What do I do if I meet a boy I don't want to fend off?"

"Oh, baby girl. I hope you do. I hope you meet someone worthy of everything you have to give." He reached over and caressed her face, something he hadn't done since she was very little. "You're destined for great things. You make sure you find a man who's up to the challenge."

***

October 1995

Dermot rubbed his hair dry with a towel. He was glad Sarah had found the sprayer that fit over the old faucet on the bathtub so they could have something like a shower. After walking through the woods and the tension of talking with Budge, it had felt good to get clean. He'd been watching Sarah all afternoon, wondering if the story had triggered some long-buried memory he might have to help her explain. He knew it was what Walter and maybe even James wanted, but he wasn't ready to turn her world upside down…not yet.

After dinner he'd left Sarah curled up by the fire and looking at her notes. They hadn't talked much during the meal. She had been deep in thought, her emotions close to the surface, and Dermot had tried to give her some breathing room. He still half expected for her to remember something, but at least he felt better able to handle it after getting cleaned up.

Coming out of the bathroom in his sweats, he was surprised the find the cabin empty. He felt a quick surge of panic. “Sarah?”

He climbed the ladder to check the loft, thinking she might have gone to bed early, but she wasn’t there. His breath coming fast, he went to check the porch. He found her there leaning against the corner post. Her cheek was resting on the damp wood and her arms hugged tight around her chest as if she were physically holding her heart inside.

The afternoon had been unseasonably warm, but the evening had turned rainy, blanketing the mountain in fog that swirled around her legs and across the floorboards. The damp air had condensed in her hair, forming tiny droplets of water that clung to her curls and sparkled in the light from the window.

The sight of her there—equal parts impossible beauty and heart-wrenching pain—gripped him like a fist around his heart. He’d been so worried all day about what she might learn or remember that he hadn’t even thought of how emotional this trip might be for her. This place was so much like her home, and Budge had known of her grandmother, knew this Duff person. They were all part of the world Sarah had left behind when her grandmother died. Of course she’d be maudlin.

As silently as he could on the creaky old boards, he made his way over to stand next to her at the porch railing. He tried to make his voice as soft and soothing as he could. “Do you want to talk about it?”

Sarah inhaled deeply, lifting her head from the post. She gave him a tender smile before shaking her head. "I don't think so. I'm not sad, not really. It just seems sometimes like I was the only one that knew them. It's easy to forget that other people knew them too, or knew of them. Most of the time, Granny's like this person that only lives inside me, something private that no one else can understand. No one down there knows what she was like or what our lives were like. So many of them grew up in suburbs in cookie-cutter houses with stoves that get hot at the flip of a switch and meat that comes wrapped in cellophane. It's all so easy down there that no one gets it. It's like I grew up in another century, in a fairy tale, and she was my fairy godmother. Budge just made her real again for me. I think maybe I was ready for them all to be real again."

There was nothing he could say to that, nothing more to add. He just wrapped his arm around her shoulders and pulled her to him, offering her the strength and safety of friendship. Sarah sighed and leaned her head on his shoulder.

***

They rested for what seemed a long time. Sarah enjoyed the warmth of Dermot's arm on her shoulders. Since that afternoon, she'd felt almost raw with longing for the people she'd lost. They had all been there with her in the woods, looking at the old still, sitting around Budge's porch. She had felt them all, and now felt their loss again—not as fresh and wrenching as before, but still there like a dull ache attached to every breath.

She felt as much as heard Dermot's low rumbling question. "Who is Old Duff?"

She smiled. "He's almost like an uncle, I guess. He's a drifter that used to run Granny's moonshine all over the mountains. He would roll in in the late fall and spend the winter on an old homestead that was above our house on the mountain. Technically it was our land, but Granny let him live there as part of his compensation. In the spring, he'd leave with his old pickup truck full of contraband and return in the fall with money for Granny, minus a small cut of course. If the stuff sold fast, he'd come back sooner and leave again. I think he also took odd jobs up and down the mountains and just…drifted."

"And your Granny let him come around ye?" He was incredulous.

Sarah shook her head. "He wasn't like that. In fact, he was one of the few people Granny trusted. I always got the impression they had known each other long before I was born."

Dermot shifted his shoulder and let his arm drop to her waist. He resettled her closer, with her head resting on his chest. "Ye told Budge ye remembered what he taught ye. What was that?"

Sarah rubbed her cheek against his soft sweatshirt, enjoying the feel of the hard muscle beneath it. "How to survive off the mountain, how to defend myself, mostly how to fend off boys."

Laughter rumbled through his chest. "Has it worked?"

"You joke, but he knows what he's talking about. He has some sort of military training; he never said where he got it."

She leaned away a little. “It’s kept me safe so far, not that I’ve been attacked or anything.”

“So he was like an uncle. Is he related?”

“Not that I know of. He was about Granny’s age, maybe a little younger. When he was around, they always seemed pretty close, not romantic or anything, just close friends. Still, I think we were the closest thing to family that he had.” She suddenly remembered one of those times that they had counted on Duff, a time when he’d been there out of season, the summer her mother had died. Her voice sounded like it was coming from a distance, from someone else. “He would do anything for us.”

Dermot made one of his speaking grunts against her cheek, and she lifted her head away from his chest to search his eyes. It struck her then, the similarities between Dermot and Duff: the military training, the understanding, the inexplicable sense of attachment that she felt. “He was a good friend to us, to me. We should all be lucky enough to have a friend like Duff.”

He lifted his hand to cradle her cheek, his eyes determined. His words sounded like they had to scrape past sandpaper to escape his throat. “Ye are. Ye do.”

Sarah looked into those blue eyes that always seemed to see too much. She wasn’t afraid of him anymore. “You have no idea how much I want to believe that.”

Her gaze dropped to his lips, and she was struck by their perfect shape. She remembered how soft they had been last summer when he had kissed her. She lifted her hand and slid her fingers through the hair at the back of his neck and pulled him down to her. Their lips met softly, gently, as if the moment weren’t entirely real, like that half second after a match is struck and the chemical reaction spreads across the head before the flame comes to life.

Then the flame burst forth. Sarah opened her mouth to breathe, but Dermot stole the air from her lungs when he surged closer, pressing her back against the post. She wrapped her arms around him in an effort to absorb his hungry assault. His hand came up to grip the hair just behind her ear, holding her in place. His other hand stole around her waist, pulling her tight against him. Adrenaline surged through her, making her quiver from her bones out. Her body hummed as if to say, "This! Yes this!"

And just as quickly as they had come together, Dermot tore himself away from her. "Agh! *Ifrinn!*" *[Hell!]*

Sarah couldn't move. He had felt so good in her arms, like he was another part of her. Without him now, she felt unbalanced and afraid that if she moved she would simply topple over. So she stayed where she was and leaned her head back against the post for support.

Dermot bent at the waist and held the porch railing in a white-knuckled grip, his arms bent and every muscle straining against what she thought he wanted. His eyes looked hard out into the darkening fog. She thought she detected an almost imperceptible shake of his head. "I—"

"Shouldn't have done that?" Her tone was bitter, and she tilted her head to the side in the hopes of seeing his face but all she got was a profile. The muscles of his jaw flexed as if he was grinding his teeth. "Yeah, that seems to be a pattern with us."

He inhaled deeply and let it out in a low groan. He spoke softly, keeping his eyes on the fog. "Dinna think that I don't want ye or care for ye. I do, more than I should."

She pulled away from the post to stand next to him at the porch rail. "I don't see the problem."

"There's someone else…" he hissed.

Hope sprang up in her chest. Sarah reached across him and turned his face to her with a caress. "But that's over. It was over a long time ago. I was kidding myself. Jon never—"

His eyes bored into hers as he gently pulled her hand away from his cheek. His voice was so low she almost didn't hear it. "Not Jon."

"Ah. You have someone else." Sarah felt the realization crash over her like a cold bucket of water. She took her hand away from his face and eased away from him. Slunk away would have been more like it. She suddenly wished the floor would open up and swallow her. "I don't know why that never occurred to me."

He stood back from the railing and looked down at her. It was getting harder to see by the meager light coming out of the window, but Sarah read his expression perfectly. Pity. "I'm sorry."

"No!" She raised her hand to cover her own blushing cheek. She knew she must be practically glowing red with embarrassment. She wouldn't dare look him in the eye. She didn't think she could bear seeing what was there. "No, I'm sorry. I've put you in an awful position."

They stood for what seemed an eternity, not wanting to leave each other but not wanting to say more, neither of them able to look at the other. Finally, Sarah drew in a sharp breath and said, "I think I'll go to bed now. Good night."

***

He waited on the porch with his hands gripping the railing like a lifeline until he heard her climb the ladder to the loft. Then he waited about ten minutes longer. The rough wood of the railing dug into his hands, but he welcomed the pain. It rooted him to the spot where he was, when everything in him wanted to go inside and climb that ladder and show Sarah how much he wanted her. A few splinters were nothing compared to the look on her face when she'd assumed he meant he had someone else.

It wasn't true, of course; there was no one else for him. But she wasn't his and never would be. It was better this way. He'd hide behind whatever imaginary girlfriend she conjured up for him and let that keep their relationship platonic. He knew too well what would happen if he gave in and did what he wanted so badly to do. Walter Stuart chose his leverage well.

When he was satisfied that Sarah was in bed and he wouldn't risk running into her again until morning, he went back into the cabin. He banked the fire and spread his blanket on the couch, doubting he would get any sleep.

Those doubts were confirmed later when he started to drift off, only to be roused by the same soft whimpering he'd heard the night before. He eyed the ladder, wondering if he should go to her, afraid of what might happen if he did. When she said "Mama?" in a voice like a child full of pain and fear, his decision was made. He was up the ladder in an instant to find Sarah in the bed, lying perfectly still on her back as if pinned to the mattress.

She wasn't thrashing about and she hadn't cried out again, but her brows were drawn together and her breath came in quick, shallow gasps. Not knowing if he should wake her, he slid under the comforter and turned her away from him. Fitting his chest to her back, he splayed his hand across her lower ribs over her diaphragm. Relieved when she didn't fight him, he changed his focus to his breath. He took slow deep breaths in through his nose and out through his mouth, pressing and releasing on her diaphragm to match his breathing. After a time she matched her breathing to his without the help of his hand.

He kept up the rhythm and began stroking her hair, whispering soothing nonsense words. He didn't stop even when he was sure she was still asleep and no longer in the grip of the nightmare. She relaxed against him and shifted closer, rubbing her back against his chest. Still, he continued their tandem breathing, whispering to her on the exhale. Eventually, his words began to make sense.

"I know ye think I don't want ye, and that's the way that it has to be…But God, Sarah, if I thought ye could be mine…if I thought for a second that I could keep ye…almost anything…"

***

…white and pink swirling around in a bright kaleidoscope. And the mumbling.

…They won't have you. I won't let them…

The dream was the same as always. The flowers floated above her in their colorful ballet. Her mother's voice rang in her ears feverish and urgent.

...let them take you away from me. I won't let...

...Mama?

Her chest felt tight, as if her airway was closing off with those familiar waves of terror and pain.

Then there was another voice, a familiar one. It flowed into her and eased the tension in her muscles, the tightness in her chest. She was still in the bath floating under the surface. Molly was still there too saying all the same words, but she could breathe now and she wasn't alone.

…I canna have ye for my own, but I can give ye…

...Not my baby...never take you...

…sent here for ye…I am yours…

Eventually even Molly's voice calmed. It was no longer frantic but soothing too. The voices blended together.

...won't do it to you...not if I...

…will always be here to protect…

...ruin your life like they did mine....

…will give my life for ye…

The sickening thunk of porcelain against flesh that Sarah had grown to expect never came. Instead she was warm and relaxed cradled and soothed by the voices.

"I'm always here." Somehow, that statement didn't scare her anymore.

***

Sarah washed her hands in the restroom sink and glanced up at her reflection. Last night had been one of the best night's sleep she could remember having in months, and it showed. There were no dark circles under her eyes, and she felt less foggy this morning than usual. Of course that might have been the shock of waking up in Dermot's arms. After that humiliating scene on the porch the night before, she would never have expected to find him snuggled up behind her in nothing but his sweatpants with the evidence of his, or at least his body's, opinion of the situation pressed up against her backside. She allowed herself just a few minutes to snuggle deeper into the cocoon of warmth that his broad shoulders made around her. Like the kiss the night before, it had felt entirely too good.

Lulled by the feel of him, she'd fallen half asleep again and turned to him. She was nuzzling the soft place just under the sharp line of his jaw when she felt him jerk awake. She'd be lying if she said she didn't get a little secret pleasure out of his stuttering embarrassment. She'd been talking in her sleep, and he'd been afraid she would sleepwalk right off the loft. That was the explanation he gave, and it actually didn't surprise her. She remembered having the dream last night, though it had felt different, and she didn't recall the terror that usually came with it. Maybe his being there had made the difference. She felt a stab of regret that it wouldn't be a regular occurrence.

It had been a morning full of careful avoidance and uneasy silences since then. They had packed up their clothes and gear, cleaned the cabin, returned the key, and were now just sitting down to breakfast at a diner, all with a minimum of words passing between them. They'd barely made eye contact. It was suddenly finding herself across a table from him in a restaurant and the prospect of a very awkward breakfast that had sent Sarah running to the ladies' room. She continued examining herself in the mirror, wondering if she could just stay there forever or at least until he was back on the other side of the Atlantic.

When she'd finished washing her hands and taken her time drying them, checked her teeth and hair in the mirror, and basically run out of stalling tactics, Sarah took a deep breath and pushed out of the door back into to dining room.

Dermot, as was his habit, was facing the dining room. She had noticed this little quirk of his before and chalked it up to his army training. Dermot almost never turned his back on a room full of people. Sarah tried to stop herself from admiring the ripple of his shoulders under his T-shirt, but it was a losing battle. There was no harm in looking, right?

While she'd been stalling in the restroom he had gotten a newspaper and had it folded on itself so he could read half a page but didn't block his view of the room. As he had last summer, he'd found the perfect solution for conquering her morning-after embarrassment. They could either use the paper as an excuse for ignoring each other, or it could be an icebreaker to put them back on solid footing. Stifling a sigh of relief, she slid into the booth across from him and started scanning the menu.

When their waitress returned, they ordered and Sarah grabbed the local section of the paper to occupy herself. They would have passed the whole meal that way in careful if companionable silence if Sarah hadn't looked up noticed the picture on the back of the section Dermot was reading. The picture was upside down and in slightly smudged newsprint, but Sarah could not have mistaken the smiling face of Bridget MacKenzie just above a headline that sent her fork clattering to her plate.

"Can I see that?" she asked with a nod at his part of the paper.

"Sure." He handed it to her, watching to see what had caught her attention.

Sarah flipped over the paper to find the article she was looking for. It was in the national section on page five just below the fold.

ME Beach Remains ID'd as Canadian Student

Ellsworth, Maine—Authorities have used dental records to identify the remains of a woman that washed ashore last month near Mosquito Harbor, Maine, as those of Canadian graduate student, Bridget MacKenzie. MacKenzie of Inverness, Nova Scotia, disappeared last August. Evidence suggests she was murdered. Authorities believe the body drifted along the Nova Scotia and Eastern Maine Coastal Currents before landing near Mosquito Bay. The time spent in the ocean destroyed the majority of forensic evidence. However Hancock County coroner, Josh Frellick, said there were marks on the body consistent with a homicide. These marks, according to Frellick, could not have been caused by ocean scavengers or the rapid decay that can occur in water.

"There are a number of injuries to the body that appear to have been caused by a knife. I'm confident she was dead before she went in the ocean," said Frellick.

According to Isobel MacKenzie, the victim's grandmother, MacKenzie left her home in Inverness, Nova Scotia, on August 17 to return to her studies at McGill University in Montreal but never arrived at her apartment there. Her roommates reported her missing on August 20. Canadian authorities have obtained security camera footage from a gas station in New Glasgow, Nova Scotia, showing MacKenzie purchasing gas. Investigators have canvassed possible routes between New Glasgow and Montreal but have found no further sightings of MacKenzie. It is believed that she never left Nova Scotia. There are currently no suspects in the case. Neither her grandmother nor her roommates were aware of anyone of MacKenzie's acquaintance who might mean her harm. The investigation is further complicated by the number of summer tourists who come to Nova Scotia for recreation.

"We could be looking for a needle that's already left the haystack," said Simon MacIsaac, the lead investigator in Nova Scotia.

The body was discovered four weeks ago on a rocky beach by an estate caretaker northeast of Mosquito Harbor. Identification of the body was delayed by its advanced state of decomposition and the fact that the body seemed to have drifted so far. Local police first attempted to match the body with missing persons reports up and down the Maine coast before widening their search to include reports as far north as Nova Scotia and as far south as Long Island, New York.

It is not unheard of for bodies from boating accidents around the southern coast of Nova Scotia to wash up on the shores of the Gulf of Maine. Although MacKenzie appeared to have been driving along the northern coast of Nova Scotia, authorities theorize that the body was dumped along the southern coast, thus allowing it to be picked up by the Nova Scotia current and driven into the gulf.

***

Dermot watched as Sarah's face went ashen and she clutched her fist to her mouth to stifle a gasp. When she finished reading, her fingers loosened enough to let the paper fall to the table. He wasted no time in grabbing it and reading the article. He struggled not to let his growing alarm show.

"Isobel MacKenzie, isna that the one that…?" He didn't have to finish the question. She nodded silently, tears pooling in her eyes.

Her hands shook as she pushed her plate away and reached for her coffee. He could hear the disbelief plainly in her voice. "We had dinner after I interviewed her grandmother. I remember thinking how much alike we were: close to our grandmothers, Gaelic speaking from a young age, ambitious…Jesus!"

Dermot reached across the table and took her hand, hoping to help still both their nerves. She turned her hand to his and gripped it. He tried to sound calmer than he felt. "When did ye meet her?"

Sarah searched her memory. "Early August. I'm not sure the exact date. I've got it written down."

Too close, he thought. "Did she say anything about anyone she'd met recently or anyone harassing her?"

She shook her head. "No, but we didn't really talk about that. We talked about growing up with our grandmothers and our plans for the future…she did seem kind of relieved about something. It was strange. Before I talked to her grandmother, she seemed friendly enough, but a little tense. After the interview she was totally relaxed. I guessed she'd been nervous about me talking to her granny, but the difference seemed like more than I would have expected."

"Did ye see or hear aught that might help them find who did this?" He dreaded and hoped for a positive answer.

He could see her wheels turning, trying to think of anything she had seen that might give them a clue. Eventually she just shook her head numbly. He could feel her hand trembling in his. "Alright. We're going. I'll drive."

He stood and pulled her from the booth, wrapping his arm around her in what he hoped was a comforting or reassuring gesture. They paid quickly and headed for the car.

CHAPTER TWENTY-ONE

"Do ye want to explain to me just how that girl was missing for more than a month an no one bloody told me?" Dermot fought hard to keep his voice level. He'd had hours of driving back to Chapel Hill and then another hour wading through James's gatekeepers to get the man on the phone. That made plenty of time he'd had to simmer, and now his temper was on full boil.

James, on the other hand, responded with calm assurance. "We honestly didn't think it was of concern. Her steward went missing about the same time she did. His last message to us was about Sarah's visit. We thought they had run off together. We learned about this the same way that you did."

"Did the grandmother not tell you that she was worried?" Dermot was incredulous.

"She did, but again we thought that Bridget had just learned that she wasn't the one. Maybe she needed to blow off some steam." Dermot wondered how James could keep his voice so even and calm.

"So the old women are important when they're telling ye what ye want to know, but when they need yer help ye ignore them?" Dermot growled low in his throat. "That's not the way it's supposed to work, James."

His cousin's tone took on a definite chill. "We have to have our priorities, cousin. She had her steward; WE have to focus on Sarah."

"And how can I protect Sarah if ye keep things like this from me, if I don't even know what might be coming?"

"Unfortunately, what we know about this case doesn't tell us much about what might be coming. We don't know who did it or who sent him. We only know that someone doesn't want us to find the Maiden enough to kill anyone they think might be the one. We've sent some investigators to Nova Scotia to learn what they can."

"Have ye checked in with the other one?"

"She's safe, and we've increased her security. I'm also sending you some backup who can watch Sarah for you when you need sleep. I need you to stay focused on keeping contact with her and making sure she comes home."

Dermot gave a frustrated sigh. "Maybe Walter is right. Maybe we should tell her. Then she'd understand and be easier to protect."

"No. You convinced me yourself that she wouldn't understand, not yet. I think you're right about that."

Dermot made a speaking grunt. "I also need information on a Grant MacDuff. He's a drifter in the Blue Ridge Mountains, probably in his sixties now. Sarah knew him when she was a child. I think he's a steward, but we should be sure."

"I'll let you know. If he's a steward, why isn't he with her now?"

"Exactly."

***

Sarah's nose twitched at the acidic laboratory air as she made her way down the basement hallway of Howell Hall. Not wanting to disturb anyone else who might be working on the brisk fall afternoon, she stepped as quietly as she could from lab to lab until she found the one where Jon was working. She studied him as she approached. Alone in the half-dark room, he sat perched on the edge of a stool at a high table. His head was bent over a lighted magnifier and his hands were manipulating something in a tray on the table. As she drew closer, Sarah could see that he was trying to fit together the pieces of a skull with a long, flat forehead. There were a couple of teeth still attached to the upper jaw. Tiny bits of turquoise were embedded in the teeth.

The sight made Sarah run her tongue along her own teeth, wondering what it would feel like to have them implanted with stones. She was so distracted by what he was working on that she didn't realize how close she was to him until he jumped, dropping the fragments he was holding, and the skull seemed to fall apart in the tray.

"Jesus, Sarah!" He was standing now on the other side of the stool with a steadying hand braced on the table.

"Sorry. I didn't mean to startle you." She gave a guilty shrug and looked down at the tray where the skull fragments lay like scattered pieces of eggshell. "I hope it's not damaged."

Jon let out a long breath. "It's okay. I was already trying to piece it back together."

They stood there looking at the skull and its many pieces in the tray, each searching for the next thing to say. Something to bridge the gap that he'd created.

Jon reached toward the tray and started rearranging his tools. His white gloved hands hovering over each one as if he couldn't quite remember what it was for. He cleared his throat and without looking at her asked, "Did you use the cabin?"

"Yes. Yeah, I turned it into a research trip…Actually got some work done…Thanks." She gave him a nod, still not quite looking at him.

"Good…good." They lapsed into more awkward silence. Sarah wished she had thought this through. His note had been so final that she didn't know how to start the conversation. This would have been so much easier over the phone, but he wouldn't return her calls. Finally, he said in a voice so soft she almost didn't hear it, "What do you want, Sarah?"

She looked up to find him watching her warily as if she were somehow dangerous. She was so startled by his look that she simply blurted it out. "I want to know why."

"I told you why." He picked up the tray and carried it to the counter that ringed the room, leaving her standing alone in the small pool of light cast by the magnifier.

"I mean why the change." She took a hesitant step toward him. "Two weeks ago, you waited at my door for hours to tell me that you wanted to work on our relationship, you planned this incredibly thoughtful weekend, and then you just dropped me. I want to know what changed your mind."

He was standing in shadow, but she could still see him bristle and shake his head. "You might ask your Scottish friend about that."

"What?"

Jon pushed away from the counter and stepped closer to her. His face was a mask of contempt. "Yeah, he paid me a little late-night visit. Pointed out to me how I didn't deserve you and continuing to work on things was just a waste of your time."

Sarah just shook her head. "You can't mean Dermot."

"Brown hair, blue eyes, built like a brick wall?" He stepped into the pool of light and his eyes told her that he didn't like admitting it. Still, he seemed to like telling her about what Dermot had done.

She fumed, stepping close to him. She'd always thought of him as taller, but today he seemed small. She had no trouble looking straight into his eyes, searching his face. "Let me get this straight. We've been dating for a year, and you gave up on me because some guy you've barely met told you to?"

That took a little wind out of his sails. He seemed to shrink further right in front of her. "Yeah, well. He can be very convincing."

She wondered just what kind of convincing and how much it had taken for Jon to give her up. She had given him the benefit of the doubt for over a year. She had defended him when her friends had questioned her taste and her patience with him when he always seemed to put work first. Now he gave her up that easily because someone told him to. He'd just proved them all right.

Sarah drew herself up and threw her shoulders back just like Granny had taught her to do when the people of Kettle Hollow had looked down their noses at them. "Well, it looks like Dermot was right. You don't deserve me, and you've clearly been wasting my time."

***

"Just who the HELL you think you are?" Sarah had found Dermot sitting at the usual table at The Daily Grind and punctuated her confrontation by slamming her bag into the chair beside him. She knew she should talk to him in private rather than making a scene, but her temper had gotten hotter and hotter with every step from the North Quad to The Pit. Meg, Barrett, and Monica were also sitting around the table and exchanged shocked looks.

Dermot, who'd been about to take sip of his tea, barely saved it from spilling down the front of his shirt. "What are ye on about?"

"I've just come from a very interesting conversation with Jon Samuels." She placed her hands on the arms of his chair and leaned close, her nose almost touching his. "I'll give you three guesses what he told me."

Dermot stood up abruptly, forcing Sarah to step back. He placed his tea on the table and with a hand on her elbow calmly steered her away from the tables and out of earshot, leaving their friends staring after them.

"I know ye're upset—" he began softly.

"Upset is far too mild a word for what I'm feeling right now." Her voice shook with fury.

He turned her to him and ran his hands down her arms in an effort to calm her. In his most soothing voice, he said, "Sarah, he's not right for ye, and I can't stand watching you try and try to make something work wi' him when he sees ye as nothing more than a pretty accessory for faculty events."

"You've barely met. How would you know how he sees me?"

He sighed. "I saw ye. The night of the mixer when ye had that fight, I was walking back to my apartment just as ye were coming out of the building."

"And what exactly do you think you saw?" Her tone was laced with skepticism.

Dermot softened his own voice. "I saw a man who used ye as a prop to get in wi' the married faculty and ignored anything ye had to contribute." Her head drooped, remembering the argument and how awful she'd felt. He stroked her arm again and stepped closer, softening his voice. "I saw a man who let ye walk home barefoot and alone in the dark rather than admit then and there that ye were right."

"He's not always like that. And it was an event for his department. If it had been a Folklore Department event it would have been different." Jesus! Even now she couldn't stop making excuses for him.

"Aye, he would hae found some excuse to avoid going." Dermot's voice hardened again and his accent got thicker.

Sarah tried to deny what he was saying, but she knew it was probably true. Seconds stretched by as they eyed each other fuming.

Dermot broke the silence. His voice was warm and smooth, but the soothing touches had stopped. He held himself apart from her, his hands tight at his sides. "You're worth more than Jon Samuels will ever be able to give ye. I got tired of seeing ye sell yerself short."

Sarah looked up at him. She couldn't be sure of what she saw in his eyes: love, friendship. She didn't know which she wanted to see, and after last weekend's revelation she didn't think it mattered. "What did you do that night?"

"Hmm?"

"That night when Jon and I argued, you said you saw us. You judge him for letting me walk home alone, but you let me do it."

He looked at his feet, a blush creeping across his face. Softly, he said, "No, I didn't. I reckoned ye wanted to be alone, so I followed you home to make sure ye were safe."

He'd followed her, and she'd never even known it. Part of her found that sweet—she had needed to be alone. Still there was a definite creep factor to being followed by someone she thought she trusted. The whole confusing situation became suddenly very frustrating to her. "I just don't get you! You say you've got someone else. You've made it imminently clear that you're not romantically interested in me, but you sure act all proprietary when it comes to my love life."

"I'm yer friend, Sarah." He stepped closer, but she stepped back.

"Not good enough!" Her eyes pierced him with a look of contempt. "A friend would be straight with me and not try to run my life behind my back. A friend would have let me deal with Jon myself not stepped in like some overprotective bully."

"Sarah, please." He looked pained. "I thought I was acting in your best interest. Can ye not see that?"

She shook her head, backing away from him. "No. No, I can't, and I'm done giving the benefit of the doubt to people who don't deserve it."

"Sarah—" he called as she retreated.

"Stay away from me, Sinclair. We're done." She stalked back to the table to grab her bag before heading toward the library.

CHAPTER TWENTY-TWO

Dermot settled down at the top of the cold stone steps of Wilson Library and leaned back against the base of one of the massive white columns. He positioned himself within sight of the door, but far enough to look like he was just enjoying a quiet fall afternoon on the steps of the great stone facade and not waiting for someone to come out. He was of course waiting for Sarah. She'd gone into the library a few minutes before, and any minute now she would be opening her assigned listening room to find the little bouquet of flowers that he'd left for her along with a note of apology. He hoped to be there when she left the library to gauge her reaction.

It had been six days since Sarah had talked to him or looked at him or even acknowledged they'd ever met…six days of awkward silences and sympathetic looks from mutual friends. He'd tried to "bump into" her in the halls, catch her leaving a class, or sitting with friends in The Pit, but she'd managed to avoid him every time. He had hoped to see her at Friday coffee at the little blue house, but Sarah had avoided that too. She'd spent the afternoon just a block away in her apartment doing heaven knows what. Once he was sure she wasn't coming, he'd spent his time across the street hiding in a mimosa bush and watching her door.

James's promised reinforcement had arrived in the form of Fleming Sinclair, another more distant cousin who had been in the army around the same time as Dermot. He'd shown the man around, taken his measure, and approved. They couldn't be too careful now, knowing that someone was out there looking for Sarah. While they didn't know each other well, Dermot at least felt comfortable enough with Fleming that he'd been able to go back to his apartment to sleep at night—not that he'd actually slept.

He had paced the length of his tiny apartment and cursed himself and cursed James for making him talk to Samuels and Samuels for telling Sarah. He'd nearly worn a trench in the concrete floor waiting for any word from Fleming about Sarah or from James about the MacKenzie case. He'd checked newspaper after newspaper, hoping to find some detail about Bridget MacKenzie's murder that would tell him what to expect.

The entire time he'd felt strung taut like a bow, like each breath he took couldn't quite fill his lungs. He knew this feeling wouldn't go away until he could talk to Sarah again and gain some kind of accord. He couldn't protect her if she wouldn't even talk to him.

But Sarah wasn't softening at all. Whenever he'd seen her on campus, she had looked the other way, sometimes even turned and walked the other way. That first day he'd tried to chase her down, but she had ducked into the ladies loo and waited him out. The note and flowers were his next attempt to at least get her to talk to him again. Best case: she accepted the flowers, read the note, and called him this evening. Worst case: she tossed both note and flowers in the bin and tried for a restraining order. It was a chance he'd have to take, and he was prepared to wait until the library closed to see the result.

He didn't have to wait that long. He was just mentally reliving the tongue lashing that Walter Stuart had given him when he told them about Sarah's order to stay away from her when one of the center doors opened and Sarah came stumbling out. She seemed as if she couldn't catch her breath and held a hand to her diaphragm as she took a few steps. She reached her other hand out, and it fetched up against one of the columns. She leaned over, gasping as if she might be sick and using her hand against the column for support. At first, Dermot thought she was ill and rose to help her. He stopped in his tracks when he saw the tears. Her face was turned away from him, but the tears caught the sunlight. Great falling drops glinted like diamonds until they dotted the marble around her feet. She didn't allow many, but they were enough. Almost as soon as he saw them, she straightened her back. Her face shifted, transforming from a mask of hurt and confusion to quiet resolve. She looked around as if to make sure no one had seen her moment of weakness.

Dermot ducked behind a column, feeling like a worm. He had put that look on her face. He had made those tears, and he knew he would make more. He turned his face to the quad in time to see Sarah descend the last few steps and turn toward home. She hadn't had the flowers. He stepped to the door and into the library. There in the ornate foyer on a table to the side lay the flowers he had left for her. His note was crumpled on the floor.

***

"Stupid, stupid! Get a grip," she told herself as her feet beat a path along the brick walk past the long, low chemistry building. "You know better. He's not for you. He told you himself…Damn him!"

She dashed an escaped tear off her cheek. All week she'd felt unmoored, like she'd been allowed to drift off course. She'd avoided Dermot like the plague in the hopes that this lost feeling would fade the less she saw him. He hadn't made it easy. He seemed to be everywhere she usually went: in The Pit, in Greenlaw Hall, the library, the blue house…Then he'd gone and pulled a stunt like today. She felt another angry tear trickle down her cheek.

The real kicker was that when she'd seen those flowers hope had exploded inside her and she realized that she wanted more than an apology. She wanted a confession, a declaration. She hated to admit it, but a part of her wanted him to say that it was over with the other girl and he wanted her. What she'd gotten had been a more than gracious apology and declaration of friendship. Now she was just as angry with herself for harboring that moment's hope as she was at him for his interference.

So she'd battened down the hatches on the storm of emotions that threatened the peace of the library and left. There was no way she would get any work done. She carefully carried the flowers that were too pretty to waste and laid them on a table in the front hall. Maybe someone would take them. At the least they would brighten the hall for a while. On the walk from the folk-life collection to the hall, she had unconsciously crumpled the note in her shaking hand. She was so focused on keeping her emotions in check that she didn't notice she'd dropped it until she heard it hit the floor. She stood there just staring numbly at the note on the floor and thinking about all the things that weren't in it, until she couldn't hold it in anymore. She made it as far as the door before the tears started.

Now her pounding feet made quick work of the walk back to Ransom Street as she alternately cursed Dermot and herself. Sarah was so busy castigating herself that she didn't realize she wasn't home alone until she bumped into Ryan coming out of her room. She stepped back and looked sharply at him.

He seemed surprised, but didn't look the least bit guilty. "Oh, Sarah…Hey."

"Uh…hey." She looked at him pointedly. "Can I help you with something?"

"Ah…" He didn't even blush at being caught coming out of her room. "I have a headache. Amy said you might have some Advil."

Sarah's eyes narrowed at the obvious lie. "Nice try. Amy knows I don't take medicine for anything."

"Uh…" He looked nonplussed at being caught out.

Sarah didn't have the patience or the self-control to be nice to Amy's erstwhile boyfriend this afternoon. She let all of her irritation with herself and with Dermot and Ryan come out in her voice. "If you have a headache, drink some willow bark tea and take a nap. And I don't care how much Amy likes you, if I catch you in my room again, I'm calling the cops."

"Hey, take it easy. I was just looking for some medicine. There's no need to get nasty." He held his hands up in a melodramatic gesture.

Sarah took a deep breath and let it out slowly, trying to summon up a little patience and keep the venom out of her voice. "Fine. Just stay out of my room."

Ryan looked at her closely, still blocking the doorway to her room. “Are you okay, Sarah? You looked a little flushed.”

She shook her head. She tolerated this guy because Amy was crazy about him, but she wouldn’t trust him to walk a dog. “Brisk walk. Chilly day. I’m fine.”

“Okay, okay. Rough week, huh?” His words should have sounded sympathetic, but Sarah thought it sounded like he relished the idea.

They stood there for a minute eyeing each other in awkward silence. After what seemed an age, Sarah waved a hand toward her room. “Do you mind?”

Ryan jumped as if he didn’t realize he was blocking her from her room and stepped out of the way. “Oh! Sorry.”

Sarah stepped into her room and dropped her bag just inside the door. She heard a breath behind her and turned to see Ryan still standing in the hall. He opened his mouth as if to say something more, but Sarah very deliberately shut the door on him.

***

Isobel MacKenzie

Inverness, Nova Scotia, Canada

Ms. MacKenzie,

I cannot tell you how sorry I was to hear of your granddaughter’s death. Though I only knew her for a few short hours, I felt a kinship with Bridget. I think our shared heritage gave us common ground and we made fast friends. She was so excited about the future that was ahead of her. I can only imagine how you must be feeling. You have often been in my thoughts since we met and even more so since I learned of your loss. If there is any help that I can offer you, please don't hesitate to let me know.

My phone number and address are below. Given the timing of Bridget's disappearance, I can only think it happened shortly after we met. I've included an extra copy of my contact information that you can give to the authorities if they have any questions for me.

Sincerely,

Sarah MacAlpin

Sarah was finally satisfied with the letter. She would take it tomorrow to get printed in Braille for Isobel to read. She'd written it in English, thinking that translating Gaelic to Braille might be a little too much to ask.

She'd spent a while going over her room with a fine-toothed comb, trying to figure out what Ryan had been after. Everything seemed to be in its place, and she'd had most of her research with her. She had laughed when she looked in her medicine cabinet. If he really had come in looking for Advil, he must have been frustrated to find nothing but an extra tube of toothpaste and some slippery elm throat lozenges.

When she had exhausted her search, she sat down to try to get a little work done, but she couldn't seem to get her mind off Dermot. She hoped writing the letter would be a diversion, and it was something she had been meaning to do for days. Between Ryan's invasion of her privacy and writing the sympathy letter, she had managed to calm down. She hoped she would get through the evening without more stress.

Thinking it would be nice to just veg out in front of the TV for an evening, Sarah poked her head out of her door and listened. She hoped Ryan was gone. She really would have to talk to Amy about him being in the apartment when they weren't home. All was silent, so Sarah crept down the hall and listened at Amy's door. No sounds came from inside. Sarah felt the muscles in her shoulders relax and she strolled back down the hall to the kitchen to forage for some dinner. She noticed that the message light on the answering machine was blinking. She pressed play.

"Yes, I'm calling for Sarah MacAlpin," came a very cultured sounding voice with a hint of a Scottish accent. "My name is Archie MacInnis and I am the managing director with Scots Preservation. We received your application for a position with our oral histories project and I would like to interview you. My telephone number is 44 131 586 7295. I look forward to speaking with you."

Sarah nearly dropped the bowl she was pulling out of the cabinet in excitement. Scots Preservation was the organization James had recommended. She had hastily sent off her resume and some samples of her work. She hadn't expected them to get back to her this quickly. Hands shaking with nerves, she reached for the phone, but then she glanced at the clock and realized it was about midnight in Scotland. Her return call would have to wait until tomorrow, but it now ranked right at the top of her to-do list.

With a little more energy than just a moment before, she went back to dishing out her soup. She took her bowl and a cup of tea over to the couch and settled in, feeling a great deal better about things.

CHAPTER TWENTY-THREE

"I must confess, Miss MacAlpin, when I got a recommendation for you from our…chief funder, I questioned Mr. Stuart's motives." Archie MacInnis's tone seemed to relax suddenly. Sarah had spent the last hour discussing the principles of fieldwork and answering the laundry list of questions MacInnis had directed at her with what she hoped was confidence and calm. When she had called at the time they had agreed on for the interview, he had started the conversation with rapid Gaelic, which Sarah was sure was meant to test her ability to speak it. She easily understood him and pointed out that she had learned Gaelic and English together as a child.

They had moved on to a laundry list of questions about her experience with fieldwork, her dissertation, and her knowledge of Scottish culture and oral traditions. Sarah felt good about her answers, and now that MacInnis seemed to have shifted from his tone from disapproving head master to colleague, she felt good about the interview. "Yes, I told Mr. Stuart that I was concerned about appearances. I appreciate him putting us in contact with each other, but I would much rather be judged on the merits of my work than on my acquaintance with him."

"Oh, I think you've more than answered the concerns that I had. Naturally, we'll have to speak with all the candidates before making a decision."

"Of course. Do you have a timeline for making that decision?" Sarah didn't want to sound impatient, but she wanted to know when she could expect an answer and when she should give up hope if things didn't work out.

"Oh, the next couple of weeks I should say to allow time for visa applications and paperwork and the like."

"Great! I'll hope to hear from you soon, then."

"Yes, thank you. We'll be in touch."

"Thank you so much for your time." Sarah heard the click on the other end that signaled he had hung up. She quietly laid the phone back in its cradle and looked around Donald's office. He had been kind enough to let her use it for the call so she wouldn't be interrupted. Like so many professors in the English department, it was crammed so full of books and papers that there was barely room for the desk and one chair. But Sarah wasn't seeing the shelves and stacks of books. She was seeing the heather covered hills and mist-shrouded crags of the Highlands that she only knew through pictures and her grandmother's stories. She felt good enough about the interview to truly believe for the first time that she would be going there. It felt so right.

"Well?" She was startled out of her reverie to find Donald poking his head through the door and watching her expectantly.

Sarah gave him a crooked smile and did her best impression of MacInnis. "Well, as you know, we'll have to talk with all the candidates before making a decision."

"Bollocks! How do ye think ye did?" he said, coming through the door and flopping down in the guest chair.

Sarah could only give him a beaming smile and a nod.

"S' math sin!" [That's good!] He burst out of the chair and came around the desk to throw a fatherly arm around her. "I knew it was a good omen having the interview on Samhain!"

"I don't know if that helped, but I'm glad I got it done early. Now I can relax the rest of the day."

"And hopefully the rest of the semester, aye?" He gave her another reassuring squeeze.

"Hmm…I feel good about it, but I don't want to count my chickens before they hatch." She slid around the desk and picked up her bag, giving Donald back his office.

"Agh! Ye did fine, I'm sure. I'll miss ye next semester," he said with a wink.

"From your lips to Archie MacInnis's ears," she said as she opened the door. "Thanks for letting me use your office, Donald. I shudder to think how this would have gone if I'd tried to do it at home."

"No worries," Donald said with a shrug as he turned his attention to a stack of student papers sitting nearest the center of his desk. Sarah stepped out into the hall and was pulling the door closed when he called her back.

"Oh, and Sarah?" She leaned back into the office and met his smiling blue eyes. "Happy birthday."

She returned his smile, thinking that it had been a great day when she had drawn Donald MacKenzie as her mentor. "*Tapadh leibh, a'Dhomnaill.*" *[Thank you, Donald.]*

***

For being the end of October, the weather was gorgeous, and Sarah couldn't help stopping as she passed from the shadow of the trees into the open area around The Pit to enjoy the feel of the sun on her face. There wouldn't be many more days like this before the weather turned cold. If all went well, this might be the last sunny Carolina day Sarah felt for a while. She opened her eyes and turned toward the tables at The Daily Grind and found Amy, Barrett, and most of the Ransom Street crew sitting in their usual spot. And just walking away in the other direction, as had become their habit over the past week, was Dermot. She stopped where she was, watching the tall figure making his way across The Pit.

After leaving the flowers in the library, he had stopped trying to talk to her and now avoided her as much as she avoided him. If he was in the library when she got there, he would shut himself in a private study carrel with his back to the door. He would leave the table at The Daily Grind before she had a chance to turn away herself, and he hadn't even tried to go to coffee at Ransom Street last Friday. Even with his avoidance, he managed to be a part of her circle of friends. He seemed to always be on the periphery. The chorus of, "You just missed Dermot," from her friends was becoming all too familiar, and she was starting to get used to the sight of his retreating back.

Today the loss of his friendship seemed even starker, as if there were a great six-foot-something hole torn out of the scenery. Today she had something to share, something he would be excited about, happy even. But the gulf seemed too wide, and Sarah wasn't sure what it would mean to let him back in. Whenever she thought about reconciling, she saw Jon's sneering face saying, "Why don't you ask your Scottish friend?" and she couldn't get past his interference, couldn't help feeling threatened by it.

Sarah continued to the table where her friends were sitting. She was determined not to let the riddle that was Dermot Sinclair ruin her day. After all, it was her birthday and Halloween, a day like none other in Chapel Hill, and she'd just had a great interview that could really move her forward in her research.

"Speak of the devil!" Barrett popped up from the table and pulled out a chair for Sarah as she approached.

"How did it go?" Amy burst out before Sarah could even set her bag down. Sarah was glad to see that Ryan wasn't with her for once. Maybe he was at the job he claimed to have. Sarah wondered about his true employment status, given the amount of time he spent at their apartment during the week.

"Very well. He seemed satisfied with my answers, and I feel pretty good about it. He said they should know in a couple of weeks. So keep your fingers crossed."

"Count on it, sister," Barrett said, giving her a reassuring pat on the back as he retook his seat beside her. Heads nodded all around the table as everyone's eyes suddenly shifted behind her. Sarah turned just as Joe, the cafe manager, arrived at their table with her usual coffee and a scone with a lit candle sticking out of the top.

Sarah couldn't help laughing as Joe set the plate in front of her and all of her friends screamed, "Happy birthday!"

She was glad they spared her the awkwardness of being sung to in the middle of the bustling campus center, but she appreciated their thoughtfulness.

"Thanks, ya'll." Sarah beamed at the group around the table.

"Make a wish!" Amy ordered.

It seemed such a silly thing for a grown woman to do, but her friends looked at her expectantly. Sarah thought of wishing for a resolution to the Dermot situation, but she was too unsure of what resolution would be the right one. So she closed her eyes and made a quick wish for the way to be cleared for her to go to Scotland before blowing out the candle.

They spent a good half hour in the usual way: relaxing, people watching, and drinking coffee. That day the conversation centered on what everyone would be wearing that night. Halloween in Chapel Hill was the closest thing to a Bacchanal. Franklin Street would be blocked off, and the crowd of young people from the university and anyone else who wanted to enjoy the festivities would come down in costume to party in the street. The police would try to ensure there was no violence involved, but there would be much drinking and debauchery. The best part, in Sarah's opinion, was seeing what people with plenty of intelligence and time but little money managed to come up with in the way of costumes. The previous year, a friend had made a very elaborate spider costume with duct tape, string, paint, and cardboard that he had dug out of a Dumpster. The more creative students would frequently take their costumes past appearance and into the realm of performance art. This year, the Ransom Street ladies were going as Muses: Meg as Thalia and Jane as Terpsichore.

"I'm going as Raoul Duke from Fear and Loathing in Las Vegas, because after the week I've had, I am due for a party."

"What do you mean the week you've had?" From the looks around the table, Sarah could tell she'd missed something.

"While you were camping out in the library, Todd broke up with Barrett," Amy said as if Sarah was the worst kind of friend for not knowing already. Sarah was startled by her tone, but not as startled as she was by the suddenness of the break-up. She looked at Barrett.

He waved a hand in the air as if to say it was nothing. "Never fear. I always land on my feet. What about you Amy, what are you going as tonight."

"Ryan and I are working on a joint costume. You'll see."

"What are you doing, Sarah?" Meg asked.

"I haven't really thought about it. I've honestly had my head down so much applying for this fellowship that it kind of snuck up on me. But I've got the better part of the afternoon off, so I guess I'll have to figure something out."

"Come by the house," offered Jane. "I'm sure if we all put our heads together we can come up with something."

"Thanks. I may take you up on that. I'm drawing a complete blank."

"Great. We'll be home around three," Monica said, looking at her watch. "In the meantime, I've got Italian."

Suddenly everyone was looking at their watches, and as they stood to leave the bell tower sounded the hour. As Amy was leaving, she left a small box wrapped in brown Kraft paper on the table. Sarah grabbed it and held it out to her. "Hey, Ame. You forgot something."

Amy stopped, looking back at the package and then at Sarah. "No, I didn't. He left that for you."

Sarah didn't need to be told who "he" was. She looked back up at Amy only to see that she was already halfway to the library and not sticking around to see what was in it. Sarah pulled the little package in front of her, flipping it around in her hand. The wrapping was plain and neat. He had written "Happy Birthday" diagonally across the smooth top. It was only a couple of inches square and probably contained jewelry of some kind. It looked right for earrings or a necklace. "Or a ring," a tiny voice inside her said.

She heard a gusty sigh beside her and realized that Barrett hadn't left. He was leaning back in his chair regarding her. Most people watching her like that made Sarah nervous, but Barrett was one of the few people who always made Sarah feel safe. He wore his many tattoos and piercings like a shield, but she saw past them. Maybe it was because, of all her friends, Barrett had seen the most tragedy when his abusive father had beaten and stalked his mother. They had both survived terror at the hands of their respective parents. They had always had an easy rapport, as if they each recognized the damaged places in the other. They didn't have to pretend as they did with some of their friends who hadn't been through that. He tilted his coffee cup at the box. "You gonna open it?"

Sarah dropped it on the table and grabbed her coffee cup, holding it with both hands. She leaned back to be closer to her friend. "Would you?"

He just gave her an understanding smile and reached over to rest a comforting hand on her arm as if he knew she had more to say.

"I mean, he told my boyfriend to dump me, Bear. And a few days later, he goes with me to the mountains acting like nothing's happened. And then when we kiss he puts me off and tells me he's got someone else. Who does that?!"

"Don't forget the part about climbing into bed with you," Barrett supplied, having heard the whole story from her shortly after her argument with Dermot.

Sarah gave a nod and emphatic gesture. “Talk about mixed messages!”

They fell into silence, Sarah staring at the box and Barrett watching a crowd gathering in The Pit. One of the street preachers who liked to shout their beliefs at the center of campus was drawing a crowd of students. It was always entertaining when religious studies majors got into heated debates with what everyone commonly called the “Pit preachers.” This one was spouting something about the New World Order and that the common symbol for an artificial sweetener was the “mark of the beast.”

“The thing is, Bear, if you take out the weird thing with Jon, I really liked him. I thought he was a good guy.” She sighed. “And I can’t condemn him for rejecting me if he’s doing it because he has someone else, even if he’s attracted to me. And if that kiss at the cabin is any indication, he’s really attracted to me. I can’t be mad if he’s trying to do the right thing.”

Sarah sipped her coffee and let her mental wheels turn. “But the thing with Jon was definitely NOT the right thing. I mean, that’s like something a stalker does.”

Barrett sat forward and looked at her. His voice was gentle. “I can’t answer it for you, honey. I’ve seen stalking first hand. Hell, my mom still has a restraining order, and it’s been twelve years since we’ve heard a word from my Dad. You’re right. That was a total stalker move. I’ve talked to him over the past few weeks,” he held up a hand to head off her interruption, “not specifically about you. I wouldn’t do that to you. Just in general conversation. He doesn’t seem crazy or dangerous. He asks about you, and Amy tells him how you are and that's it. He knows how you feel and he really seems like he doesn't want to hurt you."

He looked at her directly. His usual mask of sarcasm and easy wit was gone. "I wish I could tell you that he was a good guy and you should forgive him. It's hard to come by people you can really trust. But if he went after Jon like that, he could be playing us all. I want you to be happy, baby, but I also want you to be safe."

Sarah reached out and squeezed his hand. "Thanks, Bear. I don't think I could have had this conversation with anybody else. Are you sure you're okay?"

"I will be. You know it takes time, but you and I, we're survivors." He rose and grabbed his bag to leave. He bent down rested his forehead against hers. They stayed that way for several seconds. Sarah felt a tear land on her hand where it rested on the arm of the chair. Then Barrett sniffed and placed a chaste kiss on her forehead. "I'm always here for you, honey. Happy birthday."

With that, he rose and left her at the table alone to stare at the little box. In the face of his pain, her anger at Dermot didn't feel quite so keen. He was right. The question of forgiveness was something only she could answer. She just didn't think she was ready to answer it yet. Sarah rose too, thinking she would put in some time in the folk-life collection before heading back to Ransom Street. She picked up the box and dropped it into her bag. She would have to give it some more thought.

***

Sarah wasn't any surer about whether or not to open the gift when she got home that afternoon. She had spent a couple of hours going over transcriptions in the library, but she was ever-conscious of the small box in its plain brown wrapper in her bag. It was still there. She felt her knuckles brush against it when she reached into the bag to get her keys.

She unlocked the door, only to be struck by the almost overwhelming smell of flowers. As she turned to the kitchen she saw why. The entire pass through between the kitchen and the dining area was filled with the largest flower arrangement Sarah had ever seen outside of a hotel or funeral. It was made up of every kind of fall flower she could think of and whole branches of fall leaves. Colors ranging from ivory to gold to a deep reddish purple filtered light from the kitchen into the rest of the room, bathing it in a warm fall glow.

"Wow."

"Oh, hey!" she heard Amy call from the kitchen. She tried to look around the flowers to see her roommate and eventually spotted Amy's excited smile peeking around the bottom of the vase. "Pretty impressive, huh?"

"Yeah. You didn't get those from the flower ladies on Franklin Street," Sarah said, still marveling at the enormous display.

"Not me, lady." Amy plucked a card from behind the flowers and came out of the kitchen to hand it to Sarah. "These are for you."

Sarah looked incredulous. "Who would send me flowers?"

"Only one way to find out." Amy pointedly looked at the card.

Sarah slipped the tiny card out of its envelope and read the typewritten message.

I thought fall flowers would suit you best. Happy Birthday.

James

She handed the card back to Amy and returned her gaze to the flowers. Amy read the card and whistled. "He sure knows how to make an impression."

"Mmm…Well, I suppose he can afford it," Sarah muttered, still stunned.

"Come on. You can't tell me that deep down, there isn't a very girly part of you that's getting all gooey because Prince Charming sent you half a flower shop."

As if Amy had given it permission, that very small and much neglected girly part of Sarah that was flattered at getting flowers from a man started to bloom. "Yeah, okay."

Just then a knock sounded on the front door and Ryan strode in. He stopped at the sight of the flowers. "Damn! Who sent those?"

Amy laughed and said, "Sarah's future boyfriend, if he has anything to say about it."

"Amy!" Sarah could feel the blood rushing to her face.

"What? A man like him does not send flowers like that from across an ocean just because he wants to be your pal."

"Yeah, well, I've already told him how I feel about that," Sarah said acidly.

Amy just rolled her eyes. Ryan came to stand next to them, staring at the flowers. "So, who is this guy?"

The phone rang, and Amy answered it. Between her distrust of Ryan and James's notoriety, Sarah didn't want to tell him about James. She just shrugged and said, "A guy I met a few weeks ago."

Amy came to stand next to Sarah and held out the phone. She had a grin of pure devilry on her face and said without bothering to cover the microphone, "What do ya know? It's Hottie MacMoneybags himself."

Sarah closed her eyes tight, wishing she had not heard that. If she had been blushing before, she was sure she'd be the color of a fire engine now.

"Who?" asked Ryan, his teasing tone grating on Sarah's every nerve.

She snatched the phone away from Amy, giving her friend her best keep-your-mouth-shut look. Thinking it might be entirely too much to ask for her roommate to keep her friendship with the famous playboy a secret, she didn't stay to hear Amy's explanation. Instead she just marched back to her room and slammed the door.

Taking a steadying breath, she lifted the phone to her ear and said, "Please tell me you didn't hear that."

The laughter on the other end of the line confirmed that he had indeed heard Amy's crass name for him. When he managed to stop laughing, he tried to sound innocent, "Hear what?"

"Nothing. Nothing at all."

"Did you get the flowers?" His laughter was now little more than a pleasant chuckle; his smooth voice was a balm to her flaming embarrassment.

"Yes." She sighed, hoping she didn't sound too girly. "It really wasn't necessary to send every flower they had."

This time his laugh was a deep rumble that indicated more confidence than amusement. "I heard you've been working hard lately and thought you could use a little something to brighten things up."

"Oh, they definitely do that. They really are beautiful, and you're right I have been working hard."

"I understand you had your interview for the fellowship today." He sounded as if he were fishing for information.

"I did. Your sources are pretty good." Sarah wondered how he'd heard about what she'd been doing all the way in Scotland.

"Ah, well. Archie MacInnis called me after your interview. He had nothing but glowing things to say."

"Now you know you're going to have to tell me more."

"You'll have to wait for an answer just like everyone else," he teased.

"James Stuart, don't you dare call me with the inside scoop and then not tell me anything."

He laughed outright, and Sarah could almost hear him shaking his head. "You're the only person I know besides my mother and Uncle Walter who would dare scold me. It's incredibly refreshing. As for your Mr. MacInnis, I think the words he used were 'impressive,' 'fluent,' 'accomplished'...and something about getting an academic visa application in as soon as possible."

Every muscle in her tensed. "You'd better not be teasing me."

"It's not strictly his decision. It'll have to be voted on by a committee, but I'd say you made a conquest today. Archie will steer them your way."

Sarah held the phone away from her ear as she did a little victory dance. "James, this is fantastic!"

"I'm happy I was able to help," he said seriously.

Sarah picked up on his change in tone. "You don't sound so glad. Is everything alright?"

He paused long enough to worry her. "Of course. I'm fine."

"Okay." She didn't quite believe him, but he clearly didn't want to talk about it.

"Sarah?"

"Yes?" She tensed, thinking this was what she'd been expecting. This would be the moment when she learned the price of James Stuart's help.

"I want to talk about Dermot," he said in a gentle tone. It wasn't what she expected to hear.

She stiffened, gripping the phone tighter. "James, I really don't feel comfortable talking about that."

"I know and I understand. What he did was unconscionable. But...Sarah, he's miserable about it."

"Well, he should be." Her voice hardened.

"He was only trying to look after you." He sounded apologetic but firm. Sarah could imagine him using that tone in business meetings, bending adversaries to his plans with a minimum of conflict.

"Right. Well, I've been doing a fine job of looking after myself for a few years now, and I think I can manage one emotionally constipated archaeologist without Dermot Sinclair's help."

"I'm sure you can."

"No doubt it's hard for you to imagine being a woman alone in the world. But think about it, James. Which would you find scarier: a romantically lethargic, self-absorbed nerd or a big army veteran who corners said nerd in the dark and tells him to stay away from you?"

James didn't answer, just waited for her argument to lose steam.

She let out an exasperated sigh. When she spoke again, her voice was softer, smaller. "I miss him, James, but I can't trust him anymore."

"I hate having the two of you at odds. Even if you can't trust him, can you not forgive him?"

"I don't know," she whispered.

"I have to go, but I hate leaving you like this."

She shook off her moodiness and tried to perk up. "I'll be fine. It's my birthday, and some cute guy sent me flowers."

"Cute?" She was pretty sure from his tone that "cute" wasn't a word frequently used to describe him: dashing, gorgeous, hot, ridiculously handsome…but not cute. He sobered. "Think about it, Sarah. Will you?"

"I will." She matched his tone. "Thanks, James, for everything."

"My pleasure, love."

Sarah sat back against her headboard and relaxed for a few minutes. She could easily understand why women went all doe-eyed over James Stuart. On top of his almost criminal good looks, he made it very easy to like him even when he wasn't sending flowers and doing favors. He had a way of making her feel like the most important person in the world to him, although she was all too sure that if she were to look at the British tabloids she would see pictures of him with half a dozen different supermodels and starlets. He was an interesting friend to have, and he wanted her to forgive Dermot.

The little box that was still in her bag came to mind. She fetched her bag from where she'd left it by the door and brought it back to her room. She slit the tape with a fingernail and unwrapped the gift, liking the feel of the rough brown paper. She slid the top off the box. Resting on the little cushion inside was a small stone pendant about the size of a quarter. It was crudely carved into the shape of a boar.

Sarah lifted the necklace up by its simple silver chain and let the pendant dangle in the light from the window. It swung back and forth, and the tiny boar appeared to be rearing back and charging forward. As peace offerings went, Sarah thought it was particularly fitting. She remembered the Dermot of Irish legend, Dermot's namesake, who was killed by a boar.

CHAPTER TWENTY-FOUR

"Where did you get this bright blue eyeliner anyway?" Sarah called as she watched herself apply the makeup in the mirror of the cantaloupe colored bathroom in the blue house. She'd headed over there a couple of hours earlier to get ready for the evening's festivities.

"I think Monica picked it up for the eighties dance. I'm sure she doesn't need it anymore." Jane was just outside the door in the dining room putting the finishing touches on a cardboard lyre. Her toga showing off her lithe dancer's body.

"Please, use it!" Monica's muffled voice came from her room as she was getting dressed.

"Thanks." Sarah lined an eye in bright blue, drawing the line out past her eye and into a decorative spiral at her temple. She carefully painted the other side to match the first. After running through a few ideas with the girls, she had let her costume be inspired by Dermot's gift. She was to be a Celtic princess. They found a mustard colored sheath dress that had the appearance of being naturally dyed and sufficiently primitive. Some loose-woven green fabric normally used as a table cloth was repurposed as a shawl. Sitting on top of the toilet tank behind her was a crown that Sarah had fashioned out of fall leaves and twigs. She had even borrowed some of the colorful flowers that James had sent and wove them into the crown.

Done painting her face, Sarah leaned back and began painting the top of her chest, which was left exposed by the low scoop neck of the dress. She began with a classic Pictish upturned crescent then added what scholars called the V-bar. Sarah always thought it looked like a broken arrow or the trajectory of an arrow bouncing off its target. She painted the two ends of the arrow just at her collarbone on either side, and the bent point of the arrow just above her heart. She smiled. "No arrows are going to catch me today. They'll just bounce right off." She added decorative arches and spirals inside the crescent.

Sarah picked up the boar pendant from the soap dish above the sink and put it on, satisfied to find that the boar rested just inside the center arch of the crescent. She bent over and teased the underside of her loose curls. She righted herself and liked the way the soft curls billowed wildly around her head. Turning to add some finishing touches, she was struck by the sight of the crown sitting on top of the toilet lid. She stared at it, remembering a day twenty years ago. Her recurring nightmare meant that she never forgot that day, but she usually avoided thinking of it when she was awake.

She quietly closed the bathroom door, not wanting any intrusion. She picked up the crown and sat down on the closed toilet, holding the crown in her lap. She smoothed some of the leaves and flower petals, finding comfort in their cool silkiness.

In her mind, Sarah heard her own voice high and clear as it had been when she was a little girl. *"Tha mi a' dol a dhèanamh crùn dhuibh!" [I'm going to make you a crown!]* And she had made one, of damp vines and brown oak leaves and rue anemones like little pink and white stars. She stood on the trunk of a fallen tree to put the crown on her mother's head. That was the moment it had all changed. As a girl she had thought her mother looked beautiful, but it was hard for her now to picture her mother smiling or laughing.

Sarah blinked back tears and swallowed past the lump in her throat as she looked at this new crown in her hands. The profusion of bright leaves and flowers contrasted the dark, sharp twigs. It seemed the most natural thing in the world for Sarah to stand in front of the mirror and put it on her head. She examined herself in the mirror. After being lost in her childhood memories and with the elaborate makeup, she almost didn't recognize herself, like she was distilled into a harder, fiercer, stronger Sarah. She recalled the words she'd said to her mother years ago. "*Tha coltas bànrigh an t-sìthein oirbh.*" *[You look like a fairy queen.]*

As the words left her lips, it felt as if all the air was sucked out of her lungs with them. The bright orange walls of the bathroom faded to darkness as her heart raced and the edges of her vision went black. All Sarah could see was her reflection complete with the crown, and blue Celtic lines seemed to glitter in the darkness. Behind her the light returned, but the room reflected in the mirror was no longer the bright little bathroom, but the drab beige hospital room where her grandmother had died. She could see her granny lying propped up against the pillows, her face shone with pride. She had been so frail in those last days after her heart attack. Her skin was thin as paper and lacked the usual tan she got from working outside. She was pale, with an almost gray cast that seemed to spread out from the dark circles around her eyes. Still, her voice was clear and strong.

"Arbirainn i finaidh banaon chann ur afoinn

Ach ur pham chann ur n fawur breanain."

They were the last words Granny had spoken to Sarah, the final words of the song that Sarah had spent the last few months chasing, but she had no idea what they meant. Sarah had been furious at the time. This woman had taught her so much, had raised a poor, motherless, miserable girl with such strength and patience. Yet her last words to Sarah had been gibberish in some language that no one seemed to understand.

"I don't understand, Granny! What are you saying?" Sarah felt as if she screamed the words, though her lips didn't move.

"*Ach ur pham chann ur n fawur breanain,*" Granny said again. Her look was fierce, as if Sarah should understand the words.

Her grandmother said nothing more. She nodded slowly. Sarah looked at herself in the mirror again, wondering what her grandmother could mean. Her eyes went up to the circlet of flowers and leaves on her head. She looked back over her shoulder to where her grandmother had been, but Granny and the hospital room were gone and she was once again surrounded by orange walls.

Sarah drew in and slowly let out a deep breath, watching the room around her through the mirror. She closed her eyes and tried to settle her pulse and her nerves. Part of her hoped that the image in the mirror stayed exactly as it was, and part of her hoped to see her grandmother again. When she opened her eyes there was no change. She was in Chapel Hill not Boone, at her friends' house not the hospital, and no matter how many questions she had for Granny, she wasn't going to get any answers tonight.

She was jolted by a knock on the door as Monica's voice came through the door, "Almost ready, Sarah?"

"Yeah. I'll be out in a sec." She hoped she didn't sound too shaken.

***

"Oh, this is just bloody fantastic," Dermot muttered to himself as he stepped onto Franklin Street. The street had been blocked off from in front of the Post Office and courts building down to where it met Columbia Street. The four-block space in between was filled with people in costume by the thousands. Music spilled out of the bars along the way, and more than a few people were dancing in the street. Dermot hadn't known there were this many people in Chapel Hill.

He was glad that he and Fleming had invested in two-way radios with earphones. There was no way they'd be able to find each other in this mess otherwise. He wondered how he was supposed to find Sarah in the crowd. The only consolation was that she and her friends seemed to be moving in a big group. Fleming was following them from Ransom Street on the opposite side of Columbia. Dermot would make his way down Franklin and meet them. Then he and Fleming planned to work together, watching her back as she travelled. If he couldn't be right next to Sarah, then he was glad to have another set of eyes to keep watch in the crowd.

According to Fleming, she had left Ransom Street about ten minutes ago with four muses in white togas. He hoped the ladies from the blue house would make her easier to find. His radio buzzed, and he lifted it cupping his hand around the microphone to talk. "Go."

"We've picked up two more, the roommate and a guy dressed as a cowboy. I think it's the roommate's bloke," Fleming's voice sounded in his ear.

"Location?"

"Columbia, in front of Frat Court." A good listener, Fleming had picked up on the local names for campus landmarks quickly.

"Right. I should be at Franklin and Columbia in under five."

"Copy."

Dermot quickly shouldered his way through groups of cheering partiers to the rendezvous point. He had just reached the corner when he heard his name called. On the other side of a group of students in Starfleet uniforms he saw a wiry figure working its way toward him. As he got closer, he realized it was Sarah's friend Barrett dressed for weather much hotter than October in tan trousers and wildly patterned shirt with a cartoonishly wide collar. Gold-tinted sunglasses and a white hat completed the odd ensemble.

"What kind of a costume is that?" Barrett scanned Dermot's jeans, T-shirt, and flannel shirt.

Dermot looked down at himself and shrugged. "American college student?"

"Yeah? What's with the earpiece?" Barrett cooked his head to the side, eyeing the earpiece in Dermot's ear.

"Oh!" Dermot yanked out the earpiece and shoved it in his pocket. "Uh…a mate's visiting from home. Just wanted to keep in touch in the crowd."

Barrett studied him closely over the rims of his glasses. "Right. Ya know most people would just stay together or shout."

"Aye…well…" Dermot mentally fumbled about for an explanation.

"Sweetmeat!" Barrett spotted someone behind Dermot. Turning to see what Barrett had seen, Dermot saw the four muses with Sarah looking like a goddess in the middle of them. Amy, dressed in all black, threw herself at Barrett.

"Honey, you're going to get lost in this getup," Barrett scolded her.

She stepped behind Ryan, who looked as if he'd walked right out of a spaghetti western, and quickly disappeared behind her taller boyfriend. Cumberland struck his best gunslinger pose, and Amy's voice came around him, singing the iconic theme from The Good, the Bad, and The Ugly. After the first couple of measures she peeked over his shoulder and gave everyone a wink. The group erupted in laughter.

Barrett turned his attention to Sarah and waved a hand at her décolletage. "Oh, girl! Please tell me you're going to make that blue paint permanent."

Sarah blushed and said, "Really? You think I could rock this look for good?"

"Absolutely!" Barrett gave her an exaggerated nod.

"How are you? Okay?" she asked her friend, concerned. Dermot wasn't sure why.

"Great. Ready to party," Barrett shouted and moved on to gushing over the Muses.

Dermot felt rooted to the spot. Everything about her costume from the simple dress to the markings to the crown looked like she was born to it. She was captivating, but she might as well have been wearing a target.

When Barrett had drawn attention to the neckline of her dress, Dermot couldn't help but notice that she was wearing the boar necklace. It rested against her skin just in the center of the crescent. Sarah stopped laughing as he lifted his eyes to find her looking his way. He said just loud enough for her to hear. "*Oidhche Shamhna math leat, a Mhòrag.*" *[A good Samhain to you, Sarah.]*

She blushed slightly and returned his greeting before looking away nervously. "*Leatsa cuideachd.*" *[You too.]*

They stood, awkwardly avoiding each other's eyes until the Muses came up and the whole group moved on down the street. He watched her, letting her get just far enough ahead of him. He pulled the earpiece out of his pocket and was just putting it in his ear when Fleming gave him a gentle elbow in the ribs as he walked by. His partner walked across Franklin Street and followed the group from a safe distance. Dermot stuck to his side of the street, doing the same. At least the four girls in white togas made the group easy to spot.

For the next two hours, Dermot and Fleming followed the group up and down Franklin Street and in and out of bars. The muses danced and caroused when they came upon others dressed as Greeks. Barrett rather convincingly pretended to hallucinate all manner of colorful things, and Amy and Cumberland dazzled everyone by recreating their western scene. Twice, blokes dressed as knights knelt before Sarah and asked her to bless their cardboard swords. Several Wiccans stopped her to drool over the authenticity of her markings. Generally speaking, all appeared to be having a good time.

After another pass down the street, the group came to a stop at the plaza in front of the courts building. Here a group had formed a drum circle, and more than a few partiers were dancing to their tribal rhythm. The Muses fit right in with the Greek Revival facade of the stone building and were invited into the circle to dance. Naturally, the ladies of Ransom Street couldn't resist, leaving Sarah on the outside watching and enjoying the spectacle.

Henderson Street, which ran next to the court building, marked the end of the blocked-off area of Franklin Street. Having blocked off one of the main bus routes, the police had reestablished a bus stop in front of the North Quad on the opposite side of Franklin Street from the plaza. Buses regularly came up Henderson and turned onto Franklin to deposit and pick up more people. Dermot could well imagine the volume of students and townies alike using public transport on a night like this. He could also imagine the frustration of the drivers dealing with traffic and busloads full of half-drunk kids in costumes.

He scanned the corner, taking in the flow of traffic. He only had his eyes off of Sarah for two seconds, but that was long enough for Dermot to lose sight of her. She had been standing with Barrett near the edge of the crowd closest to the Henderson Street. He wasn't sure what had happened to Amy and Cumberland. He buzzed Fleming on the radio. "Go."

"Have ye got eyes on her? I lost her," he asked, trying to keep his voice steady despite his rising alarm.

"I've got her. She's still with that weird guy." Fleming's calm, business-like tone reassured him.

"Where?" Dermot was still looking in the direction where he had last seen her.

"Crowd shifted. They're closer to Henderson."

Dermot began walking toward the corner, so he could see the edge of the plaza. He looked down Henderson Street and saw a bus turning in their direction two blocks away. "I don't like this crowd so close to the street. Stay close to her."

"Right."

Dermot continued scanning the crowd at the street's edge, trying to spot Sarah. From the corner of his eye, he noted how fast the bus was coming up the street. About halfway up the block there appeared to be a scuffle going on in the crowd with much pushing and shoving. Dermot felt the hairs prickling on the back of his neck. Just as the bus reached the point on the block where the crowd was roiling, a scream cut through the buzzing noise, and a figure in green and gold leaned back impossibly far into the street.

Sarah! Dermot's blood turned to ice as panic gripped him. Sarah seemed to hang in the air just in the path of the oncoming bus, her head showing in stark silhouette against the bright headlights. Her mouth was open as if she was screaming, but between the drums and crowd and the blood rushing in his ears, Dermot couldn't hear her.

The driver laid on his horn, as if that could stop her from falling in his path. He began to shove his way through the crowd. Too far! She was too far for him to get to her, and in this crowd probably too far for Fleming as well. Dermot pushed on, his heart in his throat. Suddenly, an arm reached out and grasped the front of her dress and shawl in a tight grip. Sarah was yanked back into the crowd just inches before the bus would have hit her.

Dermot continued working his way toward her as he tried to force himself to breath evenly. In all, the incident probably took no more than a few seconds, but it had been an eternity for him. When he got to her she was in Barrett's arms, looking thoroughly shaken. Her crown had been knocked off and hung half off the curb. Barrett was giving dirty looks over her head into the crowd. Amy was standing next to them, looking stunned and confused.

Dermot bent and retrieved the crown, holding it out to her. "Are ye alight?"

"Yeah." Sarah took the crown without looking at him. Her other arm was wrapped tight around Barrett's waist.

"What happened?" Dermot looked at Barrett, whose earlier feigned madness had disappeared behind a mask of concern and anger.

"Amy's asshole boyfriend picked a fight with some huge guy and almost knocked Sarah into a bus."

"Hey!" Amy objected. "He didn't know that was going to happen."

"Well, he sure didn't do anything to prevent it, getting in that guy's face like that," Barrett snapped.

"Where did he go anyway?" Amy said, looking around for Ryan.

"He probably took off rather than get his ass kicked by that big dude," Barrett grumbled.

Dermot turned his attention back to Sarah, leaning down closer to her ear. "Are ye sure ye're not hurt?"

"I'm fine." She straightened up, trying to pull herself together, but she still kept her arm around Barrett. She gave Dermot a nod, looking at him for the first time, and for the first time in weeks she didn't turn away from him. She even seemed to lean toward him, as if she would slip into his arms to find the safety she needed after such a close call. Dermot lifted a hand to her arm and felt a rush of hope that maybe she would forgive him. Then the relief on her face was replaced by suspicion. Sarah pulled away from him as much as the crowd would allow. "Wait. Were you following me?"

He straightened up immediately, realizing his mistake. He shook his head. "No…I was on my way home, and I saw ye fall."

She just looked up at him, obviously not buying the excuse. Cursing himself for a liar, Dermot pointed over her shoulder toward his apartment building, which luckily was only a block away. "My building is right there. Remember?"

Sarah followed his finger to look at his building. When she turned back to him, there was still enough suspicion in her eyes to have Dermot grinding his teeth. Suddenly all the frustration of the last few weeks and the terror of the last few minutes came spilling out. His voice lashed like a whip-crack, his accent clipped and hard. "Aye, that's right. I was following ye. Because…what…I want to steal yer work? Or am I just obsessed wi' ye? Aye, I canna stand to be without ye, so I followed ye. Isn't that why I've not tried to talk to ye for weeks? Isn't that why I've spent the last two weeks trying my best to stay out of yer way? Think for a minute, Sarah! If I were that obsessed wi' ye, why wouldn't I have had ye weeks ago when ye threw yerself at me?"

Her eyes flared wide with hurt and Barrett and Amy gasped, their eyes flicking to Sarah and back to Dermot. Shit! He wished he could take it back, but the words hung there in the air between them, calling to mind the passion of that kiss at the cabin and the comfort of sleeping with her in his arms. His anger spent, his shoulders sagged with shame and he held out a hand to her. "Sarah, I'm sorry."

She shrank away from him as Amy slipped an arm around her shoulders, and Barrett stepped in front of them, blocking Dermot from getting any closer to Sarah. The look of disappointment on his face mirrored how Dermot felt. How could he have embarrassed her like that? Dermot half expected the smaller man to hit him. God knows Dermot would have taken a shot if their positions were reversed. But Barrett just stared at him with eyes as cold as stone. His voice was heavy with disapproval. “I think you’ve said enough, man.”

“Aye. More than enough.” He looked over Barrett’s shoulder to see Amy and Sarah walking away into the crowd. “I didna mean—”

“But you did, dude.” Shaking his head. “Just leave her alone.”

CHAPTER TWENTY-FIVE

Donald's house was just off Boundary Street. The lavender Victorian cottage was dwarfed by the giant oaks and poplars surrounding it. This was Sarah's second Thanksgiving at Donald's, and she was looking forward to it. Despite the turkey that tasted like sawdust and the instant mashed potatoes, there was always plenty of good conversation and wine. The guest list last year had consisted of a few faculty and graduate students who had little family or were too far from home to visit on the long weekend. That's how Sarah had been invited last year, and by the method of invitation this year—which consisted of a quick "See you Thursday?"—she could tell that Donald had taken her attendance as a given. She felt a little warm at the thought of this holiday adoption.

She stepped onto the front porch and rang the doorbell. The plastic handle of her grocery bag was cutting into her wrist, and she looked down to make sure its contents hadn't shifted. No, the sweet potato pie was still upright and snug against the bottle of burgundy. She smiled, giving a silent salute to her grandmother, who had told her never to go to a party empty handed…not that they'd gone to many parties. She heard the door creak and looked up, expecting to find Donald looking disheveled from hours in the kitchen. She froze, the muscles in the back of her neck tightening in surprise.

Standing on the other side of the storm door looking equally shocked was Dermot Sinclair. She began backing away as if he were a snake about to strike. "Sneaky Donald has been at it again," she thought. She managed to turn just in time to avoid tripping over the first of the porch steps. Her feet hit the sidewalk hard, and her legs wanted to run. She managed to control that impulse for the sake of dignity but began walking swiftly away nonetheless.

Dermot was quick and quiet and managed to get a hand on her wrist before she reached the street. "Sarah, wait."

"No, I don't think so," she snapped, trying to pull her arm from his grasp.

"Please." He tightened his grip. "I didna know you would be here, but I'm glad ye are."

Sarah succeeded in retrieving her arm with a sharp twist. "I'll just bet you are. You haven't been able to stalk me for three whole weeks. Lord knows what I could have been doing in all that time." Still stinging from her Halloween embarrassment, she spewed sarcasm at him as if it were made of verbal bullets. "How much trouble do you think a girl can get into in three weeks?"

Not wanting to disturb the house by shouting, he seized her shoulders and gave her a good hard shake, which instantly shut her up. When she was quiet he looked into her eyes. He was determined, but not angry. "I shouldna have said those things. I betrayed yer trust, and I'm sorrier than ye'll ever know."

He gave her a moment to respond, but she just stared at him. "I shouldna have said anything to your Jon either. I'm sorry."

"Well…" She regarded him with a critical eyebrow arched high. She'd been nearly on the point of forgiving him before his Halloween outburst. As much as his words had hurt and embarrassed her then, she still missed having him for a friend. "I'm glad you see it my way."

He studied her for a few seconds. "Forgiven?"

"Let's call it a temporary probation." Her tone was acid, but she didn't seem angry anymore. She cocked her head toward one of his hands still gripping her shoulders. "You want to let go?"

"Not until ye promise me that ye'll come inside. Donald's cooking us a fine meal, and he'd be hurt if ye didna stay."

She gave him that half-smile that made her eyes twinkle with mischief. "You've obviously never tasted Donald's turkey."

"That bad, is it?" Sliding a hand down her arm, he took her bag as they turned back to the house.

"Just take my advice and use a lot of gravy."

"Right."

He ushered her back onto the porch and reached around to open the door, when she turned back to him, her wicked smile still in place. "You know just because I've accepted your apology doesn't mean you're off the hook. You're still going to pay for interfering."

That was the girl he knew. He looked down at her and matched her grin. "Ah, well. I've no doubt about that. Just mind the punishment ye choose. I might enjoy it."

The creaking of the door caught Donald's attention in the kitchen. He poked his head into the hall. Sarah thought she noticed the corners of his mouth creep up just a bit more at the sight of them together. "*Failte, A'Mhórag!*" *[Welcome, Sarah!]*

"*Feasgar math, A'Dhomhnuill.*" *[Good evening, Donald.]* How's the turkey coming?" Dermot took her coat and she retrieved her bag before following a distinctly charred smell to the kitchen.

Donald looked like something from a home ec teacher's nightmare. His auburn hair and fair skin were powdered with something white, which Sarah hoped was flour, and his "Kiss the Cook" apron was smeared with stains in a range of colors that Sarah did not want to contemplate. He beckoned her to him without fully turning from the stove. He was stirring something brown and thin with odd lumps in it. A box of cornstarch lurked in silent foreboding by his left hand. Sarah tried to ignore the questionable substance as she leaned in and planted a kiss on an unpowdered spot on his cheek. "I brought wine and pie."

"And it's a good thing too. I'm sorely in need of wine, and I fear my pumpkin pie is nae more than pumpkin soup in a shell." He gave her a sheepish shrug.

"I had a feeling." She winked at him.

"Ach, ye know me well." He gave her a fatherly smile.

"What's that you're working on?" She tried not to seem too concerned while looking at the bubbling lumpy liquid.

"Weel, I forgot to get gravy at the store, so I thought to make it." He studied the contents of the pan suspiciously. "It isna going well."

Sarah eyed the pan and the box of cornstarch. Scanning the counter, she noted the seeming lack of flour. "Did you put any flour in it?" she asked as gently as possible.

"Flour, well, no. I didna think of that."

"It's kind of important," said Sarah.

"Do ye think we can save it?"

Taking the spoon from him, she stirred, breaking open some powdery lumps of cornstarch. With a sigh, she said, "Sorry, I think this one's beyond my help."

Donald looked grim. "We canna do without gravy."

Sarah thought for a moment, and with a quick nod took command. "First, Dermot can open that bottle of wine and pour us some. Put that pot in the sink to soak. Do you still have the giblets from the turkey?"

Dermot, who had come in during the gravy consultation, jumped into action, searching drawers for the corkscrew. Donald retrieved the bowl in which he'd placed the giblets and Sarah took a deep breath. "I haven't done it in years, but I think I can remember how to make giblet gravy."

Seconds later, Dermot handed her a glass of wine. "What can I do?"

The doorbell rang. Sarah smiled at him. "You can get the door and keep them away from the kitchen until it smells better."

Dermot answered the door and admitted Kendall Johnson, a young anthropology professor. He ushered Kendall into the living room and poured him a glass of wine. Sarah made quick work of chopping up the giblets and soon had the gravy started. As she was stirring it, two more guests arrived, and Dermot did well at keeping them out of the kitchen. Donald, on the other hand, had stayed very much underfoot, constructing a tray full of hors d'oeuvres. When she'd finished the gravy, he thrust the tray into her hands and ordered her out of the kitchen.

"I'll take care of the rest. You go and have a good time," he said.

She was reluctant to leave Donald to his own devices in the kitchen, but she had very little choice. He firmly rejected her offers of further assistance and nearly pushed her into the living room. It only took a brief stay in the living room to convince Sarah that she would be much better off in the kitchen. The guests consisted of Johnson the anthropology professor; Lucy King an English professor; Anne Woodcliff a painfully shy graduate student; and Dermot. They were silent as Sarah entered the room, and after everyone had tried the hors d'oeuvres and politely commented on them they fell again into the awkward silence of people barely acquainted with each other. Sarah and Dermot both attempted to make conversation, but they were unsuccessful in maintaining it. After nearly half an hour of sitting and listening to little more than the clock ticking on the mantel and the sound of five people breathing, Sarah was relieved to see Donald poke his head through the door and beckon her into the kitchen with a quick jerk of his head.

"What's going on out there?" he asked.

"Nothing," she said in frustration. "They're just sitting there like bumps on a log. We tried to get chatty, but no one seems interested in small talk."

"Damn," Donald hissed. "Well, we're sunk. The turkey is ruined. Not even yer good gravy can help it. We'll have to order out."

"Who's delivering today?"

"I checked. The only places delivering are pizza, and I dinna think that will do. The other options are Greek, Chinese, or Indian, and I'll have to pick it up."

Sarah glanced back into the living room and surveyed the guests. "Let's go for Indian. Be sure to order plenty of vegetarian dishes, just in case. We have to do something about the funeral home atmosphere, though. Do you have any board games?"

Donald's eyebrows knit in consternation.

"No, of course you wouldn't." Sarah tapped her fingers thoughtfully on the counter.

"Go on back in there. I'll order the food and try to think of something." Donald squeezed her elbow and directed her back to the silent room.

Dermot gave her a concerned look that she, not wanting to spill the beans about the change in plans, could only answer with a shrug and subtle eye roll. Moments later, a clean and apron-less Donald strode into the room brimming with confidence.

"Well, I'm sorry to say I've quite ruined the turkey, but I've taken the liberty of ordering some Indian food for us all. I hope that's alright," he said, laying on as much charm as he could.

All nodded and mumbled their assent that Indian food would be fine.

"Still, I canna leave ye here in silence. Yer all academics, so I'll give ye a topic." He thought for a moment, surveying the group. When his eyes lit on Dermot, he made his decision. "Alright, Lancelot and Guinevere, Tristan and Isolde, Diarmaid and Grainne. Discuss."

And with that, he left.

Kendall was the first to speak up. "I know the first two stories, but I don't believe I'm familiar with that last one. Can anyone enlighten me?"

Sarah looked at Lucy and Anne, who seemed equally ignorant of the legend. She gave the present-day Dermot a coquettish smile. "Dermot, would you care to share with us the story of your namesake?"

He studied her for a moment, and then said with a slight bow. "I will have to bow to your greater skill as a storyteller."

"Alright, I'll tell it to you just as my grandmother told it to me." Sarah took a long, slow sip of her wine, savoring it. She began her tale with a clear voice, her western Carolina accent just slightly more pronounced.

"Long, long ago the high king of Eire, Cormac Mac Airt, employed a great army called the Fianna. They were the boldest, bravest, and fiercest warriors in the land, and their leader was the boldest, bravest, and fiercest of them all, Fionn Mac Cumhaill. Now, Fionn was legendary even then. The bards sang songs about him, and many noble families sent their sons to serve under him in the Fianna. Some even said that because the army followed only him, he was more powerful than the king himself. Of course Cormac didn't like to hear that, but he knew it was true." She gave Lucy a conspiratorial smile.

"One winter a terrible fever struck Fionn's home, killing both of his wives. The Celts could have multiple wives back then. So the spring found the leader of the Fianna lonely and wondering what woman in Eire could be worthy of such a great man. That is, until he saw Grainne. She was the most beautiful and captivating woman in Eire, and she was the king's daughter. Cormac, knowing which side his bread was buttered on, had to give in when Fionn announced his intention to marry Grainne. Once again, the great leader of the Fianna was to have his way.

“Grainne, however, had other plans. She had no interest in marrying a man she hardly knew, much less one who was old enough to be her father. So she was determined that where her father was afraid to defy Fionn Mac Cumhaill, she wasn’t. She just needed to figure out how.

“Now, the spring was also the time when new soldiers were admitted into the Fianna. That happened to be the year that Darmaid’s family sent him to join up.” Sarah smiled at around the group, then focused on Dermot. “Darmaid was quite a sensation. He passed all of the tests to join the Fianna with flying colors. He ran the fastest and fought the hardest, but above all, he was the handsomest. Wherever he went, women could be heard sighing in his wake.

“So the spring passed and the feast of Beltain came. That night, Fionn and Grainne were married. The wedding feast went on into the wee hours of the morning, and most of the men got very drunk, including Fionn. Grainne just sat in the great hall and watched until all but a few men had passed out. That was when she saw Darmaid, and like all the other women in Eire, she sighed and said, ‘If only he were mine.’ Grainne looked around at all the unconscious men, at her father and her new husband. She decided it was time to make her move. She rose and went to Darmaid, who had not been drinking, and said. ‘Darmaid, will you take me away from this place?’” Sarah did not take her eyes off Dermot.

“Darmaid knew this was a bad situation. All his life he had wanted to be one of the Fianna, and if he chose to go with Grainne that would end. Still, she was very beautiful. In the end could not give up his ambition with the Fianna and he refused.

"'If you take me away with you, I will be yours entirely,' said Grainne.

"Now here was an offer! And from a princess, no less. Yet Darmaid could not betray Fionn, so again he refused.

"'The bards will sing about you. They will say you are the handsomest because you tempted a princess. And they will say you are the bravest because you challenged Fionn Mac Cumhaill, and even the king won't do that,' she said.

"Such temptation!" Sarah rolled her eyes in mock distress. "Fame, freedom, and pleasure, and all he had to do was take her hand and walk away. Then he thought of the shame he would bring on his father, and for the third time, Darmaid refused.

"Grainne was a young woman very used to getting her way in most things, and she would not take no for an answer. So she put a kind of spell on Darmaid and made him take her away. They snuck out of the hall and out of the fort and made their way through the forest. At dawn they stopped to rest at a cave.

"At about this time, Fionn, Cormac, and the men in the great hall began to wake up. Of course Fionn began to wonder where his new bride had gone. He looked in her house. He checked with the queen and all over the fort, but Grainne was nowhere to be found. Then a soldier stepped forward and said he had seen Grainne and Darmaid sneaking out of the fort walls and into the forest.

"At this, Fionn flew into a powerful rage. He ordered all of the Fianna to the ready and rode out at the head of his army in pursuit of the two fugitives. He would have caught them too, but Darmaid was familiar with the ways of the Fianna. He heard the baying of Fionn's hunting hounds and woke Grainne. Together they escaped, and escaped, and escaped.

"Fionn and the Fianna chased Darmaid and Grainne for nearly a year, but Darmaid was always one step ahead. Grainne had been right about being famous. Songs were sung about them all over Eire, and many of the people began to help them. They said he was the handsomest man in Eire to have tempted a princess and he was the bravest to have defied Fionn Mac Cumhaill. Eventually, Darmaid grew to love Grainne.

"One day their passion was so strong that they took shelter in a rundown house in the forest. They were so absorbed in each other that they did not hear Fionn and the Fianna surround the house. They didn't hear the leaves of the great oak above the house rustling as the leader of the Fianna climbed up to get a better look. Through a hole where part of the roof had fallen in, Fionn looked down on Darmaid and Grainne wrapped in each other's arms. No one knows what he must have thought, or what made him come to the decision he did. But Fionn climbed back down the great oak, took his army, and left Darmaid and Grainne to each other. Fionn Mac Cumhaill would pursue them no longer.

"When the young lovers realized they were finally free, they petitioned Cormac for some land on which to start their life. Given their fame and popularity with the people, he couldn't refuse. So Darmaid and Grainne built themselves a fort and spent a blissful year together. They made peace with Cormac, and even made peace with Fionn.

"As the summer began to wane, Fionn and some of the Fianna came to visit. One night over dinner it was mentioned that a great wild boar was roaming the countryside near

Darmaid's fort. Now, the Fianna being the virile and gifted hunters that they were, could not turn down the opportunity for a boar hunt. Grainne told Darmaid that she didn't like the idea, but he could not let himself be outdone on his own land. So the next day, Darmaid, Fionn, and the Fianna set out on the hunt.

"The group divided up to have a better chance of finding their prey. Darmaid and Fionn set out to follow Fionn's hounds. The dogs caught the scent of the boar and chased him down. Darmaid, being younger and more eager than Fionn, ran ahead to get the first shot at the great boar. He was only out of Fionn's sight for a moment, but that was long enough for the boar to do his worst. They found Darmaid on the ground, broken, bleeding, and dying. There was nothing anyone could have done, not even the legendary leader of the Fianna. Still, Fionn tried to save him…tried and failed. So Fionn and the Fianna carried Diarmaid's body back to Grainne. She did not wail or cry or keen, because she had known that their happiness was too good to last. She simply looked at Fionn, with an accusation in her eyes.

"Grainne had grown into a very resourceful woman, and rather than find herself widowed and alone, she found herself once again married to the leader of the Fianna. She lived the rest of her days as the wife of Fionn Mac Cumhaill."

Night had fallen while Sarah told her story, but they had all been so enthralled by her voice and the hypnotic rhythm of the tale that no one had turned on the lights. They sat a moment in silence, contemplating the tale. Then Dermot rose and flipped the switch, and everyone was thrust blinking and bewildered back into the world.

"Well," said Sarah, grinning at them. "What's the moral of the stories?"

"They're parables about pride. Fionn, Arthur, and Mark…it was Mark, wasn't it? They're too proud. They think themselves invincible and they pay the price for it," Kendall volunteered the first opinion.

"But what of Diarmaid, Lancelot, and Tristan? Are they just foils for these overconfident kings?" Lucy asked incredulously.

"That's right," said Dermot, taking a sip of wine. "All three of our lover boys are supposed to be the bravest and fairest, qualities that should be expected in a king. What if they're stories of ambition?"

"Another form of pride," Sarah countered.

"I don't think they're about pride so much as they are about the natural order of things," said Lucy. "Diarmaid, Lancelot, and Tristan tried to attain positions above their station in life, and though they were temporarily successful, in the end it proved their undoing."

Kendall grasped the idea and ran with it. "Of course, the strength of kings and chiefs was of the utmost importance to everyone living under them when these stories were popular. So the fables show failed ambition and lost love, but through it all the kings are constant and enduring. They're at the top of the food chain, and wayward wives or daughters with their ambitious lovers can't do anything to topple them. Maybe these stories are designed to show people that their kings are untouchable even when those around them fall apart."

"Or they're warnings to any subjects ambitious enough to defy their kings," offered Dermot.

"That too," Kendall agreed. "Tell them in the great hall and around the campfires, and anyone who needs reassurance gets it, while warning anyone who needs to be warned. Very efficient."

"As a folklorist, I'm the first to admit that most legends have a pretty obvious moral," Sarah ventured. "But we're forgetting something. These stories may have been popular in the Middle Ages for the very reasons that you've mentioned, but they go back much further. They're from the times before the kings of Dal Riada, before the Romans, before Christianity. What if, like other systems of mythology, they're about something deeper, something more primeval?"

"What about the women?" said Anne, who'd been listening quietly up to this point. "You're skirting around them, if you'll pardon the pun, like they're nothing more than objects for these men to pass back and forth."

"Well, they were little more than objects back then," Kendall countered.

"No, Anne's right. These women weren't just pawns. Grainne is the one who convinced or coerced Diarmaid to run away with her, and we know Isolde had a will of her own. We can't treat these women as if they just got caught up in the actions of men," Lucy asserted.

Anne gave her an appreciative nod. "And if Sarah's right about the time period, then we can't assume that women were cattle back then."

"Actually," Dermot chimed in, "we do know a bit about ancient Celtic society. Women had more rights than they did in the Middle Ages. They couldna hold office, but they could hold property and have multiple husbands, just as men had multiple wives."

"Which leads us to wonder if, like many other ancient cultures, the Celts didn't develop from an older, matriarchal society," Sarah continued the thought.

"Like the Gravettian Venuses," Kendall offered.

"Yes!" said Sarah, remembering the discussion at the anthropology mixer that had prompted her argument with Jon.

"Right," said Lucy. "We all know that at some point, our ancestors shifted from worshiping goddesses to gods. Almost every Western culture still shows some of the remnants of it."

"Why should the Celts be any different?" asked Anne.

"Okay, but what does this have to do with our stories?" Kendall, ever the professor, turned them back to the task at hand.

"Maybe these are really stories about rebellious women," Lucy offered.

"There are other Celtic legends about rebellious wives and daughters," Dermot agreed.

"Exactly," said Sarah. "It's a classic motif. The kingdom is brought to the brink of chaos by the rebellious woman."

"Right. The kings think they can treat the women like property, but the women won't have it and go about doing their own thing such as running off with their lovers."

"So who's being taught the lesson here, the kingdom or the woman?" ventured Kendall. "I mean, sure, the ladies run off, but in the end Guinevere is almost burned at the stake, Isolde dies, and Grainne ends up married to Fionn anyway."

Sarah shook her head and leaned forward. "But Guinevere isn't burned. Isolde dies by the side of the man she chose, and Grainne winds up married to a much humbled Fionn on her own terms after a couple of years of bliss. They may not seem like winners, but these women taught their lesson."

"And just what lesson is that?" Kendall asked sardonically.

Anne smiled. "You men may think you've won the war, but only because we let you think that."

"The goddess you'd nearly forgotten will rise again," continued Lucy.

"The once and future queen," said Sarah with a satisfied smile.

Dermot sputtered into his glass of wine as if he'd been stung. Sarah shot him a surprised look, but everyone else's attention was immediately directed to the front door, where Donald was stumbling in his arms filled with bags containing more wine and their Thanksgiving curry.

Once Donald's dining room was filled with the pungent aroma of tandoori spices and wine, the evening digressed into the usual friendly banter. Anne continued to come out of her shell while Donald flirted shamelessly with all of the ladies. Sarah continued to play the part of hostess by making sure that everyone's glasses were filled and that no one was left out of the conversation. Dermot occasionally caught himself watching her and marveling at how easily she slipped into the role that was expected of her even though he knew she would probably prefer to be enjoying a quiet glass of wine by herself. She looked beautiful tonight as she laughed and joked with everyone, including him.

CHAPTER TWENTY-SIX

"Shall I walk ye home, then?" Dermot got up the nerve to ask her when they'd seen the other guests off and helped Donald with the dishes. He was prepared for a set down, but she'd been so relaxed with the others he hoped she might accept. He'd much rather walk with her than after her.

He didn't expect her to shrug and say, "Sure."

Dermot helped her into her coat, and they bid Donald goodnight. As they strolled down Boundary Street they fell into an awkward silence. Sarah glanced at Dermot and asked, "So what do you think about your first Thanksgiving?"

"Och, weel it's not quite what I'd heard about it, but it was nice."

"What had you heard?"

"Drunken family members arguing at the dinner table or watching yer football. A bit like Christmas at home."

"Well, my family was never like that, but then we weren't typical."

He thought he heard a note of longing in her voice and asked, "What was yours like?"

"Oh, it was always quiet. Usually Granny and I would get up early and start cooking." She smiled a little. "We might watch the parades on TV, once we got a TV. Then Old Duff would come over for dinner."

"Sounds lonely." He was simply curious now. She seemed to be a bit more open after the evening they'd had.

"My grandmother wasn't quite what people expected of a woman of her generation. The few friends she had were other outcasts: old bachelors, hippies, people who were either too backward, too forward, or just too weird for our little town." Sarah spoke of them almost with affection, and Dermot realized that, aside from her grandmother, those people were the only family she'd had.

"Still sounds lonely."

By this time they were walking across Boundary Street in front of the arboretum. Sarah lifted her shoulders and tossed her head to the side as if it were nothing. "I survived."

She looked suddenly very vulnerable, framed by the dark tunnel of vines with the streetlight glinting in her eyes. He'd seen the plant-covered tunnel that ran along the sidewalk next to the arboretum many times in the daylight. Then it was a cozy walk in the cool green shade. At night it was an ominous black cave where very little of the light from the streetlamp penetrated.

He stepped closer to Sarah and placed a hand at the small of her back, hoping she wouldn't protest. To his surprise she moved just slightly closer to his side.

"Let's take Franklin Street instead. This way is too dark," he suggested, not wanting to alarm her.

Sarah glanced back at the tunnel before turning away to walk to the better lit main street. "Yeah. Good idea."

Just past Sarah's shoulder inside the tunnel, Dermot thought he saw something move. He looked harder into the darkness. He couldn't put his finger on it, maybe a different quality to the darkness in one spot, maybe some furtive movement or maybe just paranoia, but Dermot was sure there was someone in the tunnel.

***

By the time they reached Sarah's building on Ransom Street, she and Dermot seemed to have fallen back to their old ways. They were once again able to laugh with and at each other, and if they weren't completely at ease, it was only because weeks had passed since they had talked.

"Do you want to come in for some coffee or a beer?" she offered. If she told herself the truth, she had missed him and wasn't ready for the evening to end.

"Coffee sounds great." He grinned, and Sarah thought he must be feeling the same way she was. She smiled back at him as she unlocked the door.

"I'll just put it on, have a sea—" Sarah stopped on her way to the kitchen after turning on the lights. Sitting on the couch was a rather disheveled Ryan. Sarah gaped at him.

"Uh…hey," Ryan said, rubbing a hand through his hair.

"Hey? Amy's not here." Sarah tried not to sound rude, but she had already told Amy more than once what she thought of Ryan being in the apartment when no one else was there. Sarah had hoped that after his disappearance on Halloween, Amy would change her mind about Ryan. Unfortunately, he had turned up the next morning with all kinds of excuses for why he'd been arguing and why he'd disappeared. To Sarah's dismay, Amy had fallen for it hook, line, and sinker.

Ryan had the grace to look a little embarrassed. "Oh yeah. The company wouldn't spring for the hotel over the holiday weekend, so I needed a place to crash. Amy said it would be okay."

Sarah was seething and hoped it didn't show. She might not like Ryan, but Amy was still her friend, and she didn't want to ruin that relationship because she didn't like this guy. Guys, Sarah knew, would come and go. "Right. Why are you sitting here in the dark?"

"Oh…I guess I fell asleep this afternoon. You kind of woke me up." He looked back and forth between Sarah and Dermot. "Hey, I thought you two were on the outs."

"We made up," Sarah snapped before she could stop herself. It was none of his business, but she would do her best to be polite just like she'd been doing since she'd found Ryan in her room. She took a breath and tried for a more diplomatic tone. "I was just about to make some coffee. Do you want some?"

"Nah. I'm wiped out. I think I'll just go to bed." He got up and walked past them, toward Amy's room. Sarah noticed that he still had his shoes on. He looked disheveled enough to have slept on the couch, but his eyes seemed clear of any kind of sleep haze. He was either so tired he'd forgotten to take his shoes off…or he was lying. What did Amy see in the guy?

Sarah gave Dermot a "follow me" look and a tilt of her head as she turned toward the kitchen. She reached into the cabinet to get the coffee things. She slammed the coffee can on the counter and closed the cabinet with a bang, giving a little vent to her temper. When she reached for the glass coffee pot, Dermot beat her to it and began filling it with water. "Probably best," she thought.

When they got the coffee brewing, she turned to him as if to say something, but she stopped. She stepped closer and in a low, urgent voice said, "I know that we're still…whatever, but…" She met his concerned blue eyes, biting her bottom lip. "Will you stay here tonight?"

Before he could answer she went on, "See, the thing is, Amy's boyfriend kind of gives me the creeps. I don't really feel comfortable alone with him here."

He grinned. "So you do trust me again."

She glanced toward the door nervously. "Let's just say, I trust you more than him."

"Alright, relax. I'll stay." Dermot nodded and gave her arm a reassuring squeeze.

"Maybe I'm just being paranoid, but there's something about him that just doesn't seem right."

"It's okay. I'll stay." He looked toward the hallway as if checking if Ryan was listening. "Where did ye say he's from?"

"I don't know. Somewhere in Georgia or Florida. He works construction for this big commercial contractor. They're building that new grocery store in Carrboro."

"Do ye know the name of the company?" he asked.

She tried to remember if she'd ever heard Ryan mention the name. "You know, I don't. I guess I could check the permits on the building. They have to post that stuff, don't they?"

Dermot gave a throaty Scottish grunt that Sarah took as an affirmative. He looked around the kitchen, searching for something. "I can check on it for ye."

"Nah, I can do it." She made a mental note to head over there on Monday.

"Do ye have any biscuits?"

"Are you seriously still hungry?" She thought back to the multiple helpings of curry, naan, and at least two pieces of pie she'd seen him put away at Donald's.

He shrugged before giving her a wink. "It's a long walk across town, and I'm a growing lad."

Sarah shook her head and reached into one of the cabinets to retrieve a bag of cookies. She grabbed a handful and deposited them on a small plate that she offered to him while shaking her head. "I hope oatmeal chocolate chip will do."

"That's grand." Dermot took the plate. Sarah took her mug and made to step past him, but he grabbed her other hand to stop her. His eyes sought hers, and they studied each other for a few seconds. "I really am sorry. I shouldna have said that. I don't believe it."

She gave him a hint of a smile. "Let's sit down."

They went to the living room and sat on the couch facing each other. Sarah pulled her legs up to sit cross-legged. Dermot draped his arm across the back of the couch. She sipped her coffee thoughtfully as he seemed to wait for her to respond. After a while she said softly, "Do you have any idea how embarrassing that was?"

He turned to face the coffee table and leaned forward, resting his elbows on his knees. "I reckon it was almost as embarrassing as having everyone ye've met in America thinking ye're a mad stalker."

She let out short huff, part laughter and part exasperation. When she spoke, her voice was even. "You're not going to hear me apologize for that. A girl's got to protect herself, and that stunt you pulled with Jon was well past the bounds of acceptable friend behavior."

"I know." His voice was almost a whisper as he looked down at the coffee in his hands and nodded. He lifted his head and looked at her as if he would say something more, but in the end he just nodded and repeated. "I know."

They sat there for a few minutes quietly sipping their coffee, each lost in their own thoughts. At length Sarah unfolded her legs and scooted closer. She looped an arm under his and laid her hand on his forearm, resting her head on his shoulder. Dermot let out a long breath as if he was relaxing for the first time in ages. She felt the tension seeping out of the muscles beneath her cheek. He shifted his mug to the opposite hand and, leaning back on the sofa, wrapped his arm around her.

Sarah nestled into the crook of his arm, enjoying the warmth and security. "I missed you."

"I missed ye too." Dermot planted a soft kiss on the top of her head. "More than ye'll know."

CHAPTER TWENTY-SEVEN

Daughter,

I was so relieved to see your letter. I hope you are well and safe. I also believe that you have much in common with my Bridget. You were so alike. I miss her every day, but I am consoled to know that you are safe. I know that you are alone with little family, and I worry that you will meet a similar fate. You are very special, and there are those that would seek to harm you.

Please be careful,

Isobel MacKenzie

Arbirainn i finaidh banaon chann ur afoinn

Ach ur pham chann ur n fawur breanain

Sarah read the card again. She had heard Isobel sing those words, the last verse of "The River Maiden," the last words her grandmother had spoken to her, but why would she put them in the letter? Her fingers unconsciously rubbed the edge of the card. They were obviously significant to the woman. So why hadn't she answered Sarah's earlier question about their meaning? Sarah wished she could go back to Cape Breton and press the woman on the meaning, but she wasn't sure when that kind of trip would be possible.

Sarah slid the card back into its envelope. She could only imagine how long it must have taken for Isobel to dictate those lines to whoever had written the note for her. She had no idea she'd made such an impression on the old woman. She could understand Isobel MacKenzie cautioning her as a young woman on her own, but this note seemed to draw a correlation between Bridget and Sarah. Sarah felt a chill trip up her spine at the thought.

"Hey!" Amy's voice jolted Sarah out of her thoughts. She looked up to find her roommate leaning into her room, one hand anchoring her to the doorframe. Amy was grinning. "There's a message on the machine I think you'll want to hear." Sarah rose from the bed and dropped the envelope on her dresser as she followed Amy out to the kitchen. "I'm guessing by your face you've already listened to it."

"Yep." Amy beamed at her and pointed to the answering machine. "Just press the button."

Sarah eyed her friend with suspicion as she pushed the button on the answering machine. As the gears clicked and whirred, Amy seemed about to burst. Then Archie MacInnis's cultured voice came from the little speaker. "Miss MacAlpin, this is Archie MacInnis with Scots Preservation and I have good news for you. We have decided to award you our Oral Histories Fellowship."

Amy squealed with excitement. Sarah's jaw dropped, and she reached for her friend's hand. "Please give me a call so that we can discuss the paperwork involved with getting your visa and housing. Of course the fellowship requires that you work with our research team, and we will need to discuss those requirements with our team leader. I look forward to speaking with you."

The message ended with a beep. Sarah and Amy began hopping up and down in their excitement and talking over each other.

"I can't believe it! This is so perfect!"

"You're going to have the best time."

"I'm going to Scotland!"

"I know you're going to find your song. I just know it."

"This is going to be awesome!"

They started to calm down with their arms around each other in a loose hug. Amy leaned her head into Sarah's. "What am I going to do without you?"

"What am I going to do without you to mother hen me all the time?" Sarah laughed, then gasped. "We have to find you a roommate for next semester!"

"Actually, I might already have one lined up." Amy looked slightly guilty.

"You've already been looking? I just got the news." Sarah was shocked.

"Don't look like that," Amy chided. "I knew you were going to get it. You always get these things, like the funding to go to Cape Breton. Besides, how could you not with James Stuart on your side?"

Sarah gave her a slight pinch and a wink. "So is this new roommate going to wait until I move out or are they moving in during exams?"

"Ha, ha. It's Barrett, for your information, and he's not moving in until after you're gone."

Sarah was relieved to hear it wasn't Ryan, though she suspected he would still be in the picture. It was somewhat comforting to know Amy would have a friend to live with. "Might be nice to have a man around the place."

Amy rolled her eyes. "Where are you going to stay?"

"That is a very good question. I think I'm going to have to enlist the help of a local," Sarah said with a wink.

"I think I know a couple of locals who wouldn't mind letting you crash with them." Amy gave her a leer before turning serious. "I'm so glad you and Dermot patched things up."

"Me too. I should give him a call. He can help me out with finding a place to stay." Sarah reached for the phone, and there was a knock on the door.

Amy strolled over to answer it as Sarah dialed the phone. She found she was excited to tell Dermot that she would be in Scotland with him and started to walk back to her room rather than be distracted by the visitor.

"Sarah," Amy called from the doorway as Sarah listened to the phone ring on the other end. "Sarah!"

Sarah turned back to the living room only to find Dermot standing there looking at her expectantly. "You got a call this morning, did ye not?"

Sarah put the phone back in its cradle without taking her eyes off his. "I was just calling you to tell you about it. How did you know?"

"Did ye talk to MacInnis?" His shoulders almost vibrated with tension.

"No, he left a message. He wanted me to call him back to talk details." His manner was starting to make her nervous.

"Did he mention who was leading the research team?"

She looked at him, uncertain. He seemed to be fishing for something.

"No."

"Would ye hate me if I told ye it's me?" He cringed, prepared for her to be angry at him for not telling her sooner.

"Wait a minute." Sarah had to give herself a moment to process this news. "You mean you're leading the research team, and I got on this team because I met James through you."

"No." He took a step toward her. His look was intense. "Ye're on this team because ye're damn good at what ye do."

"Did you have a say in who is on the team?" Please say no. Please don't let her have gotten this just because of who she knew.

"Just one vote on a committee of eight." Not quite the answer she was looking for, but better than it could have been.

"Does everyone on this team have a personal connection to you or James?"

He looked as if he were waiting for her temper to explode. This time he shook his head no. "They're all qualified graduate students just like you. It was James's idea to recommend ye for this. I voted for ye, because ye can do the work better than anyone I've seen, and because I like working with ye."

"I can't have this look like favoritism. It has to be legit." She told him the same thing she had told James.

"I know that." He took another step closer. "I wouldna have voted for ye if I didna know ye would be right for the team."

"When did the committee vote on this?" Sarah kept her eyes locked on his.

“Two weeks ago.” Two weeks ago she hadn’t been speaking to him. Two weeks ago she’d thought the worst of Dermot Sinclair, and he’d still wanted her on his team.

She searched his face, assessing the truth of his words. His gaze was so open and hopeful it made her eyes sting with unshed tears when she thought about his vote. She pulled herself together—no more looking at the past ready to move forward. Sarah smiled and nodded confidently. “This is going to be fantastic.”

He grinned back at her and threw an arm over her shoulders. “It better be. Ye’ll be on my turf now. I canna have ye embarrassing me.”

Sometime later that afternoon, Sarah looked around her room in the apartment. She tried to imagine packing up her things. What would she keep? What would she store? What would she give away? Through college and grad school, she had moved countless times, but none of those places had been home. This apartment she shared with her best friend was the first home she’d ever had outside the holler. And now it was time to clear out and say good-bye again. Sure, she was coming back, but she couldn’t help thinking that nothing was ever going to be the same.

***

September 1989
Kettle Hollow, North Carolina

“The electric stove is new. She just bought that last year. The refrigerator works great. The walls are sturdy and the roof doesn't leak." Sarah was getting irritated as the realtor strolled through her home, wrinkling his nose at the rustic pine floor and threadbare furniture.

"How many acres did you say there are?" he asked, barely looking at her.

"Eighty-seven, mostly up the mountain, that way." She waved to the west where the mountain rose behind the house. "There's a primitive cabin up there too. No electricity, but it's sturdy."

He grunted thoughtfully as he stepped out the front door onto the porch. Sarah had been hard pressed to find a realtor that she didn't think was trying to take advantage of her.

The first one she'd been to, a woman whose ad in the Yellow Pages in Boone had shown a picture of her with overdone hair and a wide smile, had practically drooled over her Mary Kay–slathered lips at the idea of "helping" a nineteen-year-old country girl who suddenly found herself the owner of eighty-seven acres of land in prime Blue Ridge tourist country. When the lady suggested Sarah ask about half of what she thought the land was worth, Sarah had walked right out of the woman's office without a word. A few searches in the local paper's archives showed that the woman had made several deals with local developers by underpricing large parcels of land being sold by local families. Then she acted as the selling agent for the newly subdivided and much higher priced developments.

Sonny Hargrave might be looking down his nose at her home, but as far as Sarah could tell he wasn't outright crooked. Sarah followed Sonny onto the porch. He surveyed the front yard before turning back to her. "I think I can get you a pretty good price for it. There are a number of developers looking to invest out here. Of course, you might get a better price if you hang onto it for another couple of years."

"No, I'd really rather just be rid of it. I'm never going to live here again."

"Alright," he said giving her a level look. "Now, I don't want to sound indelicate here, Miss Sarah, but everybody in these parts knows how your grandmother made her living. Before I go listing the property, I want to make sure there are no more signs of illegal activity. That's for your sake and mine."

Sarah nodded, not surprised he already knew. "That won't be a problem. I've already made arrangements for that. By sundown tomorrow, you won't find so much as an inch of pipe on this land unless it's connected to the plumbing in the house."

Sonny nodded and made for the porch steps. Just before he stepped down, he turned back a sincere, concerned look on his face. "I know it's a hard thing you're doing, Miss Sarah. I'll try to get you the best price I can. You can count on that."

Sarah smiled at him, her eyes misting a little, unaccustomed as she was to kindness from people around here. "I appreciate that, Sonny."

The realtor left and Sarah went back inside to resume packing. She wasn't taking much with her, but she needed to clean the place out. She went up to Granny's room and started packing up the clothes to take to the Salvation Army. She resisted the temptation to moon over every housecoat and pair of shoes. She worked her way through the closet and chest of drawers.

She was just coming to the ancient trunk at the foot of the bed when Sarah heard someone rattling up the driveway. She glanced out the window to see a blue pickup truck park itself right in front of the porch steps. The engine shut off, and Russell Corbett hopped out. By the way he was moving, Sarah thought he just might be sober. She didn't think she'd ever seen Russ Corbett sober, but then his business with her today was serious. Sarah headed for the stairs, more than a little relieved to not have to go through Granny's trunk just now.

Sarah let the screen door slam behind her as she stepped out onto the porch to find not only Russ, but Johnnie and Buddy Corbett as well. Sarah nodded to the younger men before looking down at Russ from the porch. "You left it late enough in the day."

Russ wiped a rough hand over his dry lips, "Well, I had to wait for the boys to help me. Can't carry that tank down by myself. Now if you'll just show us where it is, we'll get that old thing out of your way."

"Sure. But I'll have the money first." On more occasions than she could count, Sarah had heard Russ Corbett explain to Granny that he would gladly pay her on Friday for a pint of stump water on Tuesday. She wasn't going to let a single piece of that still off her property without him paying for it.

Russ tried to look affronted, but Sarah arched an eyebrow and stared him down. After a couple of seconds, he handed her a roll of money. Sarah stood right where she was and counted out the thousand dollars. It might have been a low price for a still in good working order and whatever moonshine Granny had left, but Russ had come to Sarah shortly after the funeral offering to take it all off her hands for nothing. He'd had the gall to tell her she wouldn't even have to pay him to haul it away.

Sarah thought it was interesting how when someone died, people seemed to come out of the woodwork trying to find ways to take advantage of the bereaved. Sarah didn't know if they were any more aggressive toward her because of her youth, but between the mortician wanting to sell her his most expensive coffin and burial plot to shady realtors to shifty drunks, she was exhausted. Still, Maggie MacAlpin didn't raise a fool.

Sarah pocketed the money and stepped down toward the Corbett's truck. "Has this thing got four wheel drive?"

"Yup." Russ stepped out of her way.

"Right. We can drive it across the pasture over there. It'll be closer," she said, reaching for the handle on the passenger's side door. She was anxious to get this done and get the Corbetts out of her hair. Russ ran around the front of the truck and jumped into the driver's seat while Johnnie and Buddy climbed into the bed.

It was near dark by the time Sarah had shown Russ Corbett the location of Granny's still and her remaining store of moonshine. She had walked back to the house alone as the men worked to carry the pieces of the still down to the truck at the end of the trail. Sarah warmed up a can of soup and went back to work, this time packing up the few books and knickknacks in the parlor. She knew she should, but somehow just couldn't make herself go back up to Granny's room.

***

Sarah sat on the edge of the bluff near where the still had been hidden until yesterday; the small box containing Granny's ashes sat beside her. It was the same bluff under which her mother's body had been "found" thirteen years before, where everyone believed she had fallen or jumped to her death. It was really quite peaceful with the sun coming over the mountains and breeze coming from the west with just a little bite of cold in it.

"You aren't thinking about jumping, are you?"

Sarah glanced over her shoulder to see Buddy Corbett stepping closer, his hand outstretched as if he could grab her if she tried to jump. She chuckled. "No. I'm not gonna jump. Though if you sneak up on me like that again, you might just scare me off the edge."

Buddy gave her a skeptical look. "You and I both know I've never been able to sneak up on you."

She sighed. "It's been a while since you tried."

He sighed too and lowered himself next to her on the edge, letting his legs dangle over like hers. They sat in silence just like they had as kids, each content being in the other's presence. It had always been that way between them. As children they were both bruised and bullied and found comfort in friendship. Once upon a time, it might have been more, but that had been years ago.

He'd grown from a gawky boy into a lanky man, still a little thin to be handsome by most standards. Sarah imagined that the girls around Kettle Hollow probably liked him fine.

"How's your family?" she asked, making conversation.

He shifted uncomfortably, his voice even. "You saw Johnnie. He's doing alright. Royce is in jail for a bar fight. Ronnie's pregnant again and Tanya moved back home when she left Bobbie Cutliff. And Mama's just as bitter as ever. So everything's normal."

"What about you? How are you, Buddy?" She took her eyes off the horizon and studied him.

"I'm okay." He squinted at the sun. "Been kinda drifting from one thing to another since high school, but I think I'm settling on a plan. Do you know what you're gonna do now?"

"I'm selling the place. That's why I wanted the still gone so fast." She glanced back to where the still had been.

Buddy shook his head and looked thoughtful for a minute. "Buying that still is either gonna make my daddy…or it's gonna kill him."

"I'm sorry, Buddy," Sarah said. She hadn't thought too much about what Russ would do with the still, besides the obvious.

"It's alright. I gave up on my daddy a long time ago," he said, resigned.

They fell into silence again. A hawk flew low past them before catching an updraft and soaring back toward the neighboring peak.

"What's next then?" he prompted.

"I'm going back to Boone, back to school. I've got a scholarship, so at least that's covered. What about you? What's your plan?"

"Looks like the best plan is to get my commercial driver's license and start hauling lumber. Been doing alright digging ginseng with Johnnie, but I want something steady." Buddy squinted, his eyes on the horizon. "I reckon you ain't planning on comin' back here then."

Sarah thought she heard a note of disappointment in his voice, so she answered with a gentle shake of her head. "No. I'm done with this place. Granny's gone, Duff hasn't been back since I went off to school. I went up there the other day. His cabin was cleared out. This isn't home anymore."

"No part of it?"

Sarah looked at him for a long moment. She laid her hand on top of his. "This community only tolerated us. I might love this forest and this mountain, but you know as soon as I stepped off this property, I wasn't wanted anywhere around here. You remember those things your mother said to me that day. How could I come back to a place that viewed me that way, when there is a whole world out there that doesn't know what I came from?"

"A clean break then?" He turned his hand over and wrapped his long fingers around hers.

"Mmhmm." She patted the box on her other side. "I came up here to scatter her ashes. Then I'm going down to the house to wait for the junk truck to come and haul everything away."

"Is there anything you're gonna keep?" He kept his eyes trained on the ridge to the west.

She gave his hand a squeeze. "A few things."

They sat for a while longer, hands joined between them, and for just a little while Sarah felt like she wasn't completely alone in the world. After a time, Sarah pulled back from the edge and stood up. Buddy followed her, stepping back from the edge.

She picked up the box of her grandmother's ashes and undid the string tied around it. There was tape too, as if the person who packed it was terrified that the lid might fly off. Sarah slit the tape with a fingernail and stepped closer to the edge of the bluff. Her foot bumped some loose rocks that went skittering over the ledge, bouncing from one rocky outcrop to another on their way down. Sarah froze, and for one gut-clenching second imagined that the ground beneath her feet was giving way, and she was hanging there in the air about to follow those stones down the drop.

She closed her eyes tight and breathed deep. She wriggled her toes inside her shoes and felt the ground solid under her. It was just an illusion. She was glad Buddy couldn't see her face from where he stood, glad he hadn't seen that moment of terror.

Sarah hooked her thumb under the lid of the box and extended her arm into the empty air. She flipped the lid open with her thumb and turned the box over. The ashes spilled out in a dull gray cascade, spreading through the air as they fell. A strong wind blew in from the west and sent the ashes surging eastward through the mountain air. Sarah couldn't help thinking it was pushing them toward Scotland, toward home.

She watched, thinking of her granny and her life spent in exile on this mountain. Tears pricked her eyes and her throat ached. Granny had made the best of her life, of Sarah's life too. She'd given Sarah what she needed, if not everything she wanted.

Sarah turned away from the cliff to find Buddy waiting for her. He stretched out one long arm to his side, and Sarah stepped under it and wrapped her arm around his waist. He rubbed her shoulder as if to warm her, and they started walking back toward the house.

“Hey,” he said as they entered the trail. “Maybe I’ll give you a call sometime when I’m in Boone.”

Sarah smiled. “That would be good, Buddy.” Though they both knew he would never call.

CHAPTER TWENTY-EIGHT

Sarah loaded the canvas bags of groceries in the back of her little Honda. She was at the grocery co-op on Weaver Street and had just gotten the ingredients for some truly decadent brownies. Tonight was the last coffee Friday before exams, and Sarah wanted to make something wonderful for the Ransom Street girls as a sort of farewell. She so often thought of herself as alone, but getting ready to move to Scotland had made her realize how much she appreciated her friends.

She looked back at the market. It was a co-op of natural foods and local produce. Sarah had come to think of it as the hippy grocery store. It was one of her favorite places to shop. Growing up as she had, they had made everything from scratch and foraged for or grown a lot of their vegetables and herbs. Sarah never quite felt comfortable shopping in a supermarket full of prepackaged foods and convenient mixes.

She lifted her eyes to the roof of the building on Weaver Street, which had once housed a textile mill. Just above the top of the old brick building she could see the new roof of one of those supermarkets, the one Ryan was building. The outside was complete, but the work of fitting the inside was what Ryan said they were working on. Sarah hoped it wouldn't give the little market too much competition.

Sarah got in the car and drove around the block to the construction site. She parked on the street in front of the site with some difficulty. The brakes seemed to be a little less responsive than usual. She wondered if that last trip to the mountains had been more than her little old Honda could handle. She would have to get it looked at before she left for Scotland.

The store's parking lot was blocked off by a temporary chain link fence. There was a gate to let in construction vehicles. Hanging next to the gate on the fence was a board with the various permits and licenses hung inside plastic to protect them from the weather. Sarah scanned them, looking for the name and phone number of the builder. The plastic covers kept the papers dry, but did nothing to protect them from the sun. The print on the pages was so bleached out that they were nearly impossible to read. Sarah was squinting closely at one when a gruff voice behind her said. "I already told the newspaper that we're expecting to be done in March."

Sarah turned quickly and shielded her eyes from the sun to find a man leaning out the open window of a large white pickup truck. He looked to be in his late forties. The shoulder that was leaning out the window looked solid, and a five o'clock shadow covered his jaw even though it was just after lunch. He looked a little annoyed at having to make nice with a stranger.

Sarah gave him her most winning smile. "Oh, I'm not with the paper. I'm actually looking for someone. Maybe you can help me. Are you the foreman here?"

"That's me."

"I'm trying to verify that someone works here." She tried for a note of authority.

"Okay. This person got a name?" He got out of the truck, and Sarah noticed that while his shoulders looked solid, he was a bit thicker around the middle than she would have thought, and shorter. Now that he didn't have the height of the truck helping him, he was only a couple of inches taller than she was.

"Yes, his name is Ryan Cumberland."

"Cumberland." Sarah could almost see the personnel files flipping past like a Rolodex behind the man's eyes. "Never heard of 'im."

She gave a puzzled look. "Never? This is the site he said he was working on. Is your company working on any other grocery stores in the area?"

"Far as I know, this is the only grocery store under construction this side of Raleigh."

"Hmm…Maybe he gave me a different name. I'd say he's in his early twenties, shaggy blonde hair, blue eyes, wiry build…"

"Doesn't sound familiar," the man said with a shrug. Sarah was not happy that her suspicions were starting to seem justified.

"Have you let anyone go recently, or had anyone quit who might fit that description?"

The foreman shook his head and shifted from foot to foot, reaching to open the gate. "Nope. Don't really have a lot of turnover with this crew. Sorry, I'm not much help."

Sarah shook her head, trying to summon up her manners through all the thoughts spinning around in her head. She offered the foreman her hand. "No, you've been a big help. Thank you."

The man gave her a firm handshake and curt nod. "Sure."

Sarah slid back into her car, sitting for a minute or two and trying to process what she had just learned. It was hard to imagine a reason for Ryan to lie about something as simple as where he worked. She started the car and began making her way home still trying to puzzle it out.

Sarah could see him lying about having a girlfriend back home, maybe even a child he was supposed to be paying support for. Still, it was hard for her to justify lying to Amy about where he was working, unless he wasn't working. She wondered how much Amy had been paying for in this relationship. It would be just like Amy to pay for him without even thinking about it. She was so open and generous with her friends. It wouldn't even occur to her that he might be sponging off her. Sarah was kicking herself now for not going out with them on the couple of occasions they had invited her.

She was so deep in thought that she made the left turn onto Cameron going faster than she probably should have. Just after she turned, she saw the bars of the railroad crossing coming down and the train approaching.

There were only about one hundred feet between the corner and the railroad crossing, so Sarah immediately hit her brakes. The pedal dropped to the floor too easily and nothing happened. She didn't slow down at all. The train was going slow here, because it was coming from the nearby power station, but it was big enough and fast enough to do damage.

Sarah began furiously pumping her brakes, hoping this was just a bubble in the lines and she could get the fluid working again. The approaching train gained speed as it moved away from the power station. Sarah's car drifted closer to the bars of the crossing. With each pump of her foot, the brakes seemed to offer a little more resistance. Sarah just hoped it would be enough to keep her from running into the train, which was now crossing Cameron between the safety bars.

The conductor must have noticed she was still moving because he laid on his horn, which didn't help Sarah's nerves. Sarah continued pumping her foot on the brake pedal, hoping it would be enough. The rapid thump of her heart was nearly as loud as the train's horn and drew a sharp contrast with her slow, seemingly inexorable slide toward the moving train. Foot pumping wildly, blood singing in her ears, Sarah watched breathless as the hood of her car began to slide under the safety bar before stopping just short of catastrophe.

She came to rest mere inches from the grinding wheels of the train. She kept her foot pressed hard on the brake pedal, afraid that if she let up she might coast closer. She held her breath as the train passed, fearing there might be some part of it that stuck out farther and would snag her bumper. After the last car went by and the safety bars had lifted, Sarah tapped the gas just enough to get her over the tracks and coasted to a stop along the side of Cameron Avenue. Once she knew she was out of the way of traffic, she slumped back in her seat with relief.

She rested for a few minutes of simply breathing and letting her heartbeat slow to something approaching normal. Then she began checking to figure out what had caused the failure. She pumped the brakes and felt more resistance now than she had when she was approaching the crossing. The lights on the dash all looked right—unless a sensor or light had gone bad, nothing looked out of place. She reached between the front seats to check the parking brake, wondering why she hadn't thought to pull it when she was sliding toward the train.

Something didn't seem right about it, though. She pressed the button on the end of the handle for the brake and it descended an inch back into the center console. It had been engaged just the tiniest bit, not enough to set off the brake light on the dashboard. Was it enough to interfere with normal braking? The car was an automatic. Sarah only used the parking brake on steep hills. Maybe Amy had borrowed it and accidentally left the break engaged.

Sarah sat there for a few minutes, pumping the brake pedal and hoping to get the fluid moving again. When she thought she felt the proper resistance, she pulled back onto Cameron Avenue and very slowly and carefully drove the few blocks back to her apartment.

CHAPTER TWENTY-NINE

The chocolate smell was heavenly. It filled the kitchen as Sarah poured the double batch of brownie batter into the pans. She was bending down to put the pans in the oven when Amy bounced into the kitchen and swiped a finger through the batter that was still coating the side of the bowl. "For me? You shouldn't have."

"Ha. They're for everybody. Are you coming to coffee?"

"Mmm, that is so good." Amy pointed to the bowl as she hopped up to sit on the counter next to the bowl. "Nah, Ryan's picking me up for dinner."

"Okay. Hey, did you borrow my car recently?"

Amy thought for a second. "I don't think so. Why?"

"I had a weird incident with my brakes earlier." Sarah took the bowl and placed it in the sink, running hot water into it.

Ryan picking her up meant he wasn't in the apartment now. Sarah leaned against the counter opposite Amy and began nervously folding a kitchen towel. "Umm…about Ryan, Amy."

Amy held up a hand to forestall her. "I know you're not crazy about him, and he's definitely not perfect, but he really does make me happy. And I talked to him about staying away from your stuff."

Sarah nodded, trying to be diplomatic. "I know, and as far as I know he has. I still don't like him being in the apartment when you're not home, but that's not what I want to talk about."

Amy squared her shoulders. "Okay…?"

"So I was over in Carrboro today, and I went by the construction site. Ryan wasn't there."

Amy shrugged. "Maybe he was on a break."

"That's the thing." Sarah hoped this would go better than it had in her head while she was driving home from the store. "I asked the foreman, and he'd never heard of anyone named Ryan Cumberland."

"Maybe Ryan is a nickname."

"For what?" Sarah could not let Amy rationalize this away, but she didn't want to start an argument. "Amy, I think Ryan's been lying to you."

"No!" Amy shook her head in denial. "Look, I get that you don't like him, but checking up on him at his place of work is taking things a bit far."

"That's just it, Amy. It's not his place of work." Sarah tried to stay calm. It wouldn't do her any good to lose her temper.

"Maybe he quit, maybe he got fired and didn't want to tell us. He could have any number of reasons for not telling me about that."

Sarah took a deep breath, trying not to show her frustration. "I know you want to give him the benefit of the doubt, but think about it. At best he's lying about where he works or if he works. At worst he's lying about who he IS. Doesn't that worry you?"

Amy shook her head and waved a hand in a negating motion. "So let me get this right. You were furious at Dermot for meddling in your love life, but it's okay for you to stick your nose in mine? That's pretty rich, Sarah."

"Okay, I'll admit you're right about that. But you're my best friend, and I just don't think he's worthy of your trust, and now we have proof of that."

"I don't understand. What's he done to you?" Amy cocked her head, waiting for the next volley.

Sarah's shoulders slumped. She felt deflated. "Nothing specific, Amy. I just get a bad feeling from him. He's lying to you, he creeps around the apartment when we're not here, and then finding him in my room…I just don't think you can trust him."

Amy's look was shuttered. "You really can't stand it, can you?"

"What?"

"You can't stand not being the center of your little universe." Amy narrowed her eyes at Sarah as she slid from the counter and stalked closer. "First you think Dermot is out to get your work. Then you convince everybody he's stalking you. Now you think my boyfriend is out to get you. You can't stand that I have someone else to spend time with other than you. Are you really so self-centered and paranoid that you just can't imagine a world where people have their own agendas that don't involve you?"

Sarah was too stunned and hurt to respond. Maybe Amy was right and this was all part of some paranoid delusion. Maybe she was projecting her own insecurities onto the people around her. She'd been a target for madness in her own home for long enough to make her want to cling to that feeling like it was her natural state. She thought of her mother and the demons that had chased her that final year. Could that kind of madness be passed down?

She looked down at the towel she'd been folding and unfolding as they talked. Any conciliation, any words of apology, stuck in her throat as tears began to trickle down her cheeks. She didn't look up when Amy delivered a parting shot before stalking out of the kitchen. "You need help, Sarah."

***

June 1976
Kettle Hollow, North Carolina

"I will not let you do to her what you did to me!" Mama and Granny were shouting again. Sarah tried to sleep, but the voices from downstairs travelled right up to her bedroom.

"And I willna let ye hurt that girl." Sarah could tell Granny was upset. Her accent always came out hard when she was angry. So "girl" sounded like "guh-rul" with a short, sharp Gaelic R.

Sarah pulled the quilt up almost to her ears. She didn't want to hear them fighting, but she couldn't help being curious about it too. They'd argued all winter. Sarah had hoped that when spring came, things would ease up—but that was before. She started shivering despite the warm night and the quilt around her. It had been months since that chilly spring morning, but she couldn't think of that day without feeling cold.

"Then let me take her away, Mama." Sarah's mama talked faster and lower. It was hard to hear everything. "We'll take

Duff with us…like a family…never find us…you can tell them that we ran away."

"And ye think Grant MacDuff will go wi' ye…" Granny lowered her voice so Sarah didn't hear the last part of what she said.

"Fine, we'll leave without him." Mama was determined. She sounded so normal, so like the strong Mama that Sarah had always known. She wanted that Mama back, but she was terrified that the other Mama would come back, the gaunt, terrifying ghost of the Mama she loved.

"Ye cannae run from them, Molly. They'll find ye, and if they don't then the others will."

"Well, I can't stay here and watch her grow up thinking she's got her whole life ahead of her when she doesn't!"

"She does!" Granny snapped.

"But it's not HERS!" Mama screamed so loud Sarah could hear the windows rattle. There was a moment of silence before she spoke again softer. "You let me grow up thinking I could do anything I wanted with my life, could be anyone I wanted—"

"I thought I was protecting ye," Granny put in.

"And just when I was ready to start, you took it all away."

"Not me! I wish it didna have to happen like that!"

There was a fraught silence before Mama spoke again. Her voice cracked. "Me too, Mama. Me too. Don't you see? I don't want her to go through that. But you know that's exactly what's going to happen. She's the one they've been waiting for."

"Ye cannae be sure of that."

"I can." Mama's voice was barely above a whisper, and Sarah craned her neck to hear better. "I am. And I would rather see her dead than watch her life be torn apart."

***

The brownie tasted like ashes in her mouth as Sarah let the conversation flow all around her. She was sitting on the porch swing of the blue house. Her coffee mug sat untouched on the porch railing, a plate of sweets on her lap. She just didn't have the heart to engage in the usual banter.

"D'ye care to talk about it?" Dermot's voice was soothing as she felt the swing shift with his weight. He sat next to her, taking up much of the space and stretching his arm across the back.

"Not really." Sarah groaned and looked around at her friends laughing and talking. "This isn't really a good place anyway."

"Is it about leaving?" He leaned down so he could see her face.

She shook her head. "No, everything seems to be going smoothly, thanks to James. I might object to him getting me jobs and fellowships, but I don't mind getting his help cutting through red tape."

"Mmm. He is good at that," Dermot said with a nod. "When will ye be able to leave?"

"Well, after exams it's just a matter of getting the last of the paperwork done and putting most of my things in storage. I do have to line up a place to stay in Edinburgh. That's a challenge."

"Not really. There are always one or two empty flats in the building I live in. We could be neighbors." He gave her shoulder a little friendly squeeze.

"Will it be in my budget?" Sarah had expected to have to share a flat with someone, imagining that housing costs in a city like Edinburgh would be high.

"I doubt yer budget is much smaller than mine. I'm sure it'll be fine."

"Thanks." Sarah bit down on the niggling feeling that everything for this trip to Scotland was falling into place just a little too easily. "Don't look a gift horse in the mouth," she told herself.

They sat for a few minutes in companionable silence, Sarah occasionally taking a bite of her brownie. The more she sat with him, the more relaxed she felt. Sometime over the course of the last week or so, she and Dermot had found their footing again. They'd spent Thanksgiving night sleeping platonically in her room, and Sarah had reveled in the feeling of safety and warmth she'd gotten from him.

She couldn't forget the thing with Jon, but she just couldn't believe anymore that Dermot meant her harm. Of course, that just made Amy right about Sarah's original suspicion of Dermot. Sarah had been unfair, and she had been paranoid. Maybe she was being unfair to Ryan the same way.

"Come on." Dermot gave her shoulders another squeeze. He picked up her plate with the other hand and set it on a little table next to the wall. "Yer heart's not in this. Let's go for a walk, and ye can tell me what's bothering ye."

"Yeah, okay." She let him lead her down the porch steps and onto the sidewalk. It was getting colder, and the dry evening air stung her cheeks and burned her nose, but it felt good to move. It felt like doing something as opposed to just sitting there and letting Amy's words run through her head again and again.

"So, tell me about it." Dermot matched his pace with hers.

Sarah continued walking, trying to determine what was bothering her the most about her conversation with Amy. "Do you think I'm paranoid or delusional?"

"What?" Disbelief rang in his voice.

She took a deep breath. "I've been really unfair to you. I've suspected your motives for coming here, for befriending me, for the thing with Jon. I trust you now, but I treated you pretty badly, all because I somehow thought you weren't being straight with me. Do you think that was rational?"

Dermot slowed his pace and looked at her. "Why are ye asking this?"

"Amy said something to me earlier that just started me thinking." Sarah kept walking, afraid of the answer she might see in his eyes. "She was right about one thing. I am suspicious by nature. I don't trust people easily, and you've been the victim of that more than anyone recently. I think I've been unfair to you, and maybe I'm being unfair to Ryan too."

"Ah…so this is about Ryan." He nodded sagely.

Talking it over with him was helping her look at things more objectively. It was nice having a sounding board, though Amy usually filled that role. "Only in part. It's really more about me, and whether or not my inherent caution when it comes to people has turned into something unhealthy."

"I don't think so." He reached out and took her hand in a gentle grip. "Ye've been alone in the world for a few years, and before that ye were not exactly treated kindly by yer neighbors. Anyone who'd grown up like ye have would be wary of society. How else are ye to protect yerself?"

"But I accused you of drugging me and then stalking me."

He stopped and grabbed her shoulders. "And I have never blamed ye or said ye were mad for it. What did Amy say to ye?"

Sarah looked at her feet. "That I was paranoid and delusional." Her voice was almost a whisper. "And self-absorbed."

"What?" His voice cut through the night air. Sarah could tell he was furious on her behalf, and it warmed her a little. He used a knuckle to tilt her chin up, then waited until she lifted her eyes to his. "Why?"

"I found out that Ryan doesn't work where he said he does, and I told her about it," she said in a rush.

"What do ye mean he doesna work where he said he does?" His eyes bored into hers.

Sarah wet her lips and quickly told him about her conversation with the foreman. His reaction was more than she expected. "Shit!"

Sarah looked at him, puzzled. "So you don't think I'm paranoid?"

"No, I don't." He started walking again, though much faster, pulling her along.

"There's not much I can do about it," Sarah explained, feeling a little like she was watching a train wreck. "I told Amy, but she doesn't want to hear it. She'd rather tell me I'm crazy and delusional."

"And ye nearly believed her." He gave her a look that said she should have known better.

"Well…" How could she put it without opening up the Pandora's Box that was Molly MacAlpin? My mother was nuts and tried to kill me—maybe it runs in the family? She was just starting to feel a little better; she didn't want to have that conversation.

"I don't want ye staying there anymore if he's going to be there," Dermot demanded.

Sarah bristled at his autocratic tone. "Now, hold on." She might be suspicious of Ryan, but she didn't think he was dangerous, just shifty. "I have exams this week. I'm not going to completely disrupt my life because I think he's a liar."

"If he's lying about that, what else is he lying about, Sarah? Just stay with me until I can look into him." Dermot seemed to be getting hotter about it than Sarah had.

"I'll be fine, Dermot. I can't just uproot everything during exams. As for Ryan, he's Amy's problem now. I warned her. If she chooses to ignore it, then she'll get what she's asking for."

Dermot ran an angry hand through his hair. "At least do me this favor. Don't stay in the apartment alone with him."

"I really don't think he's dan—"

"Please." He cut her off with such urgency that she didn't dare argue.

"Okay." She nodded, wondering who was paranoid now. "I won't."

***

…pink and white swirling around in a bright kaleidoscope. And the mumbling.

…They won't have you. I won't let them…

Molly was there on the other side of the flower film, her face twisted and hideous.

...let them take you away from me. I won't let...

...Mama?...

...Not my baby...never take you...

...Mama, I can't breathe...

...won't do it to you...not if I...

Why? Sarah thought. It had been weeks since she'd had the dream. But now just as things were starting to look up, when she didn't feel so weighed down by her past, she was once again under the water with Mama holding her there.

"Why can't you leave me alone?!" she shouted in her dream, in her mind.

Thunk!

Molly's face went blank with shock and fell toward her, landing in the water just an inch from Sarah's. Her voice came through loud and clear, as if the water weren't there and Molly was whispering to her.

"Because you need me."

Sarah's blood felt like ice in her veins as she sat up, desperate for air.

CHAPTER THIRTY

Sarah read through her notes on The Devil and Commodity Fetishism in South America for the tenth time. The lines on the page were starting to blend together, and her notes in the margins were looking like gibberish. Her last exam was in an hour, and she'd stayed up the better part of the night studying. She'd been focusing so much on her dissertation and transcribing things in the folk-life collection that she'd been skating by in her few classes. Her class on religion and anthropology was one she'd managed to get through relatively easily. Still, after four days of exams and helping Donald grade final papers, her brain seemed too fried to recall anything she'd read for this class.

She had just decided to give her notes one more pass when Amy burst into the room without knocking. Her hair was a mess, and her eyes were red. "Hey, I need your help."

"What's up?" It had been a tense few days in the apartment after their argument. They had barely spoken. Sarah was surprised Amy would ask her for help.

"My granddad had a stroke last night. He's in intensive care in Raleigh." Amy dropped a pile of papers on Sarah's bed and heaved a shuddering sigh. It was clear she was fighting back tears. "Can you get these to Donald? I've looked at all but a few. I told him I'd have them to him today."

Sarah rose from the bed and put her arm around Amy. She'd lived through that frantic call from home and rush to the hospital before with her own grandmother. She tried to sound as calm and understanding as she could. "No problem. I'll finish them and drop them off. Is there anything else I can do?"

"I don't think so." Their eyes met, and it was as if their fight hadn't happened. Amy let Sarah give her a comforting squeeze. "I should be back tomorrow. I hope."

Sarah followed Amy out into the hallway where they met Ryan. He was pulling on a jacket and getting ready to leave. He put a gentle hand at the small of Amy's back as she headed for the door. Amy and Ryan grabbed their bags on the way out. Sarah followed them out onto the stoop.

"Like I said, I hope I'll be back tomorrow," Amy said, turning to face Ryan and Sarah.

"In the meantime…" Ryan turned to Sarah and dangled a key to the apartment between them. She held out her hand, and he dropped it into her palm with a saucy smile. "I will leave you to your studying and paper reading."

Amy smiled at him before leaning in to give him a quick kiss. So she had talked to him about Sarah's feelings. That was a good sign. Amy threw her arms around Sarah and got a fierce hug in return. "Call me when you know something, and tell your family I'm thinking of them."

"I will." Amy looked for a second like she might say more, but Sarah saw tears welling in her eyes. "I better go."

Sarah gave her a reassuring nod. "Don't worry about us. Drive carefully."

Amy looked at Ryan again before rushing off to her car. He stood on the stoop with Sarah as they watched Amy drive away then just a bit longer. It was long enough for the silence to start feeling uncomfortable. Still, Sarah wasn't going into the apartment until she knew he was leaving, and she didn't want to have to shut the door in his face.

Ryan released a long sigh before turning to Sarah with that too-smooth smile of his and said, "I'll be seeing you around."

He stepped into the yard and started a leisurely stroll toward Cameron Street.

***

It was jacket and scarf weather, but after spending two plus hours cooped up in a classroom furiously writing an exam essay, Sarah didn't have the heart to stay inside. She decided to camp at a table near The Pit with a cup of coffee to finish up the papers from Amy's stack for Donald. She was just settling in, coffee warming her hands when Dermot strolled up.

"Hey, there." She grinned up at him.

"By that smile, I'd say yer exams must be over." He gave her a crooked smile of his own that she found far too attractive.

"You'd be right. I just have a few papers to finish reading for Donald, and then it's all packing and moving for me. I can't say I'm looking forward to that, but it's better than blue books and cramped fingers. How about you, are you done?"

"I am. We should celebrate." He smiled at her hopefully.

"Maybe tomorrow night. I'm wiped out. I really just want to go home and sleep. Besides, Amy's grandfather had a stroke. I'd feel wrong celebrating when she's spending the night in Raleigh at an ICU."

"That's awful." He leaned forward, and his eyebrows drew together in concern. "She's gone to Raleigh, then?"

"Yep. No Amy, no Ryan. He even handed me his key to the apartment. I guess it was some kind of peace offering. Either way, I'm going to have a quiet night, a cup of tea, and hours of uninterrupted sleep." She said the last words with relish.

"I still canna believe she gave him a key without asking ye." Dermot shook his head.

"Me neither, but he's only a problem for a few more days. She'll go home for Christmas, and he'll go back to whatever creepy place he crawled out of."

"And ye'll be in Scotland." His voice betrayed no small amount of satisfaction.

"Not until January. I'll be on my own here for the holidays. She took a thoughtful sip of her coffee. You're going back next week, right?"

"Aye. There's plenty to set up for the research team and the holiday with mum."

"I bet she'll be glad to have you back on that side of the pond."

He just shrugged and made one of his patented equivocal throaty noises. "Well, I'll leave ye to yer papers. Give me a call tomorrow, and we'll celebrate."

"You're on." She spared him a final smile before turning back to her papers.

***

Sarah could hear the mumbling just like in her dream. It sounded like it was coming not from the bathroom, but from Mama's room. It seemed to echo down the hall.

...won't let them. They can't take you...

Mama? Sarah felt the rough floorboards of the old farm house beneath her bare feet as she crept down the hall toward her mother's door. She had walked this path before. She knew what she would find on the other side. A little voice inside her told her that she didn't want to open that door. It was the frightened voice of six-year-old Sarah, who had never forgotten the horror of finding her mother's body.

...Never going to get you. I'll protect...

The mumbling was new to this dream. It was usually reserved for the bathtub dream. Sarah searched her memory. Had she heard her mother say anything back then? No. She was sure Molly had been dead when she found her. A frigid breeze drifted up the hall past Sarah's feet. It curled her toes and raised the hair on the back of her neck.

Mama?

...My baby. She'll make her own...

The door was ajar, and Sarah fought with herself over the decision to push it open. The woman Sarah was curious at this new dream, but little girl Sarah, the Sarah who had been here before, shivered and cried. The wood on the door was smooth. Sarah remembered playing in the yard while Granny had painted it just the year before. The hinges creaked slightly as the door swung open just in time for Sarah to see Molly fall back onto the bed, her hand trailing down the wall at the end of the word.

Run

She had scrawled it on the wall in her own blood after slitting her wrists. The bed was a jumble of sheets and quilts all covered with blood. Granny would burn them later, and the mattress too. It had taken longer to scrub the blood out of the plaster on the wall. They had given up on the floorboards and had Duff replace them.

At this point, the little girl she had been was in tears, but grown-up Sarah felt a morbid curiosity. In her memory, Molly had been cold and dead, but in this dream she was still breathing, if faintly. Her lips moved, as if she were trying to say something, but there was no air behind it. Sarah stepped closer to the bed, her eyes scanning her mother's face. Molly's eyes had rolled back in her head and her voice was barely a whisper.

...won't let them...

Mama?

Suddenly, as if Sarah had called her back, Molly's eyes rolled forward and her gaze sharpened on Sarah's. Her voice was clear and strong.

"Wake up!"

***

"Wake up, princess!" The voice was loud and sharp in Sarah's ear. Her eyes flew open to find Ryan Cumberland just a breath away from her face. Sarah forced her sleep-leaden muscles to fight, but he quickly had her arms pinned between them, a knife to her throat. His voice was a low growl; gone was the smooth drawl that he used to charm people. "Scream, and I'll do worse to your friend than I'm going to do to you."

CHAPTER THIRTY-ONE

As the weather grew colder, Dermot was starting to understand why the rent on his little basement apartment had been so low. This dry cold only made him homesick for the soggy, frigid streets of Edinburgh. "Not much longer," he thought as he pulled a sweater over his head and hit the button on the answering machine.

He'd switched off Sarah duty with Fleming after she'd gone to bed. She had been telling the truth about being tired. Through the front window, he'd seen her stop long enough to make a cup of tea, and then she had turned the lights out and trudged back to her room. He doubted if she'd even finished drinking the tea before falling asleep.

He wasn't doing much better himself. He'd been watching over her all week, and since she hadn't had much sleep neither had he. He was thankful James had decided to bring Fleming on to watch her so he could occasionally rest. He was going to grab a bite to eat and do just that.

The first message on the answering machine was a wrong number. In a college town like this, it was inevitable that a person's phone number had previously belonged to someone else and you were likely to get residual calls for whoever had your number before you. It could make for some interesting conversations. Earlier in the semester a caller had tried to convince him that his number belonged to someone named Tasha and he really should put her on the phone. The second voice he heard was all too familiar. It was just the right balance of silky tones with clipped business-like precision, the voice of the corporate oracle that was James Stuart's chief gatekeeper, Audra Lennox.

"Mr. Sinclair. This is Miss Lennox. Mr. Stuart asked me to call you about the items you wanted us to look into. I can confirm that Grant MacDuff was a steward, but he was not Margaret MacAlpin's steward as she was considerably older. He was Molly MacAlpin's steward. He seems to have gone off the books around the time Sarah MacAlpin was born. I'm afraid that the other person you were inquiring about, Ryan Cumberland, does not seem to have existed prior to this past September. We have been unable to verify any of the information you gave us, nor have we been able to find any new information."

Dermot felt all his blood drop to his feet. The cold of the apartment seemed nothing now compared to the ice in his veins. Ryan Cumberland really wasn't who he said he was. Sarah could have been living these past weeks with the enemy just in the next room. He must have just been waiting for an opportunity. And now she was all alone in the apartment, and no doubt Cumberland knew it. Dermot made for the back door and took the steps up to the street two at a time.

***

"I'm going to shift a little. I want you to put your hands above your head and no funny stuff, or I'll gut you right here and treat Amy to more of the same." Ryan was lying on top of her with the knife to her throat and her arms pinned between them. His voice had smoothed out into a confident, almost professional rumble as if he were a doctor telling her to take a breath while he listened to her heart. Sarah's brain ran through her options, thinking back to the many afternoons Duff had spent drilling her on self-defense moves.

"You're small, so your best tool is going to be surprise. Let your opponent underestimate you, and you can use that to your advantage, but don't expect them to do it twice."

As promised, Ryan shifted, giving her arms room to move. She began to slowly move them up between their bodies. Once she got free of his chest, she suddenly rammed her forearm up under his jaw, making his teeth clack together and driving his head back. She took advantage of his surprise to bring her knee up toward his crotch. He twisted, and she only managed to get his thigh, but it gave her just enough space to squirm out from under him and slide to the floor.

In a flash, she was crawling toward the door, adrenaline pumping, trying to make ground and get to her feet at the same time. Almost there. Her blood sang in her ears.

Ryan landed hard on her back and straddled her waist, pinning her down. She pushed her chest up, calling on every ounce of strength to keep crawling. She was almost within reach of the doorframe. If she could just get a grip on it, she might get enough leverage to pull away. Ryan reached around and swept an arm out from under her and twisted it behind her back. Her chest and shoulder hit the floor hard. He pressed her down, his breath hot against her ear, and reached for her other arm. Sarah just kept pushing, kept stretching that arm toward the doorframe and hoping for some kind of leverage.

But his weight was too much, and he caught her arm as she reached for the frame. She tried to resist. Tried pulling her arm in to her chest to keep him from twisting it behind her, but he was stronger. Gripping both wrists in one hand, he bound them with a zip strip from his pocket. Placing a knee in the middle of her back to keep her still, he reached over to grab a scarf from her dresser and used it to tie her ankles. He had stopped talking to her. He sounded winded, but his movements were cold, efficient, like he'd done this before.

***

Dermot struggled to catch his breath as he drew up to their spot in the mimosa bushes across the street from the apartment. The dry December air burned his sinuses. Fleming was there, keeping watch as usual. His partner looked startled at his arrival.

"Hallo there. What's got ye in a rush?" Fleming asked as he stood from his spot in the mimosa.

"Any activity?" Dermot nodded in the direction of Sarah's building. He threw off his wool jumper, desperate to cool off after running seven blocks.

"No, no lights, no noise." Fleming shook his head, sounding like it was just another day on the job.

"The roommate's bloke is a liar. Background check says he doesn't exist," Dermot stated without taking his eyes of Sarah's building.

"Bugger!" Fleming looked from Dermot back to the building. His eyes, like Dermot's, scanning furiously for any sign of movement in Sarah's apartment.

"Right. We're checking the windows." They started across the street and crept up to the side of the building. Dermot silently motioned for Fleming to look in Amy's window while he went to Sarah's. Luckily there was a small space where the blinds had been bent, and even when closed there was just enough room to see in. By the streetlight, Dermot could see that her sheets were rumpled, but Sarah wasn't there.

Dermot glanced over, and Fleming shook his head. Nothing unusual in Amy's room. Fleming stepped closer and looked in Sarah's window. "Looks like the bathroom light is on."

The bathroom was in the interior and didn't have any windows, but that likely meant Sarah was awake.

"I'm going to knock on the door." Dermot started walking toward the front of the building.

"And tell her what? It's midnight. Could be there's nothing going on." Fleming followed. Maybe they were being over-cautious, but better that than standing out here fretting over what might be happening inside.

"I'll think of something. I just need to see her."

***

Sarah watched Ryan start the bath from her place on the floor in the corner of her tiny bathroom, wondering if she would get an opportunity to escape. He'd carried her from her bedroom to the bathroom over his shoulder. Now that she was bound, he seemed more at ease. He had even given her that smile that so irritated her when he gently set her on the floor before setting a black duffel bag on the toilet lid. "You are a hard woman to kill. Do you know that? I've been trying to arrange accidents for you for weeks now."

He held his wrist to the water to test the temperature. "I tried pushing you in front of a bus. I fiddled with your parking brake, but you haven't driven the damn car enough for that to work. Shit, I was even ready to strangle you in the arboretum a couple weeks ago, but your damn bodyguard was with you."

Sarah struggled to process what he was saying. Ryan had been trying to kill her. Was this because of Amy? She tried to keep her voice even, to reason with him. "You don't have to do this. I'll be out of your way in a few weeks, and you won't have to worry about me anymore."

He glanced over at her with a smirk. The salesman's charm was gone. His blue eyes were sharp and calculating. This was not the same slightly shifty, easygoing guy Amy had introduced her to. "You think this is about your little friend?"

"It's not?"

He gave a soft laugh and shake of his head. "Wow. You're good. You really can keep a secret. You don't let on, no matter what."

"What are you talking about?" He was making less sense the more he talked.

"You're not going to convince me that you don't know why James Stuart is interested in you." He gave her a level look. "The Canadian chick knew. She told me you were the one."

Sarah's breath felt trapped in her chest, and she felt a cold prickling on the back of her neck. She forced herself to ask, even though that cold feeling told her she already knew the answer. "What Canadian chick?"

He gave her a look that said she couldn't really be that dense. "The MacKenzie girl. Keep up, princess."

Sarah couldn't think of anything to say to that. She'd known before asking, but hearing it confirmed left her stunned. He hadn't really hurt her yet. Even for all her struggling, the worst she would have was a bruise or two, but he was so matter-of-fact about killing Bridget that Sarah began to lose hope. For the first time since he'd awakened her, she started to believe she might actually die tonight.

She pulled her knees up to her chest and tried to make herself as small as possible. If she could just get her feet under her, or at least close to her body where she could kick out, maybe she could knock him off balance. She moved slow, hoping he wouldn't notice.

When he was satisfied with the water temperature, he left the tub and turned toward her. He pulled a pair of black latex gloves out of his pocket and began sliding them onto his hands.

"Why…" Her voice was barely above a whisper, but she wanted to keep him talking. He lost some of his chilling efficiency when he was talking. "Why do you keep calling me princess?"

He shook his head and chuckled as if he was wondering when she was going to catch on. He finished putting on the second glove with a snap at the wrist. "Because I know what you are, princess. That's why you have to die, though I would prefer that it didn't look like murder so the cops won't ask too many questions. Since I'm running out of time and none of my other methods have worked, you're just going to have to kill yourself."

He let his face drop into a forlorn look and gave a slow, sorry shake of his head. "Poor Sarah. Just couldn't get over that fight she and Amy had, after that sudden breakup with Jon. I guess she just couldn't take it anymore. Slit her wrists in the bathtub."

His mock mourning made Sarah's blood boil. "No one's going to buy that."

"Oh, but they will. You've just been so stressed out lately. Emotionally all over the map. Amy even commented on your paranoid delusions."

"Not that, asshole!" Sarah didn't need to be reminded of her own doubts about her emotional state. "No one's going to believe I got in a bathtub."

He reached into the black bag and pulled out a pack of utility razor blades. He gave a soft snicker. "You may be a strange one, Sarah, but I'm pretty sure you bathe."

"I take showers. I haven't taken a bath since I almost drowned as a kid. All my friends know that." That last part wasn't exactly true, but she hoped Ryan didn't know any better. Any forced change in his plans bought her extra time. She just had to figure out how to use it.

He studied her for a few seconds. Sarah could almost see the wheels turning behind his eyes, running through his options. Slowly he set the razor blades on the counter by the sink and reached down to shut off the bathwater. "Well then, I guess we'll just have to come up with another—"

He stopped mid-sentence with his head cocked to the side. With the water turned off, the silence seemed to stretch out around them like a blanket. Sarah tried to control her breathing to hear what Ryan had heard.

There it was. A knock on the door, then Dermot's voice, "Sarah?"

She almost cried out in relief, but quick as a flash Ryan was kneeling next to her and covering her mouth tightly with his hand. His fingers dug into her cheeks. His eyes bored into hers as he pursed his lips and held a finger to them in a silent shush. Ryan waited to see if Dermot would give up and go away.

Dermot knocked harder. "Sarah, it's me. Open up."

***

Why didn't she answer? If she was in the bathroom, she had to hear him knocking. He turned to Fleming. "Go over to the blue house on the corner there and bang on the door until someone answers. Tell them I sent ye and then call 911."

With a quick nod, Fleming took off at a run.

***

Ryan leaned closer. His eyes scanned over her, taking in her nightshirt and panties, her bare thighs, as he thought and listened. After a few seconds he focused his gaze sharp on hers. "One sound out of you and he bites it. Nod if you understand."

She held his gaze over his hand and nodded.

"Looks like Sinclair just gave us the perfect solution to my little problem." There was the smile again, as if he had some secret joke that only Ryan got. He grabbed the knife and used it to cut through the scarf around her ankles. He pulled her gently to her feet. After being bound for so long, her legs weren't ready for the weight and buckled.

Sarah used her weight to tumble into Ryan, hoping she could knock him down. The fall surprised him, and he fell back toward the toilet and tub, catching the side of the tub just under his arm. Sarah struggled back to her feet, but with her hands tied, her balance was off. It took longer than she'd hoped to find her balance. When she finally made it, she hurled herself through her room and into the hall without looking back.

She was almost to the living room when she heard Ryan behind her. She ran faster, half-expecting him to tackle her again. She slammed against to door with all her weight.

"Sarah!" Dermot's voice came from the other side of the door loud and urgent.

Sarah wanted to respond, but she was too focused on getting the door open. She was turning around to try to reach the knob with her bound hands when the kitchen light clicked on. Ryan was standing by the kitchen door leaning comfortably against the wall. He crossed his arms across his chest, leaving one hand on top of the other forearm to make room for the gun. Even in the light from the kitchen there was no gleam of metal or shine of textured plastic, just a matte black, light-sucking menace.

"We probably could have gotten you to the door without this much fuss, but we're here now so I suppose there's no harm done. Now, you're going to do exactly what I tell you to or it'll go badly for both of you."

"Sarah?" Dermot's muffled voice questioned.

Ryan talked in a low voice, "Back away from the door, princess. That's it."

He pushed away from the wall and came to stand next to the door. "Now, I'm going to open this, and you're going to invite him in. No funny stuff. Play your cards right, and he might just walk out of here."

Sarah gulped and tried to square her shoulders. She spoke loudly, hoping that Dermot would hear her and be ready when the door opened. "You're going to kill us anyway. Why should I cooperate with you?"

At this, the door shook in its frame, and Sarah could only imagine that Dermot was trying to break it down from the other side.

Ryan smiled at her fondly, not even acknowledging the force on the other side of the door. “Oh, I’m killing you for sure, but your boyfriend there still has a chance. So be a good girl and stand back while I open this door, or I’ll just shoot him right through it.”

Sarah bit back her next retort. She hoped if she were patient that she might find an opening, a moment when his guard was down so she could try again to get away. At least now her feet were untied. Maybe with Dermot’s help they could get free.

Ryan watched her prepare herself. Then he undid the deadbolt and reached for the knob.

CHAPTER THIRTY-TWO

Dermot took a deep breath and stepped back and to the side. He hoped his trainers had enough padding to protect his foot from what he was about to do. He lifted his foot and kicked the door hard enough to disengage the latch, splintering the wood around the knob. The deadbolt would be harder, but it was at shoulder height. He threw all of his weight against it, expecting to have to break the frame. But the lock gave way too easily and he tumbled into the apartment.

He landed hard on his shoulder, pain radiating across his chest. He cried out and rolled onto his back to find Ryan eyeing him over the sight of a Ruger 9 mm. "Nice of you to join us, Sinclair. Sarah and I were just trying to solve a difficult dilemma."

Dermot followed Ryan's glance to find Sarah standing near his head. She was dressed in nothing but a big shirt and panties and her hands were tied behind her. He watched as her eyes filled with tears and she mouthed, "I am so sorry."

"Aw, how touching." Ryan slowly stepped around until he could grab Sarah by the arm. He was careful to stay out of Dermot's reach. He pointed the gun at her head. "Get up, Sinclair. We're going over to the table."

Dermot slowly got to his feet. As he stood up, the weight of his arm pulling on his shoulder told him it was probably dislocated. He walked slowly to the dining area.

"Have a seat," Ryan said, drawing Sarah to the opposite side of the table. He pulled out a chair and pushed her into it. Dermot tried to look calm as he sat down, cradling his useless right arm. He hoped they could find a way out of this, but he would need her working with him.

"Now, Sarah likes to pretend that she doesn't know why I'm here, but you're not going to pretend are you?"

He bloody well would pretend. He was not about to let her find out who she was at the point of a gun, not like this. Dermot looked up at Ryan, doing his best to look as perplexed as Sarah. "I don't know what ye're talking about."

"Oh, you have got to be kidding me!" he nearly shouted. "Come on. You can't even let on now, when I've got a gun on you? The game is up, Sinclair. You might as well confess."

"Confess what?"

Ryan turned to Sarah, pulling her to face him. "He's as big a liar as I am. James Stuart hired him to come here and watch you, protect you. He hasn't been stalking you, he's your bodyguard."

"He's mad, Sarah." Dermot tried to get her to look at him, willed her to believe him. "Don't listen to him."

"That's bullshit. I met Dermot before I ever met James. James Stuart couldn't have known about me before that." She sounded so sure of him it made Dermot's gut clench.

Ryan looked at her with something like pity. "Oh, princess, you really don't know, do you? Explain this then. How is it that Bridget MacKenzie gets a job offer from Alba Petroleum and winds up dead? Then you meet the CEO, and here we are." He waved his gun hand to indicate their current situation. "They led me right to you. You're the one he needs to fulfill all his plans. Stuart is going to own it all. He practically does already. But you…you're going to make him a king."

Dermot could see the fear and confusion building in her eyes. "I don't know what he's talking about, Sarah, any more than you do. Ye have to believe me."

"Bastard!" Ryan spat at him, fury written across his face. He pressed the gun to Sarah's temple and she let out a low whimper. "Tell her. You tell her right now, or I'll shoot. Tell her how he sent you. Tell her she's a princess and she's meant to be the mother of the second fucking coming. You look her in the eyes and tell her that you're not her friend, you're her keeper."

Not like this. Dermot looked Sarah in the eye and kept his expression as blank as he could. She kept her red-rimmed eyes fastened on his, sure and strong, but he could hear every shaky breath she took and see her shoulders quivering. Not like this, she can't find out like this. But Ryan was right about one thing. It was his job to protect her, and he'd be damned if he'd let that bastard shoot her right in front of him just because he wouldn't tell her the truth. In a voice devoid of any emotion, he told her, "I am your keeper. You're a princess, and James sent me to protect you."

"Was that so hard?" The bastard looked satisfied and lifted the gun away from Sarah's temple. Sarah let her shoulders slump and took a deep, shaky breath, but she never took her eyes off Dermot's. He wished he knew what she was thinking as those words hung between them.

Ryan rolled his shoulders back and gave them a little shake to loosen them up. "Alright. Here's how this is going to work. I'm going to arrange a murder/suicide between the two of you. Dermot, yours will be the only fingerprints they find." Ryan held up his other hand, still covered in the latex glove.

"Sarah already told everyone she thought you were stalking her. A murder/suicide won't surprise anybody. They'll all just think she was right."

Sarah looked horrified, and Dermot watched a tear trickle down her cheek. By now, Fleming should have called the police. They had to be here any second. "*Na bith eagail ort. Cuir earbs' annam.*" *[Don't be afraid. Trust me.]*

She gave a tearful nod, never breaking eye contact. He had to keep Ryan talking until someone got there. "How are you going to explain to them that I shot her when you're here and covered in blood?"

Ryan made his face into a mask of horror and pretended he was talking to police. "I just stopped by to check on my girlfriend and this crazy guy was fighting with her roommate. I tried to stop him. I really tried."

"And ye think they'll believe that with all the blood on ye?" Was that the faint whine of a siren he heard?

"They will when they hear about how you stalked her." A grin spread wide across Ryan's face. "They'll believe me after they talk to Jon Samuels."

Sarah let out another whimper. Dermot could see the guilt written all over her face. Between the two of them, they'd given Ryan just the narrative he needed to cover up his involvement. They'd well and truly dug this grave, but they weren't in the hole yet.

The sound of the siren was multiplying and getting louder. All of Dermot's muscles tensed in anticipation. He slid a foot out toward the table leg closest to Ryan, who was standing near the corner. As soon as Ryan knew the police were coming, he would either let it distract him, or he would get down to business. Dermot had to be ready to act whenever the chance came.

Ryan cocked his head and heard the sirens approaching, never taking his eyes off Sarah. All the previous emotion drained from his face, leaving a mask of cold determination. Dermot saw the change. In the space of a half-second, Ryan went from the raving fanatic to calculating killer. He began to lift the gun again, pointing it at Sarah's head.

Before Ryan could take aim, Dermot gave the table leg a vicious shove with his foot that sent the corner slamming into the other man's groin. Springing from his chair, Dermot reached across the table with his good arm to clamp down on Ryan's gun hand. Gritting his teeth, he managed to lift his other hand and grip the gun. He gave it a quick twist, breaking Ryan's hold.

He only had time for a half-second's satisfaction as he let to gun drop to the floor behind him. Ryan hooked his free hand around the back of Dermot's head and sent it slamming down onto the table. Dermot felt the skin on his forehead split when it hit the wood. Ryan followed with a shove to Dermot's injured shoulder that sent him crashing to the floor.

Bright white pain flared across his vision. Relentless, Ryan straddled him, his face full of rage as he delivered an elbow to Dermot's temple. Darkness began to fill his vision from the edges inward. Just before everything went black, he saw Sarah scramble to her feet from under the table and make a run for the door.

CHAPTER THIRTY-THREE

"I am your keeper. You're a princess, and James sent me to protect you."

Sarah could tell by the look on his face that he hated saying those words, hated Ryan, hated this situation. She could see the fear in his eyes as he looked at her, as if he thought she might believe any of it. She knew they were the ravings of a lunatic. He didn't know that Sarah already had experience with lunatics. Ryan could say anything he wanted.

"Sarah already told everyone she thought you were stalking her. A murder/suicide won't surprise anybody. They'll all just think she was right."

She drew in a surprised breath. She hadn't thought of that when she had opened the door. Now she was kicking herself for letting Dermot in. She should have just made Ryan shoot her then, instead of getting Dermot mixed up in this. Now she had no idea how they might get out.

"*Na bith eagail ort. Cuir earbs' annam.*" *[Don't be afraid. Trust me.]*

The sound of Dermot's deep, comforting rumble in the language of her heart gave her what little comfort she could find. She did trust him, finally. Her eyes burned, filling with tears of shame at the months of suspicion that had kept them apart. Unable to speak, she gave him the barest hint of a nod, hoping he would understand.

She let Ryan rave on about his plan, not really listening. None of it really mattered anyway. They had given him the perfect cover, and he wasn't going to hesitate to use it. She watched Dermot across the table as he watched Ryan's every move. He seemed so in control, so determined and sharp. She felt a tear slide down her cheek. It seemed so unfair to her to have survived her mother's attempts all those years ago, only to have almost twenty years of hope, twenty years of building a life, of learning to trust someone, love someone, only to die like this.

"They will when they hear about how you stalked her. They'll believe me after they talk to Jon Samuels." Sarah felt more than heard the miserable sound that bubbled up from her throat. She was so caught up in her own guilt and misery that she didn't hear the sirens. The men heard them. Her eyes on Dermot, Sarah caught a flare of his eyes just before she felt the table crash into her ribs, nearly knocking the breath out of her.

She saw Dermot reach for the gun. Sarah dropped to the floor under the table. Her ribs smarted, but she squirmed to get her legs under her. She was on her knees, almost free of the table, when Dermot crashed to the floor and landed on his back. She wished she could help him, but his eyes were already starting to glaze over. If she ran, she could get help or maybe distract Ryan from doing more damage.

Sarah scooted on her knees until her back was clear of the table and lunged to her feet, sprinting for the door. The blue house. She had to make it to the blue house and get them to call the cops. Sarah didn't think about how the cold rough asphalt stung her feet. She ran as fast as she could down the middle of the street. She just kept telling herself the only way she could help Dermot was to get the police. The porch light was on at her friends' house, calling to her like a beacon.

She made it to the intersection beside the blue house before he caught up with her. Ryan grabbed her hair first and yanked her back. Sarah screamed and fell against his legs. It felt like he was ripping her hair out. Ryan adjusted his grip. The pain lessened, but he had a firmer grasp down by the roots.

Without a word he pulled her to her feet and started back toward her building, dragging Sarah behind him by her hair. Sarah struggled to keep up with him, stumbling backward. At the blue house she could see her friends spilling out onto the porch. Good. She wanted to call to them, but just couldn't form the words.

A tall form separated itself from the group on the porch and started running toward them. Ryan must have heard the man coming, because he stopped. Turning, he wrapped an arm around Sarah's waist and pulled her close. Sarah cried out when she felt something cold and hard pressed to her temple.

"One more step, Sinclair, and she gets it."

The tall guy stopped in his tracks, raising his empty hands. Sarah didn't recognize him, but at this point she was happy for any help. "Easy, mate. Just let her go."

"You know I can't do that." Ryan's voice was right next to her ear. He was out of breath, but still kept a tight grip around her waist.

"Ye've only got seconds before the police get here. If ye let her go now, ye can avoid a very public confrontation." The tall guy Ryan had called Sinclair sounded so calm and reasonable, it almost made Sarah want to scream.

"Right. I've already fucked this up once, with that Canadian chick. You think I'm going to get out of this?" Ryan scoffed.

The tall guy took a slow step toward them as Sarah heard the sirens getting closer. "All the more reason to let this one go and disappear."

Sarah could feel his whole body tense behind her. She rolled her eyes toward campus and could see the emergency lights cutting through the night in the distance.

"Clock's ticking, mate. Ye could still get away," the tall one said.

For a second, Sarah thought Ryan might let her go. His grip loosened just a little, and he shifted to the balls of his feet. She could feel him looking behind her as if he was judging the best direction to run in. Just when she thought he might actually let her go, a police car turned onto Ransom Street, flooding it with light.

Ryan's grip tightened on Sarah's waist, nearly stopping her breath. The tall guy laced his fingers behind his head and started backing toward the police car. He shrugged, "Sorry, mate. Ye missed yer shot."

By the time the tall guy reached the police car, the street was blocked in both directions with police and emergency vehicles. The little corner by the blue house was lit up like Christmas. A police officer on a bullhorn called out to them. "Let the girl go and surrender."

Ryan took a couple of rapid breaths. When he answered the police, he sounded completely unhinged. Sarah knew it was an act. "I love her. I don't want to hurt her, but she's got to come with me."

Just like the tall guy, the police officer's voice sounded even and cool. Another officer came and said something to the one with the bullhorn. "We can't let you do that, Ryan. Your name is Ryan, isn't it?"

"Yeah." Sarah had a hard time connecting the nervous sounding voice next to her ear with the steely arm around her waist or with the gun pressing to her temple.

"Ryan, whatever this is about, this isn't the way to solve things. So why don't you let…" The officer paused as someone fed him her name, "Sarah go, and we can talk things over calmly."

"There's nothing to talk about." Ryan chuckled under his breath. "I'm in love with her, and she won't come with me."

What was he talking about? That wasn't even close to what he'd said in her apartment. He had completely believed what he said before. Sarah had seen it in his eyes, heard the conviction in his voice. Whatever his reason for wanting her dead, though, he wasn't going to tell the police. Sarah wondered what the big secret was.

"Well, son, you're not going to get your chance if you hurt her now. You're only going to make it worse for yourself."

"I can't let her go." Ryan sounded near tears. Then he whispered to Sarah in a voice as cold as ice. "You're not getting out of this that easy, princess."

***

It was the flashing of the red and blue lights coming through the window that brought Dermot out of the fog. His head throbbed, and the pain was near paralyzing. He wondered for a second what had happened. His vision kept shifting in and out of focus. He recognized Sarah's apartment. Memory of how he got there flashed in his mind. He saw Ryan on top of him, twisting to deliver an elbow to his temple and Sarah running out the door.

Sarah! Flashing lights.

He rolled over onto his side, and pain shot through his shoulder. His vision swam out of focus again and his ears were ringing. It felt like someone was driving nails into his skull. He rolled to his hands and knees and had to pause there to wait for his head to stop spinning. He closed his eyes, not wanting to see the room go by as he slowly turned and crawled to the door. He used the doorframe for support as he pulled himself to his feet. He stood, leaning his good shoulder against the frame until he was sure he wouldn't pass out again.

The flashing lights coming in the open doorway from the street weren't helping him get his bearings. If anything, they were making his head swim even more. But he had to get moving, had to find Sarah. Slowly, as he started to gain his balance, the ringing in his ears receded and he could hear some of what was going on. He heard someone talking loudly, but he was having a hard time understanding the words. He reached across the hall and used the opposite wall for support, sliding toward the outer door to the street.

He was met with a wall of bright, swirling colored lights that made his head spin and his stomach churn. He summoned all his strength and trudged toward the lights, lifting his good arm to shield his eyes the best he could. The half a block felt like miles. His feet were like lead, and it was all he could do to drag one in front of the other. Through the haze of color and light, he identified a line of police cars blocking Ransom

Street. When he reached the first car, he leaned on it to keep his balance.

None of the cops seemed to notice him. All their attention and their spotlights were turned toward the intersection, lighting it up like daylight. With some of the flashing lights behind him now, his vision began to clear. In the middle of the intersection, he could see what looked like a shadow in contrast to the bright light. He closed his eyes and counted to five, hoping that would help his eyes adjust. When he opened them, the figure was clearer and Dermot realized it was actually two figures. He recognized the back of Ryan's head. All he could see of the other person in front of Ryan was a pair of bare legs, but he was sure it was Sarah. He scanned up from their legs to see Ryan's raised arm and the gun he was holding to Sarah's head.

***

"Son," the police officer seemed to have infinite patience. They'd been locked in this standoff for almost fifteen minutes. Sarah's legs were starting to ache, and her feet were frozen from the cold asphalt. Neighbors had come to stand outside and gawk, even though several officers had been dispatched to send everyone back inside their houses.

She knew Ryan had to be getting tired. She'd felt his grip around her waist loosen on more than one occasion, only to tighten again before she could make a move. Ryan kept engaging the police in a back and forth of, "Let the girl go," and, "I can't. I love her." Which of course was a load of garbage, but only Sarah and Ryan seemed to know that.

Sarah was nearing the end of her reserves when an animal scream ripped through the night air. It was a long and painful "No!" that was so sudden, it had almost everyone turning to see where it had come from. Sarah looked too, and saw Dermot hobbling toward them, blood streaming down his face and amplifying his look of pure rage.

Ryan spun to see where the sound came from, and as he did Sarah felt his grip loosen. Just then a familiar voice from the other direction shouted, "Sarah, down!"

Sarah immediately let go of every muscle in her body, effectively turning into a rag doll. The combination of his distraction and her sudden weight let her slip out of Ryan's arm. As soon as she hit the ground, Sarah started to roll away. Ryan turned back to her, his eyes blazing, but by the time he realized what was happening she was more than an arm's length away. This left him standing alone in the bright pool of light with the police shouting for him to drop his weapon. Sarah stopped rolling and looked back at Ryan.

He gave her a chilling smile. "I'm not the only one, princess. There will always be more."

With that, Ryan raised his gun and pointed it at the police officer closest to him. Before he could fire a shot, there was a pop from somewhere behind her. Sarah watched the back of Ryan's head explode in a spray of red. His arm swung out as he fell to the ground, the gun tumbling from limp fingers. His eyes were wide and lifeless. Blood slowly seeped from a hole just above his left eyebrow.

CHAPTER THIRTY-FOUR

Sarah sat slumped on the ground where she had come to a stop in the middle of Ransom Street. It was as if the gunshot that had killed Ryan had turned off the sound. Paramedics and police swarmed the area. Someone threw a blanket over her shoulders, but she didn't see who. Another paramedic was talking to her, asking her questions. Sarah saw the woman's lips moving, but no sound seemed to register in her brain. She just stared at the woman, mute.

Then, just over the woman's shoulder, she saw a tall figure shuffling her way. One shoulder seemed to hang lower than the other and blood trailed down his face like a red mask, but his eyes showed a sharp, savage intensity. Sarah thought for a second that he had walked out of her imagination. She wondered if under that blood she would find the blue woad war paint of her ancestors. His eyes found hers and held. He was no hallucination. She let out a shriek and surged from the ground, hurling herself at him heedless of the startled calls of the paramedic or his injuries. Dermot wrapped his good arm around her as tight as he dared. Sarah buried her face in his shirt and wept with relief.

His arm felt so good around her. He slowly rubbed his cheek back and forth on the top of her head. She flattened her hands on his back and pressed as close as she could, anxious for every inch of contact. She wanted to feel every breath he took, every shift of muscle, every sign that he was alive and not lying dead on her living room floor. “You’re alive.”

“So are you.” He lifted his good hand to her cheek. “Did he hurt ye?”

She kept her other cheek pressed to him, but shook her head. “No. I’m more worried about you.”

“I’ll be alright.” She felt the words rumble through his chest more than she heard them.

The same paramedic who had been talking to Sarah brought a blanket to her and tried to pull her away. Sarah would have none of it. She looked at the woman and said, “I’m fine, but he probably has a concussion.”

The woman called over her shoulder to one of her comrades for help. After a few minutes of them attempting to separate Sarah and Dermot, and the two of them refusing to be out of each other’s sight, the paramedics relented and escorted both of them to an ambulance.

They were in the back of an ambulance, Sarah watching Dermot like a hawk as the paramedics ran him through the various checks for head injuries, when the tall guy from earlier found them. He was about the same height as Dermot, but thinner and with darker hair. Sarah hadn’t noticed it before, but his Scottish accent was unmistakable when he said, “Are ye alright then, Dermot?”

“Right as rain, mate,” Dermot said, looking into the light the paramedic was shining into his eyes. “Sarah, this is another distant cousin, Fleming Sinclair.”

Fleming bowed his head slightly and offered Sarah his hand. “I’m glad to see yer alright, hen.”

Sarah gave him a smile and shifted the blanket so she could shake his hand. “Thanks for trying to help.”

"Least I could do." He looked about to say more when Sarah heard another voice from the crowd of police officers near Ryan's body.

"Hey, MacDuff! That was quite a shot." The man grinned at another officer in uniform who was loading a long narrow black bag into the trunk of a patrol car.

The officer he'd called MacDuff had his back to Sarah, but something about the way he moved his shoulders, squared and with an easy grace, that looked so familiar. It couldn't be Old Duff. This man was too young. He looked to be in his early to mid-fifties, whereas Old Duff was around Granny's age.

The officer nodded at his comrade and closed the trunk, turning to survey the scene, and Sarah caught her first glimpse of his face. He had the same expression of flat resolve that all the cops on the scene seemed to be wearing as he scanned the area. His light brown hair was cropped short and he was clean-shaven. She had never seen Old Duff that neat, even at her mother's funeral. But this man could have been his son.

MacDuff looked around the clustered patrol cars and ambulances. He stopped when he saw Sarah staring at him, then quickly looked away and started walking in the other direction. Sarah jumped from the ambulance, forgetting she was still barefoot. "Hey! Wait!"

She reached him just as he was stepping onto the curb in front of her building and grabbed his arm. The man looked down at Sarah's hand on his arm before fixing his chocolate brown eyes on hers. This close, Sarah couldn't help feeling swamped by how familiar he was. She searched his face, looking for any sign of recognition from him.

"Yes?" If he recognized her as anything other than the hostage he'd just helped rescue, he gave no sign of it. Sarah began to doubt what she was thinking.

"You're the sniper, right?" He nodded. "I just want to thank you."

"Just doing my job, ma'am." He gave her a nod and started to step away.

Sarah glanced down at his name tag. "MacDuff. I…I know a Grant MacDuff, lives in the mountains. You kind of remind me of him. Any relation?"

"Could be. It's a big family." The half-smile he gave her was so familiar that she could almost picture him with a winter's growth of beard and long, wild hair.

"It was you that told me to get down, wasn't it?"

"Mmhmm. You did just fine." He gave her arm a gentle squeeze just above the elbow.

"Hey, Doug," a man in business casual clothes with a badge hanging from a chain around his neck and an air of authority interrupted them. "Nasty business, but that was a good shot."

"Thanks, Sarge." MacDuff nodded to the man before turning back to Sarah. "Well, I'm glad you're okay, miss."

"Wait!" He had started to walk away again. Sarah stepped closer to him and slowly wrapped her arms around his neck. He went stiff for a second before returning the hug. When she let him go, Sarah gave him a direct look. "Thank you, for everything."

He nodded mutely at Sarah and the other officer before walking away. She could have sworn she saw tears pooling in his eyes.

"Miss, will you come with me so we can talk about what happened here tonight?" the other cop asked, taking Sarah's arm and leading her toward a police car.

Sarah pulled the blanket tighter around her and got into the back seat of the car. The officer stood in the open car doorway. The inside of the car was blessedly warm, and Sarah was reminded again what little clothes she was wearing under the blanket. "Can I go into my apartment and get some clothes?"

"We have some personnel in there now. We'll send some clothes out." He leaned into the front of the car and used the radio to communicate the request to the officers inside. Turning back to her, he gave her a fatherly smile. "Now, I'd like to hear your account of what happened here tonight, starting with your full name."

Sarah took a deep breath before she began. "My legal name is Mórag NicMhàili MacAlpin, but most people just call me Sarah…"

She told him who Ryan was and about waking up to find him on top of her. She recounted their conversation with as much detail as she could remember. As she went through the events in order, she felt the energy draining out of her and being replaced with a nearly overwhelming dread. How was she going to explain this to Amy? Hell, she didn't really understand herself. She had thought at first that his attack was about Amy, but he had said it wasn't.

Sarah told the detective about his admission to killing Bridget MacKenzie and suggested that he contact the authorities in Nova Scotia. It was so hard to imagine him following her from Cape Breton and then biding his time all these months. Sarah couldn't make sense of it.

A police officer brought out a bag of clothes from Sarah's dresser, and they left her in the not-quite privacy of the police car to slip sweats on over her nightshirt. Then the detective returned, and they went through Sarah's version of events again. After going over the bullet points a third time, the detective said, "I'm going to have this report typed up, and then I'm going to need you to review it and sign it. Can you come by the police station this afternoon to do that?"

Sarah was relieved he wasn't going to expect her to go now and wait while the report was produced. She nodded.

The detective stepped back from the car, and Sarah saw Dermot there. His arm was in a sling, and the blood had been cleaned off his face. A couple butterfly bandages held closed a cut on his forehead. Again she felt the knee-weakening relief that she'd felt when she'd first laid eyes on him after the confrontation with Ryan. She rose from the car and walked into his arms.

CHAPTER THIRTY-FIVE

They finally stumbled into the basement apartment on Rosemary Street just before dawn. All the statements had been taken down and the questions answered. Dermot's shoulder still throbbed from a deep bruise, but nothing was broken. He had a mild concussion, and they had wanted him to go to the hospital, but he'd refused. He couldn't let Sarah out of his sight. It would be some time before he stopped seeing the image of her dropping to the ground at the killer's feet every time he closed his eyes.

Sarah looked wrung out. She couldn't go back to her apartment as there was no lock on the door. She had gotten dressed at some point and someone had packed her a bag. Dermot dropped it just inside the door, not really caring where it landed. Sarah sat on the sofa.

He went to the bedroom to change. When he returned, Sarah was still on the couch leaning against the arm and staring vacantly at the wall. He sat next to her, not touching. He was afraid to touch her tonight. He'd spent months denying his attraction to her, but after what they had been through he didn't trust himself to hold back. He wanted more than anything to hold her, make love to her, to affirm they were both still alive.

"Where's Fleming?" she asked softly.

"Hotel."

She made a grunt of understanding, and they returned to their stunned silence. For all they were sitting next to each other, she wore a weary, far-away look.

Remembering some of the things Ryan had told her, made him tell her, Dermot began to dread what might be going on behind that look.

When he couldn't take the silence any longer he said, "Sarah, what he said…about me, about James—"

She didn't turn to look at him, but cut him off with a slow, tired "Shh" and a hand on his arm. "I don't want to hear any more about it. It's ridiculous, and he was crazy. Maybe he was obsessed with James, and somehow Bridget and I and who knows who else fell victim to that obsession. But I'm not going to take the ravings of a madman over what I've seen and what I know about you. I'm done suspecting you of ulterior motives or nefarious plots or anything other than being my friend. You said those things to stall for time. It probably saved our lives."

He let go of a long breath he felt like he'd been holding since he realized she was in danger. He didn't know if he was relieved that she didn't believe it…or disappointed that the truth wasn't out. Still, he wasn't going to force it on her now, not today. "Even for all yer suspicions, yer better to me than I deserve."

They slipped back into silence, feeling slightly more at ease than a moment ago. Neither one of them seemed inclined to move, so they remained on the couch. It could have been twenty seconds, twenty minutes, or two hours.

"I'm going to make a sandwich." Sarah shifted and rose from the sofa like a woman three times her age. She trudged over to the tiny kitchen.

Confused, Dermot followed and watched as she pulled bread out of the cabinet and opened the fridge. He was disconcerted by how easily she made herself at home in his apartment. "A lunatic just tried to kill ye and yer making a sandwich?"

"Yep." Her face was set and her eyes burned with quiet determination. "You want one?"

He studied her for a few more seconds. "Sure."

She made two sandwiches out of the measly pickings in his refrigerator. It wasn't much, just some meat slapped between a couple pieces of bread. When she was done, they sat at the little cafe table and ate silently. Then she picked up their plates and carried them to the sink, placing them carefully as if the clatter of dishes might shatter the morning around them. Taking out a glass, she filled it with water and stood at the sink drinking it down without taking a breath. When she finished she filled the glass again, but drank more slowly this time while staring at the wall behind the sink.

"Ye're taking this awfully well for someone who was stalked by a killer." His voice was almost a whisper, not wanting to completely ruin the quiet she was so carefully preserving.

Sarah let out a sort of shrugging, want-to-hear-something-funny laugh. "Thing is, Dermot, this isn't the first time that someone's tried to kill me. And the other time…" head shaking, she looked away, "was so much worse, so much closer…I relive it regularly in my nightmares. But I survived that and built myself a good life. And I'll survive this. That psycho is lying in the morgue, and I'm standing right here."

She shifted her weight, but stayed at the sink glass in hand. "So yeah, I made a sandwich and ate, and I'm going to keep on eating and breathing and hopefully sleeping. Tomorrow, I'll get up and get dressed and go about my day just like I would any other time. And after a while, those things will be natural again, and that nut job will just be a memory. A couple of years from now, I'll say to you, 'Hey, remember that guy?' And we'll laugh about it. And it won't hurt me anymore, not like the other time."

"Who was it?" He edged forward on his chair, not sure if he should ask but he had to know.

She was silent a moment before she turned to him. "Hmm?"

"Who tried to kill ye before?"

She looked back to the wall, studying the grainy pattern of the cinderblock. Her knuckles on the hand that held the glass were white. "My mother." Her voice was a whisper. "I was six, and it was springtime."

***

March 1976
Kettle Hollow, North Carolina

"Sarah, over here. I found some." I came running up behind Mama. I was so excited to be outside in the sun after all winter indoors. It had been a long one. I don't know what they were fighting about, but Mama and Granny had been at it since Yule. They would talk hard to each other and then not talk at all. Then they'd start another round. They were careful not to do it around me, but I knew something was going on. The walls in our old house were thick enough that I couldn't understand words, but not thick enough to block out raised voices. And you know nothing sounds quite like angry Gaelic, not that Mama ever spoke Gaelic. She understood it just fine. So their arguments always happened in two sides. Granny speaking Gaelic and Mama speaking English.

That day, the sun had finally come out, and Mama and I were desperate to get out of the house. I said we should go look to see if any flowers had started blooming. I wanted us all to go, but Granny said she would stay home and tend to the chores. Mama tried to get me to wear a hat. She was always trying to get me to wear hats in the cold, but my curls were so springy I couldn't get any to stay down on my head.

So Mama and I headed out and were up the mountain from where the still was when she finally found some flowers. Just these little star shaped anemones in white and pink with their yellow centers. She called me over to show them to me, and they were so beautiful peeking out of dead leaves and mulch in the forest. They were like the Star of Hope the Burns writes about in "Ae Fond Kiss". I remember standing there thinking that spring was going to fix everything, that all the arguing and tension at home were just because we'd all been cooped up in the house too long. Once we got outside and went about the spring planting and managed to stretch our legs past the length of the parlor floor, it would all be okay. I think Mama did too. I felt her rest her hand on my head, like she sometimes did when she thought I wouldn't notice or when I was tired.

"*A bheil tuilleadh ann?*" I asked.

"Let's find out." We started walking slowly, watching for places where the flowers might be growing. We found a huge patch of them under a great oak tree, just like a carpet of stars.

I was so excited. I just wanted to snatch them all up and take them home with us. Maybe they would make everyone smile. "*Am faod mise na flùraichean a thogail a Mhamaidh?*"

"Yes," she nodded. "You can pick some."

I stopped and held out my hands and closed my eyes to give thanks. I'm not sure when I stopped doing that. It might have been that year. I don't think I felt very thankful after that day, but I was thankful for those flowers and for spring, and I lifted my hands and breathed and said so. Mama just watched me.

I smiled up at her and told her. "*Tha mi a' dol dhèanamh crùn dhuibh!*"

Then I ran ahead and picked flowers until they were spilling out of my arms. We sat down on a log and I twisted some vines into a circle and tucked the flowers and leaves into it. We sang a puirt à beul, "*Sealamh Curraigh Eoghan,*" and Mama tucked flowers into my hair. That might be the last time I ever saw her happy, and I spoiled it.

I finished making the crown and I stood on the log to put it on her head. "*Tha coltas bànrigh an t-sìthein oirbh.*"

Mama froze and got this look on her face, like I had caught her at something. It wasn't guilt, but a kind of shock and recognition. It only lasted a second before she laughed and said, "A fairy queen? A witch more likely."

She went to take it off, but I stopped her. "*Fag e.*"

I always knew my mama was sad, but she was a queen to me. I couldn't let her take off that crown. It would have been like letting her deny how beautiful, how wonderful she was.

We were frozen there with her hands on the crown and my hands on hers. She gave me a long, searching look. After a few seconds, she dropped her hands and sighed. "Let's take some flowers back to Granny."

We picked some more and carried them back down the mountain. We were singing the whole way and even dancing when the trail was wide enough. It felt so good. Like we were freer than we'd ever been.

When we got home, Granny was in the kitchen washing dishes. We tumbled in and spilled our flowers all over the table and chattered about where we found them. Granny kept looking at the crown on Mama's head, like she was pleasantly surprised that Mama was wearing it. Mama was nicer to Granny than I think she had been all winter, and it seemed for a few minutes like things might be getting better, like everything might be okay.

Granny offered to fix lunch while Mama and I went and got cleaned up. We went up to the bathroom at the top of the stairs and Mama started running the bath. "Alright. Get those clothes off."

I was so happy about Mama and Granny getting along and how much fun we'd had that morning that I threw my arms around Mama's legs and asked, "Will you and Granny stop fighting now?"

I stepped back and started peeling off my clothes. Mama looked at me. Her face was soft and she said. "We'll see. I hope so."

She helped me climb into the great claw-footed tub and handed me a bar of soap. I started scrubbing away the green stains that were left on my fingers. I looked up to find Mama staring at her reflection in the mirror. She still wore the crown on her head, but her face was so sad.

I wanted to cheer her up, to distract her. “Mama? When I go away from here, will you come with me?”

“Are you going somewhere?” She came over to the tub and pulled a pink flower from my hair and dropped it in the water.

“I had a dream about going far away. I was going to meet the king.”

Mama froze in the act of pulling another flower from my hair. She looked at me hard. “What king?”

I didn’t understand why she was suddenly so intent on what I was saying. I wondered for a second if I should go on, but in the end I said, “The king of mist.”

I watched some range of emotions sweep across her face that I still don’t quite understand. Horror, sadness, determination…and before I knew what was happening she had me by the shoulders and was pushing me under the water. She kept saying she was going to save me. “They can’t have you, not my baby. I won’t let them.”

I tried reaching up to her, but she had my arms pinned and I couldn’t get free. I was a tiny thing at six, and her grip was so strong. “They’re not going to get their hooks in you.”

My lungs were on fire and my head was swimming and she just kept muttering about them, whoever they were. Eventually, I started to black out. The last thing I remember seeing were the flowers floating on the surface above me.

When I woke up, Granny was holding me tight and rocking me, giving thanks that I was alive. Mama was on the floor unconscious. There was blood coming from her head.

***

"Do ye know why she did it?"

Sarah shook her head. "She was dead within six months. The official story was that she accidentally fell off a cliff in the fog one morning. The truth is that she slit her wrists in her bedroom."

Sarah looked down at her own wrists ringed with angry red welts left by the zip ties Ryan had used to bind them. "She wrote a message on the wall in her own blood, very dramatic, my mother. I found her. It was the last day of school, and I was going to show her my report card, but I found her on the bed in a pool of blood. Duff was the one that…" Sarah paused, biting back a sob, "threw her body off the cliff and called the sheriff. I guess it was easier for Granny to have people talking about the dangers of putting a still too close to a drop-off than it was to have them talking about how poor Molly MacAlpin did herself in."

"What was the message?"

"*Ruith,*" she answered, switching flawlessly from western Carolina twang to Gaelic lilt.

"Run away?" He could only stare at her, wondering what Molly MacAlpin had known and why she would tell them to run. "From what?"

Sarah inhaled sharply. "I don't know. From herself, from whatever was haunting her, from whatever she thought was worth killing me over. We'll never know."

She turned her hand next to his on the counter and gripped his fingers, shaking her head. He watched her throat move as she swallowed painfully. "We had next to nothing. We lived off our garden and the forest. I never had a new dress until I was in high school. My toys were sticks and corn husk dolls. I knew my mother was unhappy. Hell, it was hard to miss. But I never wanted for anything important, and I never doubted that she loved me. After that day," her voice cracked, "I can't see how anyone can love me when my own mother tried to kill me, when she killed herself to get away from me."

"Och, no. No, no, no, Sarah." He turned her around and took her face in his hands, his blue eyes fierce on hers. "Don't ye see that everyone loves ye? Everyone from Amy right down to any punter who's seen ye on a stage. I love ye."

Sarah returned his fierce blue gaze, her eyes searching his.

"I love ye." He said the words as if they had been sitting on the tip of his tongue for too long, and he was relieved to finally let them out. They stood for a long moment with those words hanging in the air between them. Dermot leaned forward. His lips pressed to hers before he pulled back to say again. "I love ye."

Sarah let out a sob as her hand slipped to the back of his head, her fingers threading through his hair. "I thought he'd killed you. I couldn't bear it."

"I know. I'm here. We're alive." He told her between quick, hard kisses.

"I love you." She pulled him to her and kissed him. The tension that was held in check over the last few months exploded. They devoured each other. She tasted like salvation and damnation all at once.

No matter how loud the alarm bells went off in his head, Dermot didn't stop this time. He was done stopping himself, done denying what was real. She had given him the hard, unvarnished truth of her childhood. He owed her the truth. She had to know that he loved her. Everything else was for another time.

"I need you." Her voice shook with the words as she grasped the hem of her shirt and lifted it over her head. She was bare from the waist up, and her breasts were just as perfect as he'd been trying not to imagine. Her skin called to his, and he yanked his own shirt off and dropped it before taking her face in his hands again.

"I'm here. I'll always be here." He pressed forward, pinning her between his hips and the counter behind her. "Put your arms around my neck."

Dermot bent to hook an arm behind her knees and lift her up against his chest, heedless of the pain in his shoulder. He carried her across the apartment and into the bedroom. Falling to his knees, he placed Sarah on the futon and moved to kneel between her thighs. He sat back to look at her, not believing she was with him. He'd spent so many months dreaming of this moment and knowing it could never be. He'd be damned in the morning. Looking at her curls spilling across his pillow and her skin flushed and glowing, he found he couldn't care about that.

***

Sarah tried to tell herself that this moment would last. He wouldn't pull back like he had before. This time was different. He knelt over her, his breath coming quick and hard. She noticed the purple bruise spreading from his injured shoulder and reached up to skim her fingers across it. "Does it still hurt?"

"Aye." He leaned over her, resting most of his weight on his good arm. His perfect lips curved into a cheeky smile. "I'll manage."

Sarah drew her fingers down his side, feeling the muscles bunch and ripple under her touch. He leaned down and sealed his mouth to hers, kissing her deeply. It wasn't the flaring passion that had ignited at the cabin, nor the tentative seeking of last summer. This was a steady burning fire of need.

He released her lips and leaned down to lap at one of her nipples before taking it between his teeth and tugging on it. Sarah arched against him, sharpening the delicious pinch. His hot breath fanned out over her ribs as he slid down her body. He drew her sweats down and she lifted her hips so he could pull them off. He pushed his own off before returning to her. His skin beneath her hands was hot as he leaned down again and took her mouth.

"Och, God, Sarah how I've wanted ye." He breathed against the hair at her temple as he slid inside her.

"Shhh…" She reveled in the feeling of fullness, in his hard weight on top of her. "I'm yours, all yours."

He drew back and pushed forward again, filling her slowly. It felt so right. Having him inside her felt like home, like this was something she'd been looking for far longer than she realized. From that first meeting last summer, something about Dermot had seemed inevitable to her. She realized now that this was it, this heart-gripping, mind-emptying need. This was what she'd been afraid of: needing him.

He slid his good arm around her back and rose to his knees, pulling her with him. They were still joined. Their bodies slid against each other as they rose and fell with the shifting of his powerful thighs. Sarah wrapped her legs around his waist and let him guide them to oblivion.

CHAPTER THIRTY-SIX

Sarah squeezed her eyes shut, trying hard to stay asleep. She curled up on her side, pulling the comforter around her shoulder and mentally cataloguing all her various aches. She didn't want to get up, didn't want to spend her day signing police reports and cleaning her apartment and explaining what had happened to Amy. She knew she could get through it all, but she didn't want to leave the warmth of Dermot's bed just yet. Although he seemed to have already gotten up. She wasn't deliciously tangled up in his rangy limbs anymore. Sarah drifted back to sleep hoping that he'd return.

You're going to make him a king.

The king was lost in the mist.

Sarah let her eyes slip open to see the mid-day sun filtering in through the sheer curtain that covered Dermot's tiny window at the top of the wall that faced the street. The sun shone almost straight down, making a keystone shaped box of sunlight on the square vinyl tiles on the floor, a network of boxes overlapping at odd angles. Occasionally, the shadow of someone walking by on the sidewalk would cross the keystone, blocking the light for a second before it reappeared.

She watched the shadows cross by from one direction then another, obscuring and revealing the boundaries of the various boxes and clamped down on the drift of her thoughts. She was still exhausted and caught in that half-asleep zone of the mind that blended dreams with reality and memory to generate any number of worries that weren't necessarily real.

You're going to make him a king.

King was lost

She liked to think she knew the difference between dreams and reality, but the last few months had proven to her that maybe she didn't. Too many of those half-dream anxieties had filtered into her life, and she had misunderstood them. She'd been so focused on her imagined danger that she hadn't recognized the real danger until it was almost too late.

What king?

King of Mist

Someone stopped in front of the window and stood blocking out most of the light box and leaving only the flat network of alternating squares. Sarah squirmed deeper under the comforter, seeking to escape the December chill radiating off the concrete walls. The person on the street walked on, revealing the box of light once again.

Make him king…

Sarah sat up with a gasp. Her childhood dream and the trigger that had set her mother off, "The River Maiden," Ryan's ramblings. They were all too close. There had to be a connection. She had to tell Dermot.

Wrapping the comforter around her, she threw open the bedroom door only to find Dermot on the phone. He stood in the middle of the room with his back to her as if he'd been pacing. He wore the same gray sweats he'd had on before they'd gone to bed. His chestnut hair was tousled from sleep. Sarah scanned the wall of muscle that was his back, remembering the feel of it under her hands. His shoulders and the back of his neck were tense. The muscles were so knotted she could see it.

He turned and took her in and the look that crossed his face before he turned away could only be described as bleak. Sarah looked down at herself. She was naked but for the comforter, and she was sure her hair was a disaster, but it couldn't be all that bad.

"Right. She's here now," he said into the phone before holding it out to her. He gave her a pleading look she didn't quite understand. "It's James."

She had hoped they'd burned through all the barriers that had been keeping them apart, but his attitude this morning suggested otherwise. She took the phone from him and slowly brought it to her ear, not taking her eyes from his. "James."

"Sarah." The smooth, patrician voice on the phone quaked with relief. "It's so good to hear your voice. How are you? Are you hurt?"

"Just a few bruises. Dermot is the one with the concussion and the hurt shoulder." Dermot turned away. He trudged into the bedroom.

"He's tough. He'll mend."

Sarah looked through the bedroom door to see Dermot pulling on a shirt, his shoulders sagging. She wasn't so sure.

"I'm pretty tough too, James."

"Still, I hate to think that I'm in any way responsible for this. You have to believe me. I don't know who that man was." The urgency in his voice touched her.

"I believe you. I never thought you did."

He sighed on the other end of the line. "How soon can you get over here? I want to see you with my own eyes. To know you're safe."

"It'll be a few weeks, James. I've got to pack up my apartment and wrap up some things here." Who knew how long that would take now that her apartment was a crime scene?

"Let me send someone to help you." There was that proprietary tone of his that made her bristle.

"James, that's really not necessary."

"I admire your independence," he said, sounding like he felt very much the opposite. "But if my name gets out, there will be press, probably a lot of it. I don't want you to be hounded or feel like you have to handle that yourself. I would feel much better if someone were there with you."

Sarah hadn't thought about that. She didn't like the idea of being hounded by press either. "Okay. You're right. I definitely have enough to deal with. Oh. You should also send someone to help Isobel MacKenzie, Bridget MacKenzie's grandmother. She could get caught up in the press too."

"You have a good heart, Sarah. I'll have someone there by tomorrow, and I'll send someone to help the MacKenzie woman. And Sarah?"

"Hmm?"

"Please take care." He sounded so concerned, so sincere that she couldn't help but melt a little.

She smiled. "I will, James. I'll see you soon."

***

She hung up the phone and laid it on the table before looking back at Dermot. Her hair was a mess. Her eyes were red-rimmed and tired, and he was sure there was nothing on her under the comforter. She was the most beautiful thing he'd ever seen. He couldn't look at her without remembering what they'd done. The taste of her was still in his mouth, and now he would have to tell her why it could never happen again.

He scooped up her bag from the floor where he'd dropped it when they'd arrived early in the morning and held it out to her.

"Get dressed. We need to talk." He tried to make his voice gentle but commanding.

Sarah looked as though she'd have none of it. She stepped past his outstretched arm and wrapped her arms around his waist. She nuzzled his neck her lips, grazing just above the collar of his shirt. "Not yet, Dermot. Whatever it is, it can wait."

He held himself stiff, not touching her, but every muscle wanted to take her again. He fought hard to control it. "It can't."

Sarah leaned back to look in his eyes. Dread and uncertainty were written on her brow as her eyes searched his. She tightened her grip on his waist. "Then tell me now, while we're close."

"Not like this. Please just get dressed."

Sarah stepped back and let the comforter slide from her shoulders, baring her torso. Her skin was nearly perfect but for the faint bruise over her ribs where the table had hit her the night before, the table he'd kicked into her. He thought it no small irony that her biggest lingering injury of the night wasn't from something that Ryan had done, but something he'd done.

"I don't think so," she said with her own special brand of quiet determination.

Dermot gritted his teeth and pointedly looked away. "Damn it, Sarah. I have to tell ye something you are not going to like. And ye'll be able to take it much better with some clothes on ye. Will ye not go and get dressed?"

Her green eyes shot fire and the muscles in her jaw worked as if she were biting back a dozen different things she might say. She let the comforter fall to the floor, baring all of herself. "Are you sure that would be for my benefit, or yours?"

She stepped close again and never took her eyes from his as she took the bag from his hand. She stalked around him, her feet barely making a sound as she padded into the bedroom. He didn't turn around, but jumped when the door slammed shut behind her.

***

She did feel better with clothes on. Something about the slide of fabric over skin and buttoning things up felt so simple and practical that it brought her back from that place of dread she'd been in moments ago. Not finding a comb in the bag, which had clearly been packed by a man, she ran her fingers through her hair and secured it in a bun with a rubber band she found on Dermot's dresser. A little makeup wouldn't have been a bad idea if she was getting ready for battle, but there wasn't any of that in the bag either. So jeans and her favorite Carolina sweatshirt worn soft by years of washing were all the armor she'd have today.

She rubbed her palms on her thighs nervously before opening the bedroom door. In the few minutes she'd been in his room, he had folded the comforter neatly and set it on one arm of the sofa. He was sitting with his elbows on his knees with his head hanging. He rose when he heard her step and indicated for her to take his seat.

When she sat gingerly on the edge, he pulled a chair from the little table and placed it in front of her. He lowered himself into the chair and took her hands in his. His blue eyes held hers with a resigned look while he took a deep breath. "What I'm about to tell ye has to be in strictest confidence. Ye cannot tell Amy or Barrett or anyone else. If he knew I was telling ye this, James would kill me. He may yet."

Sarah waited patiently for him to get to the point. "Ye'll know that MacAlpin is a verra old Scottish name."

"Of course. Kenneth MacAlpin united Scotland by marrying a Pictish prin—" She gasped. How could she have missed the connection? It was like the story of "The River Maiden." "Well, that certainly explains why Granny taught it to me."

"Aye. There's more. Yer family is actually much older. Your people have been in Scotland longer than anyone can remember and have been inter-marrying with Scots kings since before Dalriada. Royal families have changed…MacAlpin, Bruce, Comyn, Stuart. Your ancestors are the real constant." His eyes bored into hers. "The legacy of 'The River Maiden' is yours."

Sarah sat back from him, her hands sliding from his. "Okay, but what does that matter now? What am I missing?"

"Well, James is a Stuart. Aye?" At her nod, he went on. "He's descended from Charles Edward Stuart, which makes him—"

"The rightful heir to the Scottish throne. Except that Charles only had a daughter who was illegitimate."

Dermot tilted his head, acknowledging her point. “But he did acknowledge her eventually and she did have children. As to how that gets back to the Stuarts is long story that would probably require a chart.”

“It’s really a moot point, because there is no Scottish throne to speak of. I think that claim was decided a while ago.”

He made one of his throaty noises that could have been part laugh. “Ye know how ye hear old men around here arguing how the Confederates could have won certain battles of yer Civil War?”

Of course Sarah had heard them; frequently their arguments had been fueled by Granny Maggie’s best stump water. She nodded.

“Well, in Scotland ye hear the same kind of talk, only it’s usually about Culloden or Falkirk.” He took another deep breath. “In the next couple of years, Scotland will likely get its own Parliament. Home rule. James believes that true independence will follow. He also believes that Scotland will need a king.”

She couldn’t help it. She had to laugh. The idea that in the twentieth century anyone thought they needed a monarch seemed silly. “That’s so cute.”

“Ye willna think so when I tell ye that he also thinks that marrying you is essential to making that happen.” His words cut through her giggles like a bucket of icy water.

She stopped and he looked back at her. His expression was flat, deadpan. She matched his expression, but her eyes were full of ice. “Well, he can’t have me.”

He took her hand again. “I’m afraid he willna give ye a choice. He can be verra persuasive.”

Sarah stood up, shaking her head. She began pacing the room. Dermot turned in his chair to watch her. "This is the most ridiculous thing I have ever heard. This isn't 1320 or 1745. It's 1995! Countries aren't governed by kings anymore. Royals are just taxpayer-funded celebrities."

"I can see how ye might think that, being an American, but there are a lot people in Britain, and in Scotland, who care. More importantly there are some verra powerful people, and not just James, who care deeply about that."

"Well good for them." She shook her head. "That doesn't mean I have to participate."

Dermot rose slowly from his chair. "Actually, I think it does."

"No." She gritted her teeth and shook her head in small, rapid movements as if they could hold off the realization that was just dawning on her. "No!"

"Think about it, Sarah. James sent me to protect ye. But someone else sent Ryan to kill ye, and they'll send another when they know that he failed."

Sarah grabbed her head, covering her ears with her hands, her eyes closed. "No. He was not right. Ryan was not right about this. This is not happening."

Dermot came to her and grabbed her wrists, tugging them gently from her ears. She lifted her eyes to find his swimming with unshed tears. "I'm sorry. I'm so sorry."

Sarah felt the answering sting of tears. She swallowed past the lump that was quickly forming in her throat. When she spoke, her voice seemed so small in her own ears, like a child. "But...but you love me."

"Aye." A tear escaped to trickle down his cheek. "I do."

Sarah stretched toward him, her mouth seeking his, but he held her away from him with his hand on her shoulder. His next words were like lashes to both of them. “But I canna have ye. Making love to ye was the greatest experience of my life, but it never should have happened. It canna happen again.”

Sarah was startled to realize that the awful keening sound that filled her ears next was coming from her. She nearly fell to the floor where she stood, but he caught her and guided her to the sofa. She wanted so badly for him to put his arms around her, but he stepped away. So she pulled her knees up to her chest and cried in great heaving sobs.

Sarah had no idea how long she wept, but at length got control of herself. She inhaled deeply and pulled her shoulders back. She wiped her cheeks with the cuff of her sweatshirt. “So how do you fit into all of this?”

He’d been standing in the kitchen his back turned to give her some privacy. He cleared his throat. “I’m a steward. We take care of royal business.”

She huffed. “And that’s what I am? Royal business?”

“I wish I could tell ye otherwise, but aye. That’s why I’m here.” He brought her a glass of water. She drank, and he sat in front of her again. “I’m your steward, just like Grant MacDuff was yer mother’s.”

Sarah took that bit of information in stride. She thought about all the times Duff had acted as Molly’s champion, how he’d taken care of her even at the end. “Do you know where he is, Duff?”

“No. They lost track of him shortly after ye were born. Then when your mother died, they didna think he was needed.” So they didn’t suspect that Duff was still around.

"Are you really a folklorist?"

"I am. Everything I've told you about myself is true." He looked directly into her eyes. His voice was calm, patient even.

"What about the fellowship? Is that real or just a ruse to get me across the pond?" Sarah asked, wondering just how much of her life was going to be wrecked today.

"No, that's real. I was sent here because of our similar interests, but I talked James into funding that team before I ever met ye."

"But I would have been on that team even if I were the worst student who applied."

"You're not, by far. But if ye hadna been ready to go to Scotland, I would have made the offer before the semester ended." It stung her pride to know that she hadn't gotten the position on the merits of her work. She was a good folklorist and she knew it, but it didn't matter.

She dreaded hearing the answer to her next question. "What about Bridget, did she have a steward?"

He looked away. "He disappeared about the same time she did."

"So what exactly does a steward do?"

He looked distinctly uncomfortable. "We protect ye, support ye, make sure ye have whatever ye need, listen when ye need someone to talk to."

"Hmmph. You're basically a husband without any of the benefits."

He brushed a curl away from her face. "But not without love."

"Don't. Don't tell me you love me at the same time that you're telling me we can't be together." She unfolded herself and stood up from the sofa. "You can tell me you love me when you've decided that this is all bullshit and you'd rather live in this century."

"Ye're angry."

"I'm furious. This is the biggest load of garbage that I have ever heard." She squared her shoulders and her eyes bored into his. "I love you more than I ever thought possible, but you choose this, a myth and chance at a myth, over me. Yeah. I'm angry."

"There's no choice about it!" His voice echoed off the cinderblock walls. "I have no choice. People with more money and power than we could dream of have chosen for both of us."

"Not me. No one gets to choose for me," she shouted back. They watched each other in silence for some minutes. Sarah was gritting her teeth so hard in determination that her jaw began to ache.

"What are ye going to do?" he asked after some time.

Her look was shuttered. "I'm going to clean myself up and go to the police station. I have a report to sign."

"I meant about Scotland, about James." He lifted a hand as if he was going to lay it on her arm, but stopped himself.

That was a very good question, one that would require more thinking than she was capable of at the moment. "I don't know. I'm going to have to think about that."

He accepted her answer with a nod.

"Is Fleming a…steward?" she asked as she headed for the bathroom.

"Mmmhmm."

"Good. He can take me to the police station." And with that she closed the door.

CHAPTER THIRTY-SEVEN

Her eyes itched. She knew they had to be swollen, and her head was beginning to throb. After going over the events of the previous night for the umpteenth time, Sarah had finally been able to sign her statement. She was now waiting at a bench near the front desk while the guys finished theirs.

In the end, Dermot had ridden to the police station with them after pointing out that he needed to sign a report too. Fleming and Dermot were each talking to detectives, reviewing their own accounts of what happened. Sarah seethed. She couldn't stand the sight of him, but she was equally terrified of being without him.

She was feeling decidedly sorry for herself, and with good reason. Normally, she would dust herself off and keep moving, but there was nothing normal about this situation. Her life had been completely up-ended. The man she loved wouldn't have her, her home was a crime scene, her best friend was going to flip out when she heard what happened, and even her academic future seemed questionable. For the first time in a very long time, Sarah didn't know if she was going to get past this. She was just shifting on the bench, trying to find a position that didn't make her ribs hurt worse, when Officer MacDuff walked past her. In the light of day he looked even more like the Duff she knew.

He didn't seem to notice Sarah. She jumped up to follow him into the hall. He turned into the men's room. Sarah parked herself next to the restroom door to wait for him.

Within a couple of minutes MacDuff came out. Sarah waited until the door was almost closed. He was a few feet down the hall. "I know it's you."

He stopped in his tracks, but didn't turn around. Sarah walked to him, keeping her voice low. "How long have you been here?"

"'Bout as long as you have." He was paler than she remembered, but then he'd always worked outside and had worn a beard back then. She had a hard time reconciling this man in the blue uniform with the rough, often dirty itinerant Duff she knew.

"So is it true? You were her steward?" Sarah watched him stiffen.

"No one's called me that in a long time." His shoulders dropped. "I guess that means you know."

"Yeah. Although I didn't really believe it until just now." She looked toward the office to make sure Dermot wasn't coming out. "Is there any way to escape it?"

Duff closed his eyes and took a deep breath. "Not one that's worked. Your Mama wanted to try. She even ran away once, before you came along, but she didn't get very far."

"Did you help her?"

He flinched. "It's complicated."

They fell into an awkward silence, each occupied with their own thoughts. Eventually Sarah asked softly, "Why hide? Why not tell me you were here?"

"I was there when you needed me." His eyes met hers, and she saw the raw pain that he'd kept hidden from her for years.

"What about when I needed a family? All those years we were both alone when we could have had each other." Sarah tried to keep her voice steady.

A door slammed down the hall, and he looked back as if he didn't want anyone to overhear. "I don't have a good answer for you. For a while I thought I could be what you needed. But as you got older, you just..." His eyes scanned her face. "You remind me more and more of Molly all the time. I mean the way she was when I met her, all full of dreams and ready to take on the world. I started to see why she had such trouble with it, thinking you were the one. I got so I couldn't take it anymore, but I couldn't leave you alone either."

"So you watched me struggle through years of grief, thinking I had no one."

"No, Sarah-girl, that's wrong." He gripped her arm and stepped closer. "I watched you blossom. I watched you become the person I knew you could be, that your Mama knew you could be."

Sarah closed her eyes and breathed deep. "Why didn't you warn me?"

"Would you have believed me?" He started strolling back to the office area, leading her gently by the arm.

She huffed out a laugh. "Probably not."

He led her past the detective's desks to another cluster of desks deeper in the office. One of them had his name on the nameplate. "I had a feeling I'd be seeing you today. I have something for you."

He opened a drawer and pulled out a small brown paper bag. "I had a feeling I'd be seeing you again. She would want you to have this."

Sarah unrolled the top of the bag and slid out a small and worn leather-bound book. She flipped through a few pages to find that they were covered with her mother's small, neat handwriting. She was instantly swamped with too many feelings to process: grief, curiosity, dread. "Her diary? Duff, I don't know if I want to read this."

His warm brown eyes sought hers. They were as kind as always. This was one man Sarah could trust. "You do. You're going to need it."

He led her back to where Dermot and Fleming were wrapping things up. Duff nodded toward them. "Are they your stewards?"

Sarah looked up just as Dermot did. Their eyes locked. He looked away first. "The big one with the brown hair is. I think the other one is just here for back-up."

"Hmmph." He eyed the two younger men before tugging on her arm. She turned to him and he leaned down to whisper in her ear. "Go easy on him, Sarah. I loved your mother from the moment I met her, and it nearly tore me apart. If he's anywhere as good as you deserve, he's got a hard road ahead of him. You both do."

He gave her elbow one last squeeze and led her over to where Dermot and Fleming were standing. Dermot perked up when he recognized Duff. "Ye're the shooter from last night?"

Duff nodded, and Dermot held out his hand. "That was a fine shot. Thank ye."

Duff took the offered hand and gave it a solid shake. "Just doing my duty. You might know a thing or two about that."

Some unspoken message passed between the two of them. Something Sarah couldn't see, but Dermot arched a brow at the older man and said grimly, "Aye. That I do."

***

Sarah rubbed a rag dipped in stain remover over the bloodstain on the carpet...Dermot's blood. She'd been attempting to clean the spot for over half an hour, but only seemed to be succeeding in spreading it. She had started by soaking it with detergent and letting it sit while the handyman worked on replacing the door. Once the door had been closed, she had gotten on the floor and started scrubbing.

"Sarah, please let me do that," Dermot called from where he was sitting on the edge of the couch.

"No," she snapped. "Your shoulder."

"Then will ye leave it? We can rent one of those cleaners tomorrow."

Sarah sat back on her heels and looked hard at the stain. She didn't think she could leave it. She'd tried to leave Dermot earlier, but he wasn't letting her out of his sight. She wanted to leave the apartment altogether and never look back, but Amy would come home eventually and she should really be here to explain. Then there was James and the whole stupid, weird mess that she still wasn't sure she understood. Her whole world seemed to be careening out of control, but by God she could control her own damn carpet. "Then go rent one, but I'm not sleeping in this apartment with your blood all over the floor."

"Ye dinna have to sleep here." His accent thickened with emotion.

"I do! Dammit. I'm sure as hell not sleeping at your place again."

"Sarah—" He stood up and took a step toward her, but stopped as they heard someone fumbling unsuccessfully with the lock.

Sarah got to her feet, dreading what was next. She reached for the door. "That'll be Amy."

Dermot stopped her, wrapping his hand around hers on the knob. He checked the peephole in the door, making sure there weren't any surprises. She couldn't look at him, so he whispered into her hair. "It's not yer fault."

Sarah bowed her head and gave the briefest nod before opening the door. She backed into the room and Amy stepped over the threshold eyeing them both. Her eyes were red-rimmed and her clothes were rumpled. She looked like she'd spent the previous night in a hospital waiting room, which she likely had.

"How's your granddad?" Sarah asked.

"He'll be fine." Her voice sounded choked and she swallowed hard. "He's got some paralysis on the left side, but they think it's only temporary."

Sarah felt the muscles in her shoulders unclench a fraction. "Good."

Amy closed the door behind her, but didn't move past the space in front of it. She stood there watching the two of them.

When Sarah couldn't stand the wait anymore she said. "How much do you know?"

Amy took in a long breath. "Well, I know what the police told me. That was after I saw the report on the news this morning. Of course, they didn't name any names, but I recognized the street."

Sarah didn't know what to say to that. She wanted to ask how much the police had told her. She looked over at Dermot.

They hadn't really talked about how much to tell Amy. Sarah felt sure that the whole truth would have been too ridiculous for her to bear, but she didn't want Amy feeling responsible.

"It's a very disconcerting thing to see your street full of police cars on the news and not know what happened," Amy said before Sarah could think of what to say next. "But then it seems I've been in the dark about a lot lately."

"Honey, why don't we sit down?" Sarah said, waving a hand at the couch.

Amy dropped her bag and sat down. Sarah seated herself next to her friend on the couch. Dermot pulled up a chair and placed it close enough that he could jump in if needed. Sarah wasn't sure if that was to support her or to keep her from saying too much.

Sarah walked Amy through the events of the previous night in the most straightforward terms she could. She was careful to keep any emotion out of her account. Amy had plenty of her own emotions going on. She didn't need to be worried about Sarah's too. She was also careful to leave out any explanation or speculation as to Ryan's motives, Stuart-related or otherwise. She did, however, point out the connection with Bridget MacKenzie's murder in Nova Scotia.

Amy kept her eyes locked on the coffee table and listened without giving away any of her own feelings. She seemed stunned, and that continued for what seemed like ages even after Sarah had finished. "So it really was about you all along. All of it."

"I don't know. I have no idea what motivated him." The lie tasted sour on Sarah's tongue, but the truth would have only made everything worse.

Just then there were two quick knocks on the door. Dermot got up and opened it after checking the peephole. Fleming came in carrying a couple of bags of groceries, which he handed to Dermot. Then he leaned out into the hall and pulled in one of the big orange carpet cleaners that can be rented at grocery stores.

"Thought ye could use this," he said to the room at large.

"We were just discussing renting one. Thanks." Sarah smiled at him. "Fleming, this is my roommate, Amy Monroe. Amy, this is Fleming Sinclair. He's a cousin of Dermot's visiting from Scotland."

Amy eyed Fleming as if he were a rat standing in the middle of the apartment before turning to Sarah. "So Dermot brings in a guy and you trust him instantly?"

Sarah was so stung by the jab that she couldn't think of a diplomatic response. Amy was clearly lashing out due to a confusing mix of emotions. It was impossible to explain trusting Fleming so easily without giving away the whole truth. As far as that "truth" went, the only thing Sarah had seen proven was that Dermot, Fleming, and Duff believed it. Yet Amy had brought a killer home without a second thought and ignored Sarah's misgivings for months.

Apparently that was the thought foremost in Fleming's mind as he began to say, "Well, I havena tried to—"

"Let's go make the hens some tea. Aye?" Dermot cut in before Fleming made the situation any more tense. He grabbed his cousin by the arm and dragged him to the kitchen, where they began banging about looking for kettle and cups.

"I don't believe you," Amy said, her voice dripping with venom. "You're fine with two big guys we hardly know rummaging around in our kitchen."

Sarah inhaled and let out a slow breath, trying to keep her tone even. "First of all, Dermot is not a stranger anymore, not by any means, and he's known Fleming since they were children. Second, the two of them saved my life last night, and if you had been here, they would have done the same for you."

A pink flush crept into Amy's cheeks at that. Sarah was trying very hard not to give even a hint of "I told you so" to Amy, but maybe her friend needed to be reminded that people had almost died. Amy was looking everywhere but at Sarah. Her gaze landed on the stain on the floor. "Is that blood?"

Sarah nodded.

"Whose is it?" Amy asked in a very small voice.

"Dermot's. His forehead split when Ryan rammed it into the table. Foreheads bleed a lot apparently." Sarah watched Amy closely. Her friend didn't seem to react at all. "I had hoped to have it cleaned up before you got home."

Amy continued staring at the stain on the floor. "I don't think this will ever be my home again."

Sarah reached across the space between them as if she would lay a hand on Amy's where they rested in her lap, but wasn't sure her friend would welcome it. She let it drop to the cushion.

Amy closed her eyes, but kept facing the direction of the stain on the floor. When she spoke, her voice was quiet and deliberate. "The whole world lays down at your feet. You get scholarships and accolades. Hell, billionaires throw money at you. People hang on your every word. You're like a star that everyone orbits around. I thought for once that I had something that was mine, something that might last, something I didn't get by virtue of being Sarah's friend. But that's exactly why I had it. If I hadn't been your friend, he wouldn't have been interested in me at all."

"Amy, you have just as much academic success as I do. You know that I'm not a social person. All the friends I have, I have because you've introduced them to me. Most of all, you have a family that loves you. Do you know what that means? I might have academic success, and people might like me, but it would all be forgotten if I left. A couple of weeks after I'm gone, none of them will remember me at all. Everything I have is fleeting, and I would trade it all, every pal, every penny, if I could have a family like yours."

Amy bowed her head. Sarah saw a few tears fall, but her friend didn't make a sound. After several seconds, Amy stood. "I'm going to stay with my folks for the holiday. Call me when you have your things out so I can talk to the landlord about getting out of the lease. I guess Barrett and I will find another apartment."

Amy started walking toward the hallway, but stopped. Sarah could almost hear her teeth grinding around her words. "I hate that you were right about this."

"Me too." Sarah watched her friend's back as she walked down the hall and into her room. Amy closed the door softly.

***

It was just under an hour later that Amy's door opened again. She emerged towing a suitcase with another bag slung over her shoulder. Sarah switched off the carpet cleaner and watched her friend with her eyes swimming and hands gripped tight on the machine handle.

Dermot tried to catch Amy's eye as she walked toward the door, but she studiously avoided looking at anyone. Fleming stepped forward and took the suitcase from her hand. "I'll help ye with this."

"Is there anything else?" Dermot asked.

Amy turned toward him, but didn't meet his eyes. "A box of Christmas gifts on the bed."

He promptly went to fetch the box and followed them out to Amy's car. Fleming had loaded the suitcase into the trunk and was eyeing Amy. He seemed about to say something to her when Dermot stepped up, forcing his cousin to step back out of the way. "Go on, mate. I'll just be a minute."

He set the box in the car and turned to Amy. She stuck out her chin and said, "Is this the part where you tell me this is all my fault."

"No." His voice was gentle but firm. "It's not your fault, or hers. This is the part where I remind ye what it is to be a friend to someone."

"Oh, you're clearly an expert on that."

He gave her a look that stopped any further comment before it could reach her lips. "I know yer hurting, and it feels like ye've lost someone ye cared about. But think for a minute. Ye're hurting, so you turn to yer family. Yer apartment doesna feel safe, but you have somewhere else to stay. She's lost her only home, her only safe place, and now it looks like she's lost her best friend. For what? Yer both hurt by this, but ye dinna have to hurt each other."

Dermot stood there watching her as she let her head hang. She worried the corner of the box with her fingernails. He wasn't sure what good his little speech would do, but he wouldn't watch Sarah hurting so and be silent about it. There was so much about her life that he couldn't change, couldn't fix. He could try to fix this.

After a minute Amy still wouldn't meet his eyes. She lifted a hand, and he took it. She squeezed his fingers and she said a soft, "Good-bye, Dermot."

He watched her walk around the car and get in. She started the engine as he stepped back. She didn't drive away at once. She sat there a moment with her hands on the steering wheel and her eyes on the squat red brick apartment building. He wasn't sure how long she sat there. It seemed forever. Eventually, she put the car in gear and backed out of the space. With one last look at the building, she drove off.

Damn.

CHAPTER THIRTY-EIGHT

Sarah squeezed every drop she could out of her curls with the towel. The hot shower had helped a bit, though she had had to remind herself not to picture Ryan's ominous black bag sitting on the toilet in her bathroom. Her back ached, and her head was starting to get foggy. She could practically feel the dark circles under her eyes.

After Amy left, Sarah had exhausted herself cleaning every inch of the apartment that she could get to. She even had the guys move the couch so she could get behind it. She had gotten most of the blood out of the carpet and scrubbed her bathroom until she almost didn't recognize it. She had also talked Dermot into going home by agreeing to let Fleming stay with her. He'd been so helpful today. She was glad to have him standing guard.

She slipped into her favorite flannel pajamas, hoping she might actually manage to sleep, even if it was in the same bed where she'd been attacked. She had changed her sheets, so when she laid her head on the pillow she caught a brief whiff of fabric softener. She closed her eyes and snuggled into the sheets, trying to tell herself that this was still her home, at least for now. She would leave soon, but she didn't want to let Ryan Cumberland rob her of all the good memories that she'd made there.

***

September 1989
Kettle Hollow, North Carolina

The junk truck had been and gone. The goats and chickens had been sold and taken away just like the still. Sarah had unplugged all the appliances and piled the last of the things in the parlor by the front door. There was a suitcase full of her clothes, a box of her old things from her childhood: school awards, toys Duff had carved for her, a doll house she had made from a shoe box. There was also Granny's trunk. She hadn't opened it, just hadn't been able to. She'd found the key in the jewelry box where she knew Granny kept it. Still, it just hadn't seemed right to open it, not yet.

It was late afternoon, and Sarah wanted to get out of the narrow roads of the hollow before it got too dark. She knew she should go, but she sat down cross-legged on the pine boards and leaned against the back of the door. She closed her eyes and saw the farm in her mind.

She could see it all behind her eyelids. The narrow trail from the bluff cutting through the forest and across the creek. She saw Duff's cabin on the other side of the forest overlooking the small pond—not abandoned as it was then, but as it had been when he was there, the porch hung with bits of metal and wood he was saving for one thing or another and the inside smelling of wood smoke, lamp oil, and sweat. Further down the mountain she saw the rocky spot in the creek that had been a favorite place of hers when she was little.

When she turned her attention to the house, her mind pictured her little bedroom above the kitchen. Mama's room was at the end of the hall. She supposed she could have moved into the larger room after Mama died, but she never had. It sat there, empty and closed, the lighter boards in the floor highlighting where the stained ones had been replaced. Granny's room was at the other end of the hall from Mama's, empty now too. Then there was the bathroom in the center of the hall with its claw-footed tub and the mirror that never reflected right. It needed to be replaced or re-silvered. The reflection was always hazy and cracks in the painted back distorted the image.

Downstairs, she saw the kitchen with its new electric stove. Granny had used a wood stove for cooking until she finally got too old to be carrying the wood inside. She'd never quite gotten the hang of cooking with the electric one. Sarah saw the dining room that had mostly been a sewing room, and the rough pine boards of the parlor floor stretched out in front of her.

Sarah opened her eyes and looked at the things set on the floor in front of her. She took a deep breath, noting the bite in the fall air, and got to her feet. She grabbed the box and carried it outside, loading it into the trunk of the slightly used Honda that Duff had helped her pick out when she graduated from high school.

She went back for the trunk. For being so old, it felt solid in her arms and heavy. It was roughly half the size of the steamer trunks that Sarah had seen and was likely meant for holding linens. Its wooden sides were reinforced at the corners and slightly domed top with additional wood slats and metal studs at the joints. The wood was dark with age and polished with wear across the top. It fit neatly in the trunk next to the box.

Sarah went back in and picked up the suitcase and cast one last look around the empty room and up the stairs. For a second, she thought she could hear the ghost of girlish laughter floating down the stairs to her, but it must have just been a memory.

***

Sarah's eyes popped open and shot straight to the closet. She hadn't really gotten into the closet during her cleaning, but she knew the trunk was there. It was just small enough to fit on the shelf. She threw off the comforter and went to the closet. She had put it up there because she hadn't wanted it to get kicked. She shoved her clothes as far to the sides as she could and pulled down some shoeboxes she had put up there to make room. She had to slide the trunk from the corner to where it could be twisted just enough to angle it down.

After a couple of minutes shuffling and almost dropping the old thing on her head, she finally got it down. She set it beside her bed and ran to her jewelry box and found the key on the old piece of kitchen twine that Granny had tied to it. She had never used it. She'd been toting this trunk around through every move in the last six years, but she hadn't even thought about opening it. Now she had a reason. If what they were telling her was true, Granny might have something in here to confirm it.

She slid the small key into the ornate metal lock on the front. She hoped like hell it wasn't rusted closed or she'd have to break the lock to get inside. She turned the key and felt it slide ever so slightly and stop. She applied a little more pressure and felt it slip the tiniest bit more. She pressed harder. Just when she was afraid the key was going to break from the force, something broke free inside the lock and the key slipped into the open position.

Sarah flipped back the latch and lifted the lid. There was a flap inside the lid to hold small things. Sarah would leave that for last. In the main compartment the first thing she saw was the bowl. Granny's scrying bowl. She had only seen her Granny use it once, but she knew just what it was for. She had asked Granny once if she would teach Sarah how to use it, but Granny had told her that she didn't need it. If she knew how to read signs and dreams she wouldn't need a tool like the bowl. "Besides," she could hear Granny say in her clipped Scots accent, "ye've nae need to borrow trouble nor joy fra the future. There's plenty enough for today."

"Amen," Sarah said acidly.

Next there were linens, some baby clothes that could have been hers or her mother's, and a rag doll. The doll had definitely been Mama's because Sarah didn't remember it. It was carefully sewn with a face embroidered on it, and it wore a little blue rag dress. Its hair was made of yarn and was attached to the head by a crown of tiny flowers sewn all around.

The clothes appeared to be all baby clothes, little homemade gowns in varying sizes. No other fabric would have been so precious that it wouldn't have been recycled into something else. There was also a knitted baby blanket. Under a layer of rough cedar blocks were a yard or two of tartan wool and a shawl of the finest knitted lace Sarah had ever seen, as light as a cobweb. She lifted it up, amazed that it didn't seem to have any holes or damage.

Sarah turned her attention to the flap inside the lid. She untied the ribbons that held it closed and let the flap fall forward. Inside the lid was a small wooden box about the size of a child's shoebox and some yellowed papers she set aside. Sarah opened the box. An envelope rested on top; Sarah picked it up and lifted the flap to find two locks of hair each tied with ribbon. The golden spiral curl with the blue ribbon had to be hers. The dark straighter one had a ribbon that may have once been white. It had to be Mama's from when she was a baby. Sarah's throat got tighter as she held it. She put the hair back in the envelope and closed it carefully.

Clearing her throat, she set the envelope aside and turned her attention back to the box. There were small pieces of jewelry tangled and tarnished with age. They must have had some sentimental value, or Granny would have kept them in her jewelry box with her little bit of going-to-town finery. Sarah lifted some things, trying to figure out where they might have come from. Nestled in the tangle of metal was a worry stone rubbed smooth and shining. It was brownish red, with tiny salt-and-pepper flecks.

Sarah jumped up and ran to her own jewelry box. She picked up the stone that Isobel MacKenzie had given her and laid the two stones side by side in her palm. Isobel's stone was almost bowl shaped she had worn the center down so much. But the similarity was unmistakable. They could have been cut from the same larger stone. Sarah laid the two stones together in her jewelry box, wondering at the coincidence.

She went back and sat on the floor by the bed to look at the papers. What she'd thought would be official papers or legal documents turned out to be a book made up of loose sheets of paper crudely sewn along one edge with twine. "A Fairy Tale by Mòrag MacAlpin" was scrawled across the front in crayon. Sarah flipped the first sheet over and began reading. The text was in the over-neat pencil of a child who was just learning to write and trying her best. Each page also held an accompanying illustration in crayon. She shook her head. She'd been telling stories even then. Wondering what her younger self had written she began to read.

***

In the time before time, our people sprang from the footprint of a giant left in stone. He was an enormous creature with a thick red beard and wide slanted eyes that didn't recognize his own creation. He could have destroyed our people with a single step.

But the giant had a wife and she saw the wee folk springing up in her man's own wake. She smiled on our people. The giant's wife went to the river nearby and picked up some clay. She used her thumbs to form the clay into a great cauldron and she fired the clay with her own breath. She told the wee folk, "As long as our tracks live upon this stone you will never want. Whenever you are hungry this cauldron will give you food. Keep it safe and you will always live in plenty."

And it was true. For many generations the cauldron kept us free from want. Our people settled at the mouth of the river near the giant's footprint on the edge of the endless forest. Even when the terrible snows came and the whole world was frozen, the cauldron gave us food to eat and kept us warm. When the ice melted and the earth thawed, the giant's footprint remained, and our people remained beside it.

***

Long ago, before our land became an island when great beasts still roamed the wildwood, a band of men came to our shore. They made a home beside us and for a time we lived in harmony.

But as the others multiplied and more arrived, food became harder for them to find. The others began to claim the land they lived on so they could plant and keep their own food. Our folk saw this, but they did not understand. Some of the folk went to the king and asked if we could share our cauldron with the new people.

Our king had seen the new folk's grasping ways and did not trust them. "Surely," he said, "A prize such as our cauldron would be seized at once and we would lose the care of it. I fear the new folk would destroy the she-giant's gift with their fighting."

So our folk did nothing, and the new folk continued to seize the land around them and to build upon it. When they had run out of rushes and branches to build their homes they began to use stones. First, they picked up loose stones from the beach. Then they began to take larger stones and break them apart.

One morning the king of our folk saw a band of new men breaking apart the great stone where the giant's footprint showed still. The king threw himself upon the stone to block the hammer blows of the new men. But the footprint was so huge that the king could cover no more than the spot where the giant's great toe had been. The new men would not stop their work and one of their hammers struck our king in the thigh. They worked on and by the time our king was found, there was nothing of the giant's footprint left but the toe print that lay under him.

When our queen found the king on the stone he was near death. But the queen sent a girl to the cauldron with a cup. The girl dipped the cup into the great cauldron and it came up full of water. The queen dripped the water on the king's lips, and after a few moments he began to speak.

He told the queen of the new men and their hammers and what had happened to the giant's footprint. The king was sure that the cauldron had lost its power as the footprint no longer showed on the stone. "Nay," said the queen, "The cauldron's power remains, for you were near death and the water from the pot has healed you." But the water could not heal him completely for the king remained lame.

He told the queen, "I fear that we can no longer live among these people and protect our mother's gift. We will have to find a new home." The queen called on her two sisters to organize our people. One sister took charge of the cauldron, the giant's gift that sustained us. The other sister had the care of our grandparents and all of the knowledge our people had gained over many generations. The queen took care of the king and the stone that was all that was left of the giant's footprint. Our people tore the roofs off their homes and made rafts out of the rushes. In the space of one night, the old folk sailed up the river and away from the greed and warring tribes of the new folk.

In time they made a home on an island in a great loch. They built a great hall with the rafts as the roof. They set the cauldron in the great hall and built a warm place beside the fire for our grandparents. The stone was placed in a cave on the island to protect what was left of the footprint from the wind and the rains. And the three sisters called up a mist from the surface of the loch to shroud our new home and keep it safe.

***

For nearly a thousand years our people lived in peace on our shrouded isle in the great loch. Sometimes one of the new men would find his way to our shore blown over the water by a storm, but those who did saw our lives of plenty and chose to stay with us. Occasionally, one of our folk would grow curious about our neighbors and venture into the world of the new men, but they always came back.

One day a young princess of our people went swimming in the loch. She swam past the misty shroud and upstream to where the river spilled its white water into the black depths. There, sitting on a rock was a young man. He looked sad and deep in thought. Because our princess was curious she swam closer, because she was kind she thought to help him. She called to him from the water. “Why are you so sad, new man?”

The new man explained that he was a king and he wanted to unite all the tribes of the new men so they could work together. But they continued to fight like children over petty things. The princess had no solution to offer for the behavior of new men. Like so many of the auld folk, she didn’t understand their ways. Still, she tried to cheer up the new man on the rock by suggesting he join her for a swim.

They swam down the river and into the loch, past the mist curtain, and landed on the shore of the auld folk’s isle. The new man was hungry after swimming so long, so the princess took him to the great hall. She introduced him to her father, the king, but he was not pleased. He pulled the princess aside and said, "Oh, my daughter. What have you done? You have brought destruction upon us."

"No," she said, "This new man is good. He wants to unite the new men and end their fighting."

Her father shook his head. "He will unite them to take our precious gift. Our cauldron and our stone will be destroyed, our people scattered and our stories forgotten."

After a thousand years of peace, our people had no means of defending ourselves from the new men, nor did they have a means to keep the king of the new men on the island. So our king said nothing and showed the king of the new men all the hospitality of the great hall. The king of the new men was given food from our cauldron of plenty. He was entertained by the stories and songs of our grandparents.

In the morning, the princess took him for a walk. The king of the new men asked, "Where is this stone that your grandparents spoke of? I would like to see it."

The princess remembered what her father had told her, but she was sure in her heart that the king of the new men was good. She believed that he was not their enemy. She took him to the cave where the stone lay hidden and showed him what was left of the giant's footprint. "This is the heart of our people," she said. "As long as the footprint shows on this stone, we will live in plenty."

The king of the new men said, "Your people are so warm and giving. Your heart cannot be made of cold stone."

"That is how our mother taught us to be." answered the princess. "We were born by accident, but her gift is what sustains us. We give freely, so that we may be like her."

"But you do not give freely," the new king told her. "You hide your gift on this magic island when you could share.

The princess told him of when the new men almost destroyed the stone and nearly killed their king. She told of their escape from the new men and why they were hidden on the island.

"If the new men are united, if we all share, then you would have nothing more to fear," he said.

"Are you the one to unite the new men?" she asked.

"I think I can. But I also think that your cauldron could help me to do that. With plenty to eat, the new men would have no need to fight and your people would have nothing to fear."

The princess began to think that her father was right about this king of the new men. "You want the cauldron for your own."

"No. I want it for ALL." He stepped forward and placed his foot on the stone where the giant's toe had been. "Does it honor your mother for you to live in plenty while others starve? Did she say her gift was only for your people? I may honor your secret because I have eaten at your table, but one day someone may not. Then the new men will come in anger and they will take what they understand and destroy what they do not."

At that, the ground around them began to shake. They ran from the cave and out into a violent storm. The wind raged and the rain came down in sheets. Lightning struck the roof of the great hall and the rushes were set aflame. The auld folk ran to the loch to get water, but the ground shook so that they could not carry the water back to the fire. They were forced to watch their isle burn as the earth quaked under their feet.

In the morning, the princess awoke on the far shore of the great loch. Beside her lay the king of the new men. Just down the beach resting on its side was the cauldron of plenty. She knelt beside it and wept for her people and the home that she had lost. Her weeping woke the king and he came to her side.

"You were right," she said. "We were wrong to keep this gift to ourselves and this is the result. My people are gone. My home is gone."

The king took her hand and said, "You are still here. Let us see if the cauldron still provides."

He took a cup from his belt and dipped it into the cauldron. It came up filled with sweet wine. "You see? Your mother has not forsaken you. I will not forsake you either. Come with me and be my queen. With your mother's gift we can unite the tribes of the new men. Then we will all enjoy the giant's gift."

So the king of the new men made the princess of the auld folk his queen. They could not unite all of the tribes right away. It took generations, but they were united. For a time, they lived in plenty.

***

By the time she reached the end tears were sliding silently down her face. She closed the book and rested her hands on top of it in her lap. She leaned back against the side of her bed and closed her eyes to think. How could she have forgotten? Granny had told her that story a thousand times. She had written it down almost verbatim even when she was six. There it was, the story of "The River Maiden" and more.

She remembered what Dermot said this morning: "Yer family is actually much older. Your people have been in Scotland longer than anyone can remember…" If this was more than just a fairy tale, then he was right. The folklorist in her reminded her that most stories, no matter how crazy sounding, started with some grain of truth. So where was the truth in this story, and where was the fantasy? Just how faithful had the generations been to what they'd been told? And how many generations had passed this on? Why hadn't Granny told her about this as she grew up? When had she stopped retelling "The River Maiden"?

She sat pondering all of the questions raised by this find until she started to drift off to sleep. Nodding off, she nearly fell forward. She should really put these things away and get into bed. She put the papers back in the trunk lid and reached for the box. When she grabbed the lid, she felt something on the underside. She flipped it over and found a photograph wedged into the lid. The back of the photo had only a year on it: 1939. She pulled it out carefully from the lid, trying not to bend the old paper, and turned it over.

It was black and white and showed two smiling girls on a familiar looking beach. Their clothes appeared to be from the 1930s, but were modest even by that era's standards. Granny hadn't been one for keeping pictures, so Sarah hadn't seen any of her when she was young. Still, she was fairly certain the young woman on the right was her grandmother. She looked to be in her teens, so the impression was not so much from her features but from the sharp intelligence in her eyes.

Sarah quickly did the math thinking Granny would have been fifteen in 1939.

When Sarah looked at the other girl, the one on the left, she nearly dropped the picture. A chill of confusion and betrayal crept up her spine and made her hands shake. The girl was smiling, but not looking directly at the camera. Her hand rested on Granny's arm and she looked off to the side. Her face was lively, but her eyes were vacant.

It was Isobel MacKenzie.

Other Books in the Once & Future Series

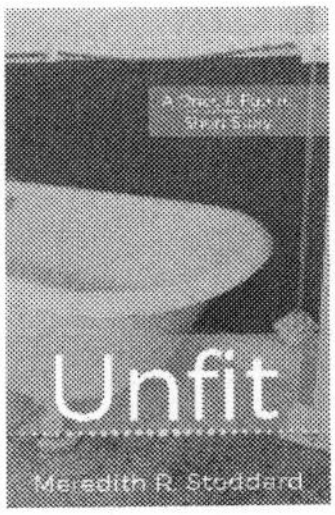

Unfit (ebook short)

When she left Kettle Hollow, Molly MacAlpin hoped never to see her remote mountain home again. She returned eighteen months later angry, pregnant and abandoned by the man she loved. So, she threw all her energy into making sure her daughter had the best life possible.

With the help and sometimes interference of her mother, she is raising a bright, sweet child she they hopes will have every possible opportunity. Until one spring day a brief conversation with her little girl brings her world crashing down around her.

Buddy (ebook short)

As the youngest of the contentious Corbett clan, Buddy has spent most of his life trying to get away from the remote mountain hollow where they all grew up. Now at the end of a long day, he can't avoid talking to them. When one of his brothers mentions their old neighbor, Maggie MacAlpin, he can't help thinking about Old Maggie's granddaughter, Sarah. She was as tough and wild as she was beautiful. And she was the first girl that Buddy ever loved.

One summer when they were barely old enough for kissing, Buddy learned just how much that love could cost them.

Cauldron

The traumatic events of The River Maiden have left Sarah MacAlpin's life in shambles. Her best friend won't talk to her. The man she loves says they can't be together. She's just discovered something that destroys the main thesis of her dissertation. To top it off, she's learned that her dream fellowship in Scotland was given to her with ulterior motives by her billionaire benefactor. Sarah has to choose whether to accept the fellowship anyway or try to find a different path.

Meanwhile she's battling her own personal demons and questions about her family. She hopes to find some answers in her mother's memoir. What she finds are some upsetting parallels to her own life. Like Sarah, Molly left Kettle Holler on the verge of making her dreams of being a dancer come true, but her ambitions were derailed by a family secret that took her across an ocean and left her a broken shade of her former self.

ACKNOWLEDGMENTS

No book is produced all on its own. There are plenty of people to thank for their help in this effort. First is, Jon VanZile of Editing for Authors. Jon's insights were crucial in refining the narrative and improving the book overall. Caroline Root of Daily Gaelic made sure my Gaelic was correct. For their support and feedback; John B. Campbell, the members of the Women's Fiction Critique Group on authonomy.com, and my beta readers.

Last but far from least my husband and kids for tolerating the many hours that I've spent working on this. Also, my extended family for their lifelong support.

ABOUT THE AUTHOR

Meredith R. Stoddard writes folklore-inspired fiction from her attic hideaway in Central Virginia. She studied literature and folklore at the University of North Carolina at Chapel Hill before working as a corporate trainer and instructional designer. Her love of storytelling is inspired by years spent listening to stories at her grandmother's kitchen table. She also advocates for the preservation of traditional fiber arts and the Scottish Gaelic language.

You can also follow @M_R_Stoddard on Twitter.

31316905R00283

Made in the USA
Columbia, SC
01 November 2018